Blood & Circuses

Manna Francis

CASPERIAN
BOOKS

This is a work of fiction. All the characters and events portrayed in this book are either fictitious or are used fictitiously.

www.casperianbooks.com

Cover illustration by Orit "Shin" Heifets.

Photographs used in the cover illustration by Doreen Simpson, Jamie Davies (www.flickr.com/photos/8374005@N02/4619277236/), and Juhan Sonin (www.flickr.com/photos/38869431@N00/4331357337/).

ISBN-10: 1-934081-49-3
ISBN-13: 978-1-934081-49-5

Thanks once again to my husband, editor, and publisher for all their help and support. Thanks also to Jessie, whose blog posts kick-started me into writing more of the Administration.

Table of Contents

Innocent Blood

Chapter One

❖

The New London offices of the Bureau of Administrative Departments looked much the same as when Toreth had last been there, almost two years before. The revolt hadn't reached this apex of Administration bureaucracy—or maybe the looters hadn't known how important the place was to the system they were failing to overthrow.

"So sorry we kept you waiting," Secretary Turnbull said when Toreth was shown into her office.

Toreth shook her hand. "Not at all."

"Rude of me, when I was the one who requested the meeting. I hope it isn't too inconvenient?"

"We're always happy to help the Bureau," Toreth said. Tillotson, when conveying the request for the meeting—summons, in reality—had made it clear that Turnbull took priority over everything else. "Have you lost another American?"

He'd meant it as a joke, but there were several intakes of breath from the people already seated around the conference table.

"In a manner of speaking," Turnbull said, and gestured for him to join them. "This is Para-investigator Val Toreth of the Investigation and Interrogation Division."

Toreth scanned the group as he sat. None of them stood out as anything other than Administration staff, albeit expensively suited ones, their manner all as immaculately polished as the table.

As Turnbull rattled off the introductions, Toreth concentrated on departments rather than names. Interesting mix of fingers in the pie: a junior official from the Bureau, another from Ext-Sec, two from the Department of International Relations, a very senior Justice rep, and a rather cheerful young woman from Socioanalysis whose pale skin contrasted eye-catchingly with her dark hair, and who had the memorably inappropriate name of Darcy Grimm. She was the only one to give him a warm smile when Turnbull introduced her.

"The Bureau has requested I&I's help with a delicate problem," Turnbull said. "A member of the European Administration's embassy in Washington has been accused of a serious crime. The authorities have refused to allow us to handle the matter entirely ourselves, even though the local investigation is obviously complicated by their suspect's diplomatic status."

The older of the two Department of International Relations reps cleared her throat. "We're keen not to have that status compromised. It would set a highly damaging precedent for an embassy staff member to be arrested for something not even a criminal matter in Europe."

"The Council hasn't yet received a formal request to remove immunity," Turnbull said, and the deliberate patience in her voice made Toreth suspect they'd already had this conversation before he arrived. "But, yes, it's possible the situation may escalate, something we'd all rather avoid. In light of our cooperation in the past, they've kindly agreed to let us send an I&I representative to Washington to observe the investigation and assure us of its thorough and fair nature."

Her voice grew steadily drier as the sentence went on. "You mean me?" Toreth asked.

"You've more than proved your ability and discretion in the past. You'll be leaving early tomorrow."

Less of a request, more of an order. "Can you give me the case files?"

"They declined to supply us with a copy of the investigation as it stands. I'm assured, though, that you'll be cleared and given access once you're in Washington." She turned to the International Relations reps. "If you would now, Ms. Kuczek?"

The woman who'd spoken before straightened the hand screen on the desk in front of her, although she didn't actually refer to it. "The embassy medic, Rebekah Campion, is accused of performing an abortion on an American citizen—and to compound the issue, the woman in question is the daughter of a national senator, which is an extremely high-level political post. Awkward for us, because he's a long-established, well-respected figure, and up until now he's been wary to neutral regarding Europe, politically speaking. Obviously if the case against Campion is proved, then he's likely to move towards the more traditionally isolationist segment of—"

Turnbull interrupted with, "I don't think that's relevant to Para-investigator Toreth. Perhaps you could return to the crimes?"

"Of course. Now, the abortion itself is legally defined as murder over there, but some complication of the procedure caused the woman to end up in hospital. Unfortunately, our access to the medical details is sketchy—our official position is that her condition has nothing to do with the embassy, so we haven't pressed for more. We know she's still unconscious, in the stabilization phase of neuroregenerative treatment, and we're led to believe her prospects for recovery are uncertain.

10

So, while it's not technically a double murder charge yet, it could become one any day."

Sounded like a mess. "Do I get a free hand to investigate?" Toreth asked.

She turned to the younger man beside her. "Cooke? What's the latest progress?"

He did check his hand screen, and then his shoulders slumped slightly. Obviously, Kuczek believed in delegating failure.

"Nothing, I'm afraid." He turned to Toreth. "You won't be allowed to become directly involved. You'll be able to interview the embassy staff, of course—" He paused, and glanced quickly at Kuczek. She nodded slightly. "Yes, of course you will, at the ambassador's discretion. Beyond that, you will just be observing, where Washington law enforcement feels it won't compromise their investigation. We are hoping to be able to negotiate a better position."

"So I have to use the evidence the Americans are willing to show me to prove someone outside the embassy is guilty?" Toreth turned to Turnbull. "Forgive me, Secretary, but that sounds like being set up to fail."

"I appreciate the difficulties that you'll be facing," Turnbull said. "And obviously, you won't be faulted if the woman did what they say she did."

The Department of International Relations officials stared resolutely into empty space, avoiding both Toreth and Turnbull. Presumably, their ideal outcome was that any blame in the situation migrated swiftly over to roost at I&I.

"And if the DIR thinks she didn't, but I can't prove that?" Toreth asked.

"As I said, I appreciate that we're making a difficult request. As long as everything possible is done, then *I* will certainly be satisfied." Turnbull looked around the table, and after a moment there was a depressingly noncommittal murmur of assent.

While, no doubt, a hundred other people outside the room would be highly dissatisfied. Still, it was an offer of protection, of a sort. And, if he pulled it off, a huge amount of kudos and the gratitude of the Secretary of the Bureau. He'd take those odds. "What kind of support do I get out there? Can I take my team?"

"If you recall, in the last case to which you were a party, two investigators were allowed as observers. The American government has indicated they would not be receptive to any expansion of that number now."

Tit for tat over the Administration's treatment of the American investigators two years ago. Toreth wondered if the American powers that be knew he'd locked the pair in a secure suite on the I&I interrogation levels.

"I'll take Jasleen Mistry." If the most he could hope for was to be allowed to talk to witnesses and suspects, he might as well take his best interviewer. "You can sort her out with a visa and so on?"

The woman from Socioanalysis cleared her throat. "Secretary?"

"Ah, yes. Toreth, I've had a request from Socioanalysis that they be allowed to supply the second member of—"

"No," Toreth said reflexively.

Turnbull's eyebrows rose; Toreth didn't imagine she was often interrupted. "Socioanalysis thinks it presents an invaluable opportunity to acquire perspectives on the American legal system not normally available. The Bureau is inclined to agree with them."

"Then, with all due respect to Socioanalysis, Secretary—" he glanced at the Socioanalysis rep, just to make it clear to both of them how little he thought that was, "— they're welcome to carry out the investigation. Without me. It'll be difficult enough for two of us to do our jobs over there with no I&I resources, without having some—" half-arsed "—impromptu intelligence operation in the middle of the case."

Turnbull looked at the rep. After a couple of seconds, Grimm shrugged. "If that's the situation, then obviously the well-being of our DIR colleague must come first." She'd lost her smile.

Toreth spent the rest of the day delegating work for his current case to allow things to run in his absence—difficult, when he didn't know how long that absence would be. By the time he took a break for a coffee in the afternoon, news of his assignment had spread through the section, and everyone wanted details. Chevril, who rarely left New London voluntarily, reacted with predictable gloom.

"Elena would kill me if I flew off to the United bloody States on some indefinite excuse of a case. Ten to one they won't even let you out of the embassy." He snorted. "I wouldn't. I hope someone's warned them to lock up their wives." He paused, no doubt expecting Toreth's customary "and husbands." "Well?"

"Not this time." Toreth sipped his coffee. "They're a funny lot over there. I'd probably end up on trial next to this medic."

Toreth had been prepared to sit through another of Mike Belkin's complaints about missing out on an interdepartmental case, but he was worryingly sanguine. "You're welcome to it," he said, when Toreth had outlined the sparse information. "Sounds like a bastard. The Bureau, Ext-Sec, and . . . Socioanalysis, did you say? That's three departments I wouldn't want to know I couldn't do my job."

"I'll sort it out," Toreth said, determined not to show any doubt.

Belkin laughed. "How? Use your fucking psychic powers? All this fame's gone to your head. I bet the Bureau thought, 'Senior Para Toreth, he was happy to kiss Carnac's arse, he'll go over there and get royally fucked for us.'"

"They'll be disappointed, then, because I told Socioanalysis where to stuff it."

"Right. And what does that leave you with?" Belkin settled back in his seat with his hands wrapped snugly around his coffee mug. "No witnesses, no evidence except what they'll let you see, and one suspect they're probably trying to fit up because of some high-level political competitive wanking. Yeah, you're definitely welcome to it."

Rays of sunshine, as ever, Belkin and Chevril both. Toreth drank his coffee, and wished he'd thought more carefully at the time about the pros and cons of stopping Carnac from killing any paras.

By the time he let himself into the flat, Toreth was wondering whether turning down the case would've been the smartest move after all, even if it pissed off Turnbull. She'd never seemed the vindictive type; probably she'd just strike him off her list of useful people and move on. For a moment, he considered calling her and saying that he'd changed his mind. Then he dismissed the idea. He'd once told Liz Carey that neither of them would ever again achieve a result as prestigious as cracking the Selman kidnapping. Solving a case in America was beyond that, something entirely unique that no other para at I&I would have on his record.

Warrick had already eaten, so Toreth filled a plate with the remains of the chicken casserole and went to join Warrick in the living room. Warrick was definitely improving, because he hardly even winced when Toreth set his glass precariously on the arm of the chair.

"Long day?" Warrick asked, which probably meant "you could've let me know you'd be late." Toreth's guess was strengthened when Warrick added, "I must've had a premonition when I chose the recipe this morning. Has it survived all right?"

"Yeah, it's fine. And yeah, it was—a long day." Toreth blew on a forkful of the casserole. "Warrick, you've been to America, haven't you?"

"North America?" Warrick set his hand screen aside. "A couple of times, yes. It's time-consuming to get a corporate visa, but not impossible. In fact, Asher was talking about making another visit, maybe next year. Why do you want to know?"

"What's it like over there?"

"I'm afraid I didn't see much of it. They were business trips, and very busy—if not ultimately very productive. I saw a lot of meeting rooms in corporate headquarters, and various restaurants, sporting events, and other places one takes one's corporate guests. And then there were a few offices belonging to government officials giving us contradictory explanations of technology trade regulations. Unfortunately, there are still export and import issues holding up the sale of the sim over there."

"So why go all that way, if you knew you couldn't sell it anyway? Flights aren't cheap, I know that." The first thing Tillotson had done after Toreth told him about Turnbull's request had been to instruct his admin Jenny to inform the Bureau that the flights weren't coming out of the I&I budget.

"Well..." Warrick picked up his hand screen again, and closed it with deliberate concentration. "It's impossible to put a value on making a personal connection with potential partners."

Toreth recognized the tone of voice people used when they were trying to talk around a politically risky subject. "Warrick?"

"No, that wasn't the whole reason. When negotiating over the comm, one's always aware that the conversation is monitored." Warrick raised his finger. "Not that we were discussing anything untoward, of course. But the Administration can be a little..."

"Paranoid," Toreth supplied.

"That's one word that comes to mind, yes. We were all debriefed on our return. On a voluntary basis," he added dryly.

"Really? Who talked to you?"

"To be perfectly honest, I didn't feel comfortable pressing for exact details. I assumed Ext-Sec—amongst others, no doubt."

Including maybe Socioanalysis, taking another opportunity to gain insights? "What did they want to know?"

"More or less everything—attitudes towards the sim, how they planned to market it over there, restrictions and surveillance they were interested in implementing. We had the opportunity to claim commercial privilege, of course, but we hoped a cooperative attitude might help our case for export licensing. So far, we've been disappointed."

"Right, I see." Toreth balanced the plate on his knee while he took a drink. "Why are you interested?"

"I'm going there. Tomorrow, assuming all the paperwork is in place. It's for a case—secondment to another department. Technically, I suppose I shouldn't tell you the details."

"Then it's probably best that you don't." Warrick paused, then said, "Do be... discreet over there. They have some rather peculiar views about certain things."

Toreth laughed. "And one of them is that fucking other men is illegal. Yeah, I know. Don't worry, I'm sure there are plenty of women in America."

Warrick shook his head. "You're impossible."

"Actually, I'm a pretty good bet." Toreth paused. "Why did you need to know who you could and couldn't fuck?"

"SimTech marketing briefings are always thorough. Whether anyone was planning any encounters—which, incidentally, I wasn't—we had to be able to talk about sim uses and chat about our personal lives without causing a chilly silence."

Toreth hadn't even thought about that. Questioning witnesses abroad could present more problems than lack of waivers. They'd be working in a world of different assumptions and social conventions. He'd have to discuss it with Mistry on the flight.

"So, how long do you think you'll be gone?" Warrick asked.

14

"Not a clue. Could be a couple of days, could be—anything, really. For all I know, I'll sit in the embassy for a month, twiddling my thumbs while everyone argues, and then Turnbull will tell me to come home."

"Turnbull?" Warrick frowned. "I feel as though I ought to know the name."

"You might. Catherine Turnbull, Principal Secretary at the Bureau of Administrative Departments."

For all that the case could turn out to be a combination of a waste of time and a pain in the arse, Toreth was glad he'd taken it just for the expression of astonishment on Warrick's face. "The Bureau of—that's who's sending you over there?"

Toreth grinned. "In person. Corporates aren't the only ones who get to move in high circles, you know." Even if Toreth wasn't moving, so much as being moved as a pawn.

"I can see that. Well." Toreth had never seen Warrick taken aback for so long. Nor so obviously curious.

"January last year, an American boy with an important father went missing from their New London embassy. Someone passed my name to Turnbull. Turned out Elliot had found himself a boyfriend. I tracked him down and persuaded him to go home without making too much of a fuss." With a little mind-fucking help from Psychoprogramming, to persuade Elliot that blowjobs really were as sinful as he'd always been told. No need for Warrick to hear about that part, though. "Now she wants another favor."

"Well, clearly you made an impression. And...good luck with your case."

"Thanks—I'm sure I'll need it." Toreth scraped up the last of his dinner, and put the plate down on the nearest table. "So, since I'll be gone for God knows how long, do you want to make the most of this evening?"

Warrick stood up and came over to pick up Toreth's plate. He swiped his hand over the surface of the wooden table. "That sounds like an excellent idea."

Chapter Two

❖

Toreth and Mistry were at the airport; what wasn't there was permission for Mistry to board the flight. After spending ten minutes fighting with the check-in screen, Toreth finally gave up.

"Shall I call the Bureau, Para?" Mistry asked.

"No, I'll do it. Or—wait a minute." Toreth accessed the system again, using his I&I authority to look at the whole passenger list. He didn't even have to run an employment check. "Bollocks."

"Para?"

Before he could explain, he heard a voice call, "Para-investigator Toreth?"

He turned to see a tall woman hurrying towards them across the wide check-in area, long dark hair swinging. Fucking, *fucking* Socioanalysis. He should've known better than to trust Grimm's meek climbdown.

"Secretary Turnbull asked me to pass on her apologies for the last-minute change of plans," the socioanalyst said breathlessly as she stopped beside them. "Unfortunately, the Americans refused to issue your investigator's visa."

"Me?" Mistry said in surprise.

At the Bureau, Toreth hadn't realized how tall Grimm was; although she wore flat shoes, standing, they were almost eye to eye. "Why the hell would they do that?" he demanded.

"The visa application requires a family history." She turned to Mistry. "Apparently your grandmother and aunt hold volunteer posts of a religious nature, necessitating additional checks that couldn't be fitted into the available time."

"Oh," Mistry said, and she glanced uncomfortably at Toreth. "I had no idea that would be a problem, Para. Mum doesn't even—we aren't close to that part of the family."

Mistry had never mentioned anything like that in her background. Of course, at I&I, she wouldn't. "I thought they liked religion over there?" he asked Grimm.

"Not the right flavor, I suppose," Grimm said.

16

"They turned Mistry down for that, but they okayed my visa, with a male registered partner on my file?"

"I'm only passing on the information I have, as relayed to me by Secretary Turnbull." Grimm stressed the name slightly, as though Toreth were too stupid to notice it.

"Fine." Toreth would bet a month of time on the interrogation rota that the Americans had never even heard Mistry's name. "Then I'll call *Secretary Turnbull* and see if I can get this sorted out."

Toreth tapped his comm, but before he could call the Bureau, Grimm reached out. Her hand stopped a couple of centimeters from his arm.

"I hate to point out the obvious—"

"Really? Carnac never had a problem with that."

She smiled politely. "But I'd hardly be here unless Turnbull thought it was an adequate compromise."

Compromise? He didn't say anything, but his expression must've spoken for him, because she winced slightly.

"Para-investigator, Socioanalysis wants me over there to collect comparative cultural and procedural data. Nothing that could interfere with your observation of the investigation. And I'm sure I'll be able to help you, if necessary. One of my specialties is data quality analysis and stratification."

"If I need evidence evaluated I'll send it to I&I. I want Mistry because she's the best I have for interviewing witnesses when there's no prospect of a decent waiver. Are you any good at that?"

"Socioanalysts are trained in the whole spectrum of information gathering techniques, including verbal modalities."

Verbal modalities. Jesus fucking Christ. For a few seconds, Toreth debated the merits of walking out of the airport and telling Turnbull to fuck off . . . no doubt shortly followed by the end of his career.

"Para-investigator? We need to go through security now, or we'll miss our flight."

"Shall I go back to I&I, and explain the situation to Nagra and Sara?" Mistry asked.

Toreth hesitated a moment longer, then nodded. "Thanks, Mistry."

"No problem, Para. Um." She looked at Grimm.

"Excuse me," the socioanalyst said. "I need to make a couple of calls."

She walked away. Well, at least the woman could take a hint.

"What is it?" Toreth asked.

"The reason they turned down my visa won't show up on my file at I&I, will it?" Mistry asked anxiously. "Honestly, I've not seen my auntie in years. She and Mum had a row when we were kids, because Auntie wanted to bring us presents for Diwali and Mum didn't think it was appropriate."

"I'll make sure it doesn't get officially recorded," Toreth said. "Don't worry about it. Odds are it's just Socioanalysis bollocks, and they never even asked for the visa."

"Thanks." She flicked her plait over her shoulder, hesitating, then said, "Shall I mention it to Sara?"

Because, no doubt, she thought he'd forget. She was probably right. "Good idea. I'll see you when I get back."

In Washington, two airport security officers met them at the exit to the plane. They steered Toreth and Grimm through a door that presumably bypassed all the security checks, because when they finally exited the largely empty corridors, they entered what was clearly the arrivals area—lots of space and lots of people, although less security than Toreth was used to seeing. A low metal fence marked off the exit, rather than the blast-proof floor-to-ceiling glass of Administration airports, and individuals and groups stood waiting on the other side. A quick glance over to Toreth was enough for most people, with some more lingering, presumably from people come to meet another tall blond man. Only one figure moved, a dark-haired man in a smart suit who lifted his hand and came over. To Toreth's astonishment, he recognized the man—one of the two American agents sent over to New London to observe I&I's search for the runaway boy.

"Good to see you again, Para-investigator."

"Agent Ruiz?" Toreth said, and the man smiled.

"You remembered. I wasn't sure you would."

His voice was as unexpectedly soft as Toreth recalled. "I don't meet enough Americans to get you mixed up."

"No, I suppose not." He shook Toreth's hand warmly. "How've you been? We heard all about the riots back in January. Just terrible. I was thinking about you, and your investigator—Barret-Connor, right?—and the guys at Psychoprogramming."

"Everything's more or less back to normal, now." Toreth touched the scar on his eyebrow. "Left me with a little reminder, but otherwise I'm fine."

"Glad to hear it. And you must be Investigator Grimm, right?" Ruiz held his hand out to the socioanalyst. "I have to say, you don't live up to your name."

Somewhat to Toreth's surprise, she smiled sweetly. "Kind of you to say so. And it's exciting to be over here."

"Great, great." Ruiz turned to the guards. "I'll take over from here."

"Thank you, sir."

"Agent Cardine isn't with you?" Toreth asked as the guards walked away.

"Why, would you rather be working with her than with me?" Ruiz grinned at him. "But no. Cardine's a specialist, and this case isn't in her area of expertise."

"How was the flight?" Ruiz asked as they walked out of the main door and towards a waiting car.

"I've never spent so long sat on a plane," Toreth said. "Five hours. My arse fell asleep somewhere over the North Pole."

"I'm sorry. And I'm pretty sure that you've wasted your time, too. The Washington police seem confident that your Dr. Campion's guilty."

"Come on," Toreth said. "At least let me unpack before you depress me. I've not even seen the case files yet."

"Really?" Ruiz sounded surprised.

"I was told that I'd get them here. I don't even know exactly who she's supposed to have murdered."

"Right, I see. Well, I could give you a summary, if you like. Once the Administration asked to send observers, Homeland Security transferred me to the case, as liaison." Ruiz shook his head. "And I gotta say, if the welcome you'll get is anything like the one I had, then it'll be tough to observe much of anything."

Their bags were already waiting by the car, with another airport security officer. Toreth hadn't paid much attention to Grimm's clothes until now, but as they took their seats in the car he realized how soberly she'd dressed, in a dark trouser suit. At some point on the flight over—when, thankfully, they hadn't had to sit together—she'd restyled her hair into a plain French plait. She fitted right in with Ruiz; Socioanalysis's briefings were obviously as good as SimTech's.

"As the police see it, your doctor befriended Judith Buchheit, the wife of a senatorial aide," Ruiz began. "Some weeks ago, Judith became pregnant. And unfortunately, she chose to do a terrible thing, to kill the child. Because unborn children are entirely innocent and entirely helpless, the law confers a higher level of protection on them than on any other human being. Something went wrong with the procedure. Judith lost a lot of blood, and she's been in a coma ever since."

"And they think all this happened at the embassy?" Toreth asked. If it had, Campion could probably kiss any help from Europe goodbye.

"Well, that's something the investigation is still trying to clear up. Judith was found in a taxi headed to the embassy. Lucky for her, it was fitted with one of the new medicalert systems; it registered that the occupant was in distress and took her to a hospital, instead. At first the police assumed she was returning to the embassy for help, but the Europeans claim Judith never entered the building."

Generally, Toreth didn't like vague crime scenes, but here it gave him a point of weakness to attack. "So if we can prove she definitely wasn't there, Campion is off the hook?"

"Not necessarily. Could be another location was involved. The police have a record of several calls made from Judith to your Dr. Campion on the day of the crime, and one on the day before that lasted almost a quarter hour. If she wasn't involved, why the contact? Why else would Judith be going to the embassy? Even if the procedure was done someplace else, having any part in what happened carries the same penalty," Ruiz added. "So if Dr. Campion advised Judith on where to go, or talked to her about what to do, or knew what she intended, then she's as guilty of murder as if she'd done it herself."

Grimm cleared her throat. "As I understand it, Agent, the embassy staff all live in the embassy, and have limited interaction with the city. Where would Dr. Campion obtain the knowledge to give advice about illegal local abortion services?"

Talking directly to Grimm about the topic clearly made Ruiz uncomfortable, but he said, "Well, women do know about these kinds of things, right?"

"But why should she? She won't be getting pregnant."

When Ruiz looked blank, Toreth said, "Investigator Grimm means that Campion will have an implant, like everyone else."

"Things like that aren't reliable."

"They are in the Administration," Toreth said. "And if it failed, Campion wouldn't need to go looking for a doctor in Washington. The DoP would sort her out—the Department of Population."

"You mean the state sanctions abortions?" Ruiz said.

"Enthusiastically, sometimes. I've probably caused a few myself. Indirectly."

Ruiz narrowed his eyes. "Indirectly?"

"A few years ago we investigated a large-scale operation bypassing population control laws. It was still active, so some of the women involved must've been taken for terminations after they were arrested."

Now Ruiz's expression had changed to disbelief. "Taken by the *government*?"

"Yes. By Department of Population enforcement officers, anyway."

"How many?"

"No idea. We were only interested in the people at the top. We kicked the client list over to Justice after we'd finished dismantling the operation, so they arrested everyone. After that, it's up to the DoP."

"Not all of them would have been eligible for terminations," Grimm said. "There's a cut-off date—twenty-something weeks, I think—although they would still lose the child and be sent for re-education. Is that correct, Para?"

"Sounds about right." Toreth shrugged. "Like I said, it's not a crime we deal with often. Mostly it's Justice-level stuff."

From his expression, Ruiz didn't find Grimm's qualifier much comfort. This, Toreth realized, was probably the kind of cultural comparison that interested Socioanalysis, relevance to his case be damned.

"So, assuming that we can rule out the embassy, where was the clinic—the place she supposedly had the abortion?" Toreth asked. The socioanalyst could make her own cultural observations, without his help.

Ruiz cleared his throat. "They never found evidence of it—if it existed. Those kinda places are pretty mobile, though. They set up, do their dirty work, and then they disappear."

"Hm."

"You're thinking not having the crime scene is enough to wreck the case?" Ruiz asked. "They don't need to arrest the doctors to prove Campion knew about it."

"No, I'm thinking it's convenient there's no one to tell their side of the story. Whoever did the abortion might know how she really found them."

Ruiz shrugged. "Like I said, women know about these things."

Grimm looked away, out of the window, and Toreth tried to catch her reflection. A frown, or a smile?

"If you can clear it, I'll want to talk to some of the people involved," Toreth said. "Family and friends of the woman in the coma, to start with."

"I can tell you right now, her family most likely won't talk to you. I hear they aren't feeling real positive towards Europeans—Senator Grant, especially."

Toreth decided the time had come to push. "How the hell am I supposed to investigate if I can't interview witnesses? I was told I'd get cooperation. Should I just get straight back on a flight to New London, and tell my bosses it was all a pile of crap?"

"Hey." Ruiz held up his hand. "I understand—I've been there, yeah? But you don't have any authority, here, and to be honest, I don't have a whole lot myself. All I can do is ask if people are willing to talk to you informally."

Unlikely, with a political heavyweight in opposition. "Can't you reinterview them and ask them questions for me?" Better than nothing. Barely.

"I didn't interview them in the first place. It's the Washington Police Department's case."

"Is there anything useful you can do?" Toreth said before he could stop himself.

"I'm sorry. I'll do the best I can, I promise. It just might not be all that much."

The view from the car's windows was disappointingly normal—Washington looked like most of the large cities Toreth had visited in the Administration. Having been primed by the previous case, he found himself looking for evidence of religious enthusiasm. Certainly, they passed numerous churches that all proclaimed their function far more obviously than he'd ever seen at home, but that was the main difference. That, and a definite lack of leg and cleavage on display—but on the other hand, it was moving towards winter.

Toreth hadn't consciously devoted any thought to the Administration's embassy in Washington, but he realized that he must have made some unconscious assumptions when they turned through the high security gates. He was surprised to see an obviously new building, nothing like the old-fashioned styling of Turnbull's bureaucratic stronghold. Here and there a few architectural flourishes of scrolls and suggestions of pillars broke up the blandness of the pale, energy-generating surface layer of mock stone, maybe meant to call to mind an older embassy. But someone in the Administration had clearly briefed the architect to make a statement about fresh starts and looking to the future.

Grimm must have noticed him peering through the windows, because she said, "It's only been a decade or so since the embassy officially opened. Before that the Administration maintained a consular office in the Australian embassy. Para," she added belatedly. Toreth wondered if Ruiz had noticed.

If he did, nothing showed on his face. He left in the car, promising to chase up the case file access and to be back at the embassy early the next day.

The air felt much colder than it had in New London as they carried their bags over to the embassy doors. The ambassador was waiting for them inside. In lieu of having anything useful to do, Toreth had looked at the security files of all the senior embassy staff and glanced at most of the rest, and he recognized the man at once. He was slender and dressed in a suit so sharp and neat it looked brand new. His thick, black hair was styled in a way that Toreth had never seen before, sculpted into a wave at the front. Maybe it was something to help blend in with the locals at diplomatic functions.

He had an expressive face, and he smiled warmly at his visitors. "Daniel Fu," he said, and then waited for them to put their bags down so he could shake hands. "Para-investigator Toreth and Socioanalyst—sorry, Investigator—Grimm, am I right? Welcome to Washington. I hope you had a good flight over, not too many security delays at the airport?"

"None at all," Toreth said, and wondered if they had Ruiz to thank for that.

"Is there anything you need? We have rooms ready for you, if you'd like to take a shower or rest for a while. The change of time zone really knocks some people out, especially if you aren't used to it."

"Thanks," Toreth said, "but we'd rather get started straight away on the case. I sent the requests for interviews on ahead. We'd like to talk to Dr. Campion first, and then to the embassy head of security."

The smile modulated into something less enthusiastic."I hope we can rely on you to be discreet and to be guided by our advice? The situation needs a delicate approach. This is primarily a diplomatic matter, and the Department of International Relations is best placed to deal with it. Not Int-Sec—in my opinion."

"The Council doesn't seem to agree," Toreth said mildly.

"Clearly. Secretary Turnbull passed on the wishes of the Council and the Bureau, and I assured her that we'd do everything we could to assist. Both of you, of course," he added, turning to Grimm with even less enthusiasm in his voice.

Toreth simply stood and waited, and after a moment, Fu nodded.

"If you'll excuse me, I'll have those interviews arranged," he said. He beckoned over a woman in a security officer's uniform. "Dixon will show you to your rooms."

"Popular, aren't we?" Grimm said under her breath as he left.

"I thought you'd be used to that."

She laughed. "You know, I doubt anyone's ever pleased to see either of us coming, in a professional capacity, at least. We have that in common, right?"

While the bedroom itself was fine—on a par with the sort of hotel where a mid-level corporate would take a casual fuck, Toreth decided as he hung up his clothes—it had one large drawback. Grimm had been assigned the adjacent room. What would've been satisfactory if he'd had a real investigator was a bloody nuisance when Toreth went back out into the corridor and, a few seconds later, Grimm opened her door.

"Are you planning to talk to Campion now?" she asked.

No point in lying when she could look at the case file. "Yes."

"Do you mind if I miss it? I can skim the transcript later, and I need to speak to various of the embassy staff."

Toreth was about to say, fine by me, then he paused. "No. You're the one who insisted on coming along to play investigator, so you can investigate."

Grimm tried the same smile she'd used on Ruiz. "And as you so correctly pointed out, I'm not a trained interviewer. I'm sure you can handle it."

"I'm sure I can. But I'm going to talk to the main suspect, and so are you. Whatever you're doing for Socioanalysis, you can do it in your own time. Looks like you'll have plenty of it, if they won't let us talk to anyone else and they still haven't produced the case files."

"Well, if you think it will help."

"I don't know, do I, until I've seen if you're any use?"

Toreth started walking before she could reply.

Fu might not have welcomed their interference, but he had already set up a pair of offices for them—adjoining, again. Toreth made a mental note to test the soundproofing on the connecting door as soon as he could. Toreth's desk had an attractive view over the city towards the river, at least as long as he ignored the distorting tint of high-security blast-proof glass, and the edge of the security perimeter blocking off the lower part of the view.

Doctor Campion was already waiting for them. She carried with her an air of no-nonsense competence, from her unfussy clothes and the lack of makeup on her pale, freckled skin to the short trim of her coppery hair. She seemed more irritated than alarmed by the accusations against her. "It's crap," she said almost before she'd finished shaking Toreth's hand. "Absolute crap. The American police are grasping at straws because they have no idea what happened to Judith, and her father is Senator Grant. Why would *I* help her break the law? I hardly knew her."

She headed for the chair across from Toreth's desk which, he realized, would cause her to be unhelpfully backlit by the large window. He intercepted her and brought the chair around to face him on his side of the desk. She raised her eyebrows as she sat, but she didn't comment. Grimm sat to one side, her attitude of polite attention presumably being her attempt to impersonate an I&I investigator.

"Apparently the police think she called you on the day she was found," Toreth said, as he settled into his own chair. "And the day before."

"Well, I didn't get any calls from her. I might have had my comm switched off. I often do when I'm working."

"So you didn't leave the embassy to meet her elsewhere?"

"Definitely not."

"And you know nothing at all about what happened to her?" Toreth asked.

"I didn't even know that she'd been hurt until the next day, when Ambassador Fu told me the police were questioning my involvement. Para-investigator, we aren't equipped for the kind of surgical procedure they're suggesting. I'm here to coordinate with the local medical services, in case any of our staff need treatment, and to oversee diagnosis. Our treatment facilities are strictly limited. There are some . . . idiosyncrasies in the American medical system around certain branches of medicine, but their overall standard is excellent."

"What idiosyncrasies?" Grimm said. "Gynecological?

Campion shook her head. "I was thinking of psychological, but yes, I suppose so."

"So, you didn't carry out any procedure here?" Toreth said.

"As I said, I don't have the equipment. And anyway, it wouldn't be necessary. I *do* have access to a medical synthesizer capable of creating any pharmaceutical I might need on demand. If Judith had approached me, which she didn't, and I'd agreed to help her, which I wouldn't have, no one would ever have known. Certainly, she wouldn't be in hospital."

"All right," Toreth said, letting a certain amount of skepticism linger in his tone. "Leave that for now. When did you last see Buchheit?"

"I suppose it must've been . . ." Toreth saw her fingers move slightly as she counted back. "Five days before she was found, at the mission. When I came here, I was asked to take over some of my predecessor's cultural outreach. It's a new policy for the diplomatic service here—well, relatively new. We're all encouraged

24

to get involved with local charities and that kind of thing. Judith volunteered at the Leahlynn Grant Foundation Family Mission. It's a sort of shelter for homeless families. Indigs. Canfield worked at a weekly clinic there, so I replaced him. That's how I met Judith."

The voluntary work was in Campion's security file, but Toreth hadn't noted the name. "Wait. The what mission?"

"Leahlynn Grant Foundation." Campion smiled wryly. "Senator Grant's grandmother, or great-grandmother, or something like that. In some ways you'll find it's a lot more like the Administration over here than you might think—political power goes hand in hand with money, elections or not. I believe the mission has a branch in Detroit, too."

"So what level of contact did you have with Buchheit?"

"Judith and I chatted while we worked. Other than that, we both attended a couple of fundraising events for the mission, and she asked me to one of her thankful socials not long after I arrived. That's all."

"Thankful socials?" Grimm asked.

"Um . . . a get-together of friends, with the emphasis on feeling grateful for their lives. As far as I can tell, that's all she and her friends do—ostentatious charity work, and endless coffee mornings and afternoons where they talk about their husbands, their children, and their churches. I went because Ambassador Fu thought it would benefit our image. They didn't know what to say to me after I told them my kids were back in New London with their father and I'd never set foot in a church in my life; I assume that's why she never invited me again. That was months ago, now. As I said, I barely knew her."

"Yet you use her first name," Toreth said.

"That's the way it's done over here." Campion shrugged. "It's diplomatic to follow the local customs."

"What did you think about Ms. Buchheit?"

"She was competent at the mission clinic. She's volunteered there for years, and she took on more than she absolutely had to if she'd just been there to be seen to contribute to the family's good works. I think she'd wanted to pursue medical training before she married, something like that."

"And personally?" Toreth prompted.

Campion wrinkled her nose as though she wasn't sure, or just didn't like to say. "She seemed nice enough. A bit dull. I suppose I did get the impression that she might not be especially happy at home—I remember she was curious about my job, and whether my husband minded that I was working out here. Maybe that's why she liked to be out of the house."

"Unhappy at home," Toreth said. "Was she seeing anyone on the side?"

"If she did, then she didn't tell me, but then I wouldn't expect her to. That's something people over here would only confide to a *very* close friend."

Toreth wished idly that he'd brought a neural scanner with him. In its absence, he couldn't find anything specifically fishy in Campion's story, even though he had a nagging sense that something didn't add up. On the other hand, he didn't have any evidence with which to make an objection. The next step was to look for some.

Grimm excused herself, muttering about making a call to Socioanalysis, and this time Toreth let her go. As it turned out, she didn't miss much. Hemmingway, the head of security, was as blasé as Campion herself.

"This American woman was never in the building." The man leaned back in his chair and folded his hands complacently over his stomach. "Never even came through the gates."

The small security office looked like a comfortable den—an expensive coffee machine with a couple of jars of real coffee, a better chair than Toreth had either back at I&I or in his temporary office here, and scuff marks on the desk that suggested the head of security spent a decent amount of time with his feet up.

"Has anyone analyzed the time frame completely?" Toreth asked. "Full movement tracking for all the embassy staff and visitors?"

"No. The access security and the internal recognition systems say that woman, whatever her name is, wasn't in the building. That's all I was asked to check. We sent that data to the police, and we told them as far as we were concerned it was nothing to do with us."

"All right. Well, maybe you could run the movement tracking now?"

"Sorry, not possible." Hemmingway made it sound as though Toreth were being utterly unreasonable in even making the request. "We don't have that kind of capability in the system—we don't need it. I've been here five years, and the only time we were told to maintain a lockdown was for a few weeks after the trouble back home. No one's ever told me to worry about whether the admins have gone shopping again. The embassy's full of grownups, isn't it?"

"Well, you don't know, do you?" Toreth said. Hemmingway just looked at him blankly. "Fine. I want all the data for that day. The I&I systems can have a crack at it."

Toreth was about to call one of his investigators when he remembered the time zone problem. Socioanalysis might still be taking calls, but Toreth's team would be long gone from I&I. On that basis, since he'd done a much longer day himself, he decided to join them. No one at the embassy apparently gave a shit that one of their staff was about to be accused of murder, including the suspect herself, so why should he give them the benefit of overtime? He sent Hemmingway's security data to Sara with instructions to have someone run the check on Campion and the rest of the embassy staff, and called it quits.

He automatically started to head for his room to change out of his uniform when he remembered he wasn't in it. He should've brought a couple along, just to wear in the embassy. Maybe someone would take the situation more seriously with a black jacket and an I&I logo on display.

At least the food in the embassy was a pleasant surprise. He arrived so early he was the only person in the long, high-ceilinged dining room, but before he'd had time to do more than look around for a screen with the opening time, a uniformed waiter arrived and directed him to a table. Even Warrick wouldn't have found fault with the menu. While Toreth waited for his food, he examined the room. Not tiny, but he couldn't imagine it was large enough for the entire embassy staff. When he checked the plan again, a much larger area elsewhere was marked as "general dining."

A series of paintings hung on the walls, all matching in size—old-fashioned, and what Cele called "proper" paintings, in that someone had actually used a brush. Curious, he went over to the nearest one and activated the discreet information screen that blended into the wall below each picture.

Apparently the woman in the painting was the last leader of the French region before unification; she'd signed the unification treaty. He checked the next one, which portrayed the final leader of part of the Iberian Peninsula. Interesting choices, Toreth thought as he looked around the room. Department of International Relations policy, replicated at other embassies around the world, or historical nostalgia on the part of someone here?

When his chicken dhansak arrived—surrounded by a fussy selection of tiny accompaniments—Toreth asked the waiter about the paintings.

"Do you ever get any Americans in here? Not very tactful, considering they bombed the Administration into existence."

The man smiled. "This is the senior staff dining room. Any visitors who matter will be eating in the formal room, and any others will only be cleared for the general canteen. Although in a way you're right—I heard that for a while they hung in the main conference room, and they were all moved in here a few years ago."

After he'd eaten, Toreth went to his room and called Warrick. When he answered, Toreth looked past him into the room in the background—it was the office at the flat, details automatically blurred by the system for security. Warrick wasn't dressed like he'd come straight back from SimTech and been in all evening, though. Should he ask Warrick where he'd been? No, that would sound unaccept-ably paranoid and insecure. He could always run a credit and purchase check later.

"How's the adventure going so far?" Warrick asked.

"*So far* it's pretty boring. Investigations are like that when you can't talk to any witnesses and there's no evidence. I'm missing sucking your cock already."

Warrick laughed. "No postcard this time? Probably wise."

"I could get it couriered by someone in International Relations."

"Most appropriate. Well, we seem to have had equally tedious evenings—or afternoons, in your case." Warrick yawned. "And that was just from thinking about it."

Warrick had provided the opening, so Toreth felt okay to ask. "Where've you been?"

"A dinner meeting with contract negotiators from a corporation with an ex-tensive cosmetic alterations portfolio—surgery and gene based. We showed them our demo system that progressively iterates the sim model in response to subcon-scious measures of user satisfaction, and they like the technology, but not the price. They've apparently decided we must be desperate for business."

"I thought you were?" Toreth said.

"Not enough to barely break even on a contract. Wheatley thinks they'll see sense, so I'm mostly leaving it in his hands, but he wanted me to put in an ap-pearance and look uninterested." Warrick smiled. "Which wasn't difficult this evening. Hopefully I sufficiently conveyed our lack of neediness."

Was that a dig at Toreth's call, when he'd only left New London that morning? Carnac's words echoed uneasily in Toreth's mind. *You want Keir to love you, and the uncontrollable need makes you sick with terror.*

"I'm sure you did," Toreth said. "Well, I should probably go. I still have a few things to do."

Warrick's eyebrows lifted fractionally, then he nodded. "Of course. Good night. And—good luck with the case."

When the screen went blank, Toreth sat back in his chair and breathed out. Need. He didn't *need* Warrick. He hadn't *needed* to call. How long would it take before the memory of that voice faded? Fuck Carnac, and fuck all socioanalysts.

Chapter Three

❖

When Toreth checked the IIP after breakfast, he found the embassy data still sitting there, unprocessed. He called Sara.

"How's America?" she asked.

"Boring. Where's that movement analysis I asked for?"

"Oh, I'm sorry, Toreth. I meant to put a note on the IIP. It's been chaos here. Systems are replacing some of the temporary repairs they did after the—from earlier in the year. It was supposed to take an hour, and all be done by the time we arrived this morning, but—"

Nagra appeared over Sara's shoulder. "Everything went tits up, and nothing's been working properly all day. Afternoon, Para—how are things over there?"

"Boring," Toreth said again. "So am I getting the analysis or not?"

Sara looked pained. "I've scheduled it five times, and then the whole queue vanishes. So, of course, every time it gets longer because there's more building up. I don't think—hm." She paused. "It's the Justice-rated secure systems that are falling over. Does it need to be evidential?"

"No. I doubt Justice gives a toss about dead Americans."

"I *might* be able to find a way of doing it, then, but it won't be submissible." Sara was still frowning slightly. "I suppose I can always run it again properly when they finally sort out the mess."

"Sara, I don't care about that. Just get it done."

And that was that. No Ruiz yet, no case files, no witnesses, and no evidence. Toreth glanced at the IIPs for the active case he'd left behind in New London, but Nagra clearly had it under control, with everything in hand that Toreth would've done in her place. He left a couple of notes on the IIP anyway, just to remind them all that he was watching. That done, he thought briefly about leaving the embassy for a look around the city, but no doubt the moment he left, something would happen.

After a while, he tapped his comm and called Grimm. She appeared in his office a few minutes later.

"Do you have a result?"

"Not yet. I don't have any coffee, either, or an admin to make one, or even a real investigator, so you're the next best thing."

"You want me to make you a coffee," she said flatly.

He smiled genially. "Please. White, no sugar."

She left without a word, and returned shortly with two mugs.

"I'd point out what a ridiculous waste of my time this is, but that's exactly why you did it, isn't is?"

"Thanks." Toreth took the mug and ignored the question. "If you wait a minute, you're about to find out how quickly you can get rid of me. If Campion was in the building and Buchheit wasn't, we're more than halfway there."

She sat down. "Para-investigator Toreth, I have no desire to get rid of you." She lifted her mug. "Not much of one, anyway. I'm sure we could work well together, if you'd give it a chance. I read my ex-colleague Carnac's report on I&I— he said you were an exemplary para-investigator. He added a highly positive note to your file."

"Lovely." The sudden appearance of Carnac's name made him want to throw the coffee right back at her. "Although he then started a revolt and tried to have me and everyone else at I&I killed, so excuse me if I'm not blown away by a commendation."

"And that's why he's my *ex*-colleague. Not to mention that—well. I heard something about his reputation for less than considerate treatment of others outside Socioanalysis."

"You mean, for fucking his 'personal liaisons'?" Toreth said with distaste. Whether they were interested or not.

She winced. "Believe me, I do understand why you have an unfortunate impression of us."

She had no idea, and Toreth certainly wasn't about to enlighten her. Even after everything, after all Warrick's reassurances, it bothered him that he was thousands of miles away and Carnac was so much nearer, somewhere in Europe. Maybe he had enough contacts left at Socioanalysis or in the wider Administration to know where Toreth was, and that it was safe to show up in New London and accidentally bump into Warrick. Maybe—

Toreth pushed the idea aside. "I don't need a personal reason. Nobody likes spooks."

She shrugged. "I won't quibble. Occasionally people do find us useful, though."

As target practice, if there was any justice in the world—which, as Toreth had reason to know, there generally wasn't. Before he could say anything to further worsen relations between I&I and Socioanalysis, the IIP alerted him about an update.

30

One glance revealed the bad news. "Fuck."

"I take it that means the case isn't closed."

He pointed at the screen. "See for yourself. There's an almost six-hour window when the timeline mapping can't place her at all." A second glance confirmed the worst. "And she's the only standout. All the other staff and visitors can be located with high confidence for most of the period."

Grimm leaned forwards and studied the screen. "I see. So, either she wasn't here, or she was keeping very still somewhere in the embassy. What does I&I procedure suggest now?"

An arrest warrant, an injector, and a neural probe, or at least that would've been Toreth's preference. "We interview her again."

To her credit, Campion didn't waste any more time keeping up the pretense that she'd been in the embassy once Toreth laid out the assessment in his office.

"All right. I left the embassy, just for a few hours. There's an archive of medical equipment at one of the museums nearby. I didn't even need a car to get there. I walked; it's only a couple of kilometers. It's a fascinating collection—really old material, including some of the first truly autonomous surgical systems, and information about more modern research on treatments that were abandoned for social reasons. It requires special permission to access, but I happened to meet someone who works there, and he arranged it for me." She looked between Toreth and Grimm, obviously hoping for some sign of them accepting her story. "It wasn't officially sanctioned, I admit. It's so tedious getting approval for professional interactions. Everyone does it, though."

So she'd been sneaking out behind the embassy's back—for *some* reason. "Quite a coincidence, you being out of the embassy at just the time Buchheit was having her abortion."

"See, this is why I didn't tell you!" Campion sounded even more exasperated than before. "That's all it is, a ridiculous coincidence. But I knew how it would look."

"Better than withholding evidence," Toreth said, trying to keep his voice level. "This is about the biggest gift you could give the Washington police, unless you walked through the doors and confessed."

"But the embassy's under no obligation to tell them, surely?" Campion asked. "Fu told me that we can't be compelled to cooperate."

"Are the police likely to talk to your helpful friend at the museum?"

Campion paused, and then said, "They might. He volunteered at the indig shelter, too, and I think he knows Judith. He may not say anything, though."

"Or he might tell them everything, and then they'll know you lied about your whereabouts."

"I'm still on the embassy staff," Campion said. "They can't walk in here and arrest me."

Before Toreth could come up with an answer expressing sufficient levels of skepticism, Grimm leaned forwards and touched Campion once on the arm. Campion looked at her in surprise.

"I don't think you appreciate the wider situation," Grimm said, no longer sounding anything like an I&I investigator. "The Administration wants a controlled, qualified normalization of relations with the United States—that's Council policy. They're allowing more open trade along with more corporate connections, and instigating a slow social realignment to support the broader economic and strategic goals. If it's a choice between putting a roadblock in the progress of what is already a delicate and complex process, and handing you over for trial, how do you think the Council will prioritize that decision?"

"I'm a diplomat," Campion said. "I have immunity from—"

"The information I have from the Bureau is that despite DIR misgivings, if the police offer enough evidence then the Council is strongly minded to waive your immunity."

Toreth and Campion both stared at Grimm; Toreth wondered if he looked as shocked as the medic.

"If you were subsequently found not guilty, then I'm sure the Council would be delighted. And if the verdict went the other way . . . well, perhaps they'd provide support for an appeal. I understand that kind of thing is popular over here. In either case, they've cooperated and made a major diplomatic concession, in return for which they can expect benefits. And there'd be no need to trouble the citizens of the Administration with news of your ultimate fate."

"That wouldn't be policy," Toreth added.

Campion looked between them, this time with bewilderment. "But I keep telling you, I barely knew the woman. I didn't *do* anything."

"Other than break embassy protocol to leave the building without approval," Toreth said. "And if you can do that, what else could you break protocol for? At least, that's how the Council might see it. The Americans definitely will. Did you see anyone at the museum? Anyone who can confirm you were there without us needing to access the museum security and blowing the whole thing open?"

Campion frowned thoughtfully. "The museum is closed to the general public on Mondays, so it was quiet. But Ben dropped in a couple of times. Benjamin Elsney—he's the one who gave me access."

"Do you know exactly when?"

"I . . . no. But I'm sure he'll remember."

"Agent Ruiz could insist on overseeing the interview," Grimm said, and Toreth nodded.

"Who?" Campion asked.

"The Homeland Security agent who's supposed to be observing us observing the police," Toreth said. "Once he knows how stupid you've been, there's nothing to stop him from telling the whole police division."

"If I may make a suggestion, Para-investigator?" Grimm said.

The way she used his title grated. He couldn't tell if he was imagining the similarity to Carnac, or if all Socioanalysts were taught the same faint overtone of contempt. "Well, go on."

"Ruiz already knows we hope to prove someone else helped Ms. Buchheit with her plans. So it would be reasonable for us to want to speak to people who knew her, as many as possible, in the search for alternative suspects. They still might not let us speak to this Elsney alone, but at least we have a plausible excuse for wanting to do so. Put his name on a list, with as many others as we can. Once we have access to the case files, there should be plenty of names."

"Or I could call him," Campion said. "There's no need to involve anyone else."

Toreth considered the options. The first disguised the name, but still carried the risk of Ruiz being there for the interview—perfect if it cleared Campion, disastrous if it didn't. The second had the appeal of speed, but carried the risk of singling out Elsney as someone of importance.

How closely would the police be watching someone with only a peripheral connection to the case? Would they be monitoring his comms? There was no immediate reason Toreth could see that Elsney would be high on their priority list. Had details of Buchheit's misfortune been released to the press? In the Administration, a politically delicate scandal would stay restricted to some of the corporate distribution services, if not be embargoed completely until the full official picture was available. But he remembered the American agents back in New London talking about a freer press. Maybe Elsney had seen the news, put two and two together to get Campion, and gone to the police himself. Surely if the police had already talked to Elsney they'd be knocking on the embassy doors, demanding they drop Campion's immunity . . . unless they were waiting until they had every piece of evidence in the IIP and could make an overwhelming case.

Too many variables.

"Call Elsney," he said to Campion, and out of the corner of his eye he saw the tiniest flicker of irritation on Grimm's face. "Don't mention us or why you're calling, just ask him if the police have spoken to him about Buchheit yet. If they have, we have no reason not to."

Campion took out her comm and called, but after a moment she shook her head. "He's not available. I don't think I should leave a message, do you?"

"Definitely not," Toreth said. "Just try again later. And while we're talking comms, what about these calls from Judith Buchheit? Anything you want to tell us about that now?"

"No, because she didn't call me," Campion said firmly. "I had the comm switched off at the museum—all calls for staff here are routed through the embassy system and monitored. If I'd left my comm on, then they would've known I wasn't in the building."

Of course, if she was off somewhere aborting babies, she'd want to keep that just as quiet. "And what about the day before? The police say you talked to her for over ten minutes."

"They're mistaken. I made a list for the ambassador—four voice calls. I spoke to my husband and kids, made two calls to the Department of International Relations Medical Division, and talked to a young woman who wanted to know if I could help some of her friends get visas for Europe to do 'missionary work' over there." Campion shrugged. "I know, I know, but it does happen. I did what I always do, which is pretend to listen and then told her I was sorry, but the DIR has no influence over the visa process and they'd have to apply like everyone else. I didn't bother to say those sorts of applications are always turned down."

"How did she get your name?" Grimm asked.

"I don't remember if she said—and I didn't recognize her name, whatever it was. I assume she'd heard about me through the clinic, or from someone I've met at an official function. For some reason, these missionaries always seem to think I'll be sympathetic."

Obviously not someone who'd met her in person, then. "But it definitely wasn't Buchheit?"

"Of course not. I know Judith's voice, and she knows me." Campion frowned, and scratched the back of her neck. "She sounded younger than Judith, I think. I suppose Judith could've processed her voice, but why would she?"

Why, indeed? Right that moment, if Toreth had had a recording of the call he probably would have sent it for high-level forensic analysis, just in case there was some shred of evidence hiding in there. But he didn't have it—or much else.

When Campion had gone, Grimm said, "What if Elsney can't confirm her whereabouts?"

"I'm not running the Americans' bloody investigation for them. We certainly don't tell them anything that makes Campion look *more* guilty."

"But if she is?"

"Then my job's to provide enough doubt that the Americans drop it. The Justice system won't get a sniff of this, so who cares what the evidence really says?"

Ruiz arrived later that morning, bringing with him mixed news.

"I knocked some heads together and waved my Homeland Security ID around. Sadly, it doesn't work as well as it did in the good old days—or so the senior agents tell us—but you have access to some of the case files."

"What does 'some' mean?"

"Well, the forensic analysis is open, but most of the witness interviews have been removed. For the privacy of the family. There are summaries of the points covered in the interviews and the investigating officers' conclusions."

The conclusion that Campion had done it, and an interpretation of the interviews that backed that up, no doubt.

Toreth opened his hand screen and scanned through the files. A glance at the summaries confirmed his suspicions about bias, and the forensic report had one rather obvious omission.

"Where's the medical evidence? There must be something from the hospital. This is...three images of her fully clothed, before and after treatment? How am I supposed to get anything from that?"

Ruiz nodded, looking pained. "I knew you wouldn't like this, but, given what happened, the physical details are of an intimate nature. And since she's still alive, there are confidentiality issues with the records, and her family—"

"Oh, for fuck's—" Toreth controlled himself. This was political muscle-flexing, and he and Ruiz were both caught in the middle of it. Antagonizing the man would only make things worse. "Well, thanks for what's here, anyway. But I'd be grateful if you could ask again if there's any way I could see more of the IIP. The investigation files," he added, when Ruiz looked at him blankly. "At least more of the medical evidence, surely? I'm flying blind here."

"If I might make a suggestion, Para-investigator?" Grimm asked.

Toreth nodded.

"Agent Ruiz, would it help our case if I were the one to review the medical evidence?"

To Toreth's surprise, Ruiz nodded. "It might, I suppose. At least it won't make it any worse. Look," he said to Toreth, "I'll talk with the police department liaison again, in person this time. They can only say no, right?"

At least according to the Washington police, everyone who knew Judith Buchheit was convinced that she would never have done such an appalling, barbaric, cruel, and completely out of character thing if she hadn't been led astray by sinful, godless heathens from the depraved European Administration. Or general words to that effect.

Of course Toreth couldn't *hear* the words, or even read a full transcript. Taking an optimistic view, and political game-playing aside, maybe the reluctance to hand over the full interviews meant they weren't as one-sided as the investigators wanted to portray them. He'd slanted plenty of Justice submissions himself in his time.

With that in mind, he reread the summaries. Assuming the police hadn't pulled the content entirely out of their arses, they suggested that the interviews had been based around a fairly standard set of questions. They covered the victim's movements on the day (largely unknown, or at least not shared with Toreth), associates who might be involved in her crime (the evil, corrupting Administration doctor, and...no one else), her state of mind (unrelentingly cheerful and satisfied with her wonderfully blessed life), her feelings about her children (she adored them more than anything except her husband and family), her feelings about her husband (see previous answer), and her spotless moral character.

Only one person stood out in any way, and that was purely because Toreth was willing to sniff for the faintest whiff of dissent in the ranks. The I&I evidence analysis system would've thrown the idea right back at him. But since a whiff was all he had...

He called Ruiz, and asked where he was.

"Still at the police department. A whole lot of people seem to be in meetings today."

"I have a couple of questions."

"Fire away."

"First, do they really have no idea where Buchheit was that day? When we needed to find that boy you lost, we just used his boyfriend's taxi journeys from the Central Transport Division records. Isn't there anything like that here?"

"Not in Washington, I'm afraid," Ruiz said. "Some other states use a central control system, but D.C. shares the Maryland system. It's a distributed network, with all the vehicles on the road figuring out the best solutions together. It's supposed to be the most efficient and robust approach."

So much for the hope that the police were hiding something they didn't want Toreth to know. "But no one keeps a record?"

"Well, I assume they've already looked at any cars she had access to and drawn a blank. And sometimes you can pull something from cab or rental companies. I'm sure the police are searching," Ruiz added. "But it takes time."

"Next, about the witnesses—"

"Toreth, I'm sorry, but they were firm about that. You can't interview them. And some of those witnesses are the kind of important that you don't want to upset when the answer is still gonna be no. It'll only hurt the case in the long run."

"Could you talk to just one of them for me? Deborah Mayhew—Buchheit's sister. Ask her if she would authorize the police to release her full interview to me. Even just a transcript."

There was a long pause, then Ruiz said, "She isn't married, right?"

"How the hell would I know? I don't have access to her security file." Or anything else.

"Her surname isn't Grant, but I thought...ah, right, I see it here. Mayhew was her mom's maiden name." Ruiz seemed to be talking out loud as he checked the file. "And, yeah . . . looks like she switched to using it when she was twenty-one. Well, as long as she really isn't married, and there's no husband to talk to . . . and I'll have to check, but I think she filed her emancipation, so there no need to involve her father, either." There was another pause, even longer. Toreth tapped his crossed fingers on the edge of his desk until Ruiz said, "Okay, I'll see what I can do. No promises, though."

"Thanks, I—"

Someone knocked on the door behind him, and before Toreth could say anything, it opened.

"Para-investigator?" Campion said. "I contacted Ben."

A male voice Toreth didn't recognize said, "Rebekah said she needed my help."

"Thanks," Toreth said to Ruiz, and cancelled the connection. When he turned around, Campion was standing in the doorway with a tall man looking over her shoulder.

Fuck. How much had Ruiz seen and heard? Would he recognize Elsney and realize Toreth was trying to run his investigation behind Ruiz's back?

As they shook hands, Toreth realized that Elsney was taller than him by a good few centimeters. He was also older than Toreth had first guessed, probably in his late forties, his dark skin showing fine wrinkles around his eyes.

"You were just supposed to ask him the question," Toreth said to Campion when the introductions were done.

"She did," Elsney said. "And, yes, the police talked with me yesterday. Rebekah said that you'd probably want to hear what I said to them, so I came right over."

"Okay, thanks." Well, any damage was already done. Toreth turned to Campion and said firmly, "Excuse us, please."

He should've guessed that she'd argue. "Wouldn't it help if I was here?"

"No, it wouldn't." Toreth put his hand on the edge of the still open door. "Go away."

That finally did the trick, and he shut the door behind her—and locked it—before she could change her mind. Thinking wistfully of a properly intimidating I&I interview room, Toreth showed Elsney over to the smart desk and comfortable chairs. He didn't bother asking Elsney if he minded Toreth recording the interview. If the man didn't assume everything at the embassy would be recorded, that was his problem.

As soon as they were settled in the chairs, Elsney said, "Val, I have to tell you, I can't believe that Rebekah would have anything to do with what happened to Judith. I mean, and excuse me for saying it, I do know what people say about Europeans, and I guess it might seem like I haven't known her for long, but I . . . well, I can't believe it."

Toreth wondered how much weight the American Department of Justice systems would put on a sincerely held belief. "Doctor Campion told us that she was at your museum on Monday."

"And so she was. When did this—when was Judith found? The police were asking about the afternoon."

"Her taxi made the emergency call around thirteen-fifteen."

"That's . . . a quarter after one, right? Well, then. Rebekah was at the museum with me from eleven until four. I arranged special permission for her to be there."

So far, so supporting of Campion's story. "Mr. Elsney, could Dr. Campion have left the museum at any time without your knowledge?"

This time, he hesitated.

"If you're worried about her, I promise that we have her best interests at heart."

Elsney looked out of the window for a moment, and then finally he nodded. "Okay. I guess I couldn't swear under oath that she didn't. I looked for her a couple times and I didn't find her. But the medical archive is a big collection. Maybe she wandered into another section following an item reference and I missed her. I didn't look too hard. She was definitely there when I went to tell her the museum was closing at four o'clock. We work a short day on Mondays."

"When you couldn't find her, was that the beginning or the end of the time she was there?"

"Around the middle, I guess? I remember right after I came back from lunch, I went to see if she was doing okay, because I'd tried to call her and she was off-net. I couldn't find her, so I figured maybe she was out getting something to eat by herself. I honestly didn't think anything of it. I had plenty to do that day at the museum—we're in the middle of finalizing next year's summer programs—and I told her to call me if she needed any help, so I pretty much just assumed she was fine."

Absolutely fine, roaming around the city getting herself involved in murders. It did at least confirm Campion's claim to have switched off her comm, for what little that was worth. "Did you tell all this to the police?"

"Well, yes. They asked me about Rebekah, so of course I had no choice but to tell them." The pain must've shown on Toreth's face, because Elsney looked at him sympathetically, then leaned forwards. "I also said I just couldn't believe she was involved."

Toreth should've said no to Turnbull right away. "How well did you know Judith Buchheit?"

He frowned. "Why?"

"I'm just trying to build up a picture of her."

"Oh, okay. Well, I met her at the museum a few years ago—she'd come to meet her cousin's wife for lunch, but Sandi was running late and she asked me to take care of Judy, show her a couple galleries while she waited. We hit it off right away, and Judy asked if I could spare some time for the mission. I help them out

38

with administration and fund-raising, that kinda thing. Judy's very popular with the mission clients and with everyone who works there. I never heard anyone say a bad word about her."

"How much time did you spend with her?"

Elsney's brow creased. "Some. I guess I put eight or ten hours a week into mission business, but not all with Judy."

"That much?" Toreth said in surprise.

"Well, the mission is my main volunteer role. Most employees can donate up to ten percent of their hours to volunteer, if they want it, plus extra at evenings and on weekends. Judy and I sit on a couple of the same committees—she's a Grant family representative—and we've worked on some fund-raising projects together. So...exactly how much time we spend together depends on what's in progress. I guess I hadn't seen as much of her for the last few months."

"But would you say you knew her well?"

"I thought so, but—" Elsney cleared his throat. "I just—if only she'd asked some of her friends for help, you know? It's heartbreaking to think of her coming into the mission, giving so much to help others but not feeling she could confide in anyone. I know it isn't a popular view, but this kind of tragedy is exactly what happens when you have a bunch of absolutist laws banning all abortions *and* limiting access to—" He stopped, and put up his hands. "Excuse me. I'm sure you don't want to hear a lot of foreign politics. To answer your question, I know Judy well enough to say that she's a great lady."

Toreth doubted he'd given that little speech to the Washington police. "Well, thanks for all your help, Mr. Elsney."

"Sure, no problem," he said with apparent sincerity. "Anything else I can do to help, just call me, okay?"

Toreth checked the interview transcript himself and put it into the IIP. Then he started composing a note to the ambassador and to Turnbull. Despite Turnbull's implied promises, this wouldn't be putting any commendations on his record. The best spin that Toreth could put on Elsney's revelation was that at least they had advance warning of what the police were keeping quiet. That gave them an indeterminate time to find some way of proving that however fucking guilty Campion had managed to make herself look, she hadn't actually done the thing he'd now carefully proved she'd had ample opportunity to do.

Toreth was still wondering how he could polish up the turd of a report when Grimm said from across the room, "So we have Campion alone and unsupervised in a museum full of surgical equipment. I'd call that an unfortunate development."

He forced himself to finish the sentence he was working on and turn around slowly, even though a spike of adrenalin had set his heart hammering. The adjoining door obviously opened quietly, because it was still standing ajar. Fuck the view, he needed to turn the desk around.

"You were watching the IIP?" he asked.

She smiled. "I thought I ought to, Para-investigator."

"So what the hell do we do now, *Socioanalyst*?" When he realized she was hesitating, he beckoned her over. "Well?"

"What would you do in New London?" she said as she sat down on the other side of the desk.

"Arrest Campion as a suspect, and get the best waiver I could. Maybe she didn't do it, but she's been lying her arse off, and if the security team here weren't actively helping her cover up her absence, then they all want sacking, anyway. She's a diplomat, not a corporate sab, so a couple of days on level D would loosen her up, even if I couldn't get a high level waiver."

"Well, I know this isn't my field—"

"It's not *my* field, either. Usually I'm trying to prove who did it, not who didn't."

"Surely it's the same thing?" she said in a patient tone that made him want to throw something at her. Maybe the desk. "Essentially, I mean. If we prove the former, and it's not Campion, then we've achieved the latter."

"And how exactly are *we* supposed to do that with no evidence?"

"We'll get more access from the police," Grimm said with confidence. "It's just political posturing."

Toreth blinked at the voicing of his own previous assessment. "I know, but it's still bloody inconvenient. Why couldn't they have done it before we flew all the way here?"

"Because it would've been at the wrong level."

"Sorry?"

"Saying no to a request from the Administration Council is an entirely different kind of snub than saying yes to the Council, and then allowing the police department to drag their feet and inconvenience the small fry—you and me. The end result might be exactly the same, but the presentation is completely different. Which is interesting, don't you think?"

Toreth wondered how successfully he was keeping his distaste—for Socioanalysis and for time-wasting politics in the middle of his investigation—from showing on his face. "Do I?"

"Well, it provides additional data about the finer nuances of the American government's attitude towards Europe. I suppose whether or not that's interesting depends on your level of engagement with international politics."

"Engagement with international politics" sounded like a euphemism for something that would win the perpetrator a nice long stretch of re-education. "Let's say 'low,' and move on. Do you think it's worth calling Turnbull and asking her to give the Americans a kick in the arse?"

Grimm frowned thoughtfully. "My spot assessment is . . . no. Not yet. I think we'll get some, but probably not all, of the information we want in a day or two. I doubt an intervention from Turnbull would significantly speed the process. The staged release is just a relationship marker, a reminder that favors are being bestowed."

Toreth waved at the screen. "And what if before then they decide to demand to talk to Campion, since she was waltzing all over Washington at the relevant time, and Fu slaps up a big red 'diplomatic immunity, do not cross' sign and tells them to fuck off?"

"Ah, well. At that point, I imagine we can whistle for it." She clicked her tongue thoughtfully. "I do think someone made a tactical error when they picked Agent Ruiz, though. He strikes me as a poor game player—someone who takes pride in his work. He may have been assigned simply to, as you so eloquently put it, 'observe us observing,' but if he can be brought around to thinking of this as a case we're jointly investigating, he might become a valuable asset, especially should dialogue with the Washington police break down completely. If I might make a suggestion, why not put some effort into cultivating a more personal relationship with him?"

"I already had a warning about trying that kind of thing over here," Toreth said.

"Not quite the kind of personal relationship I meant." Her smile was accompanied by a hint of raised eyebrows. "Although he's an attractive man, and he is married, so...."

"So what?" Toreth said coldly.

To his surprise, Grimm said immediately, "I do apologize, Para-investigator. I honestly didn't mean to cause offense, although I clearly did. I was partitioning very poorly, and I have no excuse beyond the shift in time zone."

He could just imagine her, reading through his psych file and his security file, with a sigh and a shake of her head.

"*I* have a suggestion, too," Toreth said. "Stop trying to be funny. Apparently Socioanalysis can't teach that, no matter how young they start on their lab rats." Suddenly he was as tired of Grimm as of the rest of the mess. "Why don't you stick to doing whatever the fuck Socioanalysis sent you over here to do, and I'll investigate the case?"

Grimm stood up. "As you prefer, Para-investigator," she said evenly. "But if I can assist you, just call."

When the Atlantic fucking froze over, Toreth thought as she left. Preferably after sinking Socioanalysis to the bottom of it.

The physical effort of moving his desk, and the rest of the room's furnishings that he'd needed to rearrange in order to get his back to a wall and a view of both doors to the room, burned away some of the annoyance. He replaced the screen on his desk and called up the embassy plan. Yes, there was a gym—in fact, the place seemed to be designed to give the staff as few excuses as possible to leave. At least that would give him something to do while he waited for the police to turn up and demand the embassy hand over Campion. After that, everything escalated to diplomatic point-scoring and politics beyond Toreth's control.

He half expected to have his exercise interrupted by Turnbull or one of the other interested parties from the meeting at the Bureau. In fact, the next person to call was Ruiz. Toreth slowed the treadmill and readied himself for disappointment.

"I managed to get in touch with Mayhew. She says she's happy to talk to the police about releasing her interview record, but more than that, she wants to talk with you."

Toreth blinked at the unexpected bonus. "How soon? Where?"

"She's staying at a hotel in town, so she suggested you could meet her there today. I got the feeling she wouldn't be too comfortable coming to the embassy. I guess you can't blame her, when Campion is there."

Toreth wondered if that was the real reason, or if Mayhew didn't want to draw overt attention to her dissent from the approved story. "Okay, I'll go."

"I'll go with you," Ruiz said, in a tone that made it clear this was nonnegotiable. "Don't leave the embassy until I get there."

Grimm's suggestion about trying to pull Ruiz onto their side, however annoyingly put, still might have merit. Toreth decided to test it out.

"Are you from Washington?" he asked conversationally as the car drove through the wide, oddly gridlike streets.

"No way! I was born in Loreto—that's the state capital of South California. Can't you tell from my accent?"

"Honestly, you all sound pretty much the same to me," Toreth said, and Ruiz laughed.

"I guess so. You all sounded kinda alike in New London, too."

"So you don't know Washington well?"

"So-so. I was stationed just south of here for a few years. Then I was moved to . . . another location."

"With Agent Cardine?"

"Ah, no. It was before our trip to Europe. We only worked together that one case. It's her specialty, dealing with deviant behavior. It's a tough job, I guess, but she's very dedicated to her work. Chasing terrorists and watching political agitators wouldn't interest her." He smiled wryly. "I suppose that all seemed like a pretty strange affair to you guys over there."

Toreth censored his opinion down to, "It was unusual. I&I doesn't often get involved with what consenting adults do in their own bedrooms. It's definitely different over here, especially jumping right into the middle of an investigation."

Ruiz nodded. "Well, you can get a long way if you keep in mind that the Founding Fathers Amendment to the Constitution guaranteed this is a Christian country, established on Christian principles, and that's how our laws are framed."

Unfortunate that Toreth's knowledge of Christianity was more or less limited to expressing feelings like, "Jesus fucking Christ, this case is a pain in the arse."

"I do appreciate your help." Toreth tried for sincerity, and found himself thinking just for a moment about Grimm's jibe. She was right; Ruiz was an attractive man. "I'm sure it's no fun for you either, asking people to let me interfere with their case."

"I don't mind—I even understand how you feel about it. I'm a Catholic, and I meet people who honestly think that I couldn't have been sincere when I made my pledge as a public servant—to my duty, to the Constitution, and to Jesus Christ—because I owe allegiance to the Pope in Rio de Janeiro. But there are all kinds of duty, and whatever I feel about what Judith Buchheit did, I agree with you that her case should be investigated as fairly and impartially as any other."

Toreth looked at him with surprise.

"I can see you wondering how the moral aspect affects the investigation. Yes, maybe it's easier to think that someone from outside persuaded her against her better judgement. People know about Europe—well, they think they do." He smiled again. "There are a lot of stories, anyway. Personally, I prefer to end up finding what's true, not what's easy."

"So if we find something that contradicts the police's investigation...?"

"Then I'll make sure they hear about it, and if they don't want to, I'll shout about it until they do."

"Well, thanks." Points given, however reluctantly, to Grimm.

The hotel didn't match Toreth's expectations for a daughter of a family with their own charitable foundation. The building's exterior leaned more towards old opulence than modern sharpness, but it had a shabby, faded look. The inside jarred even more, with what had obviously once been a misguided attempt at a modern update now also showing its age. The bones of the building beneath seemed embarrassed by the bright colors layered on top.

To his surprise, Mayhew was waiting for them in the lobby, scanning every new arrival intently. Toreth recognized her from the image in the abbreviated case files at the same moment as she recognized Agent Ruiz. She bore a close resemblance to the victim, except for being slightly plumper. The main difference was her healthy, pink-cheeked complexion and her light but precise makeup, a sharp contrast to the bare-faced pallor of Buchheit's hospital images. They had the same brown hair with a tight curl, in Mayhew's case kept back from her face with a band across her head.

"Hello, Ms. Mayhew," Toreth said as Ruiz introduced them.

He wasn't sure about offering his hand, but she did so first. "Good to meet you. Please, call me Deborah. How are you finding America?"

"Interesting," Toreth said. "Different."

"I guess it must be, if the things you hear about Europe are true." She blushed faintly, then said, "You want to ask me some questions about Judy, is that right?"

"If you're okay with that."

"Well, sure. If there's any chance it'll help her, I'll do whatever I can."

"I'll be here the whole time, Deborah," Ruiz said reassuringly.

"I'd rather talk to Mr. Toreth alone," Mayhew said.

"I'm afraid that isn't possible," he said.

Her demure smile didn't flicker, but a tiny bit of steel appeared in her voice. "Agent Ruiz, I'm an attorney. I know family law might not impress you much, but I think—I hope—I can answer some questions on my own."

"I'm sure you can, Deborah, but—"

"Am I under arrest? Or even under suspicion?"

"Not as far as I know," he said evenly.

Her eyes narrowed slightly, but her voice didn't waver. "Well, then. Is this an official police interview?"

"Absolutely not. Para-investigator Toreth is here as an observer only, and that's why I should—"

"So if there's no legal requirement for a second officer at the interview, and since I'm an unmarried, emancipated adult, then why can't you respect my choice?"

Stymied, Ruiz hesitated too long. Mayhew turned to Toreth. "If you come this way, I've ordered a couple coffees."

She walked away, forestalling another protest from Ruiz. As Toreth went to follow her, Ruiz put his hand on Toreth's arm.

"Listen," Ruiz said in a low voice. "If I let you talk to her now, I want to see the recording, okay?"

"Absolutely," Toreth said.

"And if she doesn't want to talk about something, then you don't press her, okay? We aren't down in your interrogation levels now."

Toreth disengaged his arm. "I'll call you when we're done."

As soon as they were out of Ruiz's sight, Mayhew's demeanor shifted subtly again. Now she was looking him right in the face, and her stride had more authority.

"There's a lounge right along here," she said. "It's public, but I've never seen anyone in there at this time of day."

When they got there, Toreth could see why. The décor was even more tasteless than the rest of the hotel he'd seen. Instead of a window, the wall was screened with a convincing view of a wide meadowland studded with pine trees and surrounded by snowcapped mountains. The view might be fake, but the sound effects were provided by a real stream of water that fell from the balcony above into a wide basin made of a colorless, cloudy material cut to resemble ice.

Mayhew looked up at the falling water. "It's ridiculous, isn't it? This place used to be my great-grandma's favorite. She remembered it when it was the most exclusive hotel in town. Even after they refurbished and put in that waterfall, she used to bring me here sometimes for lunch. And I suppose the water won't stop a really good microphone, but it's the best I can do without taking you back to my room. If my dad heard that Agent Ruiz had allowed that, there'd be hell to pay."

A tray with two cups and a self-heating coffeepot were waiting at one of the tables. Toreth noted, as he sat down, that the table she'd chosen gave them both a clear view of the rest of the lounge. Mayhew would fit right in with any corporates Toreth had met.

"How do you like your coffee, Mr. Toreth?"

"White, no sugar, please. And call me Val." He could tolerate it for the sake of a better connection. "Do you mind if I record this?" he asked.

She hesitated, pot of coffee poised over the cup. "Who gets to see it?"

"Only me."

To his surprise, she accepted the assurance right away. "All right, then. Now, you ignore whatever that agent guy said. Ask me anything you like. He said you'd only seen a summary of when I talked with the police?"

"That's right. I haven't seen a full transcript of any of the interviews. But I did notice that yours seemed shorter than the others. I wondered if there were some things that maybe the police thought didn't tie in with their view of the case."

She laughed shortly. "I bet. And not just the police's view, either."

"Agent Ruiz was keen to remind me that your father's a senator."

Mayhew nodded. "If the police can pin the whole thing on someone who isn't even American, all the better for everyone, especially my dad."

Did "everyone" include Mayhew herself? "Would it make a difference to your sister?"

"No. She'd still go to jail, or they'd put her into some kind of criminal psychiatric facility. I hate to say it, but I honestly expect my dad is praying that she dies. Without a trial there's at least a chance of him playing things down. Judy's husband has been like a substitute son for him. My mom died young, and Dad remarried, but our stepmom never had any kids."

Toreth frowned. "I thought the family background in the case file said Judith has a brother, too?"

"Oh, Maxie." She shook her head. "Well, technically, yeah. But he lives in some weird atheistic commune outside of Seattle, and he makes a living selling tourists his handmade paper models of city buildings from before the great quake."

The problem with an unfamiliar accent was that Toreth found it hard to tell if she was joking. "Paper models?"

"Sure. He folds each one out of a single piece of paper. Whenever he comes up with a new design, he sends one to me. Not the finished model—just the instructions, and a piece of paper. He makes that by hand, too. He's a sweetheart, in his own way, but he isn't exactly senator material. Lance is the one my dad sees carrying on the family tradition. Well, saw. Now, who knows?"

More political motives adding to the desire to push blame outside the country. "What about you?" Toreth picked up a paper napkin from the tray, and put in the first fold. "If you're the only one left?"

Mayhew laughed. "Val, I'm sure you've noticed that I'm not anyone's son. I'm not saying there have never been women senators, I'm just saying that my dad doesn't think there ought to be. He could barely deal with the idea that I wanted to leave home before I married and take up an unfeminine profession like law. My stepmom had to talk him into letting me go to law school without having to wait until I was twenty-one. My dad said he wouldn't waste his money on me, when I'd only quit as soon as I caught a rich lawyer. I'm pretty sure he thinks I only graduated to spite him. He's very old-fashioned in his views, and law is one of the un-Ephesian professions."

"The what?" Toreth said.

"Oh, it means . . . if women stand up in court and argue against men, that risks leading to unsubmissive thoughts outside of the courtroom, right? So, is it okay for a Christian country to allow women to put their eternal souls in jeopardy when there are plenty of men who could do the same job? Well, no, I guess not, if you don't think people can be trusted to look after their own souls. But whether it's right or wrong, that's the way it was for a long time. When my dad was young, there were no women in court, just like a woman didn't have any choice about whether she could be emancipated from her father before she married, and he doesn't see why it has to be different now."

Mayhew struck Toreth as about as submissive as Warrick—if she was, it would be on her own terms. Assuming she was telling the truth, though, she didn't appear to have gained anything from Buchheit's fall from grace.

Toreth ran his fingers firmly down the last fold—the napkin held the creases badly—and held out the finished origami bird on the palm of his hand. It had a rather drunken lean to the left.

"I'm afraid I can't make buildings," Toreth said.

46

"But it's cute!" She took the bird and examined it. "Where did you learn to do that?"

"You know, I don't remember. It's not good for much except—" a different chat-up line in bars, "—relaxation."

She adjusted the wings, trying to make the bird stand up straighter, then gave up and placed it carefully on the table. She sat back in her chair, one knee crossed over the other. "Poor thing. I don't think it could fly very far."

"I don't think your brother needs to worry about his business. So, tell me about Judith." Toreth thought about all the glowing testimonials in the case file. "Did Senator Grant approve of her?"

"Oh, yeah. She was always my dad's pet. She's done everything he thought made a good woman." Mayhew smiled sadly. "Not that it ever seemed to do her much good."

"You don't think she was as happy as everyone says?"

"I . . ." Mayhew hesitated. "Well, you have to remember that she believed everything she was told about how she'd find her true purpose in life as a wife and a mother. She always wanted to play house, and 'cause she's a couple years older than me, house was what we played. Except sometimes I could persuade her to play hospitals instead. I'd pretend I was the surgical robot, and she'd be the patient management tech and tuck the dolls in bed afterwards and bring them soup." Mayhew laughed. "Oh, and sometimes I'd have trials and send the dolls to prison, and she'd go visit them. Matthew 25:36. You know, it's amazing we stayed as close as we did, right?"

"Right," Toreth said, wondering whether the digression was deliberate distraction from something she'd decided not to say. "So, things didn't turn out as she expected?"

"My sister's other problem is that she never catches a break. Her first husband—oh yes," she said, when he raised his eyebrows. "She was married before, right out of school. And I always kinda liked Gene, I have to say, despite what happened. He was the son of one of my dad's Michigan circle. State politics, big business. And Judy really loved him, too. But, you know, they were so young, and she had no experience. They were married for four years, no kids. He wasn't exactly what you could call diligent in his duties, if you catch my meaning."

He wouldn't fuck her, obviously. Toreth went for the more Ruiz-friendly, "In the bedroom?"

"Exactly." Mayhew sipped her coffee. "She used to talk to me about it, worrying about what she was doing wrong. Well, what could *I* do? I suggested she should try to get him into some kind of counselling, to figure everything out, but in the end I got a call and she was expecting. A boy, even, which meant my dad was already picking out the right important godparents when the kid barely had a heartbeat. And not two weeks later, the police raided a hotel and arrested Gene."

"He was there with a man?" Toreth guessed.

She nodded, apparently unsurprised that he'd worked it out. But then, presumably, she was expecting him to be a louche European.

"Now you can see why I didn't want Agent Ruiz here. I bet he'd be turning colors hearing a senator's daughter airing the family's dirty laundry to you. But this is what I mean about poor Judy never getting a break. She was completely destroyed. A few days after Gene was arrested she lost the baby. My stepmom says it was because of the stress, but who knows? It was early, maybe it would've happened anyway. Of course, my dad said God knew what He was about, not bringing tainted fruit into the world. I swear, he would've had that baby adopted out, even though it would've *killed* her. And then Judy had to divorce Gene. I think, given a choice, she might have stood by him—like I said, she really loved him, and he would've gotten early probation if he repented and agreed to treatment in jail—but my dad insisted."

All interesting enough as background, adjusting for the ambient insanity, but not what Toreth had been hoping for when she arranged the meeting. "And what about her current husband?"

"Well, Lance isn't a pervert, so I guess he has that going for him. And he wasn't picked by my dad, either." From her tone, she seemed to consider the latter more important than the former. "Lance knew my cousin Simon at law school—he was a friend of Maxie's, too, until Maxie dropped out. Anyway, Judy met Lance again at Simon's birthday party a few months after her divorce, and they hit it off right away. My dad always liked Simon, so any friend of his had a head start persuading my dad he'd make a good son-in-law."

"And has Judith been happy with him?"

"Well...yes, I guess. At first. Oh, I don't know. I mean, I know for sure things haven't always been great between them, but lately she seemed pretty upbeat. She definitely felt stifled sometimes. She told me—" Mayhew looked at him closely. "Do you think she did what they're accusing her of doing?"

"I don't know," Toreth said. "No one will let me look at any evidence."

"Everyone's saying she did this terrible thing to herself, and I just...I still find it impossible to believe. Yes, she's been unhappy—sometimes very unhappy—but she wouldn't abort. She'd call it murdering a baby. I guess they have medical evidence that it happened, but someone made her do it. Forced her to, against her will. Not your doctor at the embassy, either. Why would she care if Judy had a baby or not?"

If criminals conformed in reality to what families found impossible to believe, then a lot of crime would vanish in a puff of deluded optimism. "Who did it, then?"

She sipped her coffee, and then she shook her head. "I don't know. If I had any suspicions, I'd tell you, I promise. At least it seems like you have an open mind. I told the Washington police the same thing, and they just thought I was

48

trying to protect my sister. Which, sure, I am, but I mean it wholeheartedly, too."

Toreth nodded. "So, you were telling me about why she was unhappy."

"I was going to say, she told me more than once that she felt she was a production line, pushing one baby after another through the factory doors until the right model came out. And you can see why I didn't pass that on to the police, right? It makes her sound like she didn't want her kids, but she did. She adored them. But at the same time, she felt like she'd failed—five daughters, you see? To her they were perfect, and to my dad they were all just not a boy."

"*Five?*" Toreth exclaimed. He couldn't imagine many people in the Administration, except maybe high-up corporates, swinging that past the Department of Population.

"What are the odds, right?" Mayhew seemed to take it as surprise about the gender, not the absolute number. "Although there was . . . well, they did have a son, but he died right after he was born. It was heartbreaking. He had terrible deformities—most of his brain never grew—and they knew from early on that there was no hope, not even with the best modern medical help. She carried him almost to full term, and he lived long enough to be christened before he died. They called him Jedediah—that's Lance's middle name. Poor Judy took it very hard. Who wouldn't? And people can be so judgmental."

"About what?" Toreth asked.

"Well, wondering why God would visit something like that on a family. People make assumptions that there must be a reason for it. Especially after Gene. And my dad . . . " She sighed. "I overheard my dad tell Lance there must be something wrong with Judy, that she couldn't make a son that wasn't a monster."

"Did Judith know how he felt?"

"I don't know. Maybe. Lance was pretty cold about it all, anyway. I just couldn't understand—it was his baby to lose, too, whether or not it meant he didn't have a son. I remember him telling me that she'd have another and then it would all be forgotten. But when Judy became pregnant with Abigail, she was almost out of her mind with fear it would happen again. It didn't matter how many scans she had, she got this idea fixed in her head that everyone was lying to her. I took a leave of absence from work and came to stay with her for a while, before Abbi was born and for a few weeks after. Lance asked me to."

"So her husband thought she might do something to herself?" Toreth guessed. "That's why he wanted you there to keep an eye on her."

"No. Well . . . no, I don't think so. I can't imagine . . . " She trailed off doubtfully, but then her voice strengthened. "There was nothing wrong with Abbi, and I'm sure in her heart she knew that."

"And if something had been wrong with her?"

Mayhew met his eyes steadily. "I've never had a baby. I can't imagine what it's like to carry one you know has no chance of living. If the thought entered her

49

head with Jedediah, or even with Abbi, out of fear, I wouldn't judge her. But she wouldn't *do* it. Not Judy."

None of this had shown up even obliquely in the interview summaries. "Do the Washington police know about the dead baby?"

She winced a little. "I guess. It didn't come up when they talked with me, but anyone else might've said something. And it isn't a secret—Jedediah has a grave, and a headstone."

"So when she said she felt like a production line, was that before or after the last baby?"

"Before. After Jedediah died. But..."

Mayhew stopped, and picked up the little paper bird from the table. Toreth wished Mistry was there with him. He tried to imagine what she'd do under the same circumstances. Wait? Prompt? Maybe he could've had her watching the interview over the comm, although the Americans would probably have thrown a fit about that.

His hesitation turned into a default "wait," and finally Mayhew carried on.

"After Abbi was born, Judy wasn't well. Quiet, crying all the time—some days she wouldn't even get out of bed. I did my best, but eventually Lance said it wasn't right for me to be stuck there indefinitely, and that was when he hired a live-in nanny. Judy always had help during the day, but the full-time nanny as well, that was new. Then I went home—or rather, Lance sent me home. After that I had some crazy calls with Judy. She thought the nanny was spying on her, trying to steal the kids away from her, that kind of thing. I wanted to come back, but Lance said no. Eventually Judy seemed to straighten out. She was more like herself, and she even decided she liked the nanny. But then—and this is something else I didn't tell the police—Judy told me she flat-out didn't want any more babies, at least for a while. Jedediah and Abbi had been so tough for her, and she finally decided to stand up for herself. I'm sure Lance and my dad won't tell you, or anyone, about *that*."

This time, when she stopped, Toreth prompted her. "And?"

"Well, I guess you might not know, but women can't get contraceptives by themselves. Only married men can, on behalf of their wives. But Abbi's almost two now, and she's been the last one, so I guess Lance said yes, in the end."

Toreth could just imagine Sara's face as she read the transcript of *this* interview. "In the end? Did they fight about it?"

"Honestly, I don't know for sure. She's gotten more private about her relationship with Lance. But I know she and Lance were sleeping apart, at least for a while. Judy didn't tell me outright, but she slipped up a couple times and said 'my bedroom' and 'Lance's bedroom.' I support her the best I can from California, but it isn't always easy. My dad thinks I'm a bad influence on her, and he said that to Lance so many times that I think he believed it, too."

50

Toreth poured himself more coffee while he considered the results of the interview so far. Judith was probably mentally unstable, and had also expressed a firm desire not to have any more kids which, while perfectly understandable as far as Toreth was concerned, unfortunately rather strengthened her image as a vulnerable victim-in-waiting ready to have a moment of weakness preyed upon by a European baby-killer. Now he regretted his quick agreement to let Ruiz see the interview.

On the other hand, it also meant there was ample scope for premeditation. Judith had had months to prepare for the eventuality of needing an abortion, possibly long before Campion stepped off the plane. He wondered what the odds were of being able to find evidence of such plans.

"Did your sister talk to you about Dr. Campion?"

"Not really. I heard her mention the embassy doctor a few times, that's all. I had the idea they were pretty good friends, but I don't remember anything specific. I didn't even recall the name."

Great. A contradiction to Campion's insistence that she hardly knew the woman. "Was she friends with any other medics?"

"Maybe. She's always been heavily involved with the mission—it was one of the few things she still showed any interest in when she was really sick—and they have all kinds of volunteers at the clinics there."

"Any of them particularly close?"

"Not that I know about. But like I said, for the last year or two I haven't seen so much of her." She shrugged apologetically. "Sorry, I'm not making a good witness."

"You're being very helpful," Toreth said, with a certain measure of truth.

From her smile, he suspected she thought he was humoring her. "You should talk to Lance about how Judy's been lately, and who her friends are. I admit, I didn't always have the most sisterly feelings for him, but this has changed him."

"Unfortunately, I don't think I'll get the chance. So far you're the only person who's talked to us. The Washington police don't like it."

"Really?" Her expression hardened. "We'll see about that." She stood up, her comm earpiece already in her hand. "Just wait here a minute, Val."

Mayhew crossed to the far side of the lounge, where the falling curtain of water turned her into a distorted, wavering image. Toreth waited until she turned her back, and then put the camera feed through to his comm earpiece, adjusting the detection on the microphone to compensate for the waterfall. She was right; it wasn't much protection.

When he caught her words clearly, she was saying, "Lance, since when have I ever given a crap what Dad says? And why should you? Are you married to Judy, or to him?"

The water parted briefly, and Toreth saw she was looking right at him. He kept

51

the eye contact for a few seconds—nothing said guilt like abruptly turning away—until the water separated them once more, and then picked up his coffee.

"Sure, well, you do that if you have to," Mayhew said. "But just think about this—right now the best outcome is that you can find a couple of psychiatrists to say she was weak in her faith but she's convinced them that she's sincerely repented. Then my nieces get to visit their mom locked up in a so-called hospital, *if* she isn't found to be a moral risk to them. And good luck with that. I've lost way more contact appeals than I've won, whether there was a supportive father or not. No, no, I know you wouldn't. But a court won't see it like that, trust me."

Toreth waited through the silence, wishing for proper surveillance equipment that might get him both sides of the conversation.

"I don't know. But at least he hadn't made up his mind before he even started the investigation. Well, okay. You do that. His name is Val Toreth, and I guess you'd call him at the European embassy."

By the time she came back into view, Toreth was engrossed in his hand screen. He looked up and smiled as she sat down again.

"Did you get hold of him?"

"Yes. I told him he could get you at the embassy. Apparently he needs to think about it." Mayhew rolled her eyes. "Which I'm pretty sure is Lance-talk for he needs to ask permission from my dad."

"Do you think he'll call?"

"Well..." She rocked her hand from side to side. "I hope he will. I do get the feeling it's finally sinking in that this is all for real. He's seeing what he has to lose. Just a shame that didn't happen earlier."

As they headed to the lobby in search of Ruiz, Toreth found himself wondering exactly how pro-Europeans Mayhew might be. Dinner seemed like a way to find out, even though it would no doubt be tedious to get permission from the embassy either to go out or to bring Mayhew there. Still, no one else seemed to give a shit about embassy staff sneaking out, so maybe he could just not bother.

"Do you have any plans this evening?" he asked. "If not, maybe we could have a meal together. Here, or somewhere else if you'd rather. Although I don't know anything about local restaurants, as you can imagine. Is there anywhere you'd recommend?"

She stopped walking. "You want to talk about your case some more?"

"The case, Washington, America. Europe. Anything you like, really." He gave her a friendly smile, nothing too obvious. "You're about the only American I've met who seems willing to talk to me at all."

"Don't you think Agent Ruiz would object?" she asked lightly.

"I wasn't planning to invite him. Well?"

She smiled, and Toreth knew the answer even before she said, "I appreciate the offer, but I don't think it'd be a good idea. Apart from anything, Lance needs my support right now."

She resumed walking before he could say anything else, and he took a few long strides to be able to fall in step beside her as they walked back to the lobby.

On balance, being turned down was probably for the best. Not that Mayhew wasn't perfectly fuckable, but the case was already fucked enough, in a much less fun way.

Toreth wrote up a summary of the interview, as choicely selective as the Washington police's interview summaries had doubtless been. No need to mention Mayhew's conviction that Judith had been close to Campion. He sent the interview recording itself to Sara, and told her not to rush putting the transcript into the IIP. He could always tell Ruiz about the I&I systems disruption.

Warrick was asleep when Toreth opened the connection to the flat, but he didn't use the comm. Remote access to the flat's security system would let him avoid the small talk. Warrick might see it in the logs, if he looked, but Toreth knew he wouldn't say anything. He stared at the image. Asleep, alone. No real reason to run a c&p. Still, it felt unsettling. Before the flat, he'd only ever checked up on Warrick when Warrick was away from New London, at a conference or with clients. He'd rarely wondered what Warrick might be doing when Toreth was just elsewhere.

Of course, in the past he'd been able to rely on the threat of showing up at Warrick's flat unannounced to keep him in line. The Atlantic made that inconvenient. With the urge to make the credit and purchase check still nagging at him, he closed the connection.

On his way out of the office, curiosity made him pause to listen at Grimm's adjoining door. Nothing. He eased it open a crack, but the room was unlit. Knowing she was somewhere around, but not what she was doing, made him itchy. It felt like having a lion loose in the building—nice that it wasn't standing right there staring peckishly at you, but that didn't make the claws and teeth any less sharp if the fucker crept up behind you.

Down at the reception desk by the main entrance, he found Dixon on duty. Rather to his surprise, when she checked the security system it located Grimm immediately.

"She's in storage. She asked for authorization earlier today, and she hasn't swiped out."

"Authorize me, too. I'm going there now."

He'd expected a basement; in fact, the storage room was on the top floor of the building, a long, slightly dusty room filled with floor-to-ceiling metal cabinets.

Despite the time, a row of small windows high up on one wall were surprisingly bright—probably security lighting on the building.

He found Grimm sitting on the floor by an open cabinet, surrounded by stacks of old files and folders in a multitude of colors. Many of them were old enough to have faded, with paper labels showing faint pencil or ink. Toreth wondered why the embassy still kept them around.

After the altercation earlier in the day, Grimm looked understandably wary to see him. "Para-investigator? Did you want me?"

No, I just wanted to know what you were up to. "What's all this?"

"Old paperwork. Definitely not relevant to your case."

Toreth picked up a folder. The paper inside had yellowed at the edges, and he didn't recognize the language at all. "What's it about, then?"

"Us, in a way. Our history. After the redundant nation-state embassies were closed down, some of their paper records were destroyed, some were sent back to Europe, and some were apparently put into storage." She waved her hand over them. "And remained out of sight and mind since."

"Oh." He put the folder back down. "Won't there be copies of anything important back home?"

"Not necessarily. Many of the national capitals were badly damaged by the bombings, and regional governments killed. That's why the European Crisis Administration was formed to coordinate the rebuilding, culminating in unification."

Toreth nodded. "That's all school citizenship—" crap. "Classes."

"Indeed. But the process was a little more complex and drawn out than children need to learn. Nationalistic Europe wasn't completely fragmented. It had evolved a system of international cooperation, with legal offices, elected representatives, and so on, even diplomats. Of course they held less power than the old nation-states, and focused largely on economics, but unification had begun, in part, before the bombs. There were competing interests and obligations, external pressures and threats, internal resistance. Documentation about those early days is incomplete."

"But some of it's preserved here?" Toreth crouched down. "Is that why Socioanalysis sent you with me?"

"No, no. Not at all. I only found the collection by chance, talking to one of the admins. It's largely of historical interest. Fascinating, though." She hunted through one stack of folders to her right. "Now this—see, here? This is a printed copy of the demand from an organization in the Benelux region—pre-Administration proper—that the United States government release any information they had about the origin of the tactical nuclear devices, in light of the growing belief that the initial claims of responsibility had been manufactured. Subsequently, the emergent American policy of isolationism hardened even further... well, as I said, everything here is history, now. Rather poignant history, at that." She brushed her fingertips lingeringly over the paper, tracing the signatures at the bottom. "But per-haps Socioanalysis might be able to extract something useful. Learning from the past to avoid the mistakes of the future, and so on."

"Right. Does that ever actually happen?"

"We'd better hope so, hm?" She cocked her head. "Unless we want a repetition of the events earlier in the year, the Administration will have to find ways to change."

Not a remark that most people would make to an I&I officer. He stood up. "Okay. Well, have fun."

"I'm sure I will." Grimm smiled up at him. "Good night, Para-investigator."

Chapter Four

❖

Toreth had given Mayhew's plan only a fifty-fifty chance of working, especially with the Grant family's apparently so-far unimpressive record of listening to what women told them. But Lance Buchheit called the embassy the next morning. Although he was at a desk, the furniture in the room behind him looked more like a home than an office. Of course, that was judging it by Administration standards. Maybe corporations over here went for floral wall coverings.

Lance had dark hair, already receding, and what under other circumstances would probably be a pleasant enough face—Toreth slotted him into the I'd-fuck-him-if-I-was-drunk-and-in-a-hurry category. Now, though, he looked like he hadn't slept since Monday, pale despite a light tan. The unflattering effect of the bags under his eyes and his untidy appearance was emphasized by the man seated to his right and slightly behind him. He was notably good-looking, with an angular jaw and thick, blond hair, and dressed in what in the Administration would be a smart level of business casual.

"This is Simon McGlothlin," Buchheit said, indicating the other man. "He's Judy's cousin."

"And part of Senator Grant's legal team. My uncle suggested it would be better to have someone here to make sure everything was aboveboard." He smiled with a charming sincerity that Toreth recognized at once. "Although I'm sure you wouldn't be looking to ask Lance any inappropriate questions."

Even more family; how cozy. This, presumably, was the same Simon who had introduced Lance to Judy. Toreth wondered how many nephews and nephews-in-law Senator Grant had. Probably enough to staff his entire office, if his whole family bred like Lance and his wife.

"Thanks for talking to me, Mr. Buchheit. And can I start by saying how sorry I am about what's happened to Judith." Turnbull would be proud of him.

Buchheit simply nodded, doubtless an indication of how enthusiastic he felt about Europeans right now.

56

"All right, then," McGlothlin said. "Let's hear your questions. Lance doesn't have all morning for this."

"Mr. Buchheit, I'm sorry if this seems blunt, but your sister-in-law told us that you and Judith were having some problems. Is that true?"

Lance's eyes finally seemed to focus on the screen. "*Had* some problems, maybe."

"Oh? I'm sorry. Maybe I misunderstood." Toreth tried to hit the right mix of apology and lingering disbelief. "So everything's been okay lately?"

"Look, I won't deny that Judy and I had a rough year or so." Lance sounded needled. "We lost a son—I'm sure Debby told you all about that—and then with Abbi . . . but we got through it. We went to counselling with our pastor. Judy didn't want to go at first, but it really worked. Didn't it, Simon?"

McGlothlin nodded. "Sandi—that's my wife—said it certainly seemed to. She and Judith were close," he said to Toreth. "Are close, I mean."

"We can't always see the greater plan behind what happens in our lives," Lance said. "Sometimes we might never understand it in this world. Judy still had five beautiful living children who needed their mom, and the counselling with our pastor helped her see that and move on."

"So, you'd say that your wife was happy for the past few months?"

"Yes. I'm not saying that there weren't difficult times. But we'd put all that badness behind us. We were even trying for another baby."

With one eye on the lawyer, Toreth said, "Your sister-in-law seemed to think Judith didn't want any more children."

Lance frowned. "There was a period when she wanted to use contraception, and I said no—that's when she moved into her own room. I didn't like to argue with her, when she was still kinda fragile, but I didn't think it was right. I know Judy, and what she needed was another—" He stopped abruptly, then sighed. "I even talked to her stepmom about it, to try to get her to see reason."

McGlothlin shifted, and Toreth wondered if it was personal or professional discomfort. "Lance, you don't need to—"

"No," Lance said firmly. "I want him to understand. Judy changed her mind. We'd been trying for months. We even talked about going to a clinic, because nothing had happened." He shook his head. "Judy asked me to cancel the appointment, twice. Once because she thought she was pregnant, but it turned out to be a false alarm, then a few weeks ago she told me she wanted to wait. Leave our family in God's hands, like we'd discussed with the pastor. Well, I said okay. I just told her that if nothing happened by the end of the year, we could go the medical route then, in case there was anything wrong. Women aren't always rational about these things, you know?"

In Toreth's experience, rationality was usually in short supply everywhere. "And she agreed to that?"

Lance hesitated fractionally, then said, "She didn't like the idea, but I didn't press the point too hard. I figured she'd come around with time, and she'd see I was only thinking about what was best for her. And maybe she was right, any-way—maybe we should put less faith in medical science and more in God."

McGlothlin shook his head slightly. Lance didn't seem to notice.

"Mr. McGlothlin, you don't think she cancelled the appointments because she wanted God to look after things?" Toreth asked.

McGlothlin stiffened slightly. "I'm not here to have opinions."

Lance turned to him. "You think it was because she already knew? She was already *planning* this?"

"Like I said, I'm not here—"

"No! No way. This was something on the spur of the moment. She couldn't have been thinking clearly—she wasn't herself. She was being moved by evil thoughts."

"Of course," McGlothlin said, with a smile that was probably supposed to be soothing, and came over as patronizing. "You know how I feel about Judy. She's a good woman."

"I've been praying in her hospital room every day." Lance's tone was uncom-promising. "I know the truth. My Judy would never have done this if she'd been in her right mind. It's this fucking—excuse me." He closed his eyes for a moment, then looked directly at Toreth. "The European doctor, from the embassy. I'm sorry to say it, Detective, but that's the truth. She's the root of all this evil."

McGlothlin nodded. "My wife met this Dr. Campion at the mission. She said she knew right away there was something off about her. Sandi was the one who suggested to Judith that it wasn't appropriate to have the woman at her socials."

Toreth wondered what his chances were of getting to speak to McGlothlin's wife. She might actually know something useful. "Mr. McGlothlin, if your wife has any more information about Ms. Buchheit and—"

"Mrs," Buchheit interrupted. "She's my *wife*."

"I'm sorry," Toreth said. "Mr. Buchheit, I'm not here to cover anything up. If Dr. Campion was involved in any way at all, my government wants to know."

"Right." Buchheit didn't even try to hide his skepticism. "And will she have to face up to her crimes?"

Fu—and everyone else back home—would explode if Toreth gave any hint the Administration Council was thinking about removing Campion's immunity, no matter how helpful it might be to the interview. "I'm afraid that's outside my remit, Mr. Buchheit."

He nodded, as though he hadn't expected any other answer. "Was that everything?"

"Not quite. Did your wife have any other close friends at the mission?"

"Any other doctors, you mean?" McGlothlin said before Lance could even draw breath to reply. "Who might have been involved?"

Campion was right about one thing, at least. Some things were no different over here, and it looked like annoying lawyers throwing themselves in the way of potentially productive witnesses was one of them.

If Lance had been about to give a name, he certainly wasn't now. "I don't remember her mentioning anyone."

"Are you sure? Maybe——"

"Lance already gave you his answer," McGlothlin said.

An indistinct shape appeared in the background, and Toreth suddenly appreciated what a large office the man must have in his house.

A soft female voice called, "Mr. Buchheit? Oh, excuse me."

"What is it?"

"Hannah and Lea-lea asked me if I'd help them bake a pie to send to their mom and they'd like you to come out to the orchard with them to pick some apples."

"Tell them I'll just be a few minutes." He turned back to Toreth. "The kids get nervous if they haven't seen me for a while. I guess that's probably normal, under the circumstances, right?"

Judith Buchheit being in any kind of condition to enjoy apple pie was news to Toreth. "Is your wife awake?"

"No." Buchheit smiled sadly. "But Schuyler bakes a great pie and I'm sure the staff at the hospital will be happy to eat it."

"Schuyler?" Toreth asked.

"Schuyler Finn. She's a trained homemaking assistant—actually, she worked for Simon's wife for a while before he let us steal her. Isn't that right?"

McGlothlin nodded. "It was our pleasure to be able to help. Judy was more comfortable letting someone who wasn't a complete stranger into her home," he added to Toreth. "Especially when she was unwell."

Now Buchheit's smile was warmer. "Schuyler's been *such* a blessing. I don't know how we would've coped without her since . . . with Judy in the hospital."

"I'm sure," Toreth said, and wondered how well he'd be able to process the image afterwards. This, presumably, was the nanny Judith had accused of trying to steal her kids' affection, and he'd be interested to get a better look at her. "Do she and Judith get along?"

"Oh, yes. They're great friends. Schuyler's a part of the family. If she left, it would break the kids' hearts." Lance sighed. "I haven't told them everything yet. I know they'll have to find out eventually, but even Hannah is so young and . . . we just said that Mommy is very sick in the hospital, and they should pray for God to make her well."

"Mr. Buchheit, what happens to your wife if she lives?"

"We don't know for sure yet. Legally, the state has to prosecute her. If she pleads guilty and demonstrates repentance—if she's capable of pleading anything

59

at all—we might be able to get the sentence reduced. Or if we can prove she wasn't in her right mind when she did it. I have specialist lawyers looking into the options. I'll do whatever I can to get her the best outcome."

He sounded sincere enough. But then, he was a politician, which put him high up there with corporates and senior managers—and lawyers—on the list of people Toreth wouldn't believe if they told him his own name.

Lance sighed again. "I should've done more to protect her. That's my job as her husband, right? To keep her safe, even from herself. I guess I failed." His voice broke.

"I think that's enough," McGlothlin said. "I hope we answered all your questions, Detective?"

Toreth knew a shutdown when he heard one, but he couldn't help a final attempt. "I was wondering, Mr. McGlothlin, if M—" He stumbled over the unfamiliar word. "If Mrs. McGlothlin would be willing to talk to us about Judy, and anything Dr. Campion said to—"

"Sandi isn't in town right now," McGlothlin said flatly. "She and our boys are visiting her mom. She wants to be here, obviously, to support Judy, but her great-grandmom is sick and very old."

Pointing out the existence of comms seemed futile. "I see. Thank you, Mr. McGlothlin, Mr. Buchheit."

Lance didn't respond, except to shake his head. He looked lost in grief.

"Thank you," McGlothlin said briskly, and the connection went blank.

Ambassador Fu called Toreth to his office just after ten. It was a surprisingly modest setup. Toreth would have guessed that the man's taste in expensive suits would translate into showing off whatever the Department of International Relations could supply in the way of office decoration, but although there were a few pieces of art that looked genuine and valuable, the overall effect was restrained elegance.

Campion was already there when Toreth arrived, looking uncharacteristically on edge.

"Tell Para-investigator Toreth exactly what you told me," Fu said.

Campion nodded. "Ben called me. He says he has some evidence from the museum that supports my innocence. He wants to meet me away from the embassy."

Toreth's immediate reaction was hell, no. "Call him back and tell him to send the evidence here."

Campion shook her head. "He sounded nervous; he said he'd only talk to me. He wants me to take a cab and meet him at the National Cathedral."

"So what do you think?" Toreth asked her.

"Well, he came here willingly enough yesterday." She shrugged. "I assume the police have asked him to help them. What else could he do? As far as I can tell, this ridiculous law seems to make anyone who's even slightly involved into an accomplice."

Finally, Campion seemed to be taking a realistic view of the situation. Toreth turned to Fu. "So you aren't planning to let her go?"

"All in all, no," he said drily. "But I thought you ought to know about it."

"Why the cathedral?" Toreth asked.

"I don't know," Campion said. "I've never been there. It's supposed to be impressive. Maybe he thought it would sound reassuring."

Fu cleared his throat. "In my understanding of the American system, there's nothing to prevent them from carrying out an arrest in a place of worship. It'd be perfectly legal, if unusual."

"Or the police could stop the car on the way and arrest her right there," Toreth said.

"Only if she takes a cab," the ambassador said. "An official embassy car has the same extraterritorial protection as the embassy itself. I suppose they could do it, but it'd be an extremely provocative act, and make prosecution legally tricky, even if we waived immunity." He smiled. "I had our lawyers investigate the options thoroughly, just in case we needed to get Dr. Campion out of the country in a hurry."

"So, what now?" Campion asked. "Shouldn't I give Ben some kind of an answer?"

Toreth, about to tell her to ignore him, hesitated. Yes, it was an obvious trap. But maybe it offered some opportunities. And there was the slim chance that Elsney did have some evidence that would let Toreth close the case quickly.

"Okay, I need the truth now," Toreth said to her. "The complete truth. Did you give any kind of abortion to Judith?"

"No," Campion said firmly.

"Did you have any connection at all to one? Did you give her advice, or even have a suspicion she was pregnant? *Anything*."

"Absolutely not."

"Is there anything else you haven't told me that makes you look guiltier?" Campion started to protest and Toreth added, "Even if you aren't. Think about how the Justice system would see it."

"Other than being at the museum, no. Whether Ben saw me or not, I didn't even leave the building for lunch."

Toreth studied Campion more carefully. She wasn't especially remarkable in height or physique. Her hair was somewhat distinctive, but hair was easily altered. With a decent amount of face-concealing clothing—such as someone might want to wear if they were sneaking out of an embassy for an illicit meeting—she'd be difficult to tell apart from any number of women in the embassy. Toreth could think of one candidate already.

"Ambassador, what was the name of the security officer? Dixon? Is she on duty?"

Toreth had given Ruiz a slightly edited version of his plan over the comm. When Ruiz arrived half an hour later, he stopped dead when he saw Campion standing next to a suitably disguised Dixon, and then laughed.

"Ah, now I understand." He shook his head, still smiling. "I knew you wouldn't be dumb enough to fall for that. I guess they hoped Dr. Campion would be."

Toreth decided that up-front honesty was the best strategy with Ruiz. "Will you warn them?"

"No, I don't think so. I'm pretty sure this is a plan that the police cooked up by themselves, without any authority from higher up. I don't want to get involved, and anyway, they haven't exactly been welcoming to Homeland Security."

"Thanks," Toreth said. "I was wondering, though—what are the police interrogators like?"

"Sorry?" Ruiz said.

"What can they do? Neural induction? What kind of drugs do they have?"

"Ah, right. The police here don't have access to that kind of thing. Much as I'm sure they wish they did, sometimes."

Sounded rather like Justice. "Can they send her to another department that does?"

"No. That really isn't how civilian law enforcement works. Now, I'm not saying that sometimes there might not be bad apples who can get a little rough..."

Definitely like Justice, then.

"But," Ruiz continued, "no one's gonna risk that with an Administration citizen, no matter what she's supposed to have done. They couldn't even talk to her without a lawyer in the room, unless she agreed to it. She also has right of access to spiritual counsel at all reasonable times, and precedent makes 'reasonable' pretty broad."

"Spiritual counsel?" Toreth said blankly.

"A priest or a pastor or—well, is there someone at the embassy who looks after the spiritual needs of the people who work here?"

"I'm sure there is," Fu said. "In fact, if it became necessary I think it'd turn out to be the Deputy Ambassador."

Ruiz smiled again. "There you are, then. Toreth, why do you want to know?"

"I like to be prepared. Just because it would be stupid of them to arrest her doesn't mean it won't happen."

"Won't happen?" Ruiz raised his eyebrows. "She'll be at the meeting?"

"Not exactly."

Toreth had glanced at a floor plan of the cathedral, but the size of it hadn't sunk in. The scale was more like a leisure complex than one of the churches he'd seen before. Ruiz had called ahead, and after a conversation with a rather bewildered official, they'd been given permission to park the embassy car in a private area near the cathedral itself.

The shielded, toughened car windows should protect those inside from too-close inspection. Leaving Campion in the car with a couple of embassy security officers, Toreth, Ruiz, and Dixon climbed out. Dixon pulled the scarf covering her hair a little further forwards. With that and the glasses, and wearing a coat that Campion said she'd worn to the mission, Toreth thought they had a decent chance.

"Keep looking down," he muttered as he closed the car door, and Dixon nodded.

"Which entrance?" Ruiz asked.

"They said the northwest one. But I like the look of the front better."

Inside, the white floor, patterned in squares and diamonds with green and red marble, and the tall windows high in the walls reminded him of the New London airport. But the light that splashed onto the floor was brightly colored by the window glass. Way up above, screening on the ceiling gave the impression of the walls stretching up into infinity, fading out into clouds that mirrored the overcast day outside. Hundreds, maybe thousands, of chairs stood in ranks down the central portion and in the sections to each side marked off by the massive, fluted pillars.

"Do that many people really come here?" Toreth asked.

Ruiz nodded. "For some services they run an overspill outside. Do you see Elsney?"

"Not yet. But then he's not supposed to be down here."

The place was eerily quiet for such a vast space with a fair number of people in it. They walked up the left-hand side aisle of the cathedral, and Toreth found himself trying to tread quietly so the walls wouldn't take up and magnify his footsteps. Up ahead, waiting by a pillar, a man caught Toreth's attention. He was reading a hand screen with apparent intent, but every few seconds he glanced up and around the cathedral before returning to the screen.

"Dixon, don't look up," he subvocalized into his comm. "I think I see police. Fifty meters, give or take."

"Okay." Dixon adjusted her glasses. "How many?"

"One, so far. But there's a couple of corners and a screen or two, and not many civilians, so the rest of the welcome committee is probably up there somewhere."

Ruiz glanced over his shoulder and said, "Behind us, too, now. Looks like they're buying it."

"Good. I don't want them to realize what we've done and piss off because they're embarrassed."

They walked ten meters past the watcher before the police sprang the ambush. Toreth kept still, his hands in plain sight, until at least twelve men in uniform surrounded them. He could see more ahead, covering the exits. There was an awkward pause while Toreth and the officers inspected one another warily, and Ruiz stood looking off into space with a slight smile on his face. Finally the man from the pillar stepped forwards. He had very dark skin, and a careworn, slightly jowly face, and instead of a uniform he wore a smart gray suit, with no obvious signs of rank.

"I'm Detective-Lieutenant Green."

"Of the Washington police?" Toreth asked, wondering if the suit meant he was some American equivalent of Internal Investigations.

"That's right. The Homicide Department. We're here to take Rebekah Campion back to the central Washington station."

"You want to arrest her?" Ruiz said.

"We hope we don't need to do that, Agent. We want to interview her, that's all. If she has satisfactory answers to our questions, then she'll be free to go."

"Dixon?" Toreth said.

The guard pulled off her scarf and glasses. Green took it well. The mild grimace looked more like indigestion than anger, and then he nodded. "Well, okay. In that case, you enjoy your visit to the cathedral. Benjamin Elsney isn't here either, though, I'm afraid."

"I didn't think he would be," Toreth said. "Sudden exonerating evidence that slipped his mind yesterday seemed a bit too good to be true."

"Okay," Green said again. "I guess you won this round. I take it Rebekah Campion is safe back at the embassy?"

"Actually, she's outside, in the car," Toreth said, and heard Dixon's sharp intake of breath beside him. Even Ruiz looked around in surprise. "If you want to talk to her, maybe I could ask her to put the window down for a couple of minutes."

"I don't think so." Green tapped his comm. "Brannon—don't let that embassy car leave. Tell the cathedral security to secure the exit. Keep watching it, but don't attempt to gain access."

They walked back through the cathedral in chilly silence. Outside, the car doors were still closed, but it was surrounded by uniforms. There was no way for the car to drive away without hitting at least one officer. The embassy car system might be set up for some aggressive defensive driving, but Toreth doubted Turnbull would be happy if his investigation resulted in another American citizen in hospital.

When they reached the car, Toreth folded his arms, and Green smiled, shaking his head.

"It'll make things a lot simpler if you just hand her over. All we want to do is talk with her. As we've explained to your ambassador, our district attorney acknowledges that her diplomatic immunity covers the crimes for which she's being investigated."

"It covers that car, too," Toreth said.

"Well, we can wait here as long as it takes, until you guys are feeling more cooperative."

"Why the hell *should* we cooperate with you?" Toreth said. "You've done nothing but obstruct me since I got here. I was promised full access to the case files, but I've had nothing."

"We sent the interview summaries," the detective-lieutenant said. "And you seem to have made a pretty good go of finding your own witnesses to talk to."

"I've had nothing worthwhile," Toreth repeated. "From where I'm standing, this doesn't look like a very open-minded investigation. Why should I trust you'll keep your word when you're handling a suspect?"

"All right, then. If we can talk to Rebekah, then you'll have access to the evidence. *Just* you. Deal?"

"And my investigator," Toreth said.

"Okay, and her." Green paused, and then the qualifications that Toreth had expected began. "No one else at the embassy sees it, and you don't send it to anyone outside. Not in this country, and *especially* not back in Europe."

Toreth shrugged. "Fine, I agree. I need interview access to the witnesses, too. I'm sure Agent Ruiz will let you know about anything I say to them, or they say to me," he added when he could see Green about to protest. "And I want access to any crime scenes that might turn up later. Escorted access, of course."

This time it took longer. Then the officer glanced at the car out of the corner of his eye, and nodded.

"All right. *If* the witnesses agree to cooperate, you can talk to them. I'll release the files as soon as we get Dr. Campion back to—"

"Oh, no. Do it now." With victory so close, Toreth had to work to keep his voice level. "I want to see the files, and I want a call to the ambassador and to Agent Ruiz's boss from your boss, clearing everything and with a solid assurance you can't change your mind tomorrow."

That took a few minutes to arrange, while Toreth tried not to think about the consequences of his gamble failing. Ruiz was watching him with speculation, but he didn't say anything. Finally, the call came to Ruiz, and he relayed the answer.

"Everything's arranged. And we have copies of all the files at Homeland Security now. Just as a backup."

"Great, thanks."

Toreth opened the car door and leaned in. The two embassy guards looked nervous, as well they might, heavily outnumbered by the police outside. Toreth beckoned to Campion. "Get out."

Campion stared at him. "Out of the car?"

"You're going tell Detective-Lieutenant Green here how you had nothing to do with Judith's ad hoc reproduction control. Don't worry, Ruiz assures me they're a lot more friendly than I&I."

"I thought I was just here to talk to Ben? You never said—"

"Change of plan. Come on, out."

Campion started to get out of her seat, and one of the embassy guards put out his arm, blocking her. "Did the ambassador okay this?"

"He put me in charge."

"I think I should contact him to—"

"I think you should shut the hell up and let me do my job," Toreth said evenly. "You don't have any authority here. America or not, I'm still an I&I officer. And while you're sitting in an embassy car, impeding my investigation is still an offense."

Campion climbed out, but she didn't move away from the car. Toreth put his hand on her shoulder. "Be smart. Don't talk to them at all without a lawyer—I'm sure the embassy will be sending one soon. Don't try to sell them any bullshit about not leaving the embassy. Just the truth."

Campion nodded. She still looked a little dazed.

Leaving her there, Toreth climbed into the car, followed by Ruiz and Dixon. The ring of officers parted, and they drove away.

Ruiz's bosses kept him busy on his comm for the duration of the drive back to the embassy. Toreth had half expected his own angry call from Fu. That didn't happen, but the ambassador was waiting for them when they arrived. Toreth was only surprised that Grimm wasn't there with him.

"I hope you have a good explanation for this."

"Yes—I've swapped something useless for something useful."

Fu looked at him quizzically. "Doctor Campion is 'useless'?"

"She is to me. And if anyone else needs a medic, the expert system can take care of them. I believe Campion when she says she knows nothing. The police will probably work that out soon enough, but I already have copies of the investigation files, and permission to talk to witnesses."

"And what if they don't release her?" Fu said. "What if they demand to be allowed to charge her? Then what do I tell the Council? What if they decide we have to waive immunity after all?"

Presumably having one of his embassy staff locked up wouldn't make Fu's record sparkle. Toreth shrugged. "Proving someone had the opportunity to do something's not the same as proving they did it. There must be millions of people who *could* be guilty. Campion said it herself—if she had done it, why would she do it that way? No evidence analysis system anywhere in the world would even classify her as a credible suspect at this stage. And the Justice system would probably explode."

"You do realize that they don't actually use anything like the Justice system over here?" Fu asked.

"What?" Toreth said.

"Most cases are decided by what they call guided agreement between the state and the defense," Fu said, while Ruiz nodded in support. "Where that doesn't happen, they move to a counselled peer jury system—twelve ordinary citizens plus pastoral assistance in their deliberations. I doubt a local jury will have much sympathy for Campion."

"But . . ." How could the American administration possibly run a justice system *and* a free press, if they didn't know what the verdicts would be in advance? "Seriously?"

"Justice has to have a moral dimension," Ruiz said. "Compassion and forgiveness, even, some people would argue. Even the best expert system can't give you that."

Toreth looked between them, struggling to formulate a response. Finally, he said, "Fuck."

"I'm sorry," Ruiz said, although his slight smile suggested he was enjoying the payback for the times Toreth had kept him in the dark in the past. "I guess it never occurred to me to mention it."

Fu wasn't smiling at all. "Well, I'm sure that the Council and the Bureau will be impressed by the boldness and innovation of your approach, Para-investigator."

For a few seconds more, all Toreth could do was stare at him. Then he pulled himself together. "If you need me, Ambassador, I'll be in my office, looking at the files."

The first thing Toreth opened were the medical reports. They were, at least, extremely comprehensive. Toreth guessed that the medics involved must have realized a police investigation would be the likely result of Judith's misfortune. Failing to document and report the injuries might well open them up to a charge of complicity in the crime. Everything else seemed to.

He remembered his promise to Ruiz. While he had no intention of having his case evidence filtered through a socioanalyst's inexpert eyes, it would be tactful for her at least to be able to make convincing comments about it.

Grimm looked surprised and slightly wary to have been summoned. "Can I help?"

"Probably not." Toreth turned the screen towards her.

Grimm leaned down, then tilted her head as though it might make more sense at an angle. "What's that?"

"It's the inside of Judith Buchheit's uterus."

The socioanalyst blanched.

"Yeah, it's a mess. Means nothing to me, though—it looks like something Warrick brings back from the shopping complex and swears will make an amazing casserole. Once he brought home a piece of a fucking cow's udder. From a real cow, not grown in a vat. I don't mind trying something new, but you have a draw a line somewhere. So now I usually get takeaway delivered when he's feeling experimental. But." He pointed at the screen.

Grimm swallowed. "But?"

"I know someone who will know what she's looking at. First, though, I need you to run through it and use your magical female powers to figure out what happened, or whatever the hell you're supposed to be able to do over here."

She didn't smile. Even though she still looked rather pale, she went to the beginning of the evidence and read it through.

"Any thoughts?" Toreth said when she was done, more out of malice than expectation.

"Not that will help the case," she said shortly. "But I'll be sure to tell Agent Ruiz I read it if he asks."

Frustratingly, when Toreth tried to reach O'Reilly, she had already left I&I. Toreth checked the list of forensic staff present in the building, but none of them were people he knew well enough to entrust with this case. He left a message asking O'Reilly to call him as soon as she arrived in the morning, never mind what the time would be in Washington, and went to eat a very late lunch. The morning's excitement had left him ravenous, and he ordered from his office before he went down to the dining room. The room was almost empty except for Grimm, pushing a salad around her plate.

"Not hungry?" Toreth said right behind her, and she jumped.

"No, I can't say that I am. It's... a little more visceral than my usual line of work."

Toreth sat down across the table from her. "That was just a picture. Visceral is when you're at a scene and you can smell it, too. Not just blood, all the other fluids, too."

Grimm put down her fork. "Please don't. I understand that my emotional distress has no empathic resonance for you, and is simply a source of entertainment and revenge by proxy, but... " She frowned, and Toreth wondered if she'd genuinely not thought through to a conclusion, or if she was just trying some half-arsed Socioanalysis-approved psychology.

68

"But?"

"It doesn't help progress the case, does it? In fact, it's a counterproductive distraction for both of us. Correct?"

Instead of answering, Toreth said, "Well, we've already established you've read my psych file."

She hesitated. "I was speaking from a general level of knowledge about I&I selection policy and the—"

"Oh, come off it. Why wouldn't you read the fucking thing? I'm sure you've got far more clearance than I'll ever have."

Grimm gave a little shrug, which he assumed was her admitting he was right. "My conclusion still stands."

"So did Carnac put any glowing little notes in that, too?"

She smiled very slightly. "Not to my knowledge."

"What the fuck does that mean?"

"It means that, despite your confidence, my clearance is not infinite. Parts of it were still locked."

"Really? What parts?"

"As I said, they were locked. I couldn't even speculate what might be there."

Was she fucking with him? No one else had ever mentioned anything of the kind, not the I&I psychologists at his yearly psych review, and not Warrick. But then, although he more than suspected Warrick had read it, Toreth had never talked to him about it directly. No need to know more that he absolutely had to about Warrick's forays into secure Administration files. Or maybe the high-security material was a recent addition—not necessarily a reassuring thought.

And here he was, Toreth realized suddenly, tables turned, paranoid and fretting about a fucking file back in the Administration, while Grimm had resumed calmly eating her food. So on the one hand, she was definitely cut from the same cloth as Carnac, and on the other . . . she was, annoyingly, right again. He needed to prioritize the case, and then maybe he could get back home and make sure there were no more dangerous spooks on the prowl.

He held out his hand. "I'm willing to declare a truce."

"How magnanimous of you," she said, but she shook. "So, what's happening with the case? Any positive results from your bold move?"

"Is 'bold' some diplomatic term for fucking stupid?"

"I think it probably is, yes." Grimm sipped her glass of water. "Although from my point of view, I'm impressed that you managed to gain full access to the files. Our data is frustratingly limited, but the Washington police seem to have a passably competent record. Personally, I agreed with the idea that they were focusing on Campion primarily because of a dearth of viable alternatives. Why would they expose that to us?"

"Do you know the basic principle of coercive interrogation?" Toreth asked.

"Hurting people?" Grimm suggested.

Toreth laughed. "No. That's just an option. Interrogation is about changing priorities. Making people value the things that you control. When someone will swap the information you want for five minutes' rest, or a sip of water, then you win."

"Ah. So, holding an interview with Campion had become important to them, when in fact it's not. After all, the embassy's been doing everything they can to protect her, increasing her perceived value."

"Right. Plus, you don't just say 'water.' You pour a cup and put it where they can see it, and that makes it much harder to resist. That's why I took her out to the cathedral."

She speared a cube of cucumber on her fork with a precision that reminded him of Warrick. "On that basis, one could say that their evidence seemed important to you, for similar reasons."

"Evidence is always important," Toreth said. "Unless it's giving you the answer the people higher up the food chain don't want. Then it's a fucking nuisance. But you still need to know what it is, so you can make it say what they want instead. I'm just hoping that Deborah O'Reilly—I&I forensics—can find us a straw to cling to."

Grimm nodded. "Would you mind if I looked at the rest of the case files?"

"You should have access anyway."

"I thought it would be polite to ask." She opened her hand screen and placed it beside her plate. "And I do appreciate the inclusion, thank you."

While Grimm ate, she paged quickly through the case file. So quickly that Toreth wondered if she was really reading anything, or playing spook mind games. Was she genuinely invested in the outcome, beyond seeing how the Washington police worked?

Toreth was distracted by the arrival of his shepherd's pie. He'd eaten about half of it when Grimm suddenly stopped.

"Oh!"

"What?" Toreth asked.

"Now this I guarantee you will find interesting. It's the speculative timeline, based on Judith's movements and the medical analysis. Apparently she took a car from her house late Monday morning."

"What? That wasn't in the information they sent us before."

"I'm not surprised. Guess where the journey terminated?"

"Not here?" Then an even worse possibility occurred. "Not the fucking museum?"

"Within two hundred meters of it, if I'm reading this correctly."

Toreth dropped his fork on the plate and put his head in his hands, because it was better than letting Grimm see his face. So much for his bold and innovative gamble.

70

"Well, that explains why they were so keen to get their hands on Campion once they'd spoken to Elsney," Grimm said thoughtfully. "I thought simply having her absent from the embassy seemed a little thin to prompt a gambit like the cathedral. And sound tactics for them to hold it back."

"Yeah. Fucking genius."

"I wouldn't go that far. But it was certainly well judged. I'm sure you wouldn't have handed her over if they'd shared that in advance. And the timeline itself is hardly pointed up in the case file. I suppose they were hoping you wouldn't find it quickly."

Toreth breathed out and lifted his head. "Do you think you could stop being impressed for five minutes and try to say something useful?"

"Mm." Grimm leaned back in her chair and gazed over Toreth's shoulder. He wondered if she was looking at one of the paintings. "Do you still believe that Campion had nothing to do with this?"

"Well..." Toreth thought back over every conversation he'd had with the woman. "Yes. Lying about the museum was stupid, but sometimes innocent people do stupid things. That's how they end up on level D, wasting everyone's time."

"She should consider herself lucky, then, at least if the Washington police are as considerate of their suspects as Ruiz maintains." Grimm looked back at him. "But in that case, why was Buchheit in this area? Who was she meeting?"

"Elsney?" Toreth suggested after a few seconds' thought. "Or someone we don't even know exists. But Elsney knew that Campion would be at the museum to take the rap if anything went wrong. He can't alibi her, but that means she doesn't alibi him, either."

Grimm picked up her hand screen. "Hm. He told the police exactly what he told us—he didn't check on Campion more often because he was busy in meetings all day. I don't see that they've verified that yet."

"Probably because alibis like that usually check out. I'd knock it down the priority list, too. Not many people can rustle up a roomful of colleagues willing to risk lying to I&I." Warrick might, he realized. But could Elsney possibly be as important to the museum as Warrick was to SimTech?

Grimm nodded, although Toreth could see her reluctance to abandon a pretty theory, familiar from many junior investigators on their first cases. Apparently being a socioanalyst didn't make you entirely immune to wishful thinking. "I suppose so. Still...how long a window would he need for the procedure? Less than half an hour, if the location was close by? Remember that Buchheit herself had at least some medical knowledge, so she could've carried out preparations."

"True. And if he wanted to help her out with her little problem, he has free access to a museum full of surgical equipment. Out-of-date surgical equipment, but that bloody mess didn't exactly look state of the art."

She didn't react to the reminder. "Is he a medic? Or had any medical training?"

"I don't know." Once again, the lack of resources frustrated him. Normally the answer was a quick check of a security file away. "I don't know anything about him. Of course, Campion might, but I carefully got rid of her."

To his surprise, she merely nodded. "There's nothing to be done about that. There must be some information we can access."

"I didn't see anything that looked like a security file in the case files."

"No. They don't seem to go in for that over here. Or if they do, then they don't give free access to the police. It's always possible that someone, somewhere, is keeping watch, though. I find it extremely improbable that at least a subset of the population isn't monitored."

"By Homeland Security?" Toreth said hopefully.

Grimm nodded. "Maybe you should ask Agent Ruiz."

Ruiz proved cagey about the possibility of official or unofficial government files on citizens. He didn't admit they existed, but he did offer to see what he could do in the way of background information on Elsney. Toreth threw in an optimistic request for the same information on Judith Buchheit's other close friends and relatives, and then went back to the investigation files.

Elsney's name kept distracting him from his reading, though. If this were a real case, he'd have an investigator trying to pin down Elsney's movements to the minute, if he hadn't just had the man brought to I&I for an interview. Even if his alibi was good, there were other possibilities to connect him to the case. Campion had mention banned surgical technology. Maybe Elsney had given a so-far unknown third party access to the equipment. Maybe there was even a surgical robot in the museum's collection capable of carrying out an abortion without human assistance, and Judith had been desperate enough to fly solo. In that case, someone must have tidied up and returned the device—Elsney again?

Toreth went to the connecting door and opened it without knocking. He saw the empty desk a fraction of a second before he saw Grimm herself, lying on the floor with her eyes closed and her hands behind her head, in the slanted oblong of sunlight falling through the maximally deopaqued window. Toreth walked over softly and stood over her. She was breathing slowly, her expression blank, but he didn't think she was asleep.

He'd been watching her for a couple of minutes when her eyes suddenly opened. She twitched, obviously startled, but her voice was even.

"Para-investigator?"

He thought about stepping back, but didn't. "Nice to see Socioanalysis working hard for its budget."

"I was thinking." She stood gracefully and went over to her desk, putting it between them. "It's a system based on the unscientific theory that my cat looks extremely relaxed whenever she can find a sunbeam to lie in."

"You have a cat?" Toreth asked. He'd never imagined socioanalysts keeping dumb animals around, when they could experience the same effect by talking to ordinary people.

She nodded. "Shrody—or Schrödinger II, for her full name. Schrödinger I was a present from my mum when I first entered the training program. I'd always wanted a cat, but we'd never lived anywhere one was allowed. I don't know what percentage of young Socioanalysis recruits think Schrödinger is a clever name for a cat, but I bet it's painfully high. Did you want something?"

"Fancy a museum visit?" Toreth asked. "We could get a car, but I thought we'd walk. A car will only lead to a lot of questions about what we're doing, and we can follow Campion's route."

She straightened her clothes and smoothed her hair. "Is Agent Ruiz meeting us there?"

"No, he's busy. I assume."

Her expression of speculative curiosity reminded him of Carnac. "I thought you told Detective-Lieutenant Green that Agent Ruiz would be present when you interviewed witnesses?"

Worth spending time wondering how she knew that? Toreth decided he'd file it under "fucking spooks" and try to keep his paranoia under control. "No, I said I was sure Agent Ruiz could tell the police anything he heard me say to a witness. Which he can—if he's there. But if Elsney did know Judith was planning an abortion, he won't tell Ruiz."

"Ah—because then Elsney admits he was complicit, and goes to prison."

"Exactly. Whereas I don't give a shit what he did if it exonerates Campion. So, are you coming, or do you need to do some more thinking?"

She smiled. "I'd like to see the museum. I didn't seem to be coming to any productive conclusions, anyway."

The museum guard had, trustingly, left them to wait in Elsney's office. Stealing anything would be complicated by having to find it, first. The place reminded him of Warrick's crammed office at SimTech. It even had a shelf of paper display copies of journals, although in this case they looked antique. Instead of sim hardware, the room was stacked with old books and a collection of taxidermy just large enough to have moved from impressive to disconcerting. Fake eyes watched them from every direction. On a shelf close to the door a small dust-covered glass case held an extraordinary animal that looked like a white, long-furred mole partially covered in a coat of pale orange laminated armor. No screen or even old label identified it.

Grimm joined him. "What's that?"

"No idea." On closer inspection, it was rather dilapidated. "Maybe someone made it from leftovers."

Grimm opened her hand screen, and image-matched the animal. "Apparently, it's *Chlamyphorus truncatus*. A pink fairy armadillo."

Toreth looked at her, about fifty percent sure she was taking the piss. "A fucking what?"

"A pink fairy armadillo. A South American species," she continued. "They went extinct at one point, but were successfully repopulated through a biobank project. Apparently they spend a lot of time underground."

Presumably to stop the rest of the local wildlife from laughing at them.

"My favorite animal," Elsney said from the doorway. When they turned, he grinned. "You're lucky you caught him here. Usually he lives at home, but I brought him in so one of the conservators could spruce him up. I have a mounted skeleton, too. That's almost cooler, because you can see the butt plate."

"I'm sure," Toreth said. "Mr. Elsney—"

His smile vanished. "I think I can guess why you're here. I'm sorry about the cathedral, I really am."

Before Toreth could speak again, Grimm said with deep sincerity, "We understand completely. The police asked for your help. What else could you do?"

His expression became, if anything, even more pained. "I'm afraid there isn't any new evidence, either. They just handed me a script and asked me to call Rebekah."

Grimm was already nodding. "It's okay. You know, maybe it was even for the best. I'm sure when they talk to her, they'll see that she's telling the truth."

"Oh." Elsney looked between them. "Well, thanks. I assumed you'd be pissed. I would be, if it was one of my colleagues."

"It's more that we're concerned about her." A touch of worry clouded Grimm's face, and Toreth wondered if Socioanalysis gave acting lessons to their young recruits. "We're still hoping we can find something to support her version of events. Actually, we wondered if we could see the archive where Dr. Campion was working? It's okay, we've been cleared by the police."

"Sure, sure. If you think it might help. Um." He looked around the office, then nodded. "Come right this way."

Elsney led them through the upper section of a two-level gallery that reminded Toreth of the cathedral, all tall pillars and marble. It was expensively built and well maintained, but the investment hadn't extended to the building's security. When Elsney opened a door that led into a plain, utilitarian corridor, there was no ID scan. In fact, security seemed mostly to rely on door screens reading "Museum Staff Only" and the occasional, presumably more serious, "Authorized Staff Only."

"So, this is the Tansey-Child Museum of Medical History," Elsney said as they went down a staircase. "Named after First Lady Autumn Tansey-Child, wife of President Child." He paused, one hand on the staircase rail, and looked at Toreth, who looked blankly back. "I guess you've never heard of either of them, right?"

"Right."

"Well, I guess I couldn't name many presidents of—actually, you guys don't even have presidents, do you? Anyway, the museum is funded primarily by a trust set up by Mrs. Tansey-Child." He smiled wryly. "Or Dr. Tansey-Child, to give her her proper title. She was a prominent research surgeon her whole life, including through her husband's two terms in office. But that's something the museum doesn't emphasize these days, unfortunately."

"You seem to have some pretty liberal views, Mr. Elsney," Grimm said casually.

Back home, having a supposed I&I investigator expressing an interest in the liberality of your politics would send most people into a tailspin of denial. Elsney smiled and started down the stairs again. "Ben, please. And I guess you could say that academia is famous for it—or infamous, if you like. But I don't want you guys to think we're some kind of hive mind over here. You'll find all sorts of views in all sorts of places. Like, some folks who know me would be surprised I volunteer at the mission, but it does a lot of good for some desperate people, compulsory Bible study classes or not."

"And what about Judith Buchheit?" Toreth asked. "Did she share your opinions?"

"Well...you have to take account of her world, and of the way that she was brought up. But actually, yeah, you could say so. Although maybe it's more that she focuses on forgiveness. She's a kind, very loving person." He shook his head, a sudden sadness in his voice. "Even after she lost her little boy, she still came to the mission, working with parents who had kids they didn't want and never wanted. I'm sure that was hard for her, when she'd wanted that baby so badly."

It would be nice if someone would say, yeah, she was all in favor of killing fetuses, no prompting from evil foreign medics required. So far the only person who seemed willing to back that horse was, bizarrely, her lawyer cousin. Maybe the senator should rethink his policy of hiring family.

"Did she ever talk to you about abortions?" Toreth asked, without much hope. "Recently, or maybe back when she was pregnant before?"

"Not that I recall."

"And if she had, would you have been sympathetic?" Grimm asked.

"You mean, if she'd been planning one herself, right? All I'll say is that, *as a historian,* in my view criminalizing abortion does way more harm than good." He shrugged. "But that isn't what the voting majority says, and this is a democracy, right? If you're asking if I'd take something like that to the police, then no, I would not."

The next door led them into a large open-plan area. Either they'd gone down far enough to be underground, or they were in the center of the building, because it had no windows.

"Right over there, that's the secure access historical data area where Rebekah was working," Elsney said. "Part of the terms of the trust is that we preserve and present medical history without bias—as far as anyone can do that. It means we have a substantial stock of data and equipment that outside of here would be illegal to own. Even some of the museum trustees don't like that we keep it all. But Dr. Tansey-Child had some good lawyers, as well as a lot of money, and we get by okay, even though we've had some legal challenges in the past."

The space Elsney indicated was hardly bristling with corporate-grade security—there was simply a corner of the room marked off by a head-high barrier, containing four desks with screens and a drinks machine against the wall.

"That's it?" Toreth said. "That's 'secure'?"

"Well, yeah. The screens have a shielded physical connection to the server, so getting access to them doesn't do any good unless you're authorized to see the files. Other than that, I guess you could take a coffee without paying for it."

And Campion could wander in and out without any surveillance taking note. "How about where you keep the equipment?"

The size of the room surprised Toreth. Nothing to match the hangar-like vastness of the I&I evidence storage system, but still verging on industrial in scale. The lighting was low and the air smelled of nothing—filtered, temperature-controlled, and sterile—quite unlike the embassy's casual storage room. Giant mobile racks in a dark gray maximized the storage space, and when Elsney moved the racks to demonstrate how they worked, Toreth saw that the stored items were boxed up and packed in tight. The place was clearly not meant for public browsing, and it still seemed minimally secure for supposedly illegal equipment.

"I guess," Elsney said when Toreth pointed it out. "But we've just never had a problem. Everything is tagged, so it can't leave the building. The last thing we actually lost from any storage room was a year or so ago, when we were reworking the Science of Reproduction exhibit and a couple undergrads here on assignment took Lulu, our diprosopus lamb. She'd never been tagged, because she'd never been out of her display cabinet before." He shrugged. "She doesn't say much about reproductive science, but what kid doesn't love a two-faced mutant lamb? Anyway, she reappeared a few days later, probably after the lambnappers sobered up."

"So you've never lost any equipment from in here?" Toreth asked.

"No. It's rarely even taken out for legitimate reasons." He waved to indicate the room. "Most of this junk is so old that there's probably no one who even knows how to use it. Besides, there's nothing you could do with something stolen from here that you couldn't do ten times more easily repurposing an off-the-shelf modern system."

"What about someone who couldn't easily get access to new equipment?"

"I see what you're driving at, but you know, even if someone managed to smuggle a surgical system out of here, it wouldn't help them much. The equipment here is clinically deactivated—all the control code has been archived and wiped. For procedures that would now be illegal, like abortion, assisted reproduction, or euthanasia, code access needs special permission, with an ethics justification."

Toreth touched the solid side of the storage system. "Do you get many applications?"

"No. Medics don't often research clinical dead ends, and socioethical history isn't trendy these days. I don't recall anything this year, and I sit on the access committee. Rebekah did ask me about the restricted code, but a couple of the trustees had already given me some negative comments about, if you'll excuse me—" he raised his eyebrows apologetically, "—letting a European in here. Rebekah decided she had plenty to look at already."

"Thanks." It felt like a dead end, indeed. There had to be easier ways of carrying out an abortion than sneaking antiquated equipment out of a museum. Leaving the antiquated equipment in there, for one. Toreth eyed the storage system again. It might be possible to set up a cramped space for a procedure inside one of the units, given power and light. It would certainly keep it out of the public eye.

Opening his hand screen, Toreth skimmed through the forensic evidence in the police files. The unfamiliar structure and format wasn't easy to deal with on the fly, but there appeared to be no information relating to the museum.

"Did the police bring a forensic team in here?"

Elsney shook his head. "They took a quick look around, but that was all. They seemed more interested in surveillance, of which we don't have a whole lot."

Well, Toreth wouldn't be the one to suggest Campion had set up a DIY surgery. "Who exactly knew Dr. Campion was coming here?"

"Let's see. I cleared it with the archive access committee and the medical history archivist, and of course I told the security guys on duty. Other than that..." Elsney lifted his gaze, as though seeking answers from the racks around them. "We talked about it at the mission. I might have mentioned it to a couple colleagues here, but I tried to keep it fairly quiet. European medicine has a... well, a sketchy reputation over here. Undeserved, I'm sure."

"I see, thanks." A perfect combination of sneaking Campion in without the embassy's knowledge so she looked guilty, and making sure an unknown number of people from outside could frame her. "Did anyone else come down here on the same day as Dr. Campion? Anyone that Judith knew?"

"Not that I know about. Like I told you before, Monday is a quiet day here. That's why I arranged for Dr. Campion to be here that day. Obviously, it turned out that it would've been better for her if there had been plenty of witnesses, but—" He shrugged.

"Hindsight is rarely helpful," Grimm said. "If only foresight could be made as reliable, then we'd be getting somewhere."

Which, now that Toreth thought about it, was probably the goal of socioanalysis. "I think we're done here. Thanks for your help, Mr. Elsney."

Outside, the sunshine made a welcome contrast to the gloomy storage area. Toreth stopped at the top of the broad, shallow flight of steps leading down to the pavement and breathed in deep.

"So, did we just waste our time?" Grimm asked. "Or did I miss something important?"

He looked at her suspiciously, but she seemed sincere enough. "Waste of time, probably. No." The more he thought about the question, the more he realized... "Actually, I don't know."

"No?" Grimm tilted her head quizzically. "Would you expect to, at this point in a case?"

"I like to have some idea of where I'm going, yeah." Toreth put his hands in his pockets and walked down the museum steps. More or less familiar cars drove past, punctuated by the unfamiliar red- and orange-striped taxis. "None of it feels right, and I don't know if that's because I'm looking at the wrong things in the wrong places, or it's just that everyone over here is completely fucking mad."

Grimm smiled. "Elsney struck me as fairly sane."

"For a man with an office full of dead animals and a home full of skeletons, yeah. That's exactly what I mean. What do you think?"

"About the case?"

What the fuck else? Stuffed pink fairy armadillos? Toreth restrained himself. "Yes."

"It's interesting. I didn't realize how fast-paced it would be. We have deadline pressure, of course, but the type of data we generally work on doesn't change so rapidly. And most of it's at least partly preprocessed by the researchers."

"So...no ideas, then."

"Honestly, no. Not that seem at all useful. When you interrupted me back at the embassy, I was thinking about something Deborah Mayhew told you. Do you recall her saying that her sister has no luck?"

Toreth nodded.

"I found myself wondering how her first husband came to be arrested just when he was. Very likely he'd been seeing men behind his wife's back throughout their marriage, yet he was caught at a particular moment that precipitated a particular chain of events. Pure happenstance, perhaps, but it had an outcome of potential political significance, albeit probably minor, and I suppose that's what interested me."

"Why not look into it, then," Toreth said. At least it would keep her busy.

"Me?" Grimm sounded genuinely surprised by the idea.

"I'm not your researcher—you're supposed to be *my* investigator."

"Well, yes, of course. But..."

"But? What happened to 'I'm sure I'll be useful'?"

"I *am* useful, especially if I'm supported by proper resources." Grimm sounded genuinely offended. "Still." She shrugged. "I'll see what I can do."

Waking up at three thirty in the morning felt just as unpleasant on this side of the Atlantic. Toreth couldn't complain too much, though, as it was O'Reilly, freshly arrived at I&I, calling him. Normally he would've kept the comm on sound only, but necessity forced him out of bed and into a dressing gown. Toreth finger-combed his hair approximately straight, and sat down in front of the screen.

It didn't help that O'Reilly, five hours ahead of him, looked bright and well rested. At least the weather seemed to favor him. O'Reilly's curly brown hair was damp with tiny drops that suggested drizzle, and her cheeks were pink.

"I heard you were on secondment," O'Reilly said. "What's it like over there—other than early?"

"Slightly less boring than it was. I need you to look at some medical records."

"Urgently, I assume. But you could've sent them over last night."

"Well, that's where it gets tricky. I'm not supposed to send any information out of the country, and the Bureau wants me to respect my hosts' requests."

O'Reilly nodded. "I hope you're not expecting me to fly over there."

"No. I thought, if I just happened to leave the comm open, and I also just happened to reread the report where you could see it..."

"I could just happen to give you my opinion?"

"Right. I need to know if there's anything in there that suggests this abortion wasn't screwed up by an Administration medic. There must be something—the technique, the drugs, anything."

"I'll do my best," O'Reilly said.

They sat in silence as O'Reilly read the first page, and Toreth tried to find something positive in the case so far that he could put in a report to Turnbull. It wasn't easy, when he'd been reduced to sneaking evidence out of the country to try to find an answer.

"Next," O'Reilly said eventually.

Toreth moved on through the report, and struggled to stifle a yawn.

Obviously not stifled enough. "You know, if you run through it quickly, I could *just happen* to record the call and then look at it afterwards. I might even have something for you when you wake up."

When O'Reilly had gone, promising once more to look at his evidence as a priority, Toreth braced his hands on the edge of the desk, ready to push himself up and go back to bed. Then he paused.

A quick examination of the flat security system showed that Warrick had already left for SimTech, which made it a good time for Toreth to look at the system without being caught. Warrick had come home the night before at a plausible time—and then Toreth's eyes narrowed as he saw that Warrick had gone out again. Back again just after midnight, so he hadn't been out all night. Luckily, he'd taken a taxi, not a SimTech car, so the credit and purchase check tracked him nicely to Dillian's flat and back again. Pretty as it was to imagine, Warrick probably wasn't fucking his sister.

All well, then. Toreth smiled, closed the connection, and went back to bed.

Chapter Five

❖

As he waited for the call to go through to O'Reilly, Toreth crossed the first two fingers on both hands. If O'Reilly couldn't give him fresh evidence, he was back to chasing witnesses who, official permission or not, probably still didn't want to talk to him.

"Do you have anything?"

She smiled. "Well, I can tell you one thing that might surprise you—it's extremely unlikely that woman needed an abortion."

Toreth blinked. "What?"

"She has, or rather had, a contraceptive implant. The blood analysis tipped me off. They aren't the standard screens that we'd do over here, but some values looked strange. I checked the imaging from when she was admitted, and you can clearly see where the implant had been removed. I could just about make out the original implantation point and scar tract. I assume that means she wasn't given appropriate antiscarring products. Or they use a different implant protocol—I'm afraid I'm not familiar with the procedure she'd have over there."

"As far as I know, she hasn't had any kind of procedure at all," Toreth said. "Not legally, anyway, without her husband knowing about it."

"Oh. Well—" O'Reilly shrugged. "That's for you to clear up, then. It might be something else, I suppose, but I'd be surprised, given the blood values. If the forensic team weren't expecting it, that would explain why they didn't make anything of the fresh removal incision."

"It wasn't taken out at the hospital?"

"Not according to the records. The wound was noted on admission, but it was trivial, certainly compared to her other injuries. I'd say it was contemporaneous with them."

"So when did she get the thing implanted?"

"I can't be precise from the evidence you gave me. In the Administration she's rather old for a first implant to look so recent, but the progression of scarring suggests it's been in place for a year, at least. It could well be more. Certainly long enough for fertility suppression to make a current pregnancy of any stage impossible."

A year—that put Campion nicely in the clear. Maybe they could get a better date from Buchheit's medical records. "Would it have shown up on any scans she had since then?"

O'Reilly sucked air in through her teeth, then blew it out on the first syllable of, "*Possibly.* If they were looking in detail for soft tissue abnormalities in the pelvic area. But the size and composition of the modern implants makes them transparent to some scans, and the scarring hides it further. The location is unusual, too. It's directly over bone, which makes it even harder to spot."

"Like someone was deliberately trying to hide it?" Toreth asked, and O'Reilly shrugged.

"That would be consistent, but it could also just be that they didn't know how to do it properly. From what you're saying, it could've been done illicitly by someone untrained. As far as I can tell, though, it was functioning."

"The police said she was definitely pregnant."

"Yes, that's what the blood screen said, but the type of test they did isn't compatible with an implant. Although even with what they have, it still looks a lot more like an implant false positive than a pregnancy." Her voice had a touch of disapproval. "Of course, if they don't use those implants, they wouldn't know what it meant."

Did that mean Judith herself could've taken a test and come to the same mistaken conclusion? Toreth wondered what the law had to say about trying to have an abortion when you didn't need one. "Wouldn't whoever put her back together have been able to tell she wasn't pregnant?"

"Not conclusively, I'm afraid, and neither can I. That's something *I'm* unfamiliar with. Between the original damage and the reconstruction work, the uterine damage was extensive enough that it might be possible to miss signs of an early pregnancy. I assume the actual surgery would be done by a scanner-guided robot? Anyway, I did some historical research, and while it's not inconsistent with a badly botched amateur abortion attempt, it could equally be staged."

Toreth, who'd been about to ask if there was anything to prove it hadn't been done by someone with Administration training, sat up straighter. "Attempted murder?"

"Unpleasant, I know, but certainly possible. She could've been restrained until the bleed-out caused her to lose consciousness, and then placed in the taxi where she was found. They've noted extremely minimal tissue damage around her wrists and ankles, which is consistent with that possibility . . . or with a voluntary procedure carried out under unfortunate circumstances."

"I need something more convincing than that, O'Reilly."

She looked pensively at her screen, then brightened. "Ah, there's also bio-chemical evidence of sedatives and anesthesia. While I suppose it's not impossible that a medic—especially a bad one—might need pharma *and* soft physical re-straints, I'm sure the evidence system would weight that in favor of the deliberate assault hypothesis."

"So someone who knew she had the implant took it out, and then tried to kill her, hoping that the police would be fooled by the blood assays and assume she'd gone to Campion for an abortion."

"You could definitely make that argument with the evidence I saw. Oh, wait a moment." She reached across, out of his sight, and he thought she was running her finger down the screen. "Yes. One of the trace sedatives is unusual, to me, at least. Maybe it's common over there. It's listed as a true somnambulic, so at the right dose it would make your victim extremely compliant. Could be helpful, if you need to explain how she was persuaded to go anywhere with her attacker—it was given long enough before the samples were taken that it had almost completely metabolized. More importantly, though, I'm sure it's not standard issue for embassy pharma. Check if your medic made any."

O'Reilly looked distinctly self-satisfied, but that was okay. Toreth was more than satisfied with her, too. He'd been hoping for some kind of reasonable—or even unreasonable—doubt that would satisfy the American legal system. Changing a crime by an Administration citizen into an attempted murder very likely com-mitted by someone outside the embassy who then attempted to frame Campion was an almost unbelievable bonus.

"What about the implant? How can I find out where it came from?"

"If they did remove it at the hospital and just didn't note it, then it'll have a manufacturer ID. Tell them to scan for it, and you can check the DoP database. If it's gone, then it'll be trickier. Maybe a biomarker could get you a corporation, I'm not sure. There's a long effect tail-off after removal without the appropriate secondary treatment, so she might still be positive—the problem is the amount of synthetic blood they pumped through her. Hopefully they'll have original samples. I'll send instructions for an implant-compatible pregnancy test, and the DoP validation data."

Whether Ruiz, Detective-Lieutenant Green, and their respective bosses would accept them was another question. "Thanks, O'Reilly."

She smiled. "Any time. Does this mean you'll bring me back a box of chocolates?"

"If this pans out, I'll bring you a whole shipping container full."

After O'Reilly said goodbye, Toreth called Mistry.

"Para?" she said with understandable surprise when she appeared on the comm. "Can I do something for you?"

"Yes. I need you to start tracking down a medic . . ."

83

Toreth was happy to let Ruiz take the lead in explaining the blood analysis and the likelihood that Judith Buchheit had been using an illegal contraceptive implant to the Washington police. Green's attitude of forced politeness suggested he was following a mandate from above, rather than that he believed the story was anything more than an unconvincing attempt to get Campion off the hook.

While Ruiz turned to the hopefully tempting alternative theory of the premeditated attempted murder of Buchheit, Toreth let his attention wander around the meeting room. They hadn't been invited into Green's office, but this was smart enough, at least on a par with I&I's meeting rooms. He'd expected the place to be more like Justice at home—relatively cramped and underfunded, and full of people who knew they were the second tier of law enforcement. Instead the building was as modern and smart as I&I, if nowhere near as large.

Was Campion being held in a cell somewhere in the building? Maybe they had underground detention levels.

Toreth discreetly tapped his comm and checked for messages. He'd expected something from Grimm, once she discovered Toreth had called Ruiz and left without her, but the socioanalyst was apparently sticking to his demand to stay away unless he called her. Now he wasn't so sure it had been a good idea. Lion on the prowl again.

"Where did this analysis come from?" Green asked when Ruiz finished, and Ruiz looked at Toreth.

"My investigator," Toreth said. "She's taken a lot of forensics courses."

He doubted that Green believed him, but Grimm wasn't here to cross-examine, so he had little choice but to let it go.

"So what do you think, Detective?" Ruiz asked.

"Compared to an abortion, I'd call this creative. But even if it does check out—" Green's tone suggested he found that a dubious possibility, "then it doesn't necessarily put the European medic out of the picture."

Toreth cleared his throat. "So Campion set up an elaborate plan to murder Judith in the one way that would guarantee she'd be a suspect. Do you have the saying 'grasping at straws' over here?"

Green looked at him for a long moment, then said, pleasantly enough, "If someone who had no business being in the middle of your investigation said that to you, what would you do?"

"I'd tell them to fuck right off," Toreth said without hesitation.

His snap judgement seemed to pay off. Green's expression warmed, only a few degrees away from an actual smile. "I'll send everything to the lab, and let you know what they think. We'll talk to Dr. Campion about it, too. I'm sure she's gotten bored with our other questions already."

"We were hoping we could take her back with us," Toreth said.

Green shook his head with slow mock regret. "Not just yet, I'm afraid. Sorry."

Because once they let her go, they knew they'd never winkle her out of the embassy again. Toreth would've done much the same.

Green left the room. Through the open door, Toreth could see the officer who'd escorted them up waiting.

"O'Reilly might not be getting her chocolates after all," Toreth said.

Ruiz looked at him sidelong, then said, "Let's go grab a coffee."

The coffee shop, at least, was something he hadn't seen in New London. There were a few customers but, as far as Toreth could see, no staff. A circle of enormous and elaborate machines in the middle of the room supplied the drinks, and also food. A faint, slightly sickly smell of fresh baking pervaded the place, without an obvious source. The sugary palette of the pastel décor matched the colors of the tiny, square, icing-covered cakes being enjoyed by the group of middle-aged women closest to them.

"It's all depersonnelled," Ruiz explained as he examined a selection screen. "The store sees I'm buying the drinks, and it charges my account. The coffee's brewed to order, and the pastries are baked...someplace on site. Downstairs, maybe. Even the tables are wiped down by an automatic cleaner. I assume someone must stop by to resupply the machines, but maybe that's depersonnelled, too. It's my wife's favorite chain, anyway. You want a pastry?"

Toreth glanced around at the sugary concoctions at the occupied tables. "No, thanks. Too sweet for me."

"Really?" Ruiz sounded surprised. "I thought Europe invented all that stuff—croissants, strudels and cannoli and whatever. Okay, how about a pretzel?"

They found a table in the corner, far enough away from other people for conversation. They got a couple of curious glances on the way over, and Toreth wondered if it was the sound of his accent at the counter that had drawn attention. Except for the occasional male-female couple, he noticed, everyone else in the place was in a group of two or more women.

"What do you plan to do now?" Ruiz asked when they'd settled in. "Wait for Green to look at this contraceptive evidence?"

"No. The Bureau sent me over here to get Campion off the hook. Until the police drop her as a suspect, I have to keep...observing."

Ruiz snorted softly. "That's been some pretty active observation, so far."

"I get bored easily. You should ask—" He was within a breath of Warrick's name escaping when he caught himself. "My admin."

If Ruiz had noticed the hesitation, it didn't show. "So what are you planning to observe next?"

Did he want to tell Ruiz? Toreth could probably make the next move alone. "I'm not sure."

"Really?" Ruiz peeled a glazed, flaky strip from the pastry he'd ordered, and pointed it at Toreth. "Toreth, I don't have a dog in this fight. Someone called in a favor from my director, and I had to drop an actual case and hop on a plane to Washington. The police don't want me here, and while it's great to see you again, I don't particularly want to be here. The sooner you get the result you want, the sooner we both get back to our regular jobs."

"Okay," Toreth said, thinking of his own irritation about chasing a runaway American boy around New London. "In that case, I think Deborah Mayhew's worth another interview."

Ruiz had started nodding as soon as he mentioned Mayhew's name. "I wondered if you'd be looking at her."

"For the attempted murder?"

"Sure." Now he sounded surprised. "Judith's married, she has five great kids and a beautiful house. Plenty of reasons for her sister to be jealous. Maybe she figured that with Judith out of the way, she could move in on her brother-in-law. She doesn't seem to be in any rush to get home, for someone who's supposed to be married to her work."

"Would she have the expertise to carry it out? She's a lawyer, right?"

"Ah, funny you should ask." Ruiz opened his hand screen. "You remember you asked me to look into some backgrounds? Elsney came up pretty clean, but Deborah Mayhew was arrested when she was seventeen at a pro-abortion rally. All smoothed over by her dad, of course, but he didn't get every trace scrubbed out. And some of her clients have had their parental rights terminated for so-called 'reproductive rights activism'—skirting the edge of the law, giving out misinformation about contraceptives and abortion." He shrugged. "First amendment, what can you do? Anyway, who knows what Deborah knows, or who?"

The possibility honestly hadn't occurred to him. Toreth would happily fuck Mayhew; she was at least on a par with the selection available on a night out in an average bar. Since there didn't seem to be any DoP equivalent over here, he couldn't imagine her having trouble finding someone to marry her and help her make her own brats. Maybe five ready-made ones were more appealing, though. Definitely less of an interruption to her job. Toreth pulled off a mouthful of pretzel and dipped it in his coffee while he considered the idea further.

"She was hundreds of miles away when it happened, though," he said when he'd eaten the bread. "Wasn't she?"

"Thousands. Her alibi checks out. But like you said, she's a lawyer. Lawyers know criminals."

"She said she deals with family law."

"True." Ruiz shrugged. "But hired killers get divorces, too."

"Yeah?" Toreth grinned at him. "I thought they'd have a cheaper way out than that."

86

Ruiz chuckled. "Hah, yeah. Still, the police already have her on their scanner." He leaned forwards. "If you don't think she's involved, who's your favorite suspect? Of the people we know about, anyway."

Up until now, Toreth had been distracted by all the politics and the strangeness of trying to do his job in this foreign place, but at the bottom of at all, they had an attempted murder. Basic statistics dictated who they should be looking at first, and most closely.

"Lance Buchheit?"

"Lance?" Ruiz sat back, eyebrows raised. "I don't think you appreciate how badly this would've affected his reputation. His political career would've been pretty much over, whether the senator still liked him or not."

"So everyone has less reason to wonder if he was involved. Did you read the interview transcripts? The police didn't even suggest he knew she might be thinking about an abortion. Why was that?"

"You mean, because his father-in-law is a senator? I promise you, that doesn't protect him from suspicion."

"Not even a little bit?" When Ruiz didn't reply, Toreth said, "Anyway, that wasn't what I meant. When I talked to him, he said—"

"When you what?" Ruiz interrupted.

"He called me," Toreth said disingenuously. "I think Ms. Mayhew told him about me."

"You think." Ruiz nodded once. "Right. Well, okay. What did he say?"

"He made a big deal about how they were trying for another baby. Even when his lawyer told him not to say anything, he insisted on telling me all about it. I mean, it wasn't any of my business, right? Then he went through this rigmarole about how he'd made appointments at a fertility clinic, but Judith told him to cancel them."

Ruiz's expression cleared. "Right, I see what you're driving at. Anyone who looks into it is gonna see that he *wanted* another baby, so he's the last person who'd be suspected of conspiring to carry out an abortion?"

"Exactly. And he made sure everyone knew about it. He told people they'd been fighting—that lawyer didn't seem surprised by it. He took Judith to counselling, and he even talked to her family when she wanted to use contraception. Or so he said."

"To try to persuade them to change her mind, I assume."

"But why bother? She doesn't get the contraceptives without his consent, anyway."

Ruiz chuckled. "You aren't married, are you? Maybe he was hoping for a quieter home life."

A fair point. Toreth was all in favor of that himself. He opened the file, and rather to his surprise the police had verified Lance Buchheit's statements.

"He made the appointments at the fertility clinic...and he was the one who called up and cancelled, in person. But they remembered specifically that he said it was because his wife didn't want to go. Is that the kind of thing you'd mention if you didn't have to?"

"I...no, I guess not." Ruiz sounded reluctantly impressed. "I don't see why anyone would want people to know their wife disrespected their authority like that."

Maybe, Toreth thought, he was learning the rules over here. "So why not just cancel without giving a reason? Because it gives him one more witness who can tell us he was all for more kids, and she wasn't. Any one incident could have an explanation, but all together? I've seen plenty of corporates setting up alibis, and the evidence analysis system loves to ping that kind of overkill."

"I'm not sure that 'his alibi is too good' will send the police stampeding to investigate. Anyway, what's his motive?"

"Well, for one, have you seen their nanny?" Toreth asked.

Ruiz looked interested. "No. Should I have?"

"Young, attractive, already inside the family." Toreth shrugged. "Money and power usually win over sex, but not always."

"That's all still just a theory," Ruiz said. "Circumstantial, at best. We have no *real* evidence he was involved."

"Has anyone actually tried to find any, though? Do we have proof Judith even knew about the fertility appointments?" Toreth picked up his hand screen and checked the interview transcript. "Yeah. She didn't tell her sister about it. As far as Mayhew was concerned, she thought Judith had talked Lance into contraceptives."

"We could look into that, sure." Ruiz shook his head gloomily. "Green'll say we're stirring shit up with Senator Grant just to try to confuse the case."

"I thought you said it didn't matter whether or not Buchheit's a senator's aide?"

"I said it doesn't protect him from suspicion, and it doesn't. But, yeah, it would need to be done carefully. And the Washington detectives won't want to hear that they got him so wrong—not from me, and definitely not from you. I'd rather not take it to them as a theory without something solid to back it up."

"Fair enough." Was it worth the aggravation of getting involved beyond this? So far he'd managed to downgrade serious crimes committed by an Administration citizen to unlawful contraceptives most likely provided by someone who wasn't even in the country anymore, and wouldn't be coming back. That certainly satisfied Turnbull's remit. If only he had Campion back in his possession, he'd be tempted to call it a day. "That's why I wanted to try the sister again. She was cooperative before. Besides, we can take the opportunity to spread the good news."

Ruiz's mouth quirked. "We have good news?"

"The police are taking a leisurely approach to O'Reilly's evidence—okay, we can't tell them how to run their investigation. But what looks better for a senator's aide and his senator father-in-law? Illegal abortion or illegal contraception?"

Ruiz sat back and sipped his coffee. "And once the senator hears about the implant, he'll do everything possible to make sure the police take it seriously?"

"Right. People keep telling me that Grant has a lot of clout, so let's get it weighing in on our side." Followed, with luck, by Campion's release, and a happy conclusion to Toreth's case, if not the Washington police force's. "Mayhew can get us talking to Buchheit, and hopefully the senator will listen to him."

Toreth's two birds proved to be luckily lined up for one stone. When Ruiz called Mayhew to ask for another meeting, she was already at her brother-in-law's house.

Toreth had expected to have to drive out of Washington. Even with the new zoning that had been a benefit of rebuilding New London after the bombs, Administration high-ups would need to move into the suburbs to afford a place expansive enough for a family with five kids and an *orchard*. In fact, they were still in the city when the car stopped at a pair of security gates that were almost as impressive as the house beyond. On the other side of the road, a black metal fence— old, and more for decoration than function—surrounded an immaculately manicured park. The beds Toreth could see had obviously just been replanted for the overwinter flower displays.

"Cozy little place, isn't it?" Ruiz commented as they waited for the tall gates to open.

"Very," Toreth said.

"Not the only building that Maxwell Grant owns in the neighborhood, either." Ruiz pointed down the street. "His nephew, Simon McGlothlin, lives with his wife and kids in a smaller place right down there, and over there—" He twisted around to point across the park, "is his mom, the senator's sister—divorced—in a nice little duplex. I think there are a couple more, but I heard that they're rented out since there's no family who wants them."

A smooth, even graveled driveway took them up to the house. An automatic lawn mower was shaving scant millimeters in stripes across a surface already flatter than the last pool table Toreth had played on. Lofty trees around the garden perimeter, either historic or highly growth-accelerated, provided as much privacy as if the house had been in the middle of the countryside. This kind of old money exclusivity was familiar enough from home. Deborah Mayhew and her black sheep brother Maxie had both, presumably, walked away from the chance to live in similar gilded accommodation.

With a disconcerting synchronicity, Ruiz said, "While I was looking into Deborah Mayhew's background, I checked out her current address. It's a pokey little apartment without a tree in sight. This would be a big trade up."

It wasn't Lance or Mayhew who opened the door, but a young woman in a knee-length dark blue dress that had a hint of uniform about it. Toreth recognized her as Schuyler Finn, the nanny—even more attractive in the flesh than in the background image he'd pulled up from his conversation with Lance Buchheit. Also a potential trade up.

As they followed Schuyler through the house, Ruiz cocked his head at her and raised his eyebrows. Toreth nodded. Ruiz blew out in a silent "hot," and Toreth grinned.

The large, square living room was an odd combination of exquisite high-end furniture and décor, and the mess left behind by five small kids. A detritus of toys, paper, and small screens littered the place incongruously, scattered over polished tabletops and lost under chairs with thin, delicately curved legs. Mayhew and Lance sat next to one another on the sofa, with one of the children asleep in Mayhew's lap. Ruiz glanced at Toreth, raising his eyebrows significantly. Mayhew certainly looked comfortably settled into her little domestic scene. When Lance stood up to shake their hands, she stayed seated, but she smiled up at Toreth.

"Nice to see you again, Val."

"And you." He offered his hand, and it took her a moment to disentangle herself from the child so she could shake it.

Mayhew leaned to the side, so she could look past Toreth. "Say, Schuyler, could you take Abbi? Let her sleep some more, if she can. I heard her waking up in the night."

Ruiz all but nudged Toreth in the ribs.

Mayhew passed the little girl to the nanny, who took her without waking her and retreated silently from the room.

"Can we get you something to drink?" Mayhew asked. "Coffee?"

"No, thanks, we just had one," Ruiz said as he and Toreth sat down on the sofa opposite Lance and his sister-in-law. Toreth set his camera on the arm of the sofa, and neither Mayhew nor Lance commented. "I guess you aren't staying at the hotel, now, Deborah?" Ruiz asked casually.

"No," Mayhew said. "We talked it over yesterday, and it seemed like I could be way more useful here. Schuyler's in the house twenty-four-seven, and there's the day help, too, so I don't think even my dad could say it looks bad."

Ruiz nodded. "So how long are you staying in Washington?"

"I'm not sure. As long as I can, while Judy and Lance need me here."

Lance touched her arm. "When you have to go, you just tell me."

Mayhew smiled, and Toreth thought he detected real fondness for her brother-in-law. To say more than that, he'd want a neural scanner. "I'm a junior partner in a pretty large firm. They won't even notice I'm not there."

"I guess right now it's convenient that you never married," Ruiz said casually.

Toreth expected Mayhew to take offense, but she shrugged. "It isn't a political statement. I've just never met anyone I felt that way about."

Did she steal a glance at Lance, or at least have to suppress one? Toreth wasn't sure. Ruiz obviously thought not, because a fleeting disappointment crossed his face.

"You've had plenty of offers, though," Lance said, as though he felt her attractiveness needed to be defended to the pair of detectives. "I remember when Simon—"

"No." Mayhew shook her head firmly. "Simon was trying to impress my dad by taming his little wild filly. He's much better off with what he got in the end, someone to stay at home and tell him he's always right."

"Judy always said he encouraged your career," Lance said.

"Well." Mayhew shrugged. "Maybe. But I bet you he didn't let my dad hear him do it. And I'll tell you what I told her—if Simon is such an amazing catch, why didn't she say yes to him after her divorce? Anyway, how great Simon was or wasn't as a prospect doesn't matter. My life is fine the way it is."

"I'm sorry if I offended," Lance said. "I—well, Judy and I, we just want you to find real happiness."

"I already did," she said, unmistakable irritation breaking through. "And I told her that. But Judy always thinks she knows best where her little sis is concerned."

Even if, according to Mayhew, Judith's choices hadn't done much to make *her* happy.

"Okay, well, how can I help you guys?" Lance said, looking between Ruiz and Toreth.

"We'd like to ask you a few more questions about your wife if we could, Lance," Ruiz said. He looked significantly at Mayhew.

Mayhew started to stand, but Lance put his hand on her arm. "Stay, Debby. Judy wouldn't want me to keep any secrets from you. Go ahead, please. Anything I can do to help."

"Thank you," Ruiz said. "Now, Lance—did you give permission to your wife to use an illicit contraceptive implant?"

Lance frowned. "No, of course not. I already told you, we were trying for another baby. Why are you asking? The hospital never said anything about finding any implant."

"We don't have the device itself, but she has a small wound where it was recently removed, plus supporting blood analysis. I'm surprised the police haven't contacted you yet." From the confidence in Ruiz's voice, Toreth would've assumed the Washington police had accepted O'Reilly's ideas without question. Toreth would definitely give the man a job if he wanted to move to New London. "I'm sorry if this news is a shock, but we do need to ask if you had any knowledge of it."

"No!" Lance sat up straighter. "I had no idea. None at all. She asked me about using contraception, yes. I already told you about that. But an illegal implant? No. I can't believe it. Debby? Did you know anything about this?"

Toreth had been watching Mayhew, and she appeared as genuinely surprised as her brother-in-law. "No, she never even hinted to me. Wow. Judy, of all people, getting herself fixed up with..." Toreth thought he heard a tiny trace of admiration tingeing her voice. "I never would've guessed that, not in a hundred years."

"There you are, then," Lance said to Ruiz. "Neither of us knew. And, okay, you say you have evidence, but... I don't understand why Judy would do that after everything we talked about." He looked between Toreth and Ruiz. "And if she had this thing taken out, why would she want to kill the baby after? What kind of sense does that make?"

He sounded utterly bewildered.

"Did Judy get it from the European doctor?" Mayhew asked suddenly.

"Not from Dr. Campion," Toreth said. "But that's something I wanted to ask you. You said you remembered your sister talking about an Administration medic. Do you remember when you had any of those conversations?"

"Let me think." Mayhew looked down at her hands, running her thumb over the ends of her nails. After a few seconds, she nodded. "One time I know for sure was last year, around the end of November. I don't recall the exact date, but she was talking about organizing Thanksgiving at the mission, and she mentioned that the doctor had come from the embassy, or was coming, because they didn't celebrate the holiday."

"And that's the doctor she was friends with?" Toreth asked.

Mayhew nodded. "Definitely."

"Excuse me," Toreth said, and opened his hand screen to send a message to Mistry.

Lance shook his head. "I still don't understand. So... she had this implant, and then she had it taken out, and then..." He swallowed. "Why? Why would she do that? Did it affect her brain?"

"We've gotten the evidence looked at by someone at the European embassy," Ruiz said, "and so far we have no reason to think that the implant wasn't in place and working just fine right up until last Monday." Then he sat back and waited.

In Toreth's experience, people telling lies usually under- or overestimated how long it took to work through the ramifications of a genuinely new fact. Mayhew and Lance processed at more or less the same plausible speed, and reached the same conclusion. The sudden paleness of Lance's face made the dark shadows around his eyes stand out even more; Mayhew said, "Oh, my God."

"We don't think she was pregnant," Toreth said. "We think that she was assaulted by someone who tried to make it look as though she had been."

No glimpse of panic on either face at the plain statement.

"So whoever did it must have wanted Judy to die," Mayhew said. "They wanted to kill her."

"That's the only reasonable interpretation, yes," Toreth said. "They could remove her memory of the attack easily enough, but she'd still recall having the implant. Wiping out months of global memory is difficult enough, and selective amnesia on that timescale would take time to create. Not to mention expensive equipment and someone with expertise."

Both of which he happened to know that America possessed. Of course, they might have something better than the Administration, too. If so, whether anyone had bothered to use it on Judith Buchheit they'd only know if she woke up.

"My poor Judy." Lance put his hand over his mouth. "My poor girl. This is my fault. She asked about contraception and I said no. Because of—because—"

"Because my dad wouldn't like it," Mayhew said, rather coldly.

Lance nodded. "My poor girl."

She winced. "Lance, I'm sorry. I didn't mean it to sound like that. Listen, if someone hurt Judy, it was because they wanted to hurt her, and if they hadn't done it that way then they would've done it another. How criminals choose—it doesn't always make sense, you know?"

"Thanks, but that doesn't change—"

Toreth's comm chimed in his ear, distracting him. A message from Grimm: Ask Mayhew what happened to estrange her brother from her father.

She must be watching the feed into the IIP. What had prompted that particular question?

"—and they didn't just hurt her, they hurt her character. Our memories, even. You know whatever the police report says, people are gonna talk about this for the rest of—the rest of her life." Lance faltered, then carried on, "They'll say the senator had it covered up. People will look at her and think—"

This time his voice cut off, choked, and Mayhew hugged him tenderly. Ruiz raised his eyebrows at Toreth, and Toreth studied the pair on the couch. He still couldn't see anything sexual, but maybe his perceptions were screwed up over here, and Mayhew's comforting pats to his shoulder were only one step away from clothes-ripping against-the-wall fucking.

Finally Lance straightened up and wiped his eyes. Mayhew's hand lingered on his arm as she looked at him anxiously.

"I'm okay," he said. "I'm sorry, just sometimes the whole mess hits me again."

Toreth said, "Mr. Buchheit—"

"Lance, please."

"Lance. If your wife doesn't recover, what are your plans?"

"I have been considering that." He shrugged, as though anticipating disapproval. "I have to, you know? Right now, I'm thinking about moving back to Chicago. My mom and dad live there, and they've already offered to help with the girls. Without Judy, there'd be nothing to keep me here."

"Not even Senator Grant?" Toreth said.

Lance snorted softly. "To be honest, politics was never my first choice. But

Maxwell's been so generous, and he's Judy's dad, so I felt like I owed him my support. I can find a job in Chicago, no problem. I have friends in law firms back there."

There could be all kinds of reasons for the move, some more innocent than others. "Would Ms. Finn go with you?"

"Schuyler? I—" The question seemed to surprise him. "I don't know. I haven't asked her. I hope she would—it'd be enough of an upheaval for the girls without losing her, too."

A perfectly good explanation for packing the sexy nanny along with the furniture—if Lance even owned any of the furniture. Toreth looked at Ruiz, and he gave a tiny shrug.

"I don't know how to thank you both for this," Lance said. "I know Judy's still sick, but I've been praying for some kind of a way out of this nightmare, and this news is like a miracle. Maybe the police would have come up with it on their own, maybe not, but you have my gratitude, and anything I can do for you, just name it. Can we share this with the senator?"

Ruiz made a show of considering it. "I guess so," he said slowly. "As long as it doesn't get too much exposure just yet. Not until the police have had time to assess the evidence."

"Right, sure." Lance nodded. "Well, thank you again."

"Is that everything?" Ruiz asked Toreth.

"I think so. Oh—" He turned to Lance. "Could we look at your wife's room before we go?"

"Sure. Although the police already went through it. They took a couple boxes of her stuff, then they said they were done with it."

"Maybe they missed something," Ruiz said. "Could be they weren't looking for the right evidence."

"Why don't you show us the way, Deborah?" Toreth asked.

Toreth kept the camera active and in his hand as Mayhew led them upstairs. At the bedroom door she stopped, letting Ruiz pass by her.

"Was there something you wanted to ask me?" Mayhew said to Toreth in a low voice.

Toreth looked at her in surprise, and she smiled.

"I am a lawyer, you know, and you cut me away from Lance pretty neatly."

"Fair enough. I was wondering what caused the estrangement between the senator and your brother?"

"Maxie?" That seemed to surprise her. "Why?"

Honestly? No idea. Fucking spooks and their fixation on the politically interesting. "Is there a reason you don't want to talk about it?"

"Um, no, not particularly. Okay. Well, it was dumb, really. They always had some tension after Mom died, because Maxie's older than me and Judy, and he kinda resented how quickly Dad remarried. My stepmom is great, honestly, but Maxie was just pissed that she was there at all. He used to say Dad married her because he didn't want to pay for a nanny. Nonsense, of course." She gestured down the long hallway. "Whatever else you could call my dad, 'cheap' isn't it."

Although there was a difference between generosity, and leveraging "gifts." "I can see that."

"Anyway, Maxie went kinda wild at law school. I don't think it was anything worse than the usual stupid college craziness, boys getting a taste of freedom at last. But my dad told him to straighten up, or else. I know Lance and Simon tried to keep him out of trouble, but then somehow my dad had gotten hold of a recording of Maxie on spring break. I don't know what was in it, but I heard the row. I remember my dad telling Maxie he had to think about his reputation for the future. And then Maxie said he didn't give a fuck about reputation—I think that was first time I ever heard anyone use that word to my dad—and he quit school and moved west, and they haven't talked since."

Must have been a hell of a recording. "That was it?"

"As far as I know." She brushed her hair back from her forehead. "But... yeah, I never really thought about it. I guess it seems extreme for Maxie having fun on a beach someplace. Maybe there was more to it that I didn't hear. Maxie and I talk, you know, but he won't talk about Dad. Most of the time he isn't my hottest topic of conversation, either."

Movement in the doorway made her turn away. Agent Ruiz was there, eyebrows raised.

"You joining me?" he asked.

"I'll leave you both to it," Mayhew said.

Mayhew had been correct in her deduction that Lance and Judy were sleeping in separate rooms. It seemed a perfectly reasonable arrangement to Toreth; he still wasn't convinced that separate flats wasn't the best way to go.

"So what do you think?" Ruiz asked when they were alone. "Mine, or yours?"

Suspects, Toreth assumed. "I don't think I fancy either of them that much now."

"Really? After all that business on the couch I'm starting to wonder if they planned it together. I sure don't cry on any of my sister-in-laws' shoulders like that."

The room had as high quality furniture as the rest they'd seen in the house, although plainer. Ruiz opened a couple of drawers, revealing contents that already had the disarray of an official search. While he looked through more drawers and wardrobes, Toreth went over the dressing table.

A central area seemed reserved for makeup and preparation. The space to each side was crammed with small screens, mostly showing images of people. Toreth spotted Lance and Deborah, and a small child very like the one he'd seen downstairs. The rest were presumably her other children and family. There were a few animals—dogs, a couple of horses, one cat that looked almost as foul-tempered as Bastard—and one cycling slowly through images of scenery, maybe holidays. A lot of clutter, like someone who wanted to be reminded how many good things she had in her life. One image at the back caught Toreth's eye, on paper, not a screen, in a plain glass frame. It looked old, the colors faded, with a shiny surface like a page from an antique book: a pair of familiar animals digging a nest. And, reflected in the mirror behind it, he spotted writing on the back.

Toreth picked up the picture in the frame and examined the message. The messy writing was hard to read, but Toreth thought it said, "I hope this makes you smile." No signature, but that didn't seem necessary. Toreth turned the picture back over. How old was it, and how much was it worth? Had she kept it because it was valuable, because of the sentiment, or because of the sender?

"What the heck are those?" Ruiz asked from behind his shoulder.

"Pink fairy armadillos," Toreth said, as though everyone working in criminal investigation ought to know that.

"Seriously? They aren't like any armadillos I've ever seen. They're ridiculous."

"Yeah." Toreth set the picture back in its place. "Shall we look in the bathroom?"

The room's en-suite bathroom, unused for over a week, had picked up an almost invisible layer of dust. The bathroom cabinet was patchily filled, suggesting that the police lab was probably testing a lot of innocent pharma. A plain white plastic container about five centimeters high and tucked away at one end caught Toreth's attention. Ruiz must have spotted it at the same moment; they both reached for it, and then Ruiz politely pulled his hand back.

The little box held what looked like toothpicks. Toreth took one out, revealing the flattened tab at the other end.

"That looks like a pregnancy tester," Ruiz said. "Lance did say they were trying to conceive. But there are usually instructions printed on the side."

When Toreth tapped the box lightly with the pads of his fingers one side felt slightly sticky. "It's been peeled off." He turned the box over, looking for any identifying marks. It was blank except for a conjoined male/female symbol molded into the base. "I tell you what I've seen that looks like this. Implant function test strips."

"Does everyone in Europe have these in their bathroom cabinets?"

"Not me—I've never bothered. What are the odds of an implant failing? Tiny. I get I&I medicals, anyway, and they'd pick it up. But I've seen them in other people's places." Usually while their partners were away for the night.

"But what if the implant did fail?" Ruiz asked. "What does your Department of Population say about that?"

"Well, for it to matter I'd have to fuck a woman who'd also had a failure. Tiny odds times tiny odds equals forget it, it'll never happen." He stuck the strip he'd taken out between his teeth and his cheek. "That's why the DoP doesn't accept double implant failures anymore."

"Will that work on you? I mean, since you're a guy."

"I think so." Toreth turned the box over again and showed the symbol. "Unless it *is* a pregnancy test."

"How long?"

"Thirty seconds? A minute, to be on the safe side." Toreth counted down the time, then pulled out the tester. "There you are." The flat end of the stick now displayed two black lines. "Working tester, working implant."

Ruiz grinned. "Either that, or I'm looking at a medical miracle. Okay, I'll get in touch with the police and tell them they need to come back here. This ought to strengthen the case that she had an implant."

"What'll really do that is finding the fucking idiot who gave it to her," Toreth said. "And I already have one of my investigators working on it."

They were on their way out when Lance Buchheit stopped them in the hallway. Mayhew was there with him, fastening her outdoor coat.

"I called the senator to tell him the news about Judy," Lance said, "and he wants to talk with you, if that's okay. He's heading over to the hospital to see Judy pretty soon, and he'd like you to meet him there."

"Why?" Ruiz said.

"I'm afraid I don't know any more than that. Debby and I are going, too. I guess maybe he wants to thank you in person for all you've done for us. For Judy. Please?" Lance added to Toreth.

A chance to meet someone so central to the case? "All right."

Lance gave him a relieved smile that suggested the senator was prone to messenger-shooting. "I'll tell him we're on our way. Do you want us to drive you there? We can—"

"Thanks, we have a car," Ruiz said.

Schuyler came into the hallway, holding a tray of child-sized cups. "Lance? Did you call me?"

"Yes. Debby and I are going out—I'm not sure for how long. And Schuyler, listen, this is—" Lance started speaking eagerly, then caught hold of himself. "We have some news from the detectives. It seems as though Judy might not have been pregnant after all. Someone tried to—to frame her, I guess."

The nanny put the tray down with a bump that set the juice slopping in the cups and stared at him. "Framed?"

"It's true," Mayhew said. "It's just like we all said, Judy would never do that."

Schuyler didn't seem to hear her; she was still looking at Lance, her expression bewildered. "But that's—how do they know?"

Lance touched her arm reassuringly. "It sounds pretty crazy, yeah, and they don't have all the details yet. Go back to the girls, and we can talk about it more later. Just—whatever happens to Judy, we'll never have to explain to the girls why Mommy would do something like that, because she didn't. That's what matters."

"Right." Schuyler smiled tentatively. "Okay."

"I'm sorry. I shouldn't have sprung it on you like that." He touched her arm again. "But this is the start of things going right again, Sky. I can feel it. Here, let me take these." He picked up the tray. "I'll take them up and tell the girls we're going out. I'm sure they'd rather hear it from me."

Schuyler nodded, and watched him go up the stairs, her eyes still wide. When Mayhew said her name, she jumped, obviously startled.

"Schuyler, did Judy tell you that she was using contraception?"

"That she was..." Schuyler looked between the three of them, her gaze lingering nervously on Agent Ruiz. "What do you mean?"

"Judy always said you were a good friend to her, as well as an angel with the kids," Mayhew said earnestly. "If you know anything that could help her you need to tell us."

"And it'll be much better for you to cooperate now," Ruiz said. "Unless you want to go to the police and make this all official?"

"Okay, yes, I did know." Schuyler looked appealingly at Mayhew. "I found a test, like a pregnancy test. She'd dropped it. I asked her about it—I was happy for her, that's all. I thought she wanted another baby. But instead she was upset, so I knew something must be wrong and in the end she told me about this thing that was inside her, that stopped the baby from getting started. She said it wasn't anything like an abortion, just like you don't kill a chicken when you eat an egg, 'cause there wasn't ever a chicken inside."

"Did she tell you who gave it to her?" Toreth asked.

Schuyler shook her head. "I didn't ask her. I thought maybe one of the doctors at the mission."

"And did you tell anyone else about it?" Ruiz asked.

"No, of course not," she said quickly. "I wouldn't. It's illegal, I know that, but I'd never get Judy in trouble. I guess I should've told the police, but I didn't think it mattered, that's all. They told Lance she was pregnant. I figured it didn't work, or something. Everyone always says you can't have the fun without..." She swallowed. "Am *I* in trouble, now?"

"No," Mayhew said firmly. "Not if you tell the police everything you know about this implant. I'm sure Agent Ruiz will talk to them on your behalf and tell them how helpful you've been. Right, Agent?"

Ruiz smiled. "I'll be sure to mention that when I talk to Detective-Lieutenant Green, Counselor. But, yes, Schuyler, we can work something out."

"Don't you think you ought to call the ambassador and let him know about meeting the senator?" Ruiz asked as the car pulled away from the Buchheit house.

The feeling of oversight was as annoying as hell, Toreth reflected as he tapped his comm. He might be used to Tillotson prodding pointlessly around in cases, but irritating as the section head could be, at least he was I&I, and he had a vague understanding of investigation. Even if it was mostly focused on how much it cost and whether it would upset any corporates.

Fu answered Toreth's call immediately.

"I'm on my way to talk to Senator Grant," Toreth said after they'd exchanged greetings—rather perfunctory ones on Fu's part. "He asked to see me."

Fu's expression changed to alarm. "Why?"

"Hopefully, to thank us for probably clearing his daughter's name. She might be a vegetable, but at least no one will be able to use her to smear him."

"Yes. I saw the report from I&I forensics. I would've appreciated a meeting to discuss it before you went to the police—I thought after Dr. Campion, you'd see that International Relations does possess information you might find relevant."

"You're right, I'm sorry." Fu looked like he was about to protest again, so Toreth said, "Ambassador, while we're talking, I wanted to ask you about the embassy medic you had before Campion. Presumably there was one."

Fu nodded. "Canfield. He was sent back to Europe after the trouble settled down. We rotated out quite a few staff at that point."

Campion and Canfield—similar enough to explain why witnesses hadn't remembered there were two different medics involved. "Was there any particular reason he was chosen to leave? I remember Campion saying she took over the cultural contact initiative from him."

Fu's face developed a pinched look. "Yes, and she fulfilled it better, too. Canfield became a bit *too* interested in the local culture."

"Women?" Toreth asked. "Men?"

"Churches. Not that International Relations has any official policy on employees' religious affiliations," the ambassador added. "At least, not if it doesn't interfere with their real work. But I felt a subtler approach would be helpful. A clean slate. That's why he went back."

No doubt, even after armed mobs had burned buildings across Europe in pursuit of more "freedom," Fu had felt nervous about what any new Administration might think. "And you didn't put any mention of this in his security file because...?"

"Well." Fu shifted uncomfortably, caught between the suggestion of incompetence and admitting he hadn't thought Canfield's religious fervor sufficiently serious to merit noting. "A lot was happening at the time. The unrest created an enormous amount of interest and concern over here. It must've slipped the mind of the deputy ambassador. It's her job to make those exit assessments."

Nice sidestep, with bonus blame deflection. Toreth could see how the man had reached the level he had. "Well, thanks. I'll bear that in mind when I talk to Canfield."

He cut the connection before Fu could respond. He tapped the comm again right away, and said, "Jas Mistry."

She took a few seconds to answer. "Yes, Para?"

"Did you track down the embassy medic? His name should be Canfield."

"Yes, Para, that's right. We're in luck—he's in New London. I'm at the International Relations Career Development Services building right now, just starting the interview. I put a note in the IIP."

"I've been busy. Something that might be useful—the ambassador says Canfield was kicked back to Europe because he took the cultural exchange crap seriously and started overdosing on God. Too many churches, although he might've been meeting Buchheit and screwing her senseless, for all the ambassador knows about it. And we have confirmation from a new witness that Buchheit had an implant."

"Right. Thank you for the information, Para. Are you watching?"

"Might as well. I don't have anything better to do right now." Toreth expanded his hand screen and said to Ruiz, "Do you want to see how I&I runs an interview?"

"Hm?"

"One of my investigators is talking to the embassy's previous medic. If we're lucky, we'll find even more good news for the senator."

Canfield's office looked distinctly unmedical, and rather cramped, with two desks slotted into a space barely adequate for one. Canfield himself looked as though he could barely squeeze into his chair between the desk and the wall. He was tall and well built, his fair skin had a tan, and his brown hair showed natural-looking sun highlights. If Toreth had had to guess his occupation, he would've put sports before medicine, and then Toreth recalled that his security file mentioned rugby. Maybe that would've worked out better for him as a career.

Mistry had her chair at an awkward angle beside Canfield's desk. He'd asked Mistry to keep the interview low-key for now. In Europe, with Toreth only able to back his team up from across the ocean, International Relations could decide to make things difficult. He'd suggested to Mistry she should keep in reserve the threat of making it official, in case they balked.

"What work are you doing now?" Mistry asked Canfield.

He waved at the screen. "I'm reviewing training courses. I could do it just as well from home, of course, but—" He shrugged his broad shoulders. "Not policy. And not really what I was trained for."

"Yes, I was told that you've been temporarily removed from the embassy placement roster. Why's that?"

Canfield looked at her resentfully. "Don't you have it in a file somewhere?"

"It's not entirely clear, I'm afraid. I'm working with what my boss told me, and he's in Washington. Apparently you were enthusiastic about the cultural exchange. Somehow that became a problem?" Mistry sounded puzzled.

His scowl deepened. "It wasn't a problem at all while it was useful to the embassy program. Ambassador Fu encouraged it, and, frankly, I enjoyed being able to go to church and chat with the people I met there and not have to wonder whether some idiot would decide—well. There was no political dimension to it, let's say that, not even an imaginary one. Then security tightened up after the riots over here, and suddenly asking to go out to church on a Sunday was a no-no. Nothing *I* was doing changed."

"I see. That must have been upsetting. If you'd made friends at the church, and you couldn't explain why you stopped attending."

"It was annoying, not upsetting. And I got too demanding and pissed off the ambassador, and he panicked about how the wonderful cultural exchange would look to *his* bosses. Suddenly I found out *I'd* been sneaking out to church behind his back, and he had no idea how often I'd been going. I guess he'd rather be thought incapable of keeping an eye on his staff than subversive."

Beside Toreth, Ruiz snorted quietly. Toreth looked at him, and Ruiz shook his head. "Office politics, huh?"

"No one's talking about subversion," Mistry said. "I'm here to ask about Judith Buchheit. I've been informed that you knew her well."

"'Informed that you knew her,'" Canfield said sourly. "That somehow makes it sound sinister, don't you think?"

Toreth wondered if he was imagining it, or if the downgrading of I&I's interrogations really was making suspects less cooperative. Their mistake. He tapped his comm. "Tell him you can get some guards to pick the pair of you up, and you can find an interrogator to talk to him at I&I."

"I was hoping we could get through this without having to make it any more official," Mistry said to Canfield. "That's up to you, though."

Canfield sighed. "Yes, I did know her. We both volunteered at a shelter for indigs, and we became friends. In fact, yes, I was sorry I didn't get to say goodbye to her, but as I said, they tightened embassy security and then I was reassigned."

101

Mistry nodded. "Now, we'd be interested in hearing about any medical treatments you provided for Buchheit."

"What do you mean?" he said guardedly.

"I think you understood the question." Mistry was still smiling, but her voice had hardened a little. "My boss really hopes we can move through this smoothly. You can help us, or he can dissect the entire medical records of the embassy and its staff while you sit in a cell at I&I and wait for it to be done. And knowing him, there'll probably be a charge of impeding an investigation. Once you're processed into custody I don't have any wiggle room, and the charge goes on your security file."

"Fine. Judy had a classic postnatal hormonally disregulated neurotransmitter issue, made worse by a perfectly normal reaction to grief and isolation. It was obvious. I couldn't stand seeing her at the mission, struggling to get through the day, suffering for no reason at all, so I offered to help." Canfield lifted his chin. "And it can be tricky to treat, but actually she responded fantastically to the first-line expression rebalance. A couple of doses and she was fine. I don't see why I&I would be interested."

"Why didn't she get the treatment from her own doctors if it was so simple?"

"Well, they don't use a pharma-focused system over there. Prayer is a wonderful thing but, in my experience, there are more efficient ways to shift gene expression into a new steady state." He sounded more confident now, and more antagonistic. "Yes, it wasn't my job to do it, but why shouldn't I, for pity's sake? Nothing I gave her was outright illegal, here or there."

"That's not strictly true, is it?" Mistry said seriously.

That made him pause, and when he spoke, the confidence no longer sounded natural. "I checked all the pharma I used, and everything was approved over there for use by a licensed physician. Which I am."

"I'm talking about the contraceptive implant you gave her."

"No." His voice was firm, but the flicker of panic on his face was clear over the comm. It would be far more obvious to Mistry. "That's not true. I'd never do anything to get Judy in trouble."

Obviously a lie. Equally obviously, he was ready to go down with the ship on this one. Toreth was about to suggest it was time to move to I&I when Mistry said, "Dr. Canfield, you haven't asked about Judith."

He said nothing.

"I'm sure you'd want to know that she's in hospital, in a coma."

His eyes widened. "What? A coma—no. I don't believe that."

Mistry pulled up the pictures Toreth had sworn to Ruiz would be useless, of Buchheit unconscious in hospital, her face almost as pale as the pillow. "She was hospitalized following an illegal abortion."

He sat back. "Rubbish. Absolutely impossible."

102

"You sound very sure."

"Yes, I—" He hesitated, then blurted out, "All right. She did have an implant. It was working; I gave her a supply of test strips to check it. If she conceived, she must have had the implant removed. Must have. You can't hold me responsible for anything that happened afterwards."

"And how did it come about? Giving her the implant, I mean," Mistry said, which Toreth thought made a nice paraphrase of "were you fucking her?"

"She came to see me, a month or so after I treated her. She was extremely anxious—she thought she was pregnant. She'd taken a test, of course, but she had some distorted thinking around pregnancy that was nothing to do with the expression imbalance. I tested her again—negative, by the way—and then I offered her the implant *temporarily*. It was for her mental health as much as anything else."

"Did you know it was illegal for her to have it?"

Canfield looked down, and swept a few crumbs from the desk onto the floor. He sighed. "Yes, of course I did. And she struggled with it. Judy believed it was her duty to support her husband and obey him. She never wanted to do anything behind his back, but he made it impossible."

"Why was that?"

"He was too rigid. You know, I liked Lance, the few times I met him. He seemed like a perfectly nice guy who loved his wife and children. But on one side he had the way he'd been brought up, and on the other he had Judy's father, and between them they squeezed him into the shape of an asshole. She was so unhappy that in the end I persuaded her it wouldn't do any harm. She'd get peace of mind and she could work on her relationship, and then I'd remove the implant when she decided she was okay without it, or Lance agreed to another type of contraception, or I was about to leave. Then half of Europe went up in flames and took the plan with it."

"Unfortunate for you," Mistry said.

"Worse for Judy." He sighed again. "Were you telling the truth about her?"

"Yes. She's in hospital, and they can't give a firm estimate for her chance of recovery. I'm sorry."

"I just hope they're treating her properly. There's a lot I admire about the place—am I allowed to say that?—but as I said, they have some peculiarities when it comes to medicine."

Ruiz snorted again. "Sure, you guys have room to talk," he muttered.

"However, we don't think now that it was a genuine abortion," Mistry said, and Canfield frowned. "We think it's very likely she was assaulted by someone who tried to make it look as though she'd died of accidental blood loss following a medical procedure."

Canfield stared at her, speechless.

"Can you think of anyone who might want to kill her or benefit from her death?"

"Anyone—" Canfield swallowed. "No. God, no. Judy was the kindest, most well-liked person you can imagine." He paused, then gave a crooked smile. "I suppose you must hear that a lot, but this time it's absolutely true. I can't think of anyone. She was a sweet, sweet person."

"What do you think she'd do if she wanted to remove the implant?" Mistry asked.

"She'd have to find someone with medical training she could trust to keep quiet. I don't know who that might be." Canfield was serious now, as though he just wanted to help. "There were things she'd never confide to me. That's not how it works over there. If she told anyone about the implant, it would only be a close female friend."

"Or a close female employee," Toreth said to Ruiz.

"I see," Mistry said. "When did you give her the implant?"

"Oh, let me think. It must have been...eighteen months ago? A little more than that, maybe. Obviously, I didn't keep any records."

"We understood that she was sleeping apart from her husband at that time."

The defensiveness was back. "She never told me that. Judy didn't like to talk about Lance with me."

"Doesn't it seem a little odd, though, that she'd be worrying about being pregnant when she wasn't having sex? At least not with her husband."

"Not really." Apparently he couldn't see it coming. "I told you, she had a—a fixation on the issue. Do you have any phobias? Her fear was something like that. Not entirely rational."

Mistry nodded. "So you didn't give her the implant because you were having an affair?"

"What the *hell*?"

Canfield half stood. Mistry's expression didn't change, but she uncrossed her legs and rested her hand on his desk, close to the camera recording the interview. Slowly, Canfield sat down and stared at her.

"I'd like to hear your answer, please," Mistry said.

"I was her *friend*," he said emphatically. "And even there, we had limits, lines it would've been dangerous for her to cross. We could talk at the mission, and at church, but we weren't free to just spend time alone together. She was always conscious of it, and she had her husband's position to think about, you see? Her family meant everything to her."

"I see. So, to be clear, there was absolutely nothing physical to your relationship?"

"No. Absolutely not. Not even close."

"So you have no idea why she'd run the risk of breaking the law when she wasn't sleeping with her husband?"

"They were still having sex occasionally? Maybe she was worried he wouldn't be interested in hearing 'no'? I don't know." He glanced at the camera with distaste. "She was a private person, and I respected that. I didn't pry."

"Para, is there anything else you want to know?" Mistry subvocalized.

Toreth tapped his comm. "Yes. Ask him if he gave her gifts."

Mistry relayed the question, paraphrasing it smoothly into her own words, and Canfield frowned. "No. And before you ask, not because it could've raised suspicions of something that wasn't happening anyway. We didn't have that kind of friendship, that's all. The only thing I ever gave her was a box of implant test strips, for her own peace of mind."

"That's all I wanted to know," Toreth said, thinking of the picture on Judith's dressing table. "Thanks, Mistry. I'll let you know if I need anything else."

"Thank you, Doctor," Mistry said. "If there's anything else, we'll be in touch."

"I'm sure you will."

Toreth closed the connection, then skimmed back through the interview, cutting out the section where Canfield confessed to placing the implant. He sent it to Fu with a note explaining that he intended to let the police, the senator, Turnbull, and International Relations back in Europe know about Canfield's unauthorized treatments. The latter two he copied right away. The police and Grant could wait for now.

And that, hopefully, would be that.

"Investigator Mistry, did you say?" Ruiz said. "I don't think I met her when we were over there. She's a good interviewer."

"That's why she's on my team." Toreth opened Canfield's security file and noted the interview in the appropriate section. By way of throwing a bone to International Relations, he marked him as fully cooperative, no further action. IR could make up their own minds what to do about their medics sticking illegal implants into foreign citizens.

"But—excuse me if this sounds weird, but you can just threaten to carry someone off to I&I and charge them if they don't cooperate with your investigation?"

"For actively impeding? Sure." Toreth closed his hand screen. "As long as there aren't any corporate lawyers sticking their oars in, anyway. Then it's nice to have a solid political angle, so we can strip the corporate standing first. That wouldn't help Canfield, though. He's not corporate."

"You don't have any kind of...they can't choose to refuse to incriminate themselves?"

Toreth looked at him blankly. "Why the fuck would we want to let people do that?"

"Because that's how civilized places treat citizens who haven't—" Ruiz took a breath. "It's definitely different from the way we do things over here, that's all I'm saying."

"I'm sure it is." After the open trials, Toreth wasn't even surprised anymore.

The front of the hospital complex had landscaped grass and trees laid out in front of a towering front wall made largely of energy-recovery glass. They drove around to the far less imposing rear of the building to a parking area near a door. The heavyset man waiting to meet them reminded Toreth of showy corporate muscle. Not something usually displayed by Administration officials.

"Do senators get assassinated often?" Toreth asked as they followed their guide through the hospital.

"Hm? Oh, you mean...?" Ruiz pointed to the bodyguard. "Well, they have been in the past. Not recently, though. How about in Europe?"

What would the equivalent be? Parliament of the Regions reps? Now the overt security made more sense. "Yeah. In a bad year we'll lose a couple. There are hundreds of Parliament reps, though. I doubt it affects the Administration's paperwork."

"Lose a *couple*—seriously?"

"I know. I've never understood it. The Council makes the important decisions, so the resisters are wasting their time offing reps."

"Right." Ruiz didn't seem to know if Toreth was joking or not. "Hey, are they elected, though? These parliament guys?"

Toreth nodded. "Every few years."

"Well, I guess if these 'resisters' know that most of the things they can do won't get reported by the media, then at least taking out someone from the parliament has an effect. There's a new election." Ruiz smiled wryly. "Maybe a free press would be better for the reps' life insurance."

The hospital interior matched the smart front; clearly it was a place a senator would want to care for his daughter. It had the same reassuringly expensive touches in décor and uniforms that marked out the high-end corporate hospitals from the more run-of-the-mill clinical settings at home. What would he find at the American equivalent of an Administration basic care facility?

Toreth had wondered if they were being taken to Judith Buchheit's room, but he guessed that wasn't their goal when he saw the group of men waiting up ahead. They looked like smartly suited drones clustered around their senator queen. Grant was a tall, fit-looking man in his late fifties, with a rugged handsomeness that Toreth suspected he carefully calculated to say "down-to-earth" rather than "politician." His clothes, subtly more casual than most of his minions', reminded Toreth of Simon McGlothlin, who was one of the group.

Whatever the senator was talking about, their escort seemed reluctant to interrupt. Toreth and Ruiz waited by a door that had a small window set into it. Toreth peered through into the room. A scrum of people waited inside, all with prominent ID badges. There seemed to be a lot of cameras in evidence, too.

"What's going on?" Toreth asked.

Ruiz joined him at the window. "Looks like an 'impromptu' press conference. Talking to the various media," he explained. "I guess you don't have them at I&I?"

"If we need something released to the news services, there's a different section that handles it. Media Relations. Why don't they share a single feed, at least?"

"People want to get their questions heard. Every now and then someone comes up with a fancy new automatic system. The problem is that a real live person in the room always had the edge. Even if it's just because they can taser another network's fancy new autonomous camera and flush it."

Corporate competition at its finest. Then something struck Toreth. "Is he expecting me to go in there?"

"I should think so. It's no big deal. I've talked to the media for a few cases. Just say what you want to say. If you don't like a question, ignore it. And, uh, try not to threaten anyone with interrogation, that would probably be a good idea." Ruiz gave him a quizzical smile. "Don't you want your fifteen seconds of fame?"

"Back in January they were lynching paras on the streets across Europe, so thanks, but no." A couple of people in the group seemed to have noticed their observers. Toreth stepped uneasily away from the window. "Anonymity has its perks."

Ruiz still looked bemused. "Do they watch a lot of American news over in Europe?"

"Not without bypassing data distribution laws. And funnily enough, people who do that are exactly the kind of people who dragged an interrogator into the middle of the fucking zoo and threw her in with the lions."

"With the—" Ruiz stared at him. "That really happened? Was she killed?"

"Yeah." Toreth grinned. "Not by the lions, though. They wouldn't touch her, and I'm not surprised. You wouldn't be either, if you'd met her. None of the spineless fucks in the mob dared go in after her, so they shot her, instead. *Then* the lions got involved. I guess they can't recognize meat unless it's dead."

"Wow." Ruiz shook his head. "Just...wow."

"Yeah, I know. That was definitely one of the more creative ideas. Most of the interrogators and paras who were killed they just—"

"Paravestigator Val Toreth, right?"

Toreth turned around and found Grant holding out his hand. Toreth took it, and the man shook Toreth's hand warmly with both of his.

"Para-investigator, that's right," Toreth said.

"Right, Val, right. Para-*in*vestigator, I'll remember that. I'm Maxwell Grant." The handshake evolved into a sincere squeeze. "Lance has told me all about you, and I want to thank you personally. You've done a great thing for my family."

"Thanks." Toreth retrieved his hand. "I'm just doing the job my government sent me over here to do."

"Still, I appreciate how generously you've shared your findings." Grant glanced at the group of people waiting. "Please, allow me to introduce you. You already met my nephew, right?"

"Not in person," Toreth said.

"But close enough. After Lance, he's my right-hand man. And these guys are from my communications team." He waved at the two most expensive-looking suits in the room. "They'll run through what we're planning to say, and what we'd like you to say, too, if that's okay."

"Not possible," Toreth said. "I'm sorry. There are strict rules at I&I. Paras and investigators don't talk directly to news services."

"I just need you to confirm that you have the evidence we say you have." Grant's smile didn't seem so natural now.

"Like I said, I'm sorry, but it's out of the question." A little exaggeration wouldn't hurt. "I&I would fire me five minutes after they found out about it." It might not even be that much of an exaggeration. If he said something the Administration Council didn't like, on a news service open to God knows how many people, Turnbull would no longer be a protection. She'd probably hold the door to the lion cage open while International Relations tossed him inside.

Toreth had expected a shitstorm, but after a few seconds the senator nodded. "Sure, I understand." He still sounded reluctant. "Can you at least stand in there with us?"

On the one hand don't piss off Turnbull, on the other, don't piss off the senator. "Okay." At least he wasn't in uniform. "So long as you don't mention my name or my job. Call me a representative from the embassy."

Standing behind the senator, even in the anonymity of a group, made Toreth uncomfortably aware of how far the recording could travel. Maybe back to Europe, where someone might get curious enough to try to find out his name.

The senator's explanation was heavy on sadness and disappointment that his beloved Judy's character had been mauled by the media, and light on any news about illegal contraceptive implants. Toreth wondered if Lance was about to offer the revelation that he'd given permission all along, but he and Mayhew had apparently been relegated to silent supporting roles.

"My daughter is the only victim here. We expect the police to announce in the next couple days that Judith is entirely innocent of the charges that have been talked about. Charges that never had any foundation in reality."

Grant paused, looking around the room as though daring anyone to challenge him.

"Will you be making a complaint about the way the case has been handled?" someone called.

"Simon?" the senator said.

McGlothlin cleared his throat. "That's something we'll be looking at closely as the situation develops. No official complaint has been made at this time. Our priority is justice for Judy. The senator respects the Washington police, and it is not our intention to do anything that might negatively affect the ongoing investigation."

Except, say, for making an announcement, surrounded by lawyers, to force Green to take the new evidence seriously. No one in the room pointed that out, though. Toreth had the feeling these things ran to a well-established formula.

When the media reps had been escorted away, the group around the senator broke up. One of the communications team had his screen out, apparently discussing appointments for the rest of the day with Grant. McGlothlin tapped his comm and stepped away from his boss.

"I told you not to call while—yeah, okay. I know, I know. Don't worry, I'm working on it. No, I'm with the senator right now." He glanced over his shoulder, and then moved further off.

Lance and Mayhew had also drifted away. Lance rubbed her arm and said, "Do you still want to come with me?"

Mayhew hesitated, then nodded. "Okay. I'll send a message to Schuyler to let her know we'll be a while."

"What now?" Ruiz asked. "Back to the embassy?"

Toreth almost said yes, but something still nagged at him. "I want to talk to Elsney again if we can, about that bedroom picture. Not over the comm—I want to see his reaction."

Ruiz consulted his hand screen. "The museum opens later Fridays and Saturdays; maybe we'll be able to catch him there."

Elsney wasn't in his office, but they found him in a long gallery obviously in the middle of remodelling, surrounded by half-built screen displays and empty cases. Ropes of blood vessels and strings of grayish-tan lymph nodes decorating the gallery suggested the exhibit would be focused on the circulatory system.

"We hoped you could clear something up," Ruiz said.

Elsney looked more intrigued than alarmed. "Sure."

"We found a gift from you in Judy's bedroom. A page from a book. She'd framed it—you wrote a message on the back."

"Oh! The armadillos. I sent it to her back when she was having a tough time. She always liked the little guy in my office."

"So she came here to see you?" Toreth asked.

Elsney hesitated. "Yeah, a couple times. She brought the older girls to the museum, and she stopped by to say hello."

"Did she?" Toreth said. "Because you told me that you kept that fairy thing at home until very recently."

"I—um." Elsney picked up an oversized model of a human heart; disconcertingly, it beat twice, then stopped. "Yes. Well, then I suppose she must have been at my house, too. Maybe she dropped something off for the mission. I don't remember."

"If we spoke to Lance Buchheit, would he know that his wife visited your home?" Ruiz asked. When Elsney didn't answer, he added, "Did you have an improper relationship with her?"

Elsney wetted his lips. "Does Lance need to hear about this conversation?"

"That depends on what you have to say," Ruiz said.

"Yes, Judy came to my home. And for a while, okay, we were closer than maybe we should have been. I guess it started after her son died. There was a time back then when I wondered if it could be something more. If she left Lance, if we...but it was impossible. Judy wouldn't even think about it." Elsney paused. "Well, maybe she did. We're both only human, right? But go through with it? No chance."

Ruiz nodded. "Was it a physical relationship?"

"No. Absolutely not. I respected her too much even to suggest it."

Sounded like bollocks to Toreth, but Ruiz, surprisingly, seemed willing to accept it. "So how did it end?"

"You met her nanny, right? A few months ago, Judy found out the girl had been involved with a married man—she heard it straight from the guy's wife. Apparently the wife felt guilty that the nanny was working for the Buchheits when Judy had no idea what the girl had done. Judy told me God showed her the pain at the end of the path she'd started to walk down."

"She wasn't worried about the nanny doing the same with Lance?" Toreth asked.

Elsney laughed. "Lance? Never in a million years. He's devoted to Judy. Adores her. All Judy worried about was if the nanny could be a bad influence on her kids, but at the same time she didn't want to ruin the girl's life by firing her. A couple months ago she told me that she brought it up, gently, and the girl said she'd made a bad mistake and she was sorry. Judy prayed about it and decided to let her stay. She said she didn't feel she had the right to cast that particular stone, at least not at the nanny."

"When Judy said it was over, how did that make you feel?" Ruiz asked.

"Sad. And angry—not with Judy," he added quickly. "With everyone in her life. She deserved more...more happiness. More than just living for other people. And then I realized I was being just as selfish, because I wanted her to give up her kids and live for me instead. She was right to break it off before I did any more damage."

They left Elsney standing morosely in the middle of his half-built exhibit, holding the silent heart, and walked back through the largely empty museum.

"So, are we adding Elsney to the list now?" Ruiz asked.

More targets for the police who weren't Campion would only help. "He might

110

have opportunity—his alibi's still unverified. He admits, or he *claims,* that he was looking for Campion at lunchtime. We should've asked him if he knew about the implant. He's probably the one most likely to have been fucking her when Canfield gave it to her."

"Look, we just gifted Grant back his daughter's reputation. Let's not screw that up unless we have to, okay?" Ruiz waited until Toreth nodded. "The first thing we do is ask the police to track down the people who were supposed to be in these meetings with Elsney."

Ask the police, not do it themselves. Maybe Ruiz's boss was tired of calls from Green complaining about interference in the investigation. "While they're doing that, we could check Schuyler's alibi. There are other people to look after the kids during the day. Maybe she thought with Judith out of the way, she could go after Lance—or maybe she's already gone."

Ruiz grinned. "You just don't want to let that one go, do you? Why are you so convinced he's involved?"

Toreth shrugged. "I've seen people do stupider things for less impressive tits. And what was the last thing that Buchheit did as we left the house? Tell Schuyler what we'd found. Maybe he was warning her. She didn't seem to like it, either."

"She didn't like to hear that someone had tried to murder her friend by ripping up her womb? Gee, I can't imagine why that might upset someone."

"Okay. But you remember the call that the police were so sure came from Judith Buchheit? Why couldn't Schuyler get hold of her comm the day before the attack and call Campion, pretending to be a missionary, to create a comm connection between Judith and Campion for the police to find?"

Ruiz shook his head. "She's a homemaking assistant, not some criminal mastermind."

"She knew about the implant."

"How did she hear that Campion would be at the museum, though?" Ruiz countered. "Elsney said he only talked about it at the museum and the mission. Schuyler has no reason to be at the museum, and she doesn't volunteer at the mission, at least not that I know of. Lance doesn't, either."

"Well, we could always drop in and ask Schuyler on the way back to the embassy."

"See how she reacts?" Ruiz sighed. "Sure. I guess I'd rather do that than hit Green with *another* theory for him to investigate. He'll be pissed enough about the press conference."

By the time they returned to the Buchheit house, dusk had fallen. Lights showed at the upstairs windows, but the ground floor was dark. Was Lance still at the hospital?

They weren't the only visitors. A car stood at the side of the house, and although the interior and exterior lights were off, Toreth could make out a figure inside. Ruiz directed their car to park in front of it, blocking its exit, and they both climbed out. As they approached, Toreth recognized McGlothlin, alone in the car.

Ruiz rapped on the window, and McGlothlin lowered it. "What are you doing here, Simon?"

"Looking for Schuyler."

"That's a coincidence—so are we."

Ruiz's statement didn't seem to register. "She called me right after the press conference, extremely agitated. I asked her what was wrong, but all she said was that she was in trouble. I told her I'd come see her as soon as I could, but when I got here she was already gone. Now I can't get ahold of her."

"Why would she call you for help?" Ruiz asked.

"I—I don't know. I guess whatever the trouble is, she thought she needed to talk to a lawyer."

"Bollocks," Toreth said succinctly, although the effect was somewhat spoiled by McGlothlin's expression of bafflement. He tilted his head for a better view of Toreth.

"Excuse me?"

Ruiz rested his arm on the top of the car. "She didn't think of you because, say, you two are having an affair?"

McGlothlin opened the door of the car, almost shoving Ruiz out of the way, and climbed out. "Who told you that?"

"A source we trust," Ruiz said, deadpan. "More than I'm trusting you right now, anyway."

A noise like a closing door came from the direction of the house. McGlothlin looked around, and lowered his voice. "Okay. We *had* a thing, but it wasn't an *affair*. It was just a brief—it started when I had a moment of weakness, and she took advantage of it and trapped me."

"So you're saying it's over?" Ruiz said with skepticism.

"Has been for a couple years. Right from the start, I told her we had no future. But it was hard to quit, you know? I was afraid that if I said we had to stop she'd tell Sandi what we'd been doing, out of spite." He hesitated. "Sky can be devious. She's very manipulative."

"Oh?" Ruiz said.

"Yes, absolutely. One time she even threatened to kill herself—leave a note blaming me—and make sure that Sandi or the boys found her body before I did. It was just a threat, but that's what she could be like." McGlothlin sighed. "Look, I was stupid, I know, but...well, then Sandi suggested that we should help Judy out by letting Schuyler go to her. I told Schuyler it was best we broke things off, and, thank God, she didn't make a fuss."

"So your wife doesn't know about the affair?" Toreth asked.

"No. Or . . ." McGlothlin looked anxiously between them. "Does she? Was it Sandi who told you?"

Interesting—a story failing to add up always was. Had McGlothlin's wife decided to keep quiet to her husband, but still warn her friend? Maybe Buchheit had discovered the infidelity some other way, and lied to Elsney about how. Maybe she'd guessed, or made up a story to cool things down with Elsney that just happened to be true. McGlothlin might not even be the only married man in Schuyler's past. Toreth shook his head; none of this helped locate the missing nanny.

"So do you think Schuyler might have gotten involved with Lance?" Ruiz asked. "Could that be why she called you?"

"I don't deny that crossed my mind. I never thought Sky would be able to get any traction with him. Lance is such a standup guy. But it sounded way more serious than that."

"So where is she?" Toreth said.

"I don't know. Apparently I just missed her. She left the house a few minutes before I arrived. Maybe she took a cab. I've been calling her, but there's no answer. I tried to call Lance, but he isn't picking up, either."

Schuyler and Buchheit, after all? Were they trying to make a run for it?

"Thanks for your help, Mr. McGlothlin. We'll take it from here."

"Okay." He nodded, seeming reluctant. "Could you call me if you have any news? She asked me to help her, and whatever happened in the past, I feel like that puts me under a professional obligation."

"Do you think she could get into your house?" Toreth asked.

McGlothlin shook his head. "I changed all the codes after she left, and Sandi is still away at her mom's."

Toreth looked at Ruiz. "What next?"

"We need to hand this over to the police right away." Ruiz tapped his comm and turned his back.

Still muttering about representing Schuyler if she wanted it, McGlothlin climbed back into his car and Ruiz instructed their own car to let him by. The lawyer turned left out of the driveway, towards his house. Toreth hoped that if he found Schuyler there waiting for him he'd have the sense to call them.

"They agreed to put out an alert." Ruiz rubbed his hands together; the evening was cooling down fast under a clear sky. "I'm not sure they entirely believe me, but I think I convinced Green that if we were right, then the senator wouldn't be impressed if they sat on their hands and did nothing. He wants me to come in to talk about it."

"Do you need me, too?"

"No. I'll drop you at the embassy. I'll call you if I have any news."

113

Back at the embassy, Toreth thought about putting the afternoon's work into the Investigation in Progress, and decided to write up a case summary for Fu and Turnbull instead. Overall, he didn't feel the Bureau secretary could have many complaints. In less than four days, he'd turned the abortion into attempted murder and provided the Washington police with a tasty selection of alternative suspects. Now it was up to the lawyers to extract Campion from custody, and he could close the IIP and go home.

Reports sent, he moved on to the flat security system. To his surprise, Warrick's bedroom was dark and empty. He checked the time, wondering if he'd made a mistake, but it was almost one in the morning. The office security feed had a link to SimTech, and accessing it would automatically generate a warning there. He didn't need them to know he'd been keeping an eye on Warrick.

The dining room provided the answer—Warrick, Asher Linton, and Lew Marcus sat around the table at the monthly directors' dinner. Toreth should thank Turnbull for sparing him the need to find an excuse to skip it. Then a worrying thought occurred—would Warrick have put in another security alert, since SimTech business was no doubt being discussed?

He was still wondering if he could find a way to check whether he'd tripped a security flag when the office door opened. Toreth cancelled the connection immediately, leaving him with the mental picture of Marcus laughing, wine bottle in hand as he poured.

"Hello, Para-investigator." Grimm was dressed for the outdoors. Maybe that was why she hadn't been annoying him much today.

"Busy day?" Toreth said.

"Yes, indeed." She smiled brightly at him. "Busy and interesting. I thought you might like to discuss it over dinner, if you haven't eaten yet?"

The moment she suggested it, he realized how hungry he was. Apart from the pretzel with Ruiz, he hadn't eaten since breakfast. "All right."

"As you suggested, I chased up that question I had regarding who tipped off the police about Judith Buchheit's first husband's proclivities," she said as they walked along the corridor. "It took me a while, but I finally made enough of a nuisance of myself that someone decided it was easier to track down the information I wanted than to listen to me explain why I needed it."

"Is that an official Socioanalysis tactic?"

"Primarily a researcher tactic, but yes. You recall you explained to me how interrogation works? Well, this is another way to change someone's priorities."

Toreth started laughing.

"Para-investigator?" Grimm said.

"Sorry. I just—I always thought Carnac was naturally an annoying arsehole. I didn't realize it had taken training."

"Do you want to know what I found?"

114

She might not have everything in common with Carnac, but they'd obviously been taught the same irritated glare. "Okay, go on."

"As you might suspect, there was no requirement that the informant reveal their identity. However, the message was in the case file, and it contained what I thought was a suggestive use of technical legal language."

"Legal—Lance Buchheit?" Toreth guessed. "He had her husband locked up and then married her?"

"The same possibility occurred to me, amongst others. Anyway, it piqued my curiosity further and, combined with the evidence from Ms. Mayhew, I felt justified in catching an express plane to Seattle to visit the senator's son."

"To do what?" Toreth said. "Couldn't you just call him?"

Something else she had was the classic socioanalyst's are-you-*really*-that-stupid frown. "Obviously not, or I would have done. He has no comm, and apparently the commune members travel into Seattle proper to contact the outside world. I considered trying Senator Grant or his wife instead, but I strongly suspected that the tipster would've taken care to stay anonymous, so they wouldn't know his or her identity. The question you asked Mayhew about Maxie was most helpful, by the way. Her vagueness wasn't surprising, but it did give me enough information to pursue the conversation with her brother. He's a rather charming young man, with a moderate degree of artistic talent. Oh, speaking of which, I brought something back for you."

She paused, and produced from inside her bag a roll of off-white paper secured with a bright red paper band.

"Handmade paper, along with instructions for a model of the official Seattle city bird—a type of heron. Most of his models are architectural, but I thought this would appeal more to your taste."

Toreth took the paper, despite the temptation to throw it back at her. "Is that in my fucking security file?"

"No, but I remembered the bird you made for Deborah Mayhew. This one is rather more lifelike. Quite cleverly constructed. He showed me some of the finished models." She smiled. "He seemed rather content with his life. Interesting to compare how he and Deborah have approached the problem of achieving distance from their family." Grimm tilted her head slightly. "Don't you think?"

Something about her tone made him sure she was fishing, but for what he had no idea. Toreth started walking again. "I don't give a crap. Did Maxie tell you anything that might actually help the case?"

"Ah, yes." Her fleeting smile gave him an uncomfortable feeling that he'd reacted the way she'd wanted, or at least expected. "He was somewhat bemused by my questions—he seems to have mentally severed himself from his past more successfully than Deborah—but with a little encouragement he told me that he had a strong suspicion about the origin of the recording. Apparently, out of the small number of other people present at the incident, only one of them had 'coinciden-tally' absented himself for the period covered."

"Lance again?"

"Actually, no. According to Maxie, Lance was never much of a partygoer. But it was another friend."

What had Mayhew said about Maxie's friends? "Ah...McGlothlin, then?" She nodded at the name. With the dining room in sight, Toreth stopped walking. "And you think he was responsible for the legally worded tip-off, too?"

"I do."

"I thought he was supposed to have the senator's best interests at heart. I don't see how that squares with getting his son-in-law arrested for sodomy."

"Well, I suspect that in his view, it probably does." She smiled, obviously pleased to have caught his attention. "Because a possible pattern emerges, don't you think? Over the years, McGlothlin appears to have systematically removed those standing between himself and Senator Grant. Mayhew said that Simon had always been a favorite of her father's—I imagine that he came to see the political inheritance as rightfully his. He appears to have proposed to both daughters, in a somewhat feudal attempt to secure his position, but both of them refused him, so he had to use other means."

Dinner now seemed a lot less urgent than it had a few minutes ago. "Other means."

"Exactly. The senator's son is estranged," Grimm continued. "Mayhew luckily removes herself from the game by her disinclination to marry and career ambi-tions—with, I note, McGlothlin's reported encouragement—and the first son-in-law is disgraced once he fathers the male child that would seal his place as heir. Fortunate for Lance Buchheit that he runs to daughters, don't you think?"

"Not fortunate enough." Toreth tapped his comm. "Ruiz? Come on, answer."

The silence before Ruiz answered went on for what felt like minutes, but in fact was barely long enough for Grimm to ask what was going on. Toreth waved at her to be quiet.

"Toreth?" Ruiz said. "This isn't a great time, I'm still with the police. They—"

"Just listen to this." Toreth expanded his hand screen, and added Grimm's comm to the conversation. "Grimm."

She ran briskly through her information again, in a condensed version that gave Toreth a reluctant measure of respect for how Socioanalysis trained their staff to handle evidence.

"And you think that *he* tried to kill Judith Buchheit?" Ruiz said with horror when she was done. "Just to get rid of Lance?"

"It's a possibility, yes." Grimm frowned. "Although I'm not sure why McGloth-lin might choose to move against Judith so directly now. Simply because she was planning to conceive again? Why not wait until she was pregnant with a boy, as before? No, that's weak. It requires further investigation and more evidence."

116

Toreth stared at her. "Haven't you been watching the interviews in the IIP?"

"Not since I sent you the question while you were at the Buchheits' house. The I&I secure connection didn't like the request from on board a foreign plane." She smiled slightly. "I did see you looking rather dashing on a newsfeed. I think the ambassador will probably want to talk to you about that."

"Jesus fucking Christ." Toreth crumpled the roll of paper in his hand. "Schuyler's disappeared. She knew about Judith's implant *and* she's probably having an affair with McGlothlin. Judith Buchheit found out about it."

Grimm's face fell. "Oh."

"For fuck's sake, Ruiz and I ran into McGlothlin outside the Buchheits' house. He said Schuyler had called him—and she did. I fucking heard him talking to her after the press conference. Lance told her we knew about the fake abortion before we went to the hospital, and she must've panicked."

"Oh. Yes, that does change things, rather." She frowned. "You should've let me know immediately. The threat was no longer merely the reconciliation between Lance and Judith or their hypothetical future son, but that she held evidence directly damaging to McGlothlin's reputation, and with Senator Grant's history of demanding moral rectitude from—"

"Yes, thank you, *Investigator.* Ruiz, is there any sign of Schuyler yet?"

"No, not a sniff. The police confirmed McGlothlin's story, in that Schuyler left the house. She told the other homemaking assistant that she had to go out, but the woman didn't actually see Schuyler leave, so we don't know if she took a bag."

"I'll guess no. *Bollocks.*" McGlothlin, parked outside the house—he'd been right *there.* "She's become a liability to him. She could've been dead in the boot of that car while we were talking to the smooth fucker."

"Or unconscious," Ruiz said optimistically. "Maybe he still has the drugs he used on Judith."

"The police must start searching for his car," Grimm said. "If it's active and near other vehicles right now, it surely must be possible to find it?"

"I'm taking an embassy car to McGlothlin's house," Toreth said.

"Wait for me," Ruiz said. "I'll pick you up on the way there. I don't think he's gonna just let us in, so the police will need a warrant. We can't go kicking our way in there, okay?" He raised his eyes and sighed. "Yet another suspect. Green is gonna love us."

Despite Ruiz's pessimism, Green had proved surprisingly amenable to the appearance of a brand-new name on the list, even if it was the name of a senator's nephew. What he wouldn't budge over was allowing Toreth to set foot inside McGlothlin's house.

"This isn't a crime scene," he said with undeniable satisfaction. "Not yet. And I don't remember agreeing to opening up searches, too."

"How about the interview?" Toreth said.

"We'll have to find him first. He isn't home. Yes, yes—" Green held up his hand. "His car's still there—first thing we looked for. We're checking for cab pickups."

"Senator Grant owns a bunch of properties in the neighborhood," Ruiz said.

"And we're checking all those out, too," Green said. "We already called his mom and his cousin-in-law. I promise you, we're taking this seriously. Would I have all these guys searching his house if we weren't?"

"Have you found anything yet?" Ruiz asked.

"Not a whole lot. Some unlabelled drug injectors hidden in his study, but we'll need to see what's in them before we jump to any conclusions. Lawyers, you know?" He shared a smile with Ruiz. "Oh, this might mean something—he set a route from here to the docks at Baltimore in his car, and then he cancelled it. Must have been around the time you saw him at Lance Buchheit's house. That's as good a place as any to make someone disappear."

And then McGlothlin thought better of it, once he'd been spotted by Toreth and Ruiz. Where was he now, though? Had someone warned him about the application for the search warrant? He was a lawyer, and politically connected. If they'd spooked him any more than he had already been, the slim chance that he hadn't yet killed Schuyler diminished even further.

Green and Ruiz went back to the search, leaving Toreth to stand and fume, with only mounting frustration to keep him warm in the chilly autumn weather. The expensive neighborhood was quiet at night, magnifying any individual sounds. Cars passed occasionally, some kind of garden maintenance machine started up and then stopped almost at once, and a few insomniac birds were making noise in the park. Sadly, no obvious sounds of a murder in progress.

All the rooms in McGlothlin's house were lit up, but the partly opaqued windows gave no clue as to what was happening inside. A couple of figures moved in the dimly lit garden, scanning for recent soil disturbance. Of course, McGlothlin had already had plenty of time to drive elsewhere and he could be out of range of detection while he buried Schuyler's body somewhere they'd never find it. Then he'd pop up again in a day or so, probably with a story about how he'd decided to surprise his wife with a visit. Sorry, but he'd turned off his comm for a weekend of privacy.

Fuck. As long as there was a reasonable chance of an innocent verdict, the senator would probably do everything he could to protect McGlothlin—including trying to push the blame back across the Atlantic again. Toreth eyed the gatepost, but it looked much too solid to punch.

There was one other place to try for information, not far away. Ruiz's comm was busy; Toreth left a message to say he'd be at the Buchheits' house.

"I'm sorry I didn't answer your calls," Lance said as they walked through to the living room. "I was—well, it's a long story. But to put it in a nutshell, my grandmom is Catholic, and I've been lighting a candle for Judy every day at the shrine to Mary in the local Catholic church because I knew it would make my grandmom feel better. And I guess it can't hurt, right?"

Lance Buchheit, people pleaser extraordinaire. "Right," Toreth said.

"But I didn't think the senator needed to know about it, so I've been turning off my comm. Anyway, what can I do to help?"

"Well, the police are looking for Schuyler and—"

"I know," Lance interrupted. "They already called. We're worried about her, too. It's so weird. The security system doesn't even show her opening the gate, and anyway, it just isn't like her to go out without telling someone where. The police were looking for Simon, too. They said she called him or something?"

Sounded like the police hadn't mentioned anything more sinister. "Where's Ms. Mayhew?"

"Upstairs, with Becca. Poor little kid came downstairs—she heard a monster outside." Lance smiled, a thin veneer over the worry clearly visible underneath. "The girls are already freaked out about their mom, and now of course they want to know why Sky isn't here to put them to bed." They'd reached the living room, but Lance didn't sit. He went over to the window and peered out into the darkened garden. "It's kinda hard to tell the kids there aren't really any monsters out there, you know?"

"Lance." How to approach this without loyalty shutting the man down? "Are there any family houses away from Washington? Somewhere Schuyler might have heard about while she worked here—or when she was working for Simon McGlothlin?"

Lance turned. "Well. I guess, yeah. There's the senator's home in Lansing—that's in Michigan—and he does own other real estate. You'd need to talk to him. I don't know how many would be empty, though, or how Sky—"

He stopped speaking as Mayhew appeared, holding a little girl by the hand. The girl—five or six, Toreth guessed, and wearing pajamas printed with green horses—started to run over to Lance and then stopped when she saw Toreth.

"It's okay, Becca," Lance said. "This is Val. He's come to help look for Schuyler."

Becca came over, giving Toreth a mistrustful inspection, and Lance rubbed her shoulder, a little awkwardly.

"What's up?" he asked.

"She won't settle down," Mayhew said. "I said you'd read her one story, and then she had to go back to bed. I didn't realize you were here, Val, sorry."

"It's okay," Toreth said. "Maybe you could help—I'm trying to get a list of family properties that Schuyler might know about."

"I heard a monster outside tonight," Becca said suddenly. "It roared."

"No." Lance crouched down. "It was just the mower starting up, that's all. It does that sometimes, and then it shuts right down when it realizes it's nighttime and it should be asleep. Just like you." He looked up at Mayhew. "The senator changed the maintenance service this summer, and it's been going on ever since. They don't seem to be able to fix the problem. The old mowers never did it."

"But there are monsters over the wall," Becca insisted. "Sky told us about them. She said they were very fierce, and we should never go there alone."

"Now, honey, don't tell stories." Lance looked apologetically at Toreth. "She has a vivid imagination. I asked Schuyler not to encourage her."

"It's true," Becca said indignantly. "There *are* monsters. Sometimes Sky went out there at night to scare them away. Hannah saw her going, and Sky told her it was a secret. Because she went through the *secret* door."

Lance's eyes narrowed. "Becca, are you telling the truth, now? Schuyler really went out through the door?"

Becca nodded, and Lance stood up slowly.

"There is a door," he said. "In the wall beyond the orchard. It leads out into an old alley that runs along the back of the houses. It's pretty overgrown. There was talk a while ago of tidying it up, but it never got anywhere. When the neighborhood was built all the houses had a door leading to it. Some of them are sealed up, but we still have ours. It's bolted shut, mostly covered by ivy—I honestly thought it'd be rusted solid by now. There's nowhere much out there for Schuyler to hide, but I guess she could've left that way if she wanted to risk the briars."

Becca shook her head, but she didn't say anything.

"Maybe that's why Simon didn't see her," Mayhew suggested.

An unobserved route between here and McGlothlin's house—perfect for carrying out an affair, or maybe for quickly hiding a body.

"Lance, could you show me this door?" Toreth asked.

"It should be in the wall at the back of his garden," Toreth subvocalized over the comm to Ruiz. "Probably hidden. If that's how he was still screwing his ex-nanny, I don't think he'd want to draw his wife's attention to it."

"I'm heading that way right now. I'll let you know if I find anything."

A rotting apple squelched under Toreth's foot, almost causing him to slip on the grass. "Fuck," he muttered.

"Sorry," Lance whispered. "Listen, there are yard lights—we only put them on if we're out here late. Shall I?"

Toreth debated. He'd told Lance to be quiet in case McGlothlin was out in the

120

alley, but crashing around in the dark wasn't helping, either. "Can they go on low? Just enough that we don't walk into a tree."

"Sure."

A few seconds later, lights dotted around the garden began to come up. Toreth turned to look for the increasingly unsecret door, and froze.

Beneath a sturdy tree dotted with a few late pears, Schuyler stood balanced on the squat block of the garden mower. A rope looped around her neck and ran up to the thick branch above her. She stared towards them, her face blank, her hands hanging limply at her sides. For a moment everything was still, and then the mower's motor sprang to life with another monster growl. This time it didn't stop.

Lance dashed forwards, and caught Schuyler just as the mower started to move. She didn't fight him or grab for the rope at her neck; it looked like he was manhandling a life-sized doll. Toreth turned, scanning the orchard, and caught a glimpse of movement at the end away from the house.

Witness or suspect? After a second's agonized debate, he tapped his comm and ran towards the wall.

"Ruiz? I think McGlothlin's coming your way. Better find that door fast."

Back by the wall, the garden lights barely cut through the tree-shadowed darkness, but Toreth could just make out McGlothlin as he pulled the curtain of ivy back to reveal a small arched door beneath. He was fumbling to find the handle when Toreth reached him.

"Stop right there," Toreth called, and the ivy swung back down as McGlothlin let it go and turned.

McGlothlin swung a clumsy punch that barely grazed Toreth's lip. Toreth caught his wrist, twisted his arm straight, and then smashed the back of McGlothlin's elbow with the his other hand. He felt the satisfying crunch as the joint gave way, the sound itself masked by the lawyer's scream as he dropped to his knees.

The door slammed open, barely missing McGlothlin, revealing Ruiz, flanked by two Washington police officers.

Ruiz stared at the scene. "What the—Toreth?"

"I'm fine." Toreth touched his mouth; his lip was bruised but not cut. "Corporates can usually put up a better fight at home."

"Great." Ruiz looked down at the sobbing McGlothlin, cradling his right arm. "What did you do to him?"

"I broke his elbow. He'll be fine." Toreth expertly hauled McGlothlin to his feet, which got another cry of pain. "Shut the fuck up. Someone check his pockets."

Ruiz was already wearing gloves. He pulled out four single-use injectors, three of them emptied, and a tiny fob remote with a button in the middle.

"Press it," Toreth said.

Ruiz clicked it once, and the mower in the garden behind Toreth cut out.

"Apparently the senator arranges the outdoor maintenance for his properties," Toreth said. "My money says that's the remote for McGlothlin's mower, rekeyed to Buchheit's."

"I did it for the senator," McGlothlin said in a choked voice. "He needs to be protected. That bitch was guilty, she's the one who tried to kill Judy. I couldn't let her get into court, spewing her lies."

"Like the one about how you've been having an affair with her for years?" Ruiz said.

"I told you, it was nothing like that."

Ruiz nodded. "I'm sure the forensic tests they're carrying out in your house right now are gonna back you up."

"Fuck—" McGlothlin drew in a deep, shaky breath. "I'm not saying anything more. I want a medic and a lawyer."

Ruiz pulled a sealable bag from one of his pockets and dropped the remote into it. "Oh, you're gonna need both."

"Can I get some help over here?" Lance called from the orchard. Ruiz looked quizzically at Toreth.

"Oh, yeah," Toreth said. "You won't believe this."

Leaving McGlothlin in the two officers' care, Toreth went to rescue his witness. Lance was where Toreth had left him; needing both arms to keep Schuyler from tightening the noose further, he didn't have a hand spare to free her. Between them, Toreth and Ruiz managed to loosen the rope enough to lift it over Schuyler's head. Lance lowered her carefully to the ground, and she stood there, swaying but still upright, blank-faced and dead-eyed.

"Schuyler?" Lance said. He put his hand on her face, thumb rubbing her cheek. "Sky? Listen, whatever happened, we can help you."

"She's drugged." Toreth put his fingers to Schuyler's throat and found a steady, slow pulse. She didn't react, staring past him. "Probably the same somnambulic they found in Judith," he said to Ruiz. "Now, guess where she was standing when we found her."

"On the mower?" Ruiz looked up into the branches and checked the knot on the rope. "That was his actual plan? Seriously?"

"I know. What are the odds it'd survive the forensics?" Toreth scanned the ground and found a second remote fob lying not far away, just where Schuyler might have dropped it if she really had committed suicide. No doubt her fingerprints would be on it. "Still, if he made sure he pressed his own button somewhere that he had a witness to swear he wasn't here when the mower started, and if the mower recorded time of activation... I've heard stupider ideas. Just about."

"I guess he was improvising," Ruiz said.

Lance now looked thoroughly bewildered. "I don't understand. Who was improvising?"

"Didn't you recognize the scream?" Toreth asked. "That was—"

"Detective-Lieutenant Green will explain it to you," Ruiz cut in. He looked significantly at Toreth, and Toreth shrugged and shut up. If Ruiz wanted to keep Green happy by letting him handle the witnesses, he was welcome. "I'm gonna call him right now. Toreth, I think you should go wait inside—no, how about by the main gate?"

Chapter Six

The rest of the evening and all the next morning were full of police. Green allowed Toreth to watch a few minutes of McGlothlin's interview—silence alternating with demands to be able to talk to the senator—and Schuyler's. She was being far more informative between tearful protestations of innocence and clumsy excuses for guilt. Toreth watched politely, but he didn't really care. The important thing was being allowed to walk out with Dr. Campion in tow. The autumn sunlight felt cheerfully bright as he hustled her into the diplomatic protection of the embassy car.

"I suppose I should thank you," Campion said ungraciously.

"If you like," Toreth said, as he got out his hand screen to report success to Turnbull.

The indifference silenced her for most of the journey, until she said, "I assume you found them an alternative suspect?"

"Yes—Simon McGlothlin."

"McGlothlin...that seems vaguely familiar."

"He's Judith Buchheit's cousin."

"Oh, of course. I think I met his wife at Judith's social. If it was her, I remember her being very tense."

Toreth snorted a laugh. "Not as tense as she is now, I bet."

❖ ❖ ❖

With Campion delivered to the ambassador, Toreth went looking for Grimm. He'd already sent an official note to Socioanalysis for her file, thanking Grimm for all her help with the case. Turnbull would expect it, and it gave him a malicious satisfaction to pay back Socioanalysis for Carnac leaving his slimy fingerprints all over Toreth's own file. They probably wouldn't like a commendation from a para.

After an unsuccessful hunt through the embassy, Toreth was left standing in

124

the entrance hall. Where the hell was she? Not investigating the case, not now, unless she'd found something else politically interesting to study under the Socioanalysis microscope. Toreth put his hand to his comm, and then paused.

Wherever it was, maybe he could find out another way.

He located Hemmingway outside by the embassy perimeter wall, discussing sensor recalibration with a technician. Toreth wondered if this was routine, or if the head of security's dismal failure to keep track of staff leaving the building had prompted a burst of enthusiasm.

Or just a show of it. Certainly he didn't seem any more eager to help.

"She went out," was the only information he offered.

Tempting as it was to give the man a shake, he wasn't I&I. "Where?"

Hemmingway shrugged. "We were told not to interfere with her. If that's what Socioanalysis wants, that's what they get."

Toreth supposed he couldn't argue with that; he'd fucked Carnac long after it had stopped being fun for much the same reason. "Is her comm switched on? Can you find her?"

The idea seemed to come as a surprise, but Hemmingway agreed it was possible. "But if her comm's on, why don't you call her yourself?"

"Maybe I'm just curious to see if you can do your fucking job."

The technician busied himself with a camera, but the comment didn't dent Hemmingway's placid demeanor. "Come back inside and I'll see what I can do."

Hemmingway's trace led Toreth to the river. A pedestrian bridge arched out over the water to where a single building many stories high grew like an improbable tree from the water, only a skirt of solid ground surrounding it.

Toreth hesitated at the start of the bridge. The thing was almost a tunnel, entirely enclosed. The bars were narrow, though, and instead of a solid floor the walkway was made of a metal cobweb. Heights generally didn't bother him. Heights over water, that was different. Even in the sunshine the river looked dark, flowing fast, an ebb tide revealing muddy foreshore. It made him think of retrieving bodies from the estuary at home. Usually sab victims, not drownings, but still...

The enclosed walkway made it worse. Logically, the bridge must be safe. But if it collapsed, the impact from this height wasn't sure to kill him. He'd be dragged under the water, down to the river bed, and as delicate as the metal looked, it would trap him there while—

"Excuse me?" a voice said. He blinked and focused on a young man in dark green uniform. The logo on his right shoulder was a tiny version of the building and bridge, with the letters PT under the bridge.

"My name's Seth," he said. "Can I help you, sir?"

Toreth deliberately turned away from the water. "No. I was just looking at the building. Land must be as expensive here as it is at home if they're building out in the river."

He thought Seth might ask where he was from, but presumably that wasn't part of his job. "No, the Tower used to stand on a much bigger island. Way back when, so the story goes, there was a law limiting the height of buildings in Washington to the width of the street plus so many yards. No skyscrapers here. But someone figured out there on the island, the road is the river, right? The rising sea levels flooded it all in the end, of course, but they underpinned the Tower and raised up that area right around it. These days it's mostly apartments and leisure." He tapped the logo. "I'm working over here at the satellite office today. We take deliveries, escort guests over, that kind of thing."

Seth looked questioningly at Toreth. Saying he wasn't looking for someone meant admitting defeat, if only to himself. "I'm supposed to meet a friend there, but she didn't say where, and I left my comm behind."

"Is she a resident?"

"No."

"Then you'll probably find her on one of the public leisure floors." He pointed up. "See where the Tower gets narrower? There are a whole three floors with restaurants, shops, that kinda thing. Try the terrace bar, that's always popular with tourists."

"Right. Thanks." Toreth looked back at the river.

"There's a ferry," Seth said. "If you don't like the look of the bridge."

If he hadn't added the second part, Toreth might have said yes. Instead he turned away and forced himself to take the first step onto the walkway.

"Have a great day, sir," Seth called.

"Thanks," Toreth said through clenched teeth and, eyes locked on the far end of the bridge, he started to walk.

Toreth was glad Seth had suggested he try the bar, because after the bridge he wanted a bloody great big drink. He limited himself to a beer; he was technically still working but, more importantly, he had to get back over that fucking bridge.

Although the terrace was sheltered by moveable screens, the wind was still stronger and colder than it had been down on the ground. Grimm had found a snug little corner, where she was drinking a glass of something clear and picking over the remains of an artfully arranged selection of nibbles. Warrick would definitely approve of the complex interlocking of tiny compartments on the platter.

The layout of the table and two chairs suggested she might have had, or be expecting, company. But if someone else had been with her, the evidence had been cleared away. In any case, she didn't seem either surprised or dismayed to see him.

"Not watching the IIP anymore?" Toreth asked as he sat down.

"I didn't think I'd be able to offer much. I'm sure the Washington police will tidy everything up."

"Probably. Schuyler's being helpful. Apparently Judith asked if she knew someone who'd be able to remove the implant, and Schuyler told McGlothlin about it. Judith thought she was meeting a medic, which is why she didn't tell anyone where she was going. Of course, Schuyler's claiming that all she did was use Judith's comm to call Campion the day before, when McGlothlin told her to do it. She had no idea what he was planning, and he was the one who tried to kill Judith. She thought he just wanted to blackmail Judith—she kept quiet about his affair, he kept quiet about the implant."

"A plausible enough explanation," Grimm said. "I did wonder why he hadn't tried blackmail, if he knew about the implant, but everyone's account of Judith's character suggests she would've resisted strongly. I suppose he knew her as well as anyone. So what's his story?"

"He's saying she did it all, he knew nothing until the hospital press conference, and after that it's dueling crappy alibis. Her alibi is two years old and was taking a nap after lunch, but he left the office for a couple of hours to pick up a piece of antique furniture—a surprise present for his wife. Private sale, so no delivery service. McGlothlin borrowed a van from the senator's office and sent it to his home after he loaded the wardrobe."

"Where he could clean the interior thoroughly at his leisure that evening. Interesting. I suppose between them they may be able to create a reasonable doubt."

"Or not. McGlothlin's wife's not talking, but all Buchheit's thankful social friends are. They all remember how upset Sandi McGlothlin was about Elsney sharing banned medical tech with Europe. She thought it was disgusting, and she asked Simon to use the family pull with the museum to stop it."

Grimm nodded. "That should help Schuyler's case. Still, I suspect blame will fall hardest on her. You have to feel sorry for the girl, at least on some level. McGlothlin planned to become the senator's heir, and I doubt that marrying a professional homemaking assistant featured in that. Schuyler was a convenient tool that would've become less convenient with time."

"I think she worked that out when he tried to murder her." Toreth picked the solitary remaining olive from the tray and ate it, licking his fingers afterwards. "At least the police believe one of them did it, and that's what matters to Turnbull."

"And what about the investigation? When I spoke to Fu, he suggested you might have to stay on for a while."

"I don't know yet. I gave my statement. Green's not happy that I managed to find McGlothlin before he did." He touched his slightly tender lip. "And McGlothlin's lawyers are claiming that breaking his arm was 'excessive.'"

"Well, perhaps there's a cultural difference. They might encourage their officers to turn the other cheek."

"To do what?" She had to be taking the piss, but her tone was too bland for him to tell. "The stupid bastard tried to punch me. What was I supposed to do? Duck and let him run away? Stand around yelling for help?"

"Oh, I'm not disagreeing. Just considering a hypothetical." She smiled gently. "On reflection, it might've been good to know the definition beforehand."

"I was only supposed to be observing, remember? They should've found him first." The more he thought about it, the more annoying it became. "Even if they let me go home in a few days, they might want me back if they have one of these open trials." Then something else occurred to him. "Do they let anyone into those things?"

Grimm nodded. "I believe there's also live and archive access to courtroom feeds, in the name of open and fair justice. Sometimes there's expert commentary for high-interest cases."

"Bollocks." Toreth rubbed his temple. "Maybe Turnbull can do something about it." Like agree to everything to keep the Americans happy.

Grimm probably shared his optimism, because all she said was, "Well, we'll have to see how it turns out." She sipped her drink. "I think everything I contributed can be verified in my absence."

"All right for some." God, he sounded like Chevril, but no one at I&I would be cheered by the idea of sitting around in the embassy, trying to run cases over the comm or losing good cases to other seniors. All while having his name and face splashed around in public. "What are you doing up here?" he asked, trying to distract himself from the gloomy prospect.

"Satisfying my curiosity. A long time ago, this used to be a favorite meeting place for spies of all kinds—national, commercial, technical, informational. Supposedly, this is where the final plans were made before delivery of the stolen nuclear bombs later used in Europe."

"Really? So who are you meeting?"

"Well, as I said, that's the story. It seems overly romantic to me. As a location for espionage, this is ostentatious, and even given the time, rather vulnerable to long-range monitoring. I thought I'd just come to soak up the atmosphere and see if it helped me think."

She hadn't, he noted, actually denied she'd met someone. The plate looked like it could've been for two. "Does your cat like rooftop bars, then?"

128

She laughed. "She's naturally friendly, and she goes crazy over olives, so I'm sure she would."

Grimm picked up the tray and offered it to him, and Toreth looked over the remaining scraps. The olive had tasted good, maybe even natural, and Toreth wondered idly what percentage of food over here was field-grown. He picked out a thin spiral twist of spiced cured meat, and sat back to nibble it slowly.

Grimm was gazing out over the city. Toreth hadn't read her security file, because he didn't want to give Socioanalysis the satisfaction of knowing he cared, but she definitely looked young for a fully qualified socioanalyst. Maybe late twenties or early thirties. Spooks started their training young—Carnac had claimed his began at five, and Toreth reached back, trying to remember more of their conversation from years ago at I&I. Carnac had said he'd been fully qualified for thirteen years. A memorable number, for it being an unlucky thirteen for Toreth to find the bastard inflicted on him. And he'd been...forty-one? Forty-two? Something like that. So assuming all socioanalysts followed roughly the same path, Grimm must be a relatively new graduate of the Socioanalysis lab for producing devious shit-stirrers.

Young, but not naive, Toreth would bet. Experienced enough that she'd been picked to send on a solo assignment to another continent. To do...what, exactly? While focused on the case he hadn't thought about it, but he certainly hadn't noticed much gathering of comparative cultural data happening over the past few days. What had been worth her time to come all this way?

"What are you thinking about?" Grimm asked suddenly.

The hangover of dislike that thinking about Carnac always gave him made him snappy. "Don't you fucking know?"

Her eyebrows rose. "Some socioanalysts enjoy performing party tricks. I don't, much. I could *guess*, of course, and I might have a good chance of being right, but none of us are really mind readers. Do you want me to guess?"

"I was wondering why Socioanalysis really sent you with me."

Annoyingly, the question didn't seem to surprise her. "As you were told, to observe something about systems over here."

"You didn't, though, did you? I told you to fuck off, and you did, without a protest. If you'd said Turnbull wanted you to stay on the case, I would've had to say yes every step of the way. Okay, you were watching the files, but you could've done that in New London."

"Yes." She looked at him with the same air of surprised curiosity you might give a city pigeon that had worked out how to use a street crossing. "That's almost always true, though. Meeting people is at best pointless, at worst actively detrimental. Humans are predisposed to make snap judgements and blow them out of proportion. We meet Agent Ruiz, and he's charming and helpful, so we think kindly about Homeland Security. Ambassador Fu is defensive and territorial, so we subconsciously begin to ascribe those qualities to International Relations as a whole. Elsney has a mildly unusual hobby, so we ascribe to him an unknown degree of social deviance. You suspect the victim's husband, and Agent Ruiz suspects her sister, partly because of existing prejudices, but also because of how they struck you when you met them. First impressions may or may not happen to coincide with reality, but they're rarely *helpful*." The wind blew a strand of hair across her face, and she tucked it behind her ear. "This is why it's so unfortunate that clients usually insist we meet the people involved in our cases. It introduces a layer of misdirection that even we need to spend effort consciously clearing away to see the real data beneath."

Toreth was about to explain that meeting suspects was extremely helpful to anyone who'd bothered spending time to work out how human beings acted in the real world... and then he recognized the different kind of misdirection.

"If Socioanalysis thinks meeting people is pointless, why are you here?"

"Because sometimes we *don't* have the data we need, or it's hopelessly contaminated by others' personal impressions. Then some lucky soul—" she tapped her breastbone, "—needs to get out there and get her hands dirty making the observations in the first place."

Trying to pin down a socioanalyst was like trying to catch an eel in a muddy pond. A deep muddy pond. At night. "Can't International Relations get your data?"

She shook her head. "Sadly, not always."

"So if you aren't bothering to observe the case firsthand, who are you observing? Or what?" Was that why she was up here?

"Ah, well. I'm afraid that, Para-investigator, is not pertinent to your case."

She smiled at him, a sharper amusement in her eyes. She might be younger than him, and with less practical experience in her job, but she still had decades of training behind her. And with the authority of Socioanalysis invoked, he had no right to question her any further.

Grimm stood up, and drained the last centimeter of her drink. "I'm heading back to the embassy; it's getting rather chilly up here. I'll be taking the ferry, if you'd care to accompany me? I don't like heights enough to enjoy the view from the bridge."

"Okay," Toreth said, wondering if she was telling the truth, or if it was another insight from his psych file.

As they stepped off the ferry, Toreth was surprised to see Agent Ruiz waiting for them.

"The embassy told me where to find you," Ruiz said. "I'm here to pick you up."

"Do the police want me back again?"

Ruiz laughed. "About as far from it as you can imagine. They had a call from a reporter, asking would they like to comment on the involvement of a Val Toreth from the European Investigation and Interrogation Agency in the case?"

"Oh, dear," Grimm said. "That's unfortunate."

Unfortunate didn't really cover it. "How did they get hold of my fucking name?" Toreth demanded. "Did the senator call someone?"

"I really doubt it," Ruiz said. "Not after the guy stood there with you behind him for the whole world to see."

"Yeah, thanks. The whole world is exactly what I was worried about."

"Well, I don't want to add to your worry, but they also asked Green if he knew about your personal life. He sounded pissed that he'd been blindsided." Ruiz screwed up his face, like he was preparing to deliver the *really* bad news. "This reporter told him that you share an apartment with some guy called Kieran Warrick."

"Oh." Of all the years he could've become someone's registered partner. This was entirely Warrick's fault. Okay, also the Department of Population had to take some blame, and fucking Sara, who'd made him fill in the forms right when citizen registration was such a mess the DoP might never have noticed anyway. "How the hell did they find that out?"

"I'm afraid I don't know. Protected sources and all that. But there was definitely an insinuation that you were, uh . . ." Ruiz cleared his throat, glancing at Grimm as though he were hoping not to have to spell it out in front of her. "Much more than friends."

"They can insinuate whatever they like," Toreth said, trying to hold on to the important point. "Campion's still in the clear."

"The thing is, the prosecution could never call you as a witness now. You see?" Ruiz paused, still looking pained. "The defense would find a way to bring it up and destroy your credibility. Green will have to try to scrub you from the case. He said the ambassador already agreed the Administration would refuse to cooperate regarding your testifying in court, if that would help."

"Refuse?" Suddenly, what was supposed to be a problem looked an awful lot like a perfect solution.

"I don't see how that could negatively affect the Bureau's view of the case," Grimm said. "You were only supposed to be an observer, after all."

Toreth grinned at her, hostilities temporarily suspended. "Yeah, that's true."

Ruiz looked at him oddly, and Toreth realized he probably sounded too cheerful about what ought to be a snub.

"The police care about successful case closure," Toreth said more soberly. "Tell Green I understand. I'd do the same."

Not that Green was likely to care about the opinions of some European pervert. Toreth managed to resist another grin.

"And they want you out of the country ASAP, I'm afraid," Ruiz added. "I was ordered to take you directly to the airport to wait for the next flight. The embassy is packing up your belongings, and they'll send them on to meet us."

"What about me?" Grimm asked.

"I don't have any instructions regarding you, I'm afraid, ma'am. I guess you should go back to the embassy."

"I see. Well, there it is, then." Grimm offered her hand to Toreth, a tiny smile hiding at the corners of her mouth. "I'm sure I can handle wrapping things up here, Para-investigator. Have a good flight."

Ruiz looked around, as though he were expecting the media to descend at any minute. "The car's right over here."

Toreth was in the middle of sending a message to Sara to let her know that he was on his way back and he'd see her in the office on Monday, when Ruiz said, "You broke McGlothlin's arm."

Toreth looked up from his hand screen. "Yes?"

"I mean, he's a red-blooded kinda guy, for a lawyer, and you just—" Ruiz mimed a creditable version of the same move Toreth had used. "Snapped his arm. I mean..." He trailed off.

Why was I&I training suddenly a surprise? "It's part of the job. Guards can't do everything. Anyone who deals with prisoners has to go on a lot of boring refresher courses, because it embarrasses I&I if some sab kicks the shit out of one of us when we try to arrest them."

Ruiz was silent for long enough that Toreth had gone back to his message, before he said, "You know, I was sure I saw you looking at Deborah Mayhew in an appreciative kinda way. And Agent Cardine, come to that."

The pieces suddenly snapped together, and Toreth had to stifle a laugh. "Like I told B-C, Cardine had great legs. And Mayhew... well, I asked her out for dinner, but she turned me down. Probably a good thing, considering who her father is."

That seemed to stump him again. Toreth finished the message to Sara, adding a request to stall any meetings Tillotson tried to schedule until Toreth heard from the Bureau. It was only after he closed his hand screen and tucked it away that he noticed Ruiz had, for the first time, sat opposite him in the car, not beside him.

"This, um. This 'registered' guy," Ruiz said awkwardly.

"Warrick?"

"Were you—I mean, you and he—back when Cardine and I were in New London?"

"Yeah, we were. Although we weren't registered partners then. That has more to do with some resister arseholes who looted my flat, trashed everything I owned, and made me homeless. If you'd ever tangled with the Central Housing Division, you'd know why I didn't want to wait for them to pull their fingers out and find me a new place. Warrick was much more convenient." Toreth stretched out his legs nonchalantly. "He's a great cook, among other things."

"I see." Ruiz looked torn between curiosity and disgust. "And do the rest of your team know?"

"That I'm fucking Warrick? Or just that I fuck men in general? I should think the whole division knows that." Given the wide circulation of the head of security's popular New Year party recordings at I&I, that probably wasn't far off the truth. "Although I don't do it in the office, you know." Well...not often.

Ruiz's lip twitched, like he'd smelled something bad. "But the investigator in your team, Barret-Connor, he suggested the reorientation treatment. Wasn't he worried you'd be offended?"

B-C suggested it, Cardine jumped on it. "It got that idiot Elliot boy out of I&I. Psychoprogramming does a lot worse, every day. Or did, before most of them were strung up by the resisters."

Ruiz seemed not to be listening. "Still, it must've seemed—well, you have to understand that as far as we were concerned, what Luke Elliot was doing was immoral as well as illegal. But I guess it must've felt kinda awkward for you, considering the circumstances."

Tempting as it was to play up to it and try to squeeze out a full apology, Turnbull probably wanted him to leave a good impression. "Not really. The Bureau asked me to do a job, I did it."

"Oh. Did you tell your, uh, partner about it?"

"No. He's not interested in I&I cases. I won't be telling him about this one, either. I'm just planning to get home—" Toreth checked the time. "Get home, wake him up, and fuck him until he screams."

Okay, not *that* good an impression. The rest of the drive to the airport passed in silence.

Chapter Seven

"Pancakes?" Toreth said.

Warrick must have heard the front door of the flat open, because he didn't even pause in whisking the batter. "Fresh orange juice, too."

Warrick was making pancakes. Not unusual for breakfast on a Sunday morning, but why the hell was he making them when Toreth wasn't there? On the morning after the one night when Toreth hadn't checked the flat surveillance . . .

"I'll have a shower before we eat," Toreth said.

"Mm-hmm." Warrick glanced over his shoulder and smiled. "Although you look fine to me as you are."

Much too relaxed for there to be any evidence upstairs for Toreth to find—or a good bluff? "I'll be ten minutes."

❖ ❖ ❖

The bed was immaculately made; the sheets and pillowcases smelled fresh, but Warrick's clean linen fetish meant that wasn't evidential. Toreth even checked the selection of lube in the drawer of the bedside table, but he couldn't remember the levels they'd been before he left. He weighed one bottle in his hand, almost sure some was missing. Maybe Warrick had used it on his own. Fuck. He threw the bottle back in the drawer and slammed it in disgust, then paused, waiting to see if the noise would attract Warrick's attention. Better get in the shower.

Toreth was drying his hair in the bathroom when the obvious answer hit him. Sara had woken up and seen his message, she'd called Warrick, then Warrick had checked the flights and worked out his arrival time at the flat. She probably thought she was being helpful, if she thought about it at all. Just her normal efficiency. Thank fuck he hadn't said anything downstairs.

Toreth dropped the towel on the floor and went to clean his teeth. He examined his reflection in the mirror and shook his head. He looked knackered, so maybe

134

that would do as an excuse for missing something so obvious. Still, he could verify the security record later, just to be sure. Not that it provided absolute proof. If he wanted to, Warrick could alter that almost as easily as he could change the sheets.

Back in the kitchen, the promised oranges sat in a bowl on the table, ready for juicing in Warrick's antique press. Toreth picked up the knife from the board beside them and started slicing. He loved how sharp Warrick kept his knives.

"How did the case work out, then?" Warrick asked.

"Much better than I expected." He'd enjoy the expression on Mike Belkin's face in the coffee room tomorrow.

"And is Principal Secretary Turnbull pleased?"

"Yeah." Toreth put an orange half in the juicer and pulled the lever. As cooking went, it had a satisfying physicality. "Or at least she bloody well should be. Perfect result in record time."

"Can you let me know any details, or is it all confidential?"

"Do you want to hear about it?" Toreth asked, surprised.

"If you're allowed to tell me."

Toreth considered. "I don't see why not, as long as you don't spread it around."

Warrick turned the pancakes. "Of course not."

Toreth sometimes forgot what a good listener Warrick could be. He didn't need anything repeated, and he rarely interrupted with questions. Pity he couldn't get the I&I pool investigators trained up to the same level of intelligent attentiveness. Of course, if they could be, they'd probably all leave I&I and become successful corporates.

"Just extraordinary," Warrick said when they reached Toreth's abrupt escort to the airport. "After everything you did to help their case."

"When do people ever make any sense?" Toreth took the last slice of bacon. "They're all fucking mad over there, anyway—I told you the crap about suspects not having to answer questions, right? Anyway, there were four guards waiting for us at the airport, and they stuck me in a deportation cell to wait for the flight. They even locked the fucking door—as if I wanted to stay. No comms, but they didn't take my screen so I wrote a final report for Turnbull. At least that meant I could try to sleep on the flight."

"And did you?"

"Not much." Just thinking about it made Toreth stifle a yawn. "Thank fucking Christ it's Sunday. If Turnbull asked to see me, I'd be staggering into the Bureau like a zombie."

"Well, I'm sure you wouldn't want to disappoint her." Warrick plucked at the shoulder of the T-shirt he was wearing along with loose-fitting black trousers. "I have to confess I skipped the gym yesterday, so I planned to catch up this morning. I suppose we could both go, to help you stay awake."

"Fuck off," Toreth said, and Warrick laughed.

"More coffee, then?"

Warrick went over to the sink for water to refill the brewer. Toreth stood up silently and moved over behind him. When he put his hands on Warrick's shoulders, Warrick made a startled sound. He set the jug down and started to turn, freezing when Toreth's grip tightened. After a moment he relaxed, submitting to the silent instruction. Toreth cupped Warrick's throat, right beneath his jaw, and ran his thumb along Warrick's jawbone, pressing firmly enough to catch the rub of stubble even though he'd shaved not long ago. Warrick braced his hands on the edge of the sink, and Toreth felt him swallow.

"Keep still."

Warrick nodded.

Toreth kissed the nape of his neck. "Very still."

"Yes," Warrick whispered.

He kissed Warrick again, touched him, trying to keep the contacts unexpected and force Warrick into a reaction. He managed to provoke a few abbreviated twitches, followed by the whitening of Warrick's knuckles as he gripped the sink. After a few minutes, he slid his hand flat down Warrick's stomach and under the edge of his waistband. No underwear. Warrick shifted, his feet moving apart and his back arching slightly.

"Sorry," he whispered at once.

"We'll see."

When Toreth finally touched his cock, fingers whispering over smooth skin and then curling to grip, Warrick breathed out a happy *mmm*.

Then an idea occurred, and he smiled. He released Warrick's throat and brushed his hand down Warrick's arm, from the point of his shoulder until he could take hold of his wrist and press his fingers over the pulse point. The beat fluttered fast, mirrored in Warrick's panting.

"Tell me what you did while I was away," Toreth murmured.

"What I—" Warrick shifted, trying to look over his shoulder. "What do you mean?"

"Tell me everything you did. Not at SimTech. In the evenings, when I wasn't here. Where did you go? Who did you see?"

Warrick laughed, breath stuttering as Toreth stroked faster. "You could just look at the flat surveillance."

Fuck. Had Warrick checked? Did he already know?

"I want to hear it from you." Slowly, slowly, Toreth shifted his grip and twisted Warrick's arm up behind him. Warrick breathed in shudderingly. "And make sure I believe it. Well?"

136

"Very well. On, ah—" Warrick swallowed.

"Tuesday," Toreth prompted.

"Tuesday, yes. Dinner with clients. I told you about it on the comm."

"Oh, yeah. I forgot." Toreth didn't mention that repetition was the easiest way to test interrogation answers. "Wednesday."

"Ah . . ."

Warrick's hesitation made Toreth tense up. Yes, this was ninety percent game, but ten percent of him wanted to hear the answers. "Fucking Wednesday."

"I stayed late at SimTech, to help one of the graduate students. She's having problems with her project—not getting results. I suggested some adjustments, she's talking it over with her university supervisor and we're meeting on Monday. Then—" Warrick hesitated.

"Then you gave her a lift home," Toreth said, suddenly remembering Warrick's alibi from the old case at SimTech. A more caring corporation.

Warrick nodded. "I didn't even get out of the car."

"Of course not," Toreth breathed in his ear, drawing out another shiver.

"I came home, cooked dinner, wrote up some more ideas for her study. I—" Warrick's breath hissed as Toreth pulled his wrist higher. "That was everything."

Don't sound like the answer matters too much, Toreth told himself. Only a game, after all. "Thursday?"

"I spend the whole evening with Dillian. We—" Warrick broke off and moaned as Toreth repaid the quick answer with three fast strokes. Rewarding—or distract-ing—his subject.

"That wasn't on the calendar," Toreth said.

"No. But since I had an unexpected free evening, I called her and she was free, too."

Discussing Dillian with his fingers around Warrick's cock had an appealing novelty. "Did she cook?"

Warrick made a sound half laughter, half gasp. "No. I did."

"Right." Toreth kissed his neck, a light brush of his lips, then bit the exposed shoulder at the neck of Warrick's T-shirt. He bit again, hard enough to feel the muscle yield to his teeth, not quite hard enough to bruise. "What did you talk about?"

"Um. Nothing in particular." Toreth could feel the effort it took Warrick to keep his voice even approximately level. "Family, mostly. Tarin, Jen, the house—there are some, ah, some legal problems with Kate's finances and . . . obviously it's tricky when Jen and Dilly don't know why Kate disappeared."

Novelty wasn't enough to stave off boredom once the rest of Warrick's family showed up in the conversation. Toreth twisted Warrick's arm again, just enough to stretch tendons and ligaments, and then relaxed his hold again the moment War-rick's breath caught. "Friday."

"Director's dinner, here. I'm sure you're glad you missed it. And..."

"Yes?"

"Afterwards I couldn't sleep, so I opened up the cabinet and I touched the chains, and thought about—about using it with you." Warrick's voice cracked. "I didn't use the cuffs, just stood inside. Held the chains. It wasn't—I need you there, to make it work. I thought about calling you. I didn't know if it'd be safe." He heard Warrick swallow. "So I thought about you fucking me."

Fuck. If only Grimm hadn't decided to tell him about her adventures that evening, he might have had something more interesting to watch than Lew Marcus pouring wine. On the other hand, the police would probably still be investigating Schuyler's "suicide," and Toreth wouldn't have the chance to be here in the flesh. Flesh was good. He pressed his cock against Warrick backside and breathed, "Nearly there. Saturday."

"Saturday. Yesterday. I don't—I was at SimTech most of the day. That's why I missed the gym. Oh, God. Please."

Toreth moved his hand faster, Warrick's cock slick in his hand now. "Saturday evening."

"I don't know. I cooked. I watched something—there's a production corporation, UnLTD Ent, we're thinking—thinking about approaching one of their marketing psychologists to—it was nothing." His voice cracked again, desperate. "That was everything. Nothing important. Nothing—"

Warrick cried out, the sound bouncing back from the tiles in front of him, as he came.

As soon as Warrick lifted his head, Toreth put his hands on Warrick's shoulders, turning him and pushing him down. His grip felt light, though—Warrick was already moving. It only took him a moment to deal with Toreth's zip and underwear, and then slide Toreth's cock deep into his mouth in one smooth movement.

Less than a week away and *fuck* he'd missed this. Toreth dropped his game control, braced himself against the sink, and closed his eyes. Abandoning himself to the moment, he let Warrick set the pace. All the aggravation of the past week, the Bureau and Socioanalysis, disappeared, magicked away by the heat of Warrick's mouth. He squeezed the edge of the sink, fingernails slipping on the smooth ceramic as Warrick took him in deeper. The heat and pressure washed out, pushing at his lungs, making him pant, shivering out through his whole body until he couldn't hold it in any longer and he came, gasping Warrick's name.

Warrick held him tight, thumbs pressing into his hipbones as Warrick swallowed. Finally, Warrick released him and sat back on his heels. Toreth managed to loosen his grip on the sink, and turned around so he could slide down the cupboard door to sit beside him. He sighed happily.

"Welcome home," Warrick said, a touch breathlessly.

"Mm. Good to be back." Toreth sagged back against the door, fighting to keep his eyelids open. "They don't know what they're missing in America. What do you think, worth a couple of years of restrictive detention?"

Warrick shifted to sit on the floor and leaned against Toreth's shoulder. "Definitely."

"I agree." Probably a good thing they hadn't done this in the bedroom. If he was lying on a bed right now, he'd definitely fall asleep and fuck his schedule for days. "So. What about that coffee?"

Weekend Plans

❖

Friday

Material Evidence Storage was possibly Sara's least favorite part of I&I. She hated the creepy solitude of the place, somehow managing to be disorientingly vast and claustrophobic at the same time, because despite being largely above ground, the place didn't have a single window. And it was built not for people, but for machines.

In the past that had been a bonus, because the automated systems took care of everything. Evidence requests were sent in from elsewhere in the building, and by the time the person making the request had reached ME, the case evidence box would be waiting, ready to be signed out. Behind the long evidence desk, a glass wall overlooked the closest of the cavernous storage rooms, shelving dropping down out of sight to the floor below. Conveyor belts ran around the walls and between the shelves, evidence boxes occasionally moving into sight, coming to the desk or heading away to be stored for the prescribed length of time. Even with the glass and desk between it and her, ME had always given Sara the shivers.

Before the revolt, the system had worked well. Then the looters had gone through the place, leaving a strange, frozen sea of smashed boxes and damaged infrastructure. In places, so Sara had heard, the rubbish had been piled up to twice the height of the people trying to clear it. Even now, teams were working in there, collecting evidence, trying to tie it to a case, and either restoring it to its proper place or adding it to the enormous new classification of "unidentified case."

"Unidentified" was now Sara's least favorite part of her least favorite place. The ME systems weren't designed to work with thousands of items that couldn't be assigned to case containers. The solution had been to split some storage cells into multilevel warrens of temporary stairs and walkways, and fit the shelving with lockers and security doors. It was like restrictive detention for evidence and, as

141

she'd often told Kel, I&I couldn't pay her enough to go down there alone. Thank God management mistrusted their employees enough to require a double ID scan to open anything.

Toreth and Sara climbed another staircase, the echoes of their footsteps confused by the shelves, and she checked the unit numbers with her torch. Low lighting to save money—another great feature of ME.

"This is it," she said.

Toreth and Sara scanned the cage open, then the indicated locker inside, and Toreth started checking the rack of tiny drawers. He fished out a plain gold ring and peered inside the band.

"Fuck it. Not a thing." He tossed the ring back in the drawer and closed locker and cage. "This is such bollocks." Toreth checked his hand screen. "Thirty-six more potentials. Which won't be the right ones either, because the inscription would've shown up in the pattern match and the ring would already be back in the case crate, and we wouldn't have all these shitty low confidence matches. Right, come on."

"They might not have done a three-sixty scan," Sara said.

"Or the looters took it, or one of the light-fingered bastards stole it in the cleanup, or it's still lying somewhere under a heap of bloodstained clothes and blunt instruments. Why couldn't this idiot, this—"

"Heckman," Sara supplied.

"Right. Why didn't he ask for his wife's fucking ring back before? It's been down here for what? Eight years?"

"Well, General Criminal never closed the case," Sara said, and Toreth made a dissatisfied grunting sound. "And his daughter's getting married, so..."

"So? It wasn't *my* case. And whether some corporate brat is getting married or not, that won't make the bloody ring magically appear when it isn't here. Fucking Tillotson. If he loves corporations so much, he should piss off and get a job in one, instead of deluding himself that if he kisses enough corporate arse, they'll start inviting him round for drinks and nibbles."

"I'll do the rest, if you like. I can find someone else to help me." Andy Morehen had offered, before Toreth swept off in a spectacularly foul temper to do the section head's bidding, dragging Sara along behind him.

"There's no point. When you can't find it, Tillotson will only ask me to do it again, 'just to make sure,' which wastes even *more* time. Tosser." Toreth sighed sharply. "And it's not like I have anything better to do this evening."

"No?" Sara skipped to keep up as Toreth strode off along the walkway. "I thought Friday was kinky sex night?"

"Yes, it should be. But Warrick's pissing off to some vitally important corporate shindig. Potential new contracts or something. God knows what time he'll be back."

"Oh. Well." That explained the excessive crankiness. Sara hesitated, with the suggestion that it didn't matter so much now that they were living together hovering on her tongue, waiting for her to decide if she wanted to risk it. Although Toreth and Warrick's experiment in cohabitation seemed to be working out better than Sara had expected (in that both of them were still alive, and Toreth didn't spend too many more nights on her sofa bed than he had in the past), it was also a topic Toreth didn't like to dwell on, especially when things weren't going well. "There's always another night, right?"

"That's not the point, though, is it?" Toreth didn't elaborate on what the point was, and Sara decided not to press.

"Shall we do something, then? I wasn't planning anything special tonight, but I'm sure we can go out somewhere and—"

"No, forget it. I can amuse myself for one fucking evening. Okay, we must be nearly there."

The second ring was as blank of inscriptions as the first. But instead of throwing it back, Toreth stood with the ring in his palm. He angled it under the torchlight, then showed Sara the screen.

"What?" she said,

"It's the best physical match on the list by far. Right weight, right color, right purity and alloy, right cross-section, even. Neither of them were ID chipped— which would've saved all this fucking about in the first place."

"But it isn't the right ring," Sara pointed out. "Just look at the original case images. There's no inscription on this one."

"Not yet, anyway." Toreth raised his eyebrows a little.

"Oh, no. You can't do that! The poor girl wants to get married with her mum's ring." With someone else, Sara might've asked how he would feel in the girl's place, but that was clearly a nonstarter.

"So? What she doesn't know won't hurt her, or Tillotson, either. But . . ." Toreth was still peering at the ring, comparing it to the screen. "It's a microinscription, so you were right, it could be missed if someone imaged it carelessly. The text is 'Do Everything In Love ~ 1 Cor 16:14.' What the hell does that last bit mean? Looks like a code."

"I don't know—it sounds vaguely familiar, though. I'm sure I've seen something like it somewhere else. Another case or something, maybe? Hang on a minute." Sara clipped her torch to the cage mesh and searched on her own hand screen. "Oh. It's religious. Christian, from the Bible."

"Fuck, not again," Toreth said. "And no wonder he didn't want it back before. But it's a quotation, right? Even the numbers at the end?"

"Yes." Sara scanned up and down the screen, trying to pick the sense of the text out of the unfamiliar document format. "I suppose the 'Cor' is an abbreviation for 'Corinthians,' and then it looks like . . . it's part of a message to someone? Or

143

something like that. It's all about sending people to different places, anyway, nothing about marriage. Weird. Macedonia—that's an Administration subregion, I think. The section around the line on the ring says, 'Be on your guard; stand firm in your faith; have courage; be strong. Do everything in love. You know the household of Stephanas—' "

"All right, all right. I don't need the whole bloody thing. The point *is*, it's a quotation. Anyone could have it inside a ring, right? So if Heckman figures it out and kicks up a stink about it, well, it was just our bad luck we found the wrong one." Now Toreth sounded almost cheerful.

"But how could you do it?" Sara asked. "It'll look a bit suspicious if you take a taxi out to a jeweler's and then show up in Tillotson's office with the ring."

"You're right, but—" Toreth grinned smugly. "There's an engraving system down in the Interrogation stores. At least there used to be, a few years back. Remember when they brought in a new model of induction probes and they kept breaking down?"

Sara nodded. "I remember. The whole section was complaining about interrogators stealing other people's probes."

"Right. So stores bought an engraver, because they were sick of people sneaking in and swiping new probes, swapping labels and chips around. It was probably shoved in the back of a storeroom somewhere, so it might've survived, if no one threw a grenade on top of it. We give it the image to copy, stick the quote on the ring..." He held the band between thumb and forefinger, checking the inside. "Depending on how good the engraver is we might need to rub it down a bit so it looks worn, like the original, but any scratches that weren't there before could be damage from when it was kicking around here in the rubbish. I mean, Heckman hasn't seen the ring for eight years, and it was his wife's, even then. She won't be looking at it. So, what do you think?"

"It'll take a while to do all that," Sara said, still reluctant.

"Got to be quicker than checking thirty-five more cages and coming up blank, though. Especially if Tillotson decides to send us around again afterwards, just for fun. He'll probably give us a longer list of even worse matches, too."

Sara looked up and down the gloomy walkway. Checking the whole of the list would definitely take them until long after she should've gone home. She didn't mind staying late for a good reason, even on a Friday, but so that Tillotson could do a favor for a corporate, over something that wasn't even associated with one of their cases?

"I'm going to talk to someone in stores," Toreth said. "You stay and keep looking, if you like."

The shadows fading back into darkness suddenly seemed to loom closer. "I can't open the cages on my own."

"I'll send Morehen down. If I bump into him." From Toreth's malicious smile,

144

she knew he'd guessed how much she didn't want to be here alone. "Or maybe a guard will wander past. Eventually."

"I don't—" A cool draft across the back of her neck made her shiver. Preservation requirements kept the temperature and humidity low. "I suppose engraving it could work."

"Great." Toreth tossed the ring up and caught it, then put it in his pocket. "Once it's done, we can get out of here, and I'll buy you a drink."

Saturday

Not enough sleep, too many drugs, too much alcohol, and far too much light. Toreth scrunched his eyes tighter closed and ignored the smell of coffee. Normally fresh coffee on a morning after drew him like a beacon, but today it made him feel sick. A very, very bad sign.

Warrick set something down on the bedside table with a soft sound—a tray, Toreth guessed—and even that was too loud for comfort. "Go 'way," Toreth muttered.

"Why on earth do you do it?" Warrick asked.

Exhaustion made him tactless and the spiking headache put a petulant edge on his voice. "Why the fuck do you think? Because I might feel like shit now, but I fucked three guys—four—oh, Christ knows. But it was fun." His tongue felt thick and uncooperative. "What the hell has it got to do with you, anyway?"

"Normally, nothing. You're free to abuse your body in any way you see fit. And mine too, of course." The sheet over him shifted and Toreth tensed for a moment until Warrick's hand stroked gently and hotly up his inner thigh. He must've warmed it on the mug. "If you can manage to squeeze me onto your busy schedule," Warrick added.

Toreth couldn't help smiling, although even *that* hurt. God. His cheeks had hangovers. "It's your fault, anyway."

The bed shifted, not much but also far too much, as Warrick sat down. "I'd love to hear the chain of logic that gets us there."

"Friday night is fuck night, right?"

"Right."

"And you were busy. So I had to get my entertainment somewhere."

Warrick stroked his thigh again. "I wasn't exactly out enjoying myself. I didn't even have a drink. SimTech needs those contracts, and Asher—"

"Warrick." An involved discussion of SimTech's financial woes was not what Toreth needed at that moment. "Maybe you could just fuck off?"

"Well, again, normally..."

"But?"

"But today—in a little over thirty minutes—there will be decorators arriving to redecorate your room. Which is, in case you're not exactly sure where you are, this room."

It took a good ten seconds for the words to make any kind of sense. Then he checked again to be sure and, no, Warrick really had said—"Jesus fucking Christ in heaven." He tried hopelessly to string together something that expressed his opinion of the idea, then gave up. "Fuck. Off."

"But—"

"No buts." He pulled the pillow over his head. "Cancel them."

"Just into the other bedroom." The bed shifted again, and there was a gentle rattle, something against china. "Hangover tablets."

The thought of swallowing even tablets made his stomach spasm. Actually, of so much as putting anything in his mouth—and then the memory of all the things he'd put in his mouth last night surfaced, and he really did almost puke. "No," Toreth said when he dared try to speak. "No fucking way. 'M not moving."

"I'm paying a premium already, because they happened to have a Saturday slot free." Warrick's voice was still reasonable, although the edges were starting to fray. "Corporate security-cleared decorating companies with available booking slots aren't easy to come by. Not at the moment."

Not with corporates still scurrying from secure housing complexes to even more secure ones. And the decorators were only coming at all because Toreth had decided that he didn't like the wallpaper, on the wall for less than six months, which technically gave Warrick the upper hand in the situation. In any other room that would've been cancelled out by the fact that Toreth didn't give a crap about wallpaper or anything else in a bedroom, beyond it being weatherproof and having a flat surface suitable for sleeping. But if he opened his eyes, he'd be reminded again about why this time was different.

"I'll do it myself," Toreth said, only because maybe that would persuade Warrick to leave him alone. Right now, he'd rather die than argue any longer. "I'll do it tomorrow. Today. And take that coffee away before I throw up."

There was a pause, then Warrick said, *"You'll* do it?"

Even through the sick headache, the level of disbelief in Warrick's voice was staggeringly offensive.

"Yeah. *I'll* do it," Toreth said, then moaned quietly because that had been far too fucking loud. "Any reason why not?"

Warrick stood up. "I'll call the decorators," he said, and thankfully left without further comment.

146

By late morning Toreth felt recovered enough to down some of his selection of postrecreational pharma and stagger out to the bathroom. On the landing, a new feature had appeared—rolls of wallpaper stacked in a corner, neatly out of the way. Toreth contemplated them for a minute or so, then detoured back to the bedroom.

He stood in the doorway and looked around slowly. Could he live with it after all?

The green and grey striped pattern had been harmless enough on the screen in the selection Warrick had waved under his nose. In daylight, sober and now only mildly hung over, it wasn't bad either. But under less controlled conditions it had a distressing tendency to pick up the effects of bed spin and magnify them horribly. As he frequently used the bedroom when he was pissed and home late, he'd been forced to admit it had been a bad choice.

Warrick hadn't even blinked. He'd just offered to arrange redecoration as soon as possible and suggested Toreth use another bedroom until then.

A reasonable enough idea, except that when he was plastered or tired enough, Toreth homed unerringly to the room with the mess on the floor and the bolts in the wall and his old sofa lurking in the corner, unloved and largely unsat-upon and thoroughly trashing the carefully coordinated décor. Maybe it smelled like his old flat. Sometimes he remembered not to turn any lights on, and he made it to bed safely. Even then, though, he'd wake up and the pattern would kick him between the eyes all over again.

Right now, it was putting the edge back on his fading hangover. He went to try to soak the rest of it away in the bath.

When he got back to the bedroom, feeling almost human again, he found the furniture pulled away from the walls and positioned neatly in the middle of the floor. The place was covered in plastic sheeting, including every square centimeter of carpet and even his sofa.

He dressed, accompanied by constant rustling whenever he walked across the room or opened a wardrobe. Where had he put his jacket last night? He found it draped over a chair, under a plastic sheet, with his comm earpiece in its usual pocket. He pulled the jacket on and left the bedroom, closing the door firmly behind him.

Toreth knocked on the study door and then called, "I'm going out."

"Wait." After a moment, the door opened. "Where?" Warrick asked.

"To buy the shit I need for the bedroom. Unless it's already hidden somewhere."

"No, they only delivered the paper—they'd made that up before I cancelled so I had to pay for it in any case." Warrick paused for a moment, then added, "Would you like me to come along?"

"What, you don't trust me to get what I need? Or do you think I'm doing a runner?"

"Not at all," Warrick said evenly. "I was merely offering company. Possibly advice, if required."

"Decorated a lot of walls?"

"Actually, no. Although Lissa and I did one room together, once, and then we realized it wasn't an activity we enjoyed sharing. After that, she spray-coated the whole place in inoffensive neutral tones. Back then we couldn't even afford to screen the walls."

"In other words, you have no idea. So you won't be much help, will you? Anyway, I don't need advice. I know what I'm doing," Toreth finished with as much confidence as he could manage. Sounded pretty convincing, he thought.

Possibly Warrick even believed him. Or possibly not, because he quirked the corner of his mouth and then his eyebrow.

"Very well, I'll see you later," Warrick said, and closed the door.

Outside, the October sky was overcast. Given the residual hangover manifesting in the scratchiness behind his eyelids, Toreth didn't mind the grey. He caught a taxi, wondering whether Warrick was watching on the office screen.

Once safely in the taxi, he fitted the earpiece and made the call. Sara answered at once.

"Toreth?" He could hear other voices over the comm, laughter in the background. "Oh, no—is this work? And if it is, is it really important? Because I'm over with my sister at—"

"No, nothing like that. I've got a quick question, that's all."

"*Shush,*" she said forcefully. "Not you. What is it?"

"Have you ever stuck wallpaper onto a wall?"

"Have I ever what?" Before he could say anything, she went on, "No, of course not. Why would I want to do something like that? But...wait just a sec. I think I remember—"

The connection muted, and Toreth sat, tapping his fingers on the seat beside him.

After a couple of minutes, Sara came back. "I'm just going to pass you over to Jojo—John Joseph—he's the brother of a friend of Fee's. Fee says he knows all about it."

Decorating was a piece of piss, Toreth decided.

Stripping was almost fun. A spray dissolved the old adhesive and the wallpaper peeled off, leaving the walls smooth and mostly clean. The process held the deep satisfaction of effortless destruction, and every rip made the walls that little less eye-warpingly ugly.

Washing the walls was both more effort and more boring. Sara's sister's friend's brother—Jesus, how did Toreth get into these ridiculous situations?—had listened to Toreth's vague description and assured him that a sympathetically restored building of that era would have genuine gypsum plaster finish, no matter what security features had been layered behind it. And that, unfortunately, meant handwashing. By the time Toreth was three-quarters done, the sun had set and his stomach was rumbling. With the lingering remains of the hangover, he'd skimped on lunch. He considered taking a break for a snack, then decided there was no way he'd be bothered to do any more tonight if he stopped now. This wasn't DIY—this was a *competition*. Warrick wouldn't win it because Toreth threw in the towel.

Toreth put enough muscle into getting the last wall done quickly that his T-shirt was damp with sweat by the time he dropped the sponge in the bucket. He barely had time to look around to check he hadn't missed anywhere before Warrick arrived with tea, cake, and the same kind of appreciative gleam in his eye that appeared after Toreth had been at the gym.

Toreth took one mug of tea, then Warrick set the tray down, leaving his own tea on it. He came up close and put his hands flat on Toreth's chest. Feeling him breathe, Toreth thought, and confirmed it by taking a deeper breath and watching the fleeting smile appear and disappear on Warrick's lips.

"How's it going?" Warrick asked.

"Fine. Just done, in fact." Toreth swallowed a mouthful of tea, ignoring the heat. "Give it a bit more to dry, and I might even be able to start putting the paper up tonight, if the house system can get the lights bright enough. I—"

"Ah. The sweat of honest toil," Warrick said, slightly muffled by Toreth's shoulder. His breath felt cool through the thin cotton as he inhaled deep and slow, then hot as he breathed out. Toreth switched hands on the mug so he could rest his left hand on Warrick's hip, pulling him closer. After last night, he hadn't been planning any fucking today, and possibly not Sunday either, but on the other hand, the drugs had definitely—

He jerked slightly, almost spilling the tea, as Warrick scratched his nails lightly over Toreth's left nipple. It verged on unpleasant, when two minutes earlier Toreth had been concentrating on plasterwork. Experimentally, he nudged his thigh forward, between Warrick's legs, and Warrick pressed forward against him at once. Definitely further up the arousal curve, which made Toreth wonder why. And then wonder how Warrick had known when to turn up with tea. Too damn convenient to be coincidental.

"How did you know I'd finished?"

Warrick didn't hesitate. "Security system. There are cameras in all the rooms, you know that. The bedrooms are usually off when it's only us here, but it's simply a matter of turning them on."

Toreth paused, mug at his lips. "You were watching me? All the time?"

149

"Good God, no. I've been working." Warrick was pulling Toreth's shirt out of his jeans, centimeter by precise centimeter, around from the small of his back. "I simply set up a program to monitor the area of wall washed. Tricky, because there isn't much of a color change and the plaster dries quickly. So I tracked the sponge and mapped that onto the walls."

Sometimes a taste for being tied up and tortured for fun seemed like the most normal thing about Warrick. "How long did all that take you?"

"Mm. Twenty minutes or so to get the system running fully." Having finished with the shirt, Warrick ran his thumbs around the top of Toreth's jeans. He paused at the button, flicking his fingers over it, then apparently changed his mind and went back to rubbing over the seams and stitching. "After that it was just a question of checking every so often and fine-tuning the variables—how often you rewashed the same area on average, how often you paused, and so on. An hour ago it gave me a prediction of when you'd finish that was only off by a couple of minutes. Which was good, in a way, because I spilled the milk and I lost about that mopping it up."

Toreth snorted. "You are absolutely fucking insane."

Warrick looked up and grinned. "I'll admit it wasn't the most productive time I've ever spent. But I enjoyed it. By the way, I hope you're feeling recovered from this morning?"

"More or less, yeah."

"Oh, good." He scratched again, and this time Toreth smiled.

"What about the papering?" Toreth asked.

"Jen had a saying," Warrick murmured. "When we wanted to stay up late to finish doing something. If I remember correctly, she learned it from her grandmother—my great-grandmother."

"Yeah?"

"Tomorrow is also a day."

Sunday

Papering, Toreth decided, wasn't quite as easy as it looked. The adhesive went onto the wall rather than the paper, so at least what he was handling was dry. The paper peeled off cleanly too, allowing him to reposition the strips easily. He'd scoffed at the instructions when he read them, but everything worked as advertised. Jojo had sworn that brand was the only thing to buy. Apparently he'd spent a summer working for a company that refurbished historic buildings, which he'd then proceeded to tell Toreth about in entirely unnecessary detail. Tempting as it had been to cut him off, Toreth had decided that under the circumstances he'd better listen with a pretense of polite interest.

"If you tell anyone about all this, I'll kill you," he'd said to Sara yesterday when Jojo had finally run out of things to say about lining paper. He hoped she believed he meant it. If Chevril or any of the other General Criminal seniors found out, he'd never live it down.

He'd wasted most of the time so far fucking around with the laser measure, which took the exact room dimensions and planned the most efficient paper layout. Toreth had decided to start with the long flat wall on the principle that working around windows and the door must be more difficult, so it would make sense for him to leave them until later. Despite the fact that the entire exercise was a stupid waste of time and energy, it needed to be done perfectly.

Competition.

"How are you doing?" Warrick called from the foot of the stairs.

"Still on the first wall, but I think I'm getting the hang of it."

"I thought I'd make us an early brunch—or a late breakfast—if it's convenient."

"Definitely. I'm fucking starving."

Toreth had woken up at some obscenely early hour and missed their usual Sunday morning fuck, because he'd told Warrick the paper would be done today. And it would be, Toreth was sure of that.

He stood up and shuffled back, careful not to trip over the assorted junk on the floor, and surveyed the results. Maybe he wouldn't have to reposition it again. If everything wasn't exactly right, even with the backing paper, Warrick would only bloody complain. Toreth wouldn't put it past Warrick to be right that moment programming something to keep an eye on progress while he was out and let Warrick know if Toreth misaligned a section by a micrometer. He'd need to deal with the camera in the room once Warrick left.

Footsteps on the stairs prompted him to look busy again, and he picked up the adhesive spray and shook it.

"It looks good," Warrick said from the doorway.

"You know, you could sound less surprised." Toreth touched up a couple of places where he'd missed patches for the next strip of paper. "Aren't you watching me, anyway?"

"I do have other things to do with my time." Warrick smiled. "Unfortunately for me. If you remember, I'll need to leave soon to meet Philly and Jen. We're visiting Tarin—Valeria's coming, too. It'll be the first time she's been able to be in the same room as him."

"Sounds like a bundle of laughs. Anyway, I thought he was still in intensive care?" Toreth sifted through his mental file of how-much-do-I-have-to-worry-about-Tarin-Marriot-surviving-to-cause-more-trouble notes. "Bone infection?"

"They cleared the last of it a couple of weeks ago. He's back in the contact isolation unit. Of course, it still meant they've had to delay the limb grafts, but—" Warrick shrugged. "He's doing better. Things have definitely been a lot worse, anyway."

Fuck. It was true that Toreth had gone to a lot of trouble to make sure Tarin had at least the potential for a viable future. On the other hand, it would save a lot of danger and aggravation to everyone concerned if the man would be considerate and just die. Preferably for some unimpeachably medical reason that would ensure Warrick didn't feel the need to poke around in Citizen Surveillance business yet again. Toreth had toyed with a few ideas himself over the months for bringing the matter to a satisfactory conclusion, but they all ran up against the problem that Warrick was smart, and already primed to be suspicious.

"Is he getting out of hospital soon, then?" Toreth asked.

"No. Not for a while—months, at least." Warrick sounded as faintly surprised as he always did when Toreth asked about Tarin. "They're talking about moving him to a dedicated rehabilitation facility some time around New Year, assuming that the final grafts take well and they can stabilize his immune system. Then he'd be nearer to Val and Philly, which would be something."

"Yeah, that'd be great for them." Nearer to his wife and daughter—and nearer to his idiotic resister friends, too, at least the ones who'd escaped arrest and re-education. "Is he getting many visitors?"

Warrick shook his head. "And he won't be for a while. Family only, on a strict schedule. And no, I still haven't said anything to Tarin about what happened, beyond the accident with the transporter. There's no need, not yet. While the doctors are telling him no nonfamily visitors, he has no reason to wonder why other people can't, or won't, come."

"So what will you tell him when he starts asking?"

"I don't know. Philly knows there were arrests, of course, as does Jen, and while they don't know the whole story, Philly agreed with me that it would be better to keep that aspect of it from Tarin for as long as possible."

Toreth put down the spray gun. "Warrick . . ."

"I *know*," Warrick said. Then he added more evenly, "I know. But it's difficult. It needs to be done right, if it's done at all. If Tarin found out what you did to protect him, he'd be . . . at the very least, it could affect his recovery."

Maybe Toreth should send Tarin a "Get well soon, congratulations on having your friends sent to re-education" card, and hope for the best. "It had nothing to do with Marriot. Cit was picking them all up, anyway. All I did was make sure he didn't go down with them."

"And of course I'm grateful for the risks you took." Warrick sounded as formal as if he were in the middle of corporate negotiations. "Right now, though, he's still far too ill to hear anything about it."

Toreth didn't need to say anything. He looked Warrick steadily in the eyes, and Warrick was the one to break contact first.

"I have no idea how to tell him," Warrick said, his voice unusually subdued.

"Well, it's starting to look a lot like you'll have to think of something, eventually. He's bound to work out something's wrong. He might be a fucking idiot, but he isn't actually that stupid."

After a moment, Warrick said, "I'll go make breakfast."

Toreth sighed and picked up the adhesive again. Someday he'd need to dedicate some serious thought to Tarin. Not today, though. Today he had other plans.

Under other circumstances, Warrick didn't mind solo travel. It gave him a welcome break from people wanting a piece of his time; comms could be switched off at SimTech, too, but with an office door to knock on, even Gerry and his co-admins couldn't guarantee peace and quiet. Some people were too important to turn away. A car journey with his comm set for emergencies only could be a haven.

Travelling to Tarin's hospital was different. Worries intruded, and he couldn't maintain the level of concentration he liked to give to SimTech.

The conversation with Toreth hadn't helped, although that wasn't Toreth's fault. Toreth had taken personal risks to protect Tarin, and while there was an undoubted element of self-interest those risks had been real, and larger than absolutely necessary. Warrick owed an answer to Toreth's perfectly reasonable questions, but the truth was that he had none to give.

Was he really delaying because of Tarin's health, or because of what his reaction might be?

The New London scenery passed outside, familiar from repeated journeys. The slow change from spring to summer and now into autumn had marked Tarin's equally slow journey back towards health. A particularly stately beech tree that grew in a small park where the cars habitually halted to allow pedestrians to cross had turned into a patchwork of brown and dying green. Just as the car moved on, a shift in the largely still air swirled the morning mist and carried away a handful of leaves.

At least these days he looked forwards to reaching his destination. In the first weeks after Tarin's accident, a day with no news from the hospital had seemed like some bizarre blessing. The milestones of progress had come so slowly, and far more frequent had been a call from Philadelphia or Aunt Jen, announcing some new medical crisis. Each journey to the hospital had been a torture of anticipation of the decisions he might have to help make when he reached it.

At first Warrick hadn't even been sure if they were doing the right thing. Sometimes, looking back, he found himself trying to blur the memories, to convince himself that he'd always known Tarin could recover. He remembered the conversation he'd had with Toreth, though, wondering what Tarin would have wanted, whether it might be better to stop treatment.

It had been the same conversation in which Toreth had mentioned his own patient directive to never be put in an ICU tank. The two memories had become inextricably linked over the following weeks, every visit to Tarin calling Toreth's phobia of drowning to mind. Somehow, that association had kept Warrick's recollections too clear to pretend he hadn't once been absolutely sure that Tarin would die.

When the first organ grafts—respiratory system and esophagus—had failed to take, Warrick had hesitated to back Philly's request for one more attempt. Philly had looked at him for support, doubting herself, but before anything could be said, Dillian had spoken up.

"Of course, Philly. Of *course* you're right, they have to."

Even Cele had faltered then, her usual optimism wavering. She'd taken him and Dillian aside, out of earshot of Philly and the medic she was talking to, and he'd been shocked to see tears in Cele's eyes, even though her voice was steady.

"Dilly, you know I'll support whatever you want, but sometimes…people try to let go, and just because someone can't speak, it's still selfish not to listen to them. Are you sure you're doing this for Tarin, not because you and he—"

Dillian had begun shaking her head before she finished. "This isn't because I feel guilty, I promise. Look." And she'd touched her palm to the monitoring screen, fingertips underlining the graph analyzing Tarin's heart rhythm. The lines dipped and rose, marking each beat. "See how determined he is? He needs us to believe he can do it."

And yes, Tarin's heart had always stayed strong, beating with an unyielding persistence in the face of every crisis. Intellectually, Warrick knew a heart was merely a lump of tissue made up of muscle cells with slightly unusual properties, but Dillian's conviction stirred an echo in him. Warrick had been so absorbed by the graph that he hadn't said anything until Cele prompted him.

"Keir?"

"No, I agree with Dilly." He put his hand next to Dilly's, noting absently how similar they were in shape. "Tarin deserves the chance."

Logically, he knew it wasn't a position he could defend. Luckily, the defense hadn't been needed.

The chamber-flow pressure graph of Tarin's heart on the screen by the tank had become the first place his eyes went on every visit. The steady rhythm in the face of the physiological devastation the transporter fire had wreaked around it seemed like a kind of contact with Tarin, when Warrick couldn't even touch him.

Now, though, Tarin was conscious, and every drive to the hospital was filled with grim anticipation that this would be the time when Tarin would ask the questions Warrick still didn't know how to answer. Why had some of Tarin's closest friends not tried to contact him or even sent their wishes for his recovery? What had happened to them?

"They probably all hate you because they think you were an Administration agent," Warrick said out loud, in the privacy of the corporate-grade security taxi.

"And they think that because it's what Toreth made them think while he was interrogating them, before he handed them over to the Justice systems for sentencing."

Practicality demanded he must find some lies, or at best half-truths, that would cover the facts and perhaps even create a shield protecting Tarin from any accusations he might hear in the future (although please, God, Tarin's friends would have the sense to stay away from their supposed betrayer). Warrick was forced to admit, though, that he didn't want to lie. He'd already kept so much from Tarin in the past—what Carnac had called his "sins of omission."

And then the car arrived at the hospital, and another journey was over, with Warrick's dilemma no closer to a resolution.

Sara hadn't visited the AgriStem Solar Bio-repository Gardens at Kew since the previous autumn. It seemed like far longer than a year, though. Time, like everything else, was distorted by the lens of the revolt. Life before, and life after. To her relief, the revolt seemed to have left the gardens untouched. Either the rioters had had better places to be in January or the guards belonging to the corporate structures underground had protected the historical buildings, too.

Her first stop was always the aerial walkway. As a child, she'd stood with her hands on the bars at the foot of the shuttered staircase, looking up past the screen warning of structural weakness, and imagining being on eye level with the bird's nests and squirrels in the trees. After the walkway had been restored, Sara never tired of climbing the tower and seeing the park stretching out around her.

The back and forth of the stairs reminded her of Friday's trip to Material Evidence Storage, but she ran up the last flight, already smiling, and stopped to catch her breath and admire the view.

A mist hung in the air, so low above the walkway that it tempted her to reach up to try to touch it. In reality, it would be higher than it looked, lit a soft glowing yellow by the sun as it struggled to break through. The leaves were as beautiful as ever: evergreens and a few deciduous trees still clinging to their late-summer green, the autumn rainbows of reds, yellows, oranges and browns, and here and there bare branches above a skirt of grass scattered with leaves. Years ago, she'd taken pictures of the park and ordered a cardi-coat custom knitted in the same colors. It had burned up with the rest of her possessions in the flat during the revolt, and she hadn't even thought about it until she saw the trees.

"Stop that," Sara said out loud. "You can just take another picture and order a new one."

The squirrels were busy, stocking up for winter, running through the branches of the chestnuts and sending fragments of shells to patter on the ground below. Sara tried to call to the nearest one, squeaking through her teeth, but it ignored her.

Andy Morehen finally appeared at the top of the stairs, making his way slowly up the last flight and leaning on the railing beside her.

"That felt a lot higher than it looked," he said.

"A hundred and eight steps," she said. "Worth it, though."

With his hands braced on the wood, Andy didn't look as though he entirely agreed, but he nodded. "Fantastic view. So many colors."

"Yes." Sara had planned to come alone, after a sociable Saturday, but at Friday coffee the conversation had turned to weekend plans. Sara had mentioned Kew, Andy had said that he'd never visited it, and she'd been so surprised that she'd invited him along. "When I was a kid they treated the trees with something that made their leaves all turn at exactly the same time. I like it a lot more like this."

They stood admiring the park together, their arms touching, until Andy said, "What next?"

Sara pointed to the rust-colored walkway stretching away through the treetops. "If we go to the other side, and then along the extension, there's a place where we can get a drink. See how many squirrels you can count on the way."

Buying the coffees required a couple of minutes' debate deciding who last bought drinks, before Sara paid.

The last time had been at a bar near I&I, after work, half an hour of chatting and unwinding before Daedra and the others had arrived. That was where they seemed to be stuck—drinks and a chat, without things ever moving forwards. Mostly, Sara had to admit, because she hadn't pushed them forwards. Andy seemed willing, but she had the same doubts she'd had with Rob McLean, minus Andy telling her that she was some kind of monster for doing the job the Administration paid her to do.

Was this just because of the revolt? A temporary fear of being alone, brought on by the nights she still woke up with her heart hammering and no one to tell her she was safe. No one to hug her, or be hugged—just like a typical cat, Bastard had stopped trying to sleep on her bed, probably deciding the abrupt awakenings were a personal attack on his beauty sleep.

She'd known Andy for over three years now, since he'd come from Political Crimes to join the team. And she'd always fancied him; Toreth never seemed to grow bored of bringing up that fact so she'd feel forced to deny it. But Andy had had a girlfriend, and she'd...well, she'd been busy with her plan, which in ten years had failed to deliver anything more substantial than an extensive collection of jewelry, now also lost to the resisters.

"Nice to have a whole weekend off," Andy said as they walked.

"Yes, it is," Sara said. "I try to get here every year, but sometimes if there's a big case I can't make it until it's too late and all the color's gone. Then it's just depressing—bare trees, and piles of soggy leaves rotting everywhere."

"I can't believe I've never been before."

"It's one of those funny things, isn't it? You never visit the places nearby, even if it's something all the tourists see."

"I suppose it's always been out of the way for me. I didn't even know it was free on Sundays."

"It was like that when I was a kid, too—all weekend, though." Sara paused for a mouthful of coffee. "Then for a while you had to pay every day. I expect it depends on what corporate tax deductions there are, or something like that."

"Well, thanks for inviting me. I—hang on a minute." Andy handed her his coffee, then bent down and rubbed his right calf. "Ow, shit. Sorry, it still cramps up sometimes."

"I didn't think." With both hands occupied with cups, she felt oddly helpless. "Do you want to find somewhere to sit down?"

"No, it'll be fine." He straightened up and put his weight gingerly on the leg. "It's easing off."

He held out his hand, and Sara returned his coffee. Actually, she wouldn't have minded stopping for a while at the last minicomplex, rather than getting their coffee to take away. The thin cup—made from a revolutionary new AgriStem Solar ligniplastic compound, according to the bright green informational panel on the side—might be cutting edge, but there was such a thing as being too insulating. It wasn't even warming her fingers.

Andy was walking on the spot, shifting his weight from leg to leg. He winced again.

"Are you sure you're okay?" she asked.

"Yes. Walking it off's the best thing, anyway, if we go slowly." He set off, limping slightly, and Sara walked beside him. "The hospital said it's normal. Hyperexcitability of the new nerves—takes a few months to settle down. Sort of self-calibration, that's how they explained it. The graft grew in isolation, and the nerves have to learn how to function as part of me. It's much better than it was."

Sara hadn't seen him during the revolt. She'd been locked in the coffee rooms—lucky, really, compared to so many others—and then she'd been busy helping Toreth save I&I from Carnac. But Andy had been there, down in the interrogation level medical unit, delirious and in agony, according to Mistry. Then he'd been transferred out to a hospital, and still she hadn't gone to see him until he'd been sitting up in bed, waiting for the labs to have space to grow him a graft, and at least able to fake cheerfulness.

"I wasn't sure you'd want to come back," she said.

Andy, cup to his lips, raised his eyebrows. "Mm?"

"To work, after everything that happened." She looked down at her own cup, swirling the coffee. "You were in such a bad way. And lots of people didn't come back. Wrenn didn't."

His expression hardened slightly. "Well, that was her choice. I never even thought about it, to be honest. I love I&I. I've always wanted to work there."

"Really?" That wasn't something Sara heard often. "I only applied because there were plenty of admin vacancies—of course, that was before I knew what bastards some of the paras are to their admins. I was just lucky I got Toreth."

"Actually, I applied to the interrogator and the para courses, but I didn't pass the psych requirements. They offered me a trainee investigator post instead, so I decided that was the next best thing." He paused for a moment, then added, "My dad was an interrogator at Justice, before the reorganization."

Sara stared at him in surprise. "I never heard that."

"It's a long story, and I got tired of telling it back in training."

"So...does he work at New London?" Sara couldn't believe the admin network would miss that. "Oh—he wasn't, you know, was he?" Andy looked at her blankly, until Sara said, "Killed?"

"Oh! No. He's older than my mum, so he must be past retirement age now. And I'm sure we would've been notified if anything happened to him."

"You aren't in touch, then?"

"Not really. Well, not at all. He and Mum split up when I was eight, and after that he wasn't interested in seeing me. He wasn't much interested before, to be honest." He shrugged. "But that's the way it goes, sometimes."

His defensive front reminded her of Toreth, only with what had to be assumed indifference replacing Toreth's anger. Well, she was used to tiptoeing around the subject of families. "I'm sorry. I won't mention it again."

He looked at her, appearing surprised. "No, it's okay. It was a bit shit at the time, but I got over it. My mum tried to talk me out of I&I because she thought I was just trying to do something to impress Dad, or at least get his attention. She might've been right—she usually is. Either way, it didn't happen. But before I finished training I realized I made a pretty decent investigator, and I liked it, thank you very much."

"Well." Sara swapped hands with the coffee cup and tucked her arm cautiously through his. "*I'm* very glad you did."

After ten minutes, they reached Sara's second-favorite part of the gardens— the playzone, arranged in a series of clearings through the faux wild woodland. On Sundays the place was busy, but Sara took a smaller path to the oldest section of the zone, which was as quiet as usual. All the play furniture was shaped to represent important food crops, with integrated small screens giving information no one ever bothered to read.

Sara finished her coffee and dropped the cup into the recycling point, then led the way over to the swings. They were shaped like the curved pods of bio-oil engineered soya, swing seats hanging from green ropes. She and Andy took a seat each, next to one another, and Sara set herself swinging.

A minute or so later, she turned to make a comment about the algae cell bounce rings, and realized Andy was watching her, smiling.

"What?" she said.

"This doesn't seem very like you."

"No? What's 'like me,' then?"

"You know—party girl Sara. Rings and rich boyfriends. Or work Sara, serious and organized, second in charge of the team."

"Nagra is—"

"She's a junior para. Technically she might be the next most senior rank on the team right now, but juniors come and go. She could get a promotion or a transfer next week. Okay, how about this—who writes up our assessments?"

Sara laughed. "Toreth authorizes them all, so officially, he does. Anyway, who says you can't be efficient *and* like swings?"

He grinned. "I don't think many people who've been on your bad side at work would imagine you like this, that's all."

"Well, I've been coming here for a lot longer than I've worked at I&I." She kicked her legs and swung higher. "It was a special treat for me and Fee when we were kids. Aren't you going to swing?"

"I can give it a try." Andy put his hands on the ropes, then added, "We never lived near a playground, I suppose, or no one ever had time to take me."

"It's easy. Push yourself off—your legs are longer than mine, anyway—and then you just kick. Forwards when you go forwards, back when you go back. Like this."

He watched her for a minute, then copied her. Sara swung higher at first, but with the advantage of longer legs he quickly caught up with her. Sara wasn't a great fan of exercise, but she loved this, pushing herself higher with the wind messing up her hair and rushing damply over her cheeks until she started to feel breathless. She slowed down, and Andy slowed with her, swinging in and out of sync. No one else had come into the playground yet, and Sara felt selfishly glad. Just as Andy couldn't imagine her in a playground, she couldn't imagine the ex-Political Crimes investigator still doing this in front of a bunch of kids.

"So, have you been here with Toreth?" Andy asked.

Sara glanced at him, but his expression was as bland as his tone. "I don't spend all my time outside work with him, you know."

"That wasn't really an answer."

He might've failed his psych assessment, but he definitely had the right tone for interrogation. Sara wondered how he'd scored in his investigator interview tests.

"No, I haven't." Sara looked around at the trees and the leaf-dotted grass between them. "It isn't his kind of thing. Nature." Then as she swung up, a distant glimpse of white and glass caught her eye, and nudged her brain. "Oh, no, wait. I think we did go to something at the Temperate complex—maybe one of those big club events they used to run. God, that was *years* ago, though. Let me think . . . that must've been when we had the first junior, the one that was already in the team when I got the job. Oh, what was his name?"

"Long before my time, sorry."

"He wasn't there long. It'll come to me. Anyway, no, I never come *here* with Toreth. Or the walkway, either."

Andy let his swing slow down further, and Sara did the same. They swung out of phase for a while, and she watched the breeze ruffle his hair as he swooped away from her. It definitely suited him more when it was longer like this. She wondered why he hadn't had it cut again after he came back to work.

Finally, they both stopped. Sara could barely touch the padded ground from the seat; Andy rocked himself backwards and forwards slightly, from heel to toe. She was about to suggest they moved on—her cheeks were getting stiff from the damp cold—when he spoke.

"I always thought the real reason my mum didn't want me to join I&I was that she was worried I'd pass the psych test for the para or interrogator courses. She couldn't even pretend not to be relieved when I didn't. I think she'd feel like she'd failed if I'd turned out that much like my dad. But like I said, I'm happy with where I am. And it would've been inconvenient now if I'd passed, wouldn't it?"

"Why?"

He rubbed his hands up and down the swing rope. "Well, you don't date paras, do you?"

"No. And definitely not interrogators."

"So how about investigators?"

"Well." She hesitated, poised like the weightless moment at the top of a swing. "I never have before."

He raised his eyebrows. "Want to give it a go?"

Breathing out, Sara let go of the worries, and smiled. "Okay."

A corporate car had traffic system priority over the public taxis, although on a Sunday the difference was negligible. Still, since he'd had to use a taxi, Warrick had allowed extra time for the journey, which wasn't needed in the end. When he reached the hospital, the others weren't yet there. Better to be early than late, but early was still an annoying scheduling inefficiency. He stood outside the Burns Center door and debated trying to get in early to see Tarin alone. Maybe he should take this chance to say . . . something. At least try to lay some subtle groundwork to prepare Tarin for any necessary explanations later.

He still couldn't come up with the words, though, that would allow him to make a start without risking the explanation spiralling to reveal far too much. More pertinently, it would be terrible to spoil Valeria's first time at the unit. That was a good enough reason not to talk to Tarin today, Warrick told himself, as he found a corner seat in the familiar waiting area and tried to let the pastel yellows and greens of the décor soothe him.

Warrick took out his hand screen, not to try to work, but to see how Toreth was getting on alone at the flat.

The plan was thwarted by the discovery that Toreth had done something to the security cameras which Warrick couldn't work out. At first he thought the flat system had simply turned them off because no unregistered occupant was present. He turned the surveillance on again to be surprised by blank images, not only from Toreth's room but from the landing, stairs, and hallway, too, where he might have been able to manipulate a camera for an oblique glimpse of the room. Visual spectrum and infrared were equally uninformative. The system reported no blocks on any feeds, and the other rooms displayed normally. The tomographic motion detector showed one person in the flat, in Toreth's room. Warrick watched the motion plot for a while, moving between the wall and a spot in the center of the room that presumably equated to the papering table.

It lacked a certain something, however, compared to watching Toreth working up a sweat with a bucket and sponge.

Mildly intrigued, he set about discovering what Toreth had done to the system. The SimTech head of security wouldn't be pleased if he had found a way to disable the flat cameras. He'd just established that he couldn't detect a single abnormality about the system when he heard a voice call, "Uncle Keir!"

He closed the screen and tucked it away, standing up just in time for Valeria to run over and hug him. "Hello, there."

Philadelphia and Aunt Jen followed more sedately.

"Are we still going to see Dad?" Valeria asked anxiously.

"I don't know. I was waiting for the rest of you." Warrick looked questioningly at Philly, who gave a little shrug. "I'm sure they would've called someone to say if we couldn't."

"Now, remember what we talked about yesterday?" Philly said.

Valeria turned to her mother and nodded. "About how Dad's still very poorly?"

"Yes. He'll probably be very tired, and we might not be able to talk to him for too long. It's important he has lots of rest so he can keep getting better. And you remember we were talking about some of the treatments he's had, because of the accident and the fire?"

"Just like when Saskia at school had the accident, and they had to grow a new hand for her."

"That's right. You know they're having to do a lot more than that for Dad, though?"

"Yes, of course," Valeria said. "That's why he looked different on the comm. But he's still Dad, just the same."

It broke Warrick's heart to see her trying to be so brave, and he suddenly found himself wishing that he'd asked Toreth to come along after all. Sometimes Toreth's emotional severance from suffering was a steadying influence, even though hospitals bored him, and he'd probably end up trying to pull one of the medical staff.

"Will it be okay if I give him a hug?" Valeria asked.

"We hope you can, yes," Philly said. "But remember we'll have to put on special clothes, so we don't give him any infections."

"Because of all the bacteria on our skin," Valeria said. She looked up at Warrick. "This year at school we all sequenced the microbiome on the backs of our hands."

"Really? That must've been fun."

"It was. I've decided I'm going to be a doctor when I grow up. Not a patient technician—someone who investigates new treatments."

Behind her, Philly smiled. Warrick wondered if Valeria had ever informed her mother of her previous determination, years ago, to be a para-investigator. He doubted Philly would like that idea any more than Tarin had. "I'm sure that would be an interesting job, Val," Warrick said.

Valeria looked around the adults. "So? Can we go in now, please?"

Of course, they couldn't. First they needed to have another conversation with one of the medical staff who had the same calm, sympathetic professionalism, no matter whether the news they were delivering was good or bad.

"He's still experiencing some sensory processing issues," the treatment coordinator said to Philly. "We'd like to keep his stress levels controlled, so no more than two visitors today. And we still might have to cut the visit short."

"Two?" Val asked. "That's me, isn't it, Mum? Me and you?"

"Of course," Philly said. "That's why we came."

Warrick hoped his relief didn't show. Another conversation avoided. "Aunt Jen and I'll wait for you. We can see him another day."

Philly and Val went with the coordinator. Warrick and Jen were left behind, with a screen from which they could watch the reunion. Warrick turned off the sound; Tarin must know the room was monitored, but if he didn't definitely know that Warrick and Jen were watching, it felt wrong to eavesdrop.

Valeria had, no doubt, listened carefully to the instructions. She rushed across the room to him, but at the very last second pulled up so that her hug was gentle, if no less heartfelt. Tarin hugged her in return. He was wearing gloves, not to protect his skin but to hide that fact that his lower arms were temporary prosthetics, driven by neural sensors translating intention into movement and feeding back a limited range of sensation. Another part of his treatment that had parallels in the sim. How must it feel to hug his daughter and know that the contact was to some extent an illusion? A subset of sim users consistently scored the sim low on satisfaction based on exactly that, and Warrick sometimes feared they might never be able to overcome the issue.

If Tarin was thinking about the neural sensors, it didn't show on his face. He had his eyes closed, and the broadest smile Warrick had seen from him probably since he had introduced Warrick to Valeria for the first time as a newborn. Even when Tarin relaxed his hug, Valeria didn't move away. She stayed kneeling by his chair, leaning her head against his chest. Tarin kissed her, and then looked up to say something to Philly.

"Well, that's a relief," Warrick said.

Jen looked up at him. "Mm?"

"I was worried she might react badly. He does look . . . well, somewhat strange."

"Philly and I showed her plenty of pictures, don't worry. And they talked on the comm." Jen smiled at the screen. "Anyway, Tarin's her daddy."

Every time Warrick saw Tarin he wondered if he'd recognize his half brother if he hadn't know who Tarin was. Perhaps a picture from before the accident would've helped him find the sameness underlying the reconstructive work. None of the skin replacement had yet been differentiated into follicles. There was a reason, Warrick remembered from his investigation of the medical procedures Tarin had had to undergo. Something about infection, or matrix stability? The exact detail escaped him; medical technicalities kept sliding down his list of things about which he needed to worry.

They watched for another minute, then Jen spoke again.

"Keir, I need to talk to you about something." She lowered her voice. "I wanted to wait until I saw you in person. I thought it might be a bad idea to discuss it over the comm."

Tarin's medical insurance had proved surprisingly comprehensive; Warrick had initially worried that a charity working on behalf of the indigent homeless might skimp on their own staff, but it had bought an excellent insurance package, paying for appreciable upgrades to Administration basic care. The grounds reflected that, with a quiet garden set aside for patients and visitors. Pathways wound between low, precisely trimmed evergreen hedges, and one section was laid out as a sensory garden, where the damp air held on to the scent of the lavender bushes.

Warrick and Jen found a bench set against a building wall with a clear view of the rest of the garden. The gloomy layers of mist had finally started to break up, making a patchwork of white and pale, autumnal blue. Still, the air was cold, and he and Jen were the only people in sight.

"What's wrong?" Warrick asked.

"Maybe nothing, I'm not sure. But I had a message from a legal firm—not the usual group that Kate used—saying that she's transferring the house to my name. Did you know about that?"

Warrick shook his head. "I haven't heard anything from her since my birthday."

"But why me?"

"You're the one living in it, I suppose."

"Tarin does, too, or he will once he's better. That's what I can't understand. She and Tarin were always so close. She bought the house with his father—Marriot's life insurance cleared the mortgage. Do you think she knows what happened to Tar? I've had one letter since it happened, and she didn't mention it."

Warrick shrugged. "I'm sorry. I just have no idea."

Jen frowned. "Even if she somehow knew about the accident, why wait until now and then give the house to me?"

"Perhaps..." Automatically, Warrick glanced around. "Well, there were the arrests. You were never even slightly political."

"So she didn't want us to lose the house if Tarin's arrested, too? But do you think he still might be?"

"No. Not after all this time. Tar's safe—Toreth thinks the same." Even as he said it, Warrick realized that in trying to reassure he was making the house transfer sound even more odd. "Mother might not be so sure, though. Perhaps it's what she always meant to do, and this is just the first chance that she's had."

"Yes, that could be true." Jen didn't sound entirely convinced. "It must be difficult, dealing with everything from outside Europe. But if things are so bad that she can't come home, why would they let her transfer property?" Her expression changed to alarm. "Are they trying to identify her associates?"

"Mother wouldn't do anything to put us in danger. Even if someone was watching, what would it tell them? That she's given her house to her sister, who's shared it with her for decades already."

After a moment, Jen nodded. "Yes, you're right. It just makes me nervous, having to second-guess everything. At least in the old days, you knew what was right and what might get you in trouble." She sighed. "Like Kate. She never *did* anything, Keir. All she did was talk, and she'd agree with Tar and his friends, sometimes. Not that I'd ever suggest to him that he might've had something to do with why she left, of course. Poor Tar."

Sometimes, like now, the weight of the secret felt too heavy to keep bearing alone. So tempting to use the excuse of letting Jen make sense of all this loss. *Kate left because she was a Citizen Surveillance agent, at risk of being exposed*—that explained so much on its own. Jen might even be able to accept it, eventually. She was clever, though, and soon she'd look beyond that one truth and find the others. At the very least, she surely couldn't avoid seeing Tarin's status in Kate's eyes, as a surveillance tool first, and her child a very distant second, if even that.

He and Dillian had won the maternal love race, Warrick thought morbidly, with Tar a "did not finish."

"It's a funny coincidence, isn't it?" Jen said. "Tarin and his father. Marriot was killed in a traffic accident, and now—I thought about it before, of course, but I didn't like to mention it. At least it doesn't look as though things will end the same way."

"There've been so many medical advances since then." Warrick wondered if John Sable had got the idea from Kate's file. And, suddenly, if what had happened to Kate's first husband had been as much of an "accident" as Tarin's misfortune. "Is there anything else you wanted to talk about?" he asked, desperate to divert the conversation.

"Not that I can—oh, yes. You remember TAM Logistics?"

"Marriot's old company?" Warrick said in surprise.

"Yes. Kate inherited his shares in it. I'd written them off, because the company shut down—the directors were arrested at the same time as Tarin's friends."

"Did you know them?" Warrick asked, with a twinge of guilt. Irrational, since everyone who'd been arrested would've gone to I&I no matter what Toreth had done.

"Not well—hardly at all, really. They both founded the company with Marriot, but I haven't seen them since . . . since after Leo died, I suppose. They came to the house once or twice for New Year, but I doubt you'll remember them." She smiled suddenly. "Did you know they're how Kate met your father?"

Happy family reminiscences were not what he wanted at that moment, but flat disinterest would sound strange. "I think she mentioned something like that."

"Marriot's death was so sudden, and TAM was only a few years old and still struggling for business, so they were desperate to replace him. Kate insisted on being involved—everyone told her there was no need, but you know how stubborn she was." Her face fell momentarily. "Is. She said she had to look after Tarin's interests, in case he wanted to be involved in the company some day. I suppose we should be glad *that* didn't happen. Anyway, when Leo came along he had experience and contacts, and some money he was looking to invest. Kate was at the first meeting."

A logistics company—perfect for smuggling materials, information, and even people in and out of the Administration. And a perfect entry point into the resister network for a pair of Citizen Surveillance agents. "And it was love at first sight. Has something happened with the TAM shares, then?"

"What? Oh, yes, of course. I had a message from the receivers saying that I should get some kind of payout, probably by the end of the year. The Administration takes most of it, because the other shareholders were sent to re-education. I thought they'd take it all, but apparently..." She sat up straighter. "Now, that's as strange as the house, and not just because Kate gave Marriot's shares to me instead of Tar. If the other shareholders were convicted, I suppose it must be true they were mixed up in something political. But if Kate had to leave, why are the receivers acting like she did nothing wrong? If she broke the law, why not have a trial without her and take her assets? They can do that, can't they?"

"I don't know," Warrick said, although he suspected she was right. "Listen, Jen—"

"Kate knew Marriot's old partners far better than I did. She did accountancy work for them. But why—"

"Jen." He took her hand, and she stopped and looked at him, a different kind of doubt growing in her eyes. "We have no way to get in touch with Kate, and she's the only one who knows the answers. Maybe it would be better not to think about it—not to worry about it."

Her eyes narrowed. "You do know something, don't you? Was it on Kate's system? Tar told me you looked at it."

Oh, she had no idea how close she was. "*If* I found anything strange—maybe from a long time in the past—you wouldn't want me to put other people in danger by telling them, too. Would you?"

"No. But..." She sighed. "I can't really say 'just tell me,' can I?"

"I'd rather you didn't." Then, taking a risk, he said, "If you really want me to, then of course I will."

Jen looked up at the sky, then finally shook her head. "I trust you to do the right thing."

Which was more than Warrick did himself, these days. "Good." He released her hand. "Now I was thinking, about the house and Kate's shares and so on. I could try to find a financial specialist to help sort all of that out. So you don't have to worry about it." Someone discreet and not too curious—and willing to become involved with a corporation closed down because of political crimes, which would probably be the hardest part. "Apart from anything else, it would be good to have professional advice. There's no reason why you or Tar should lose out, just because of... the situation. I'm sure Kate wouldn't want that. Asher might know someone. I could talk to her on Monday."

"Would you?" Jen said with obvious relief. "Kate always dealt with that kind of thing. She was the accountant, not me."

"There we are, then. You won't have to worry about it, and I won't have to worry about you."

She smiled a little wanly. "You don't need to do that anyway."

"I can't help it—it's the way I was brought up. Now, shall we go back in? It's cold out here, and I could use a cup of tea."

As they walked back to the door, Jen said, "Just now, you called your mother 'Kate.'"

"Oh." So many ways to make a mistake around this topic. "Did I?"

"Yes. I've never heard you do that before. There's no reason why you can't—you're certainly old enough. It just seemed odd."

"It's been an odd few months," Warrick said, and fortunately that seemed enough to close the matter.

Inside, Val and Philly were still with Tarin; that must be a good sign, if the medical assessment was positive enough to allow such a long visit.

While he waited, Warrick opened his hand screen and called Dillian. She didn't answer, but ten minutes later she called back, looking a little mussed.

"Sorry, I was, um." She tried to smooth her hair with her hand. "Busy."

"With me," Cele called faintly from somewhere in the background. "Very busy."

Dillian laughed. "Yes, all right. I was trying for a smidgen of decorum—Keir's at the hospital. Aren't you?"

"Yes, I am."

"Did you tell Tar I'm sorry I can't be there?"

"I didn't have the chance. And as things turned out, it was probably for the best that you couldn't make it. You wouldn't have got much out of the journey. They've only allowed two visitors in the room with him, so Jen and I won't get to talk to him either."

"Oh, that's a shame."

"It doesn't matter. I saw the others. We'll probably go back to Jen's place for a late lunch. I'm sure Val will want to tell me all about her visit. Speaking of which, do you want to come to the flat for dinner tonight, and I can pass it all on to you?"

She thought about it for a moment, then shook her head. "I'd love to, but I have to get up early. I'm flying out to see a client for an emergency consultation contract, and—" She glanced to the side. "I still have to do most of the preparation for it that I was planning to have finished already."

"I thought you would've noticed by now that I'm a bad influence," Cele said.

Dillian smiled. "Oh, we've all definitely noticed that. Maybe when I get back, Keir, we could go see Tar together, and then I'll treat you to dinner?"

"All right." Warrick smiled in return. "Enjoy your Sunday with Cele."

"Warrick?" Toreth called as he opened the door to the flat.

Warrick almost said, "Who else?", but there were a few other people with the code. "Yes."

"I wasn't expecting you back yet."

"Yes, the traffic was very quiet. I don't know why; just one of those things."

Warrick took off his jacket and hung it neatly in the tiny cloakroom. He reached the foot of the stairs just as Toreth came down them. His T-shirt was more or less clean, but a shaving of paper had stuck to his sleeve. Warrick picked it off.

"Looks like you've been busy. I can't wait to see the results."

"Yes, you can," Toreth said. "Close your eyes."

Warrick shut them, waiting to be led to the bedroom, but a few seconds later he jerked in surprise as something touched his face. "What—" he began, but the familiar pressure of a blindfold answered the unfinished question.

"I'm not quite done," Toreth said.

"Then I can wait down here."

"Yeah, and you can spy on me from the office, too."

"I wouldn't if you don't want me to—and anyway, I can't, because you did something to the security system that you need to explain to me before I have to tell Emma Queen."

The name of the SimTech head of security made Toreth laugh. "She won't be very impressed by my technical skill. I know where the cameras were installed, so I stuck a square of wide-spectrum blocking tape over them."

"Ah." Simple explanations are usually the best. "The only thing I could get working was the tomographic motion detector."

There was a pause, then Toreth said, "Fuck, I forgot all about that."

"It's less riveting than you might think. I watched for five minutes while I was waiting at the hospital, and you definitely lose some appeal as a mass-centered dot. I thought about trying to recalibrate it for a more detailed scan, but I didn't have time."

Toreth laughed again. "See, that's why I need the blindfold—you should've been a sab. But you can still keep me company if you like."

Toreth guided him up the stairs—although by now Warrick could walk confidently up alone blindfolded—and into the room. The plastic sheeting crackled beneath Warrick's feet, and he caught the faint background smell of adhesive.

"Hands behind you."

Warrick obeyed, and the edge of his hand brushed cool paper. He stroked it with his fingertips, just to confirm he was against a wall, and then he touched metal, and chain clinked softly. Toreth took his wrist and clicked a manacle around it.

"Toreth—"

"I'm still finishing off the last strip." Toreth secured his other wrist. "And we can't have you peeking."

168

"I told you—"

Toreth took his chin in a firm grip and kissed him hard, pulling back almost before Warrick could open his mouth. Warrick went very still.

"Patience," Toreth said. "I'll get to you when I'm done with the paper."

Warrick's lips tingled. "All right."

Toreth took a few steps away, then said, "Crap. I knew there was something. Wait here. I'll be five minutes."

Footsteps headed loudly to the doorway, over the crackling plastic, and then went more faintly over the landing to the stairs. A moment later, straining to hear, he caught the faint sound of a door opening and closing. The front door of the flat? The kitchen? He couldn't tell.

Well. Five minutes. Just the time he needed to put the rest of the day behind him.

Being chained to a wall shouldn't really be relaxing, Warrick thought. And in one way, it definitely wasn't. Like the background sound of plastic sheeting when he shifted his feet, his mind held the anticipation of what might happen when Toreth returned. At this point, though, the helplessness was more calming than erotically charged. There was nothing he could do. Everything was up to Toreth now. Warrick leaned against the newly papered wall and tried to let his mind go blank. One by one, he set aside the worries and problems of the day.

All that would still be there tomorrow. Tonight he would have nothing more stressful to do than pretend not to notice any defects in Toreth's papering. He could always call someone in to fix them, when Toreth wasn't there.

Warrick was almost dozing, buoyant in a warm sea of anticipation and relaxation, when the sound of someone in the flat pulled him back to the present. He opened his eyes to the blackness of the blindfold, which confused him for a moment. He concentrated, hoping it *was* Toreth, and not Dillian deciding to take him up on his invitation after all. No voice, only a faint suggestion of footsteps. After a few seconds, he heard plastic crackle again.

"Toreth?"

"Mh-hm." Glasses chinked together. "I thought I deserved a the-wallpaper-is-finally-up-thank-fuck celebration. But I forgot to put a bottle in the fridge, so I stuck one in the fast chiller."

What kind of mood was Toreth in? Warrick couldn't tell from his voice. When Toreth touched his arm, the shock of it made Warrick shiver after all the time standing alone.

Toreth chuckled softly. "Missed me?"

"Oh, yes."

The shift of Toreth's feet on the plastic warned him, and he was ready for the kiss. This time, it went on, mouth against mouth, Toreth free to touch at will and Warrick blind and bound. Finally, Toreth's hands brushed over his chest, and Warrick whimpered; Toreth broke the kiss as though he'd been waiting for the sound.

Panting, Warrick waited, expecting Toreth to move away. Instead, he tugged Warrick's shirt free all around, pulling the front straight, then said, "Keep very, very still."

Warrick held his breath, trying to work out by touch what Toreth was doing. The breath had started to turn into a pressure in his throat when Toreth swept his hand down, and something pattered softly onto the plastic. Buttons, Warrick realized a moment later, when his shirt fell open.

"Decorating knife," Toreth said economically, and Warrick breathed out sharply. "It didn't even nick the shirt." Warrick heard a metallic click, and then another. "Nice. I like this."

A shadow of movement brushed Warrick's right cheek. He leaned his head to the side a little, and found the muscle-over-bone firmness of Toreth's forearm. He was about to say something when the prick of metal against his other cheek stopped the words in his throat.

"Do you remember that party at the Shop?" Toreth said conversationally. "That couple with the hooks?"

"I remember," Warrick said, trying to speak without letting his head move a millimeter.

"Well, we've got the plastic down anyway."

Warrick had to swallow before he could say, "Still too much damage. Too many explanations, as well."

The blade stroked down his cheek, real metal, not the nerve induction toy, and then lifted away. "That's what I thought, or I would've bought the hooks."

Warrick heard a thump at a distance—Toreth throwing the knife somewhere?—and then Toreth groped the front of his trousers. Warrick gasped.

"Still liking the idea, though?"

"Oh, yes."

"You stay there and think about it. I need to finish and tidy everything away."

Every time Warrick thought the final plastic sheet had been folded, the rustling started again. Then, he heard furniture sliding.

"I could help, if—"

"Shut up."

Warrick shifted in the chains, and suddenly Toreth's footsteps came closer. Warrick barely had time to brace himself before Toreth grabbed his upper arms, squeezing tightly, and pushed him back flat against the wall. Warrick parted his lips, expecting another kiss, but instead Toreth spoke right against his ear.

"You know, we could've used that other stuff—the instant paper. Sprayed the substrate on the wall and scanned on the pattern. That would've taken no time at all. Remind me again why we aren't doing that."

"Because . . ."

"Come on, I know there was a reason." Toreth pushed his thigh between Warrick's. "Well?"

"I wanted it to be in keeping with the period of the building."

"That's right." The touch of Toreth's lips against his ear made Warrick want to squirm away, but he had nowhere to go. "So, really, this is all your fault, isn't it?"

"Yes."

"I put a lot of effort into this."

The room, or planning what he'd do with the rest of the evening? "Believe me, I appreciate it."

"Mm. Appreciate it quietly. Or I might just leave you there all night."

Warrick nodded, then gritted his teeth against the sudden feeling of abandonment as Toreth stepped back, all contact withdrawn in one smooth movement. Warrick's skin itched, wanting the touch back again.

Finally, the room fell silent. Warrick held his breath, straining to listen, and then twitched in surprise as Toreth said right next to him, "That's about done."

Warrick closed his eyes as Toreth unlocked the chains and removed the blindfold, and then carefully squinted at the lights. They were turned down low, brightening slowly in what must have been a preset program.

"It looks . . ." Warrick had been ready to say "perfect" no matter what, but the sentence trailed away halfway through because, well, it *did*. "Very good."

"Go on, then," Toreth said. "Check it. I don't want to hear tomorrow about how it isn't right."

He looked over every strip of paper, trying to find an edge where the subdued pattern of vines didn't match up, but even in the corners and around the windows he couldn't find a flaw. Maybe from up close there might be something. Even Warrick, though, could accept that decoration didn't have to stand up to scrutiny with a magnifying glass to be acceptable, at least when he wasn't paying for it.

Still, why had he thought Toreth wouldn't stick it out? Domesticity might bore him, and he might never grasp why the floor wasn't the perfect storage area for most items, but at I&I he did his work with dedication and attention to detail.

"Any complaints?" Toreth said when Warrick straightened up from examining the window sill. He stood by the dressing table, holding the bottle of champagne, ready to twist the cork.

"None whatsoever."

"Good." Toreth smiled, and the cork popped. He poured the first glass, the bubbles spilling over and running down to pool on the surface of the dressing table. All the plastic sheeting in the room, and nothing under the glasses—precisely why, when Warrick had been picking furniture for Toreth's room, he'd gone for something period with marble tops.

"Thanks," Warrick said as Toreth handed him a glass.

"Enjoy." Toreth switched hands with the glasses and licked his fingers. "So. What are we going to do with the rest of the weekend?"

"Well, it is Sunday." And, tempting as the chains were against the new wallpaper, Warrick had missed their usual relaxed Sunday fuck. It had become so much a part of the routine of their lives.

"True," Toreth said. "And?"

"You've been working hard all day. I feel I should contribute something to the effort."

Preparing the room yesterday had made up to some extent for their missed morning at the gym. Toreth liked the faint aches in his back and arms, a reminder of muscles working together in subtly new ways that made him pleasantly aware of his body. And he certainly didn't mind the opportunity to be lazy and let Warrick do all the work for once.

Not that he seemed to need much encouragement. He'd stripped Toreth and spread him out on the bed on his back, and gone to work with a dedication that was already going a long way towards compensating for missing their usual Friday night. Toreth relaxed and luxuriated in Warrick's fingers and mouth, the occasional brush of Warrick's cock against his own a reminder of more to come. Warrick could fuck him, Toreth decided. Nice and slow, or maybe not so slow, but still very, very nice…

Kneeling over Toreth, Warrick ran his hands along Toreth's arms, up to his wrists. Warrick's grip lingered there for a moment, tightening; Toreth opened his eyes, then flexed his arms as though he was about to pull free. Then he relaxed, but Warrick let go of one wrist anyway.

"Do it," Warrick said in an echo of Toreth's thoughts.

Toreth smiled, loving it, loving this especially. One of Warrick's little quirks—one of the things Toreth enjoyed knowing about him. Knowing Warrick so well.

"Do what?" he asked.

"You know what."

"Of course. But I want to hear it."

"Put it in."

He shook his head—at the phrasing, not the suggestion.

"Put—" Warrick swallowed. "Put my cock inside you."

"Mmm...okay." He held still, pretending to think about it, then he curled up his legs, reached down, and guided Warrick into him.

"Ah, God." Warrick's voice, no more than a breath, laid over the delicious feeling of him thrusting home. "God, yes."

Why did he get so much out of that? A touch of obedience and submission on Toreth's part, something to go along with the hand still on his wrist, and Warrick's fantasies about tying him up? Or just liking the words? Or even just because it felt so good—which it did, whether that was the reason or not.

He was so absorbed by the idea that he almost didn't notice Warrick's hand enclosing his cock—just another one of the wonderful sensations. The part of his mind that did notice also appreciated. Nothing to do but lie back and *feel*.

Which he did, revelling in the heat and hunger for completion as the feelings began to build. He rested his hands in the small of Warrick's back—just to feel the muscles moving, because he didn't need directions. Beautiful rhythm, exactly how he liked it. Not bad payment for a few hours of DIY. If he could get this from all his clients, Toreth thought, he might consider a career change.

"Open your eyes," Warrick said, breathless and strained.

When he did he found Warrick watching him intently in return. Toreth smiled, and shook his head—turning it into a challenge.

Warrick smiled too, recognizing it, not stilling his movements. "Oh, yes you will."

"Won't."

"Yes, you will."

"You first."

"No, I'm...going to watch you come. Keep your eyes open."

In this position, Warrick had the advantage as far as dictating timing, but that could be changed. He took a deep breath and looked straight into Warrick's eyes.

"Fuck me. I—"

"That's cheating," Warrick gasped, but didn't stop.

"No such thing. Fuck me. Harder." Silly, bad-porn dialogue, which he knew Warrick couldn't resist. "I want to feel your cock inside me—deeper inside. Yes. Fuck me. More."

It wasn't doing much for his own self-control either, especially as Warrick's hand tightened on him, moving faster. If he could have closed his eyes, looked away from Warrick, he might have held out longer. But that would have been a bigger admission of defeat than surrendering to the inevitable.

Soon...very soon. He was so close, but was Warrick closer?

"Fuck me. I want you—" No he wasn't, not quite, and the tension broke in a flood of pleasure. "Ah, *Warrick*."

"Don't shut your eyes!"

Toreth managed to comply, at least for the second or two before Warrick's eyes widened, his face flushing as he thrust in hard. He ducked his head and screamed into Toreth's shoulder.

"Draw," Toreth said when he got his breath back.

"Rubbish." Warrick's voice was muffled, breath hot against his skin. "Absolute and unmitigated rubbish." He lifted his head. "Admit it: I won, you lost."

"Well... best of three?"

After a minute Toreth got out of bed and went to fetch the rest of the champagne, leaving Warrick still laughing.

Monday

Waiting for Sara at work on Monday was a message of thanks from Heckman for finding his wife's ring. It had been forwarded by Tillotson's admin Jenny; left to his own devices, doubtless Tillotson wouldn't have bothered.

The message had been sent on Saturday. Since there were no newer, less happy ones—which Sara was certain Tillotson would've slung their way immediately—she decided that their deception had, so far, passed scrutiny. And wasn't it better for the girl to be able to get married with what she thought was her mum's ring, instead of being miserably disappointed that it was lost forever at I&I?

It was early enough for the rest of the office still to be mostly empty. Sara heard Toreth's atrocious whistling before she saw him across the room. She hadn't called him last night to check how the decorating had gone. She'd been... busy.

"What are you doing here?" he asked. "Alarm set wrong?"

"No." Actually, she'd badly overestimated the time it would take to get from Andy's flat to her own, and from there to I&I. "I just woke up all enthusiastic about work. Don't worry, I'm sure it won't last. Did the papering turn out all right?"

"Absolutely fantastic. Your sister knows some very useful people." He raised his eyebrows warningly. "By the way, not a word to Warrick about Jojo. If he shows you the room, just be impressed by what a multitalented boss you have."

"You mean he doesn't know? He thinks it was all you?"

"Yeah, that's right." Toreth sat down on the edge of her desk. "Lucky for me he was out all day. Although I nearly blew it, because I forgot about the tomographic motion detector. If he'd looked at the right time, he would've seen two people in the flat. Pure coincidence that I must've been over at the complex when he was snooping."

"But Jojo left me a message asking if you needed him to come back. He said Warrick came home while he was still there."

"Yeah, but Jojo didn't talk to him, did he?"

"I didn't call him. I just assumed—Toreth?"

Toreth laughed. "The bloody plastic was still all over the floor. I told Jojo to stand very still, then I blindfolded Warrick and chained him up in the bedroom. Then Jojo and I walked out in step, and I took him downstairs and paid him. Warrick never suspected anything."

"You chained him up while—" Sara put her hands over her face. She couldn't help grinning, though. When she lowered her hands, Toreth was grinning, too. "You are so *bad*. I'll never be able to look at Jojo again without thinking about that. Did you hang any of it?"

"Some backing paper at the beginning, to start it off, otherwise Warrick might've been suspicious. Oh, and one little bit at the end that Jojo didn't have time to put up. That probably helped, to be honest. Authentic adhesive on my hands. So, did you have a good weekend?"

"Yes. Well, not bad. Nothing special." Sara adjusted her coffee cup, because she didn't feel entirely confident meeting his eyes. That was the problem with working for a trained interrogator. "By the way, you have a few messages waiting already. You might want to take a look before the case conference."

"Okay, thanks." Toreth stood up and stretched. "Well, here we go. Back to the grind. You know, some Mondays it feels like the weekend never happened."

"Yeah." Some Mondays; not this one. Across the office, she spotted Andy arriving. "I'll make you a coffee, shall I?"

175

Constellation of
Falling Stars

❖

The last song of the last encore at the last performance of the tour. Better than sex, with the noise of the audience rolling over him, resonating through his sweat-sticky body, making him hard, making his heart thunder. The lights in front of the stage filled the whole world, stopping him from seeing the stadium clearly, but he didn't need to do that to know how much they loved 343, wanted them—wanted him. Kit hadn't taken any painkillers tonight because he knew he wouldn't need them. The vast screens gave the show back to him, showing him how good they were, the faces of the screaming arena crowd amplified as the cameras swept in and over. Every note was perfect, every harmony pure. It was like flying.

Kim and Jase were flying, too—he could feel it. When they finally stumbled off the stage, Kit had to stop for a while, to try to breathe himself back into his thrumming body. He grabbed the drink bottle offered to him, and downed it as fast as he dared, craving the sugar and electrolytes. Sometimes he fainted after shows and he hated the fuss, hated the too-soon loss of the glorious high.

Better than sex, although some people didn't see it quite the same way. Barely off stage, only half hidden by equipment, Jase had his back to a lighting tower, with Kim up against him, Jase's hands on his buttocks pressing him close. They were kissing, open-mouthed, hungry.

Automatically, Kit looked around. Yes, there they were—backstage journos looking bored and exuding seen-it-all-before cynicism. The corps would choose which pictures they were allowed to use. Geoff Cheung was watching, too, a little way away, his expression more anxious. It made Kit sad to think anyone could've seen such a perfect show and still be worrying about anything, but that was why the corps paid him.

When Geoff saw Kit looking, he raised his eyebrow. This time, though, it wasn't his manager's signal or the demands of PR that made Kit drop the drink bottle and go over to Kim and Jase.

When he reached them, he wasn't in the least surprised to find they had their hands down each other's trousers. Not totally oblivious to the journos, but just oblivious enough. Effortless playing to the gallery, although they looked entirely absorbed in each other, panting and flushed from the show and from this.

When Kit tried to worm his way into the tight embrace, Jase looked down and frowned. "Kit?"

Kit shook his head. "I just want to be here."

"Okay." Jase smiled, eyes a bit glazed, and put his free arm around Kit. "You sounded great tonight. Really—ah—damn good. I didn't hear one wrong note."

Jase ducked his head and kissed Kit on the mouth, friendly, not sexual. Then he bit his lip and gasped as Kim, presumably, reminded him what they were doing. Kit grinned and buried his face in Kim's shoulder, feeling them both moving, trembling and urgent. Sweat stung his eyes and mouth, stifling. Every centimeter of contact between them felt seared into his skin. Jase was swearing, a low litany of "fuck, fuck, ah, fuck," luckily too soft for the journos to hear.

Borderline porn was allowed, bad language wasn't. To Kit, it didn't even seem strange anymore.

Then Jase bucked forwards and Kit looked up, because he always thought Jase was at his best when he was coming, relaxed and beautiful, none of the cynical lines that sometimes spoiled his face. Jase caught him watching and laughed, pulling Kit tight against him.

"Weird little freak," Jase said fondly, then his expression changed to concentration. He twisted his arm and Kim gave a choked cry, shuddering as he came.

Kit hung on, burying himself in the inferno of sweat and noise and laughter. This was it. This was better than sex, knowing that there were two people in the world who would never really hurt him.

Geoff was waiting for them outside the entertainment complex's main dressing room. Kit had sandwiched himself between Jase and Kim, their arms over his shoulders, and Kit felt them both stiffen as they saw Geoff.

"Hello, *sir*," Jase said.

Kit felt a bit sorry for Geoff sometimes, because he was only their direct manager, not senior corporate, and he worked for the corps as much as they did. And while he probably didn't have as much to lose if they fired him, he was far more disposable; mobs of girls didn't run screaming towards *him* if he poked his nose out in public. The idea made Kit want to laugh, but he didn't dare. When he looked up, Jase's expression was closed, hard, and Jase's fingers tightened, digging into Kit's shoulder.

Geoff stepped backwards into the dressing room, and Kit noticed the hand screen for the first time. In one movement Kim and Jase separated from him and followed Geoff, leaving Kit cold in his sweat-damp performance clothes. He wanted to grab hold of Kim and Jase again, cling on to that high of togetherness. Instead he trailed after them, his legs heavy and reluctant. He hated having to watch Jase try to fight the corps and lose, but afterwards Jase would need someone to tell him that things would be okay, that it would all work out.

As soon the the door had shut behind them, cutting off the arena noises, Geoff said, "Jase, have you thought any more about it?"

Jase nodded. "I'm not having the vocal snip. This is my voice, I've worked on it, and you can process it however you like but you're not making *me* into a squeaky little girl again, like—" He waved his hand.

Like Kit's voice, he meant, but Kit didn't hold it against him because Jase said stuff like that when he was wound up about the corps.

Geoff didn't look like he'd expected any other answer. "Then this is a termination of your contract with the corps. It's already authorized—it's final. You have twenty-four hours to agree to the surgery and accept a new contract, and after that there will be no more negotiation." Geoff held the screen out, and Jase took it, his face blank. "We don't actually need you to put your name to it—there's nothing you can do to stop it from happening. The twelve-week closedown period started fifteen minutes ago."

The moment the show ended. Kit's stomach felt hollow, and he held his breath, not wanting to disturb the silence.

Jase looked down at the screen, fingers running over it like he could actually change something that the corps wanted.

"You know what's unfair?" Jase's voice stayed low, and for once Kit couldn't read it. "What's so *fucking* unfair?"

Geoff frowned at the swear word, and Kit wished Jase wouldn't antagonize him like that.

"You could pull this shit any time. But I couldn't leave. I couldn't quit."

"You signed the contract," Geoff said harshly.

"Yeah. I signed the contract." Jase turned away suddenly, and Kit wondered if he was crying and really hoped he wasn't. Time passed, slow seconds, then Jase turned back and no, he was smiling. "I signed then, and I'm signing now."

Kit giggled. He couldn't help it, because his brain didn't really—couldn't yet—grasp what Jase meant, but Geoff's bug-eyed, unbelieving expression was impossibly funny.

"What?" Geoff asked after a moment.

"I'm leaving." Jase threw the hand screen on the floor, right at Geoff's feet. "I've countersigned it and I've sent a copy of that to my *new* manager. And you—you can kiss my arse and blow me, because there isn't a fucking thing you can do about it. You'd better make the most out of the last twelve fucking weeks you get of my life, because there won't be any more after that."

Then Kim started yelling and shaking Jase's shoulder, and Jase was laughing like he was insane, and Geoff had his hand to his chest, his face ashen. Kit moved to the side, out of the way, clinging tight to a costume rack as he watched everything happen, big but far away, like images on the show screens.

Kit had pictures of how he'd looked right before all the surgery started—an unremarkable eleven, wide-eyed and excited by the incredible new life. He had progression shots, step by step, as he'd transformed. Years afterwards he'd watched a documentary about butterflies, and after that he'd decided to think about it as pupating, even though it had hurt like heck sometimes and he'd cried himself to sleep. Maybe it hurt for butterflies, too—how would anyone know, as they dissolved and reformed inside their cocoons? When they came out and opened their wings, though, they were gorgeous, and that was all that mattered. No one remembered the caterpillars they'd once been.

It was hard to look at the old pictures and find himself in them. He didn't really want to—he didn't want to feel that he'd once been an unremarkable eleven, because now he looked outside time, infinitely exotic and untouchable by mortal hands. Someone had said that in a documentary about him.

He couldn't understand why Jase had always fought so hard against treatments, grudging every one the corps forced on him. Kit looked in the mirror and thought he was beautiful. The corps had taken things, yes, but they'd given him so much more.

There was only one thing the corps had wanted that Kit hadn't surrendered to them.

Kim preferred men, but when he occasionally slept with women it seemed to be easy for him, and he always sounded like he enjoyed it. Jase said it didn't matter whether or not someone had a cunt, but whether or not they *were* one, and it made Kit giggle every time, even though the swearing always scared him.

Kit liked women, and he didn't like men. Jase called him chronically straight. It puzzled Kit sometimes, when it was so easy for the other two. He'd gone on psych assessments, and a few treatment courses, but nothing had done any good. He'd watched his fifteenth birthday approach with dread; he hadn't even wanted to go to the party the corps had organized in case there'd be someone there they wanted him to be seen with. Soon after, Geoff had suggested more radical treatment. Kit hadn't really understood the process they wanted him to undergo, but his parents no longer needed to sign the consents with him, so he'd shrugged and agreed. Then he'd mentioned it to Jase, and Kit could still remember the look of stunned horror on his face.

"No way," Jase had said. "Over my dead body, kid."

"It's not a big thing," Kit had told him.

"You have to stop believing everything they tell you. All they're interested in is what's best for them, not for us." Jase had given him a hug, and Kit had curled into it, blissful, until Jase pushed him away and put his hands on Kit's shoulders, looking him anxiously in the face. "You won't do it, will you?"

He could never deny Jase anything. "Of course not. Not if you think I shouldn't."

"Promise me that you won't let them sneak you off and do it?"

"Okay, I promise."

Then Jase had gone away and researched it, and found the statistics, the chance of failure and what failure might mean. "Is this the ultimate fucking plan? We all end up brain dead and drooling?" he'd shouted at Geoff, waving the hand screen like he wanted to hit Geoff with it. "What then? You put chips in our motor cortexes and make us dance like puppets? Oh, yes, you'd fucking *love* that."

Geoff promised it was only a really tiny chance, but even Kit couldn't pretend that the thought of what might go wrong didn't make him sick. So he'd let Jase fight it out with management on his behalf, promising that they'd all three fake it really well, until finally the corps relented.

It was only then that Kit had let himself feel the relief. He hadn't really wanted to be that different, to change so much, and he couldn't imagine that it would ever seem okay to want men like that, that there wouldn't always be buried deep inside him the knowledge that the feelings weren't really his at all.

So Kit had bought Jase a piano, a old-fashioned one made of specially engineered vat-grown wood, flawless and polished like glass. An exquisite thing full of warm, living music that Jase would never have bought for himself because he was so careful with money. He'd had it delivered as a surprise, and when it was installed in Jase's flat, Jase had sat down and played it for an hour straight, improvising, completely absorbed by the music, while Kit leaned on the side of the piano and just watched him, his hands and his strong face, the faintest hint of a five-o'clock shadow starting to show on his jaw. It had been the best hour of Kit's life.

Finally, Jase had closed the piano lid and looked up, and Kit had been startled to see tears in his eyes. He'd worried for a moment that he'd done something wrong, but then Jase had smiled and said, "It's absolutely beautiful, Kit. Amazing. Thank you."

Then he'd spoiled it a bit by telling Kit all over again how important it was that Kit saved his money, "because the corps won't look after us forever, kid." Kit hadn't minded, though. Jase only said things like that because underneath his tempers and his abrasiveness, he truly cared.

And at the time, Kit had wanted to show, really show, how grateful he was for Jase's intervention. Now Kit wished that Jase hadn't done it.

It was late, because Kit had had to wait until everyone had gone to bed, and their floor of the hotel had been buzzing with all kinds of representatives from the corps, and bodyguards making sure that the awful news didn't escape prematurely. One of the corps's psychologists had come to check on Kit, and he'd told her that he was fine, that he was sure Jase would come to his senses and everything would be okay in the morning. That had seemed to please her, or at least she'd gone away and left him to sit on his bed, alone, until the last noise outside his room died away.

After that he'd waited for almost another hour, because he couldn't risk being interrupted. And because he was scared.

Now Kit stood outside Jase's hotel room and tried to stop himself from shivering. He tried for five minutes, and then when he realized it wasn't going to happen, he put his hand on the door and took deep breaths until at least it wasn't shaking so much that he couldn't scan the passcard. Everything was way too clear, too real. He needed the alcohol and music and drugs and pretty, awestruck girls around him so he could slip into his fantasy world. He should have taken something, at least, but he was pretty sure that Jase would ask him if he had, and Kit was hopeless when it came to lying to Jase.

The room was dark, which was a relief because the plan hadn't included what he was going to do if there was someone in there with Jase. There often was, and it was only sometimes Kim. Kit didn't really mind what Jase did, or who he did it with, but it still disturbed him when he caught Jase actually with someone else, an outsider, most especially because it didn't bother Jase at all.

The air in the room tasted cool and sterile. Nothing like the sweaty exuberance of the concert, although Kit's heart was beating almost as fast as it had then. This wasn't flying, though. This was falling, and he couldn't see a way to stop it, just waiting to hit the ground and smash into pieces.

Kit stripped off, and for once he didn't feel beautiful and sexy. He knew Jase didn't like the corps's perfectly tuned bodies, that he made fun of some of the other groups. Never of Kit or Kim, though, never where they could hear, or someone else could hear and tell them.

But sometimes Jase still climbed into Kit's bed in the middle of the night, and that had to mean something, right? Maybe, deep down...

"Kim?" Jase murmured sleepily when Kit climbed in beside him and moved determinedly close, putting his arm around him. The sheets were expensively smooth and soft, and chilly to Kit's skin everywhere that Jase wasn't.

"It's me, Kit." The words felt weird in his mouth. But he loved Jase so much. He could love him like this, too.

"Kit." Jase rolled over, then sat up suddenly. Kit felt Jase's stomach muscles tense under his hand. "What are you doing in here? The corps will play hell if they catch you with me."

"I came—" He'd had a speech prepared and he couldn't remember it. It felt like the early interviews, tongue-tied and terrified with the consequences of forgetting the carefully coached words. "Stay with the group, Jase. Please. Stay with me. Us. Me and Kim. They'll let you come back, I know they will. We'll both talk to them, and—"

"Lights, low," Jase said.

"Lights, out," Kit said quickly, before he caught more than a glimpse of Jase's bewildered expression.

Kit moved forwards and mouthed over Jase's shoulder, tasting shower lotion and skin. "Please, Jase. I want you to stay."

"You don't want this," Jase said gently. "You don't want me." When he sounded like that, Jase seemed so old, far older than the six years that actually separated them.

"I do. I want it." The wrongness hurt like a surgery knife. "I need you."

Jase reached down and put his hand between Kit's legs, palm right over Kit's limp cock, and Kit couldn't, couldn't stop himself flinching away.

"I'm sorry," Kit said, and moved back, letting Jase touch. "Let me try."

Jase pulled his hand away, and Kit thought he might have wiped it against his thigh. "Kit...ah, Kit, this has got nothing to do with you. Besides, you're really not my type."

He sounded amused, almost, and Kit prayed he was putting it on. It couldn't be funny to Jase that he was destroying everything they all had, burning everything down, not even to get back at the corps.

"We know about your girlfriend," Kit said. "Me and Kit do. And we haven't told Geoff—we haven't told anyone. You can have her, you can have a real relationship, I promise we can find a way to make it work, just, please—"

Jase put his finger gently against Kit's lips. "It's not about Ann, either. Or the group—not even the music, not really. I have to take this chance to get away. I have to. It's the only one I'll get. They won't let me go again until it's too late, not now." He wrapped his arm around Kit's shoulders, holding him close, breathing ticklish air onto Kit's neck that made him shiver even more. Kit closed his eyes. "I'm sorry, too. I'll miss you so much, both of you. But they can recast me. Maybe T-boy will finally get his chance. I'm not the big 343 name—that's you. You're the star, no? You'll be okay, Kit. Everything will work out for the best."

Going on with a replacement almost seemed worse than not going on at all. Trying to think of life without 343 brought nothing, just empty blackness, while Kit could just about imagine the awfulness of being trapped inside a rebuilt 343, endlessly missing someone he'd believed in with all his heart.

"Please don't leave," Kit whispered hopelessly. "Don't leave me. I don't want T-boy. You're the only one I can trust."

There was a long silence, then Jase released him.

"I'm going to find another room," Jase said. He wasn't angry, and maybe that was something, but he sounded sad and a little pitying, and that cut worse than it ever had when he'd lost his temper and shouted.

Kit didn't open his eyes until the door had closed, leaving him so, so alone in the middle of the huge bed.

For Your Entertainment

Chapter One

I suppose this is almost like a retrospective Investigation In Progress. I'll start at the beginning, chronologically, and fill in background information in the side notes where they seem relevant.

It began as just another Monday morning meeting. A recap of last week, an overview of the state of the case—or cases—and assignments for the coming week if they'd changed. If the plans last any longer than Tuesday it's a rarity, but it's still a good idea. We're a team, and the meetings make a regular start to the week. The only problem is that they often come right after the Para has been summoned by the section head, which means we all tread carefully until we can work out what kind of mood he's in.

If anyone messes up and upsets him, it's usually one of the pool investigators or juniors who hasn't worked for him before. You'd think they'd know to be careful around a senior para-investigator, but of course there has to be a reason they haven't managed to find themselves a permanent posting yet.

Not that Senior Para Toreth's bad to work for. Far from it. If he tears a strip off someone, he might not be tactful but he usually has a good reason. He doesn't humiliate people in public purely because he gets a kick from it. Sometimes I look around the General Criminal section and I thank my lucky stars I ended up in the team I did. It's pretty much a lottery at the new graduate cattle markets, although Sara picked me out early on so I should probably be thanking her or the Para.

Anyway, I digress. Because the job is so fluid, the Para doesn't waste too much time on the assignments. That Monday he got to me last. The room was crowded because it had been a busy couple of weeks for the team, with a large and active case, and a lot of pool investigators tied up in it. Not that anyone complained—at that time, not even a year after the Investigation and Interrogation Division had been wrecked by an Administration-wide unrest, we were all happy to be busy. As the Para had gone through the current case assignments I'd begun to wonder why I hadn't been mentioned. The previous week I'd been liaising with the Department of External Security, but the Para had given that to Nagra, his then-junior para, almost at the beginning of the meeting. I couldn't see what was left for me, which left me with a sinking feeling: a secondment or an unexpected training course, rather than anything more sinister, but even so.

"Investigator Barret-Connor," the Para said finally, and I guessed from his amused expression that I must've looked nervous. "You're in luck. Tillotson passed me this when I saw him. It's just for you."

I looked down at my screen as he transferred the IIP. Investigators, especially senior investigators, do get to run their own cases, and I'd been a senior for five years at that point. But it wasn't often that I'd been given a fresh case without either the Para or his junior para-investigator involved at all. To have something completely new thrown at me without any preamble was a little disconcerting. I glanced at the case summary while everyone waited. The Para was tapping his finger silently on the edge of the desk, so I didn't take long.

"Death threats against a singer?"

The Para nodded, looking sour. "Justice Department case, or it ought to be. Someone at the corporation pulled strings and Tillotson dumped it on me. Odds are it's all a marketing setup anyway and they just want the I&I name to help sell the story. I'm not wasting my time doing PR work for corporates. Sara's set up the initial interview already, for later this morning. Get over there, B-C, sort it out for me quick and shut it down, then get back where I need you, doing real cases."

There's a compliment in there, if you look at it the right way. Still, I remember feeling a little disappointed that I'd been thrown a solo case purely because it looked like such a lame duck.

A case can take a convoluted route to ending up at the Investigation and Interrogation Division. An initial investigation might have been carried out by Justice, or another part of Int-Sec, who then deemed the case to fall inside our remit (or, sometimes, desperately didn't want it to fall inside their own). Technically, we deal with criminal activity that is of political significance to the European Administration. But what does that cover?

Sometime it's quite obvious, or appears to be—a resister bombing is an overtly politically criminal act, and of course we'd be called in immediately. What if it turns out that the bomb was actually planted by corporate saboteurs employed by one corporation to attack another corporation? Well, odds are that we'd keep the case, because when corporate sabbing becomes that frisky, it's a de facto threat to the political stability of the Administration, whether or not that was its intent.

Illegal pharma, illicit provision of otherwise legal services such as gambling, loans, or prostitution, counterfeiting of various types—these can all be a source of funding for resisters. Moving beyond clear political motivation, it's often a question of scale. A local gang of troublemakers extorting money from small service providers or selling illegal pharmaceuticals would probably be a Justice matter. The same activities carried out by a large criminal organization stretching across Europe and even beyond would belong to I&I, and probably to General Criminal, at that. (How a crime that reached I&I is assigned to a section is an essay in colorful division politics in itself.)

Fraud carried out against the Administration, or within Administration departments, tends to come directly to I&I. Individual criminal acts like murder or kidnapping might be investigated by I&I when the victims are important enough to shake up the Administration, or corporations, or the delicate balance between them. If a crime poses a viable threat to the Administration's ability to provide good government and security to the citizens of Europe, then it will probably end up with us. It can be an eclectic mix, and that's one of the reasons why working at I&I is so interesting.

Now, all that said, if you'd stopped me on my way out of that case conference and asked me to explain the political importance of probably spurious threats made against an entertainment sector employee, I might have struggled. But that's the other part of the equation. I&I isn't just about political significance, it's *of* political significance. If it weren't we wouldn't have been targeted so hard in the revolt. Our name carries weight; our presence in a case means something. That can be both useful, and a colossal irritation.

Don't get me wrong, though, the fact that the Para trusted me with the case was still a good thing. Not all senior paras are so generous, and a solid record as a case lead is a necessary part of being a senior investigator; it's an absolute prerequisite if you're hoping to rise to the top grades. That made me happy enough, not that I'd spoken to him about my career ambitions. None of us have ever asked the Para about promotion—he submits names when he's ready and he usually gets what he wants. We do as well as, or better than, any other team in General Criminal.

I read the case file thoroughly before I left, which meant I was cutting it fine for the interview. I was on my way out of the building when Sara caught up with me in the corridor. She hadn't been at the meeting that morning—she's often busy dealing with mysterious admin necessities—but of course that didn't mean she'd missed anything that had gone on there.

"Off to see 343?" she asked.

343—or "three for three"—was the trio group in the case. You might remember them. They were huge at the time, but they're long gone, now, of course, except for the occasional name-check on some ghoulish celebrity feature. "That's right."

189

She grinned up at me. "Lucky you."

"Oh?"

"Of course. They're all three cuter than a sack of kittens. Don't you think so? No, I suppose not," she added without a pause. "Trust me, they are."

"I'm afraid I have no idea *who* they are, never mind how cute they are." Actually, I did vaguely know their music, but all I could remember was not thinking much of it. That in itself made me feel old—comes to us all, I suppose.

She rolled her eyes, still grinning. "Don't give me that crap. You're the same age as me, B-C, you know."

Sometimes the mind reading is disconcerting. She does it most often with the Para—the way she *understands* him can be quite creepy—but all the rest of us get it from time to time. I looked at my watch. "Did you want something?"

"Just to ask if you could get their autographs. Not for me, for Fee. My sister. Steffanie, with two *f*s. She thinks they're God's gift—especially Kit. Mind you, if they've got time, a set for me wouldn't hurt."

"I'll do my best."

"Thanks! See if you can get them to make mine something generic I can sell easily."

Even when she's being mercenary, Sara somehow manages to sound sweet. I like her. I've always had a feeling that we'd get along well personally, as well as professionally. In a relationship, I mean. Pity, in a way, that we're neither of us the other's type.

My appointment was at the headquarters of the corporation that managed the singer targeted by the threats. It was housed in part of an achingly modern building which had taken the clean, pale minimalist look to the point where there were no chairs in reception. Even the receptionists were perched on elegant little half-stools, and very annoyed about it they looked. Or maybe their manner, a thin whisker from outright rudeness, was affected too. Most people manage to show a little respect for an I&I uniform.

I know that many people think I'm dull, or at the least a little old for my age, as it were. By I&I standards, I am. There's a lot of hard playing there that goes along with the hard work and the hard people. It's not my scene. But one of the better things about the place is that in order to get singled out for comment you have to be outrageously peculiar. So I go on my own way and the most I've acquired is a reputation for being mildly staid.

I was probably showing my premature middle age that day, but few of the faces on the screens around the reception area were familiar. The screens were the only things to look at, though, so I watched. Most of them were showing clips of performances. There seemed to be a lot of different faces, belonging mostly to groups with the occasional solo and duos, so the corps was obviously doing well.

I'm not calling it "the corps" to protect the names of the not-so-innocent. The actual name of the corporation was "the corps." Spelled exactly like that, in lowercase. It was, if you like, a clever play on the abbreviation for corporation and the idea of a corps as a group of performers. That would have been fine, except that everyone pronounced it with a silent s but an audible p, which grated like hell. I like language, and it pains me to hear it being abused like that. "343" was another naming abomination, although at least it made some kind of sense. It's an example of the kind of weak pun favored as musical group names since forever.

I wandered around the room from screen to screen, trying to match faces to the pictures I'd seen in the case file. I finally found them on a screen in a corner, although I had no idea if prominence of display reflected their worth to the corporation. The trio were at a live concert, looking sweaty and slightly dazed as an unfeasibly large crowd of mostly teenaged girls gave it their all in the enormous auditorium somewhere in Europe.

I waved my hand over the sensor and the system fed the sound into my comm earpiece. I did recognize the song, or I thought I did. After about thirty seconds I turned it off again, and stood watching the three boys dancing until I heard my name called.

Some corporates are offensively confident. They go out of their way to remind us that they have important friends who can make our lives difficult. Sometimes that's true. At the same time it apparently surprises them that corporations aren't popular at I&I.

Geoffrey Cheung, however, had the tense, harassed manner so common to lower-middle corporates in places where advancement is by cutthroat competition. It's an awareness that any slipup could mean an end to dreams of promotion. Layered on top of that I could see a thick coating of stress and lack of sleep. His security file said he was thirty-one, but he looked ten years older, with a sprinkling of gray threading his black hair at his temples.

While we talked, he fiddled with the top right-hand drawer of his desk, sliding it open and closed a few centimeters. Once he lost his grip on the edge and it slid further back. I spotted at least four different medicinal-looking tablet containers before he pushed it hastily closed again.

"And you have no clue about the sender?" I asked when we'd gone once through the sequence of events.

"We could only trace them to a general area—the central Benelux region, which is rather close for comfort. All signed with the same letter, which is the other way we can link them. Security says there's an escalating threat pattern with a sharp peak."

"This message, the last one, mentions a possible breakup." There was no official note about that in the corporate files I'd seen.

"Not a possible one, no." He pinched the bridge of his nose wearily. "The trio has dissolved." Even getting the words out made him look like he had a major case of heartburn.

"When?"

"Jase's contract has already terminated. It's not common knowledge. There are plenty of rumors, but we're hoping to keep things officially denied for now. There's an upcoming awards ceremony that they'll sing at, and then the announcement will be made the day afterwards."

"What happens to them then?"

"Kit and Kim are still under contract and we're discussing their future."

"And Jase?"

He frowned. "I don't see what this has to do with I&I."

"Mr. Cheung, the threat was directed towards him. And you've just given me a major complicating factor. This should've been included in your request for I&I involvement."

"I know. I'm sorry." His right hand strayed back to the drawer, then he steepled his fingers in front of him. "The files were prepared rather hastily by the security division and I, ah, didn't have time to review them."

There, I felt fairly sure, he'd lied, and interestingly, it was pretty readable as such. It gave me a benchmark for the other things he'd told me.

"Whose idea was the breakup?" I asked.

His expression soured. "Jase's."

"And you're still hoping he'll change his mind?"

"Of course we are. The trio is one of our—" He expression froze. "That is . . . we have no interest in his staying unless he's committed to the group and the corps." He looked at me hopefully.

I decided to try honesty. "Mr. Cheung, from a statistical point of view, the likelihood of this threat being serious enough to merit I&I resources is vanishingly small. You have no evidence of a corporate vendetta or active sabotage. We have records of dozens of threats to kill made against artists, and in the majority of cases the motive behind them was—"

"Publicity," he interrupted. "Yes. I know that. And I know that you've probably heard rumors of the corps being involved in such stunts in the past. But not in this case. This is nothing to do with publicity and *certainly* isn't pressure directed by us against Jase. I give you my word."

I could imagine the Para's derisive laughter when he read *that* in the IIP. This seemed like a good moment for the speech I'd roughed out in the taxi over.

"Making false reports to I&I, fabricating evidence—these are criminal offenses, Mr. Cheung. I can give you a detailed summary of the charges you, personally, would risk if you've lied to me. And the penalties you, personally, would face if convicted. Something else I'm sure you know is the track record of corporations in selecting scapegoats when ploys like this blow up in their faces. If you decide there's been, shall we say, an error of judgment in calling in I&I, then now would be a very good time to let me know, and we can go our separate ways."

He'd gone progressively stiller and more sickly looking while I talked. But when I finished, he shook his head.

"The trio is my responsibility," he said. "And I have no reason to think the messages aren't real. So, yes. I want you to carry on."

Either the threats genuinely worried him, or he was a much better actor than my previous assessment suggested. Of course, his lack of knowledge of a setup meant little. If I were a senior corporate wanting to use I&I as a tool in a tacky marketing game, I'd put someone like Geoffrey Cheung between me and the investigation, too.

"Very well. I'll have the communication specialists look at the notes. And I'll need to speak to, um, Jase, Kim, and Kit." Their lack of second names made referring to them politely rather difficult.

That idea seemed genuinely to baffle him. "Why?"

"Because they might know something about the identity of the message sender."

That seemed to parse just as badly. "They don't know anything. They're product, Investigator. They have no idea about the business. We shield them from involvement. All they have to do is perform."

"Even so, I have to speak to them. It's procedure."

For a moment, I thought he was about to say no. Then he shrugged. "I'll arrange a corps lawyer to take you to the flat."

Which would cut to zero any chance of hearing anything interesting from them. "I'd prefer to speak to them alone."

"That isn't our policy," he said with a finality that implied he'd had the instructions direct from the Administration Council themselves.

"If you aren't willing to offer cooperation, then I&I will have to decline involvement in the case." I admit I sometimes get a kick out of flexing my lead-investigator muscles, and that was definitely one of those times. "As there's absolutely no political angle, we have ample justification. Justice might be a better place to look to for help."

"No! Investigator, we are taking this very seriously. Very." He sighed. "I'll get someone to drive you over there right away. To the flat where we're k—where Kit and Kim are staying. Seeing Jase might take a little longer to set up."

"He's at a secure location?"

Cheung grimaced. "Something like that." He was fingering the drawer again. "I'll contact him, and call you as soon as a meeting's arranged." He looked up. "Thank you for agreeing to look into this—I promise you, I appreciate it."

I didn't doubt that he did. Whether he'd appreciate the actual investigation or the possible consequences remained to be seen.

I felt old all over again when I saw Kit on the flat security screen. The case file had said he was eighteen, but he looked at least a couple of years younger, with huge green eyes and a face that, close up, had an ethereal quality—elfish or maybe alien—that made him pretty rather than handsome. He was more like some-one's cartoon idealization of a teen-market singer than anything real. He did look genuinely nervous and, standing out as the single flaw in the disconcerting per-fection of his pale face, he had a dry-looking rash at the side of his mouth that must be a nuisance to brush out when he was on screen.

"I'm Senior Investigator Ainsley Barret-Connor," I said, "from the Investiga-tion and Interrogation Division."

He nodded. "Geoff told us you were coming. Just give me a minute to figure the door out." His voice was as light as I'd expected from listening to the music.

When he opened the door there were no guards with him; I'd half expected there might be, given the present threat. Of course, the whole expensive residential complex was sealed tighter than the I&I detention level, but a lot of high-level corporates like to keep guards around. It's a status symbol. Half the time they drop the guards' backgrounds into the conversation, too—ex-Service, ex-Justice. Ex-I&I sometimes, and they usually look embarrassed to see an I&I uniform. They shouldn't, with the amount they can make compared to me.

I'd been prepared to grit my teeth and be nice whatever happened, but on first impression, I liked Kit. I've been accused of having a protective streak, and he did look like someone's kid brother. Apart from his childish face, he had a thin build that was emphasized by the baggy clothes he wore. I wondered how much it had cost him to get that picked-up-my-clothes-from-a-secondhand-shop look.

I could hear music from inside the flat.

Kit nodded down the vast, bare hallway. "Kim's working on something. Do you want to...or I was just about to make coffee." He looked at me anxiously, pushing his tumble of thick dark hair out of his eyes. "If you want coffee? Other-wise there's tea. Or other things, in the fridge."

"Coffee will be fine, thank you."

I followed him into the kitchen.

It took Kit a while to find everything in the echoing kitchen. The flat was huge, and oddly bare. The furniture didn't fill it, and the place was ultra-modern, the

walls all indefinable shades away from white, and the fittings in intricately seg-
mented wood. The Para sometimes comments on how buildings smell, and I've
heard him say you can smell money. That place smelled of almost nothing, expensively empty and unlived-in—a blank canvas with a single rich line of coffee
painted across it.

I'd wondered if he'd offer me something to eat, too, and what I'd do if he did.
I'd missed lunch and not had time to pick anything up on the way. Normally it's
frowned upon to accept meals from interviewees, but I was getting hungry. As it
was, he didn't mention food.

I carried the coffee through—Kit simply walked off, as though it hadn't even
occurred to him to pick up the tray when there was someone else to do it for him.

As we went into what I guessed was the living room, the music stopped. In
the far corner, another boy, presumably Kim, was seated at a representational keyboard in front of a large screen. He smiled and beckoned us over.

The area surrounding the keyboard was the most lived-in part of the flat I'd
seen up to then. As I moved around the keyboard desk I almost stepped on a thick
pile of paper, covered in handwritten musical notation done in different colored
pens. There were half-empty glasses of carbonated drinks gone flat lined up along
behind the keyboard, and a few expensive-looking silvered cartons of delivered
food.

Kim brought up a new page on the screen. I admit I know nothing about music.
All I can tell you is that there are horizontal lines and lots of dots on sticks. Eventually he found what he wanted and started playing. Kit sang along with him.

The flat, even if they'd been moved there as an emergency, had an amazing
sound system. To be honest, it seemed a shame to waste it on their music. It
sounded pretty much the same as the 343 songs I remembered, only with one less
voice. Dull, formulaic, something I wouldn't give house room to. But what did I
know about the music industry? Clearly not much, given that the corps was running a stable full of very lucrative horses and had the clout to snap their fingers
and call up an investigator from I&I.

In lieu of listening to the music, I looked at the musicians. On the screen at
the corps, I'd had trouble telling one of the pair from the other; they'd looked almost like twins. In the flesh, the differences were far more obvious—Kim reminded me of Sara, with a mix of Western European and East Asian genes in his
background—but they were still enough alike that I could've believed someone if
they'd told me they were cousins. According to their security files they weren't
even distantly related. Kim didn't have quite as striking a face as Kit, although
he had an odd combination of sharp-boned beauty and adolescent softness. I
caught myself staring at him, trying to spot any flaw in his honey-and-cream skin.

I drank my coffee and gave them ten minutes of playing before I started cough-
ing politely. Kim picked up the hint at once—Kit, who had been singing with a

closed-eyed intensity, opened his brilliant green eyes wide when the music stopped.

"It's about the anonymous notes, isn't it?" Kim asked.

"Yes."

"I suppose we'd better sit down."

He led the way over to an area laid out with seating in impractical pastel colors. Kit fussed around for a bit asking if the heat was okay, and whether I wanted anything else, until I told him we'd better start the interview. Kim seemed more reserved, a listener and a watcher. He had already coiled himself up on a sofa, hugging a cushion to his chest. I took one of the too-soft chairs, and Kit sprawled on the floor in front of Kim, lying on a thick cream rug, his elbows propped on a long, pastel-pink bolster. It's the only interview I've ever conducted like that.

Kit started talking without any prompting.

"The first one turned up a few weeks ago, or at least that's what Geoff said. He's our direct manager—I guess you met him?" His perfectly delineated eyebrows quirked interrogatively until I nodded. "We didn't get to see it, though. All our messages are screened. Friends and family as well as fans." Kit sounded quite matter-of-fact about the rule. "Then there were a couple more quite quickly, and then nothing for a while, until last week there was the other. The nasty one. That's when we heard about it."

As Kit spoke, Kim nodded agreement every few seconds. When Kit finished, Kim took up the conversation almost without a pause.

"They moved us to this new flat. We thought corps security would handle everything, but they said they were calling someone in from outside."

Kit looked me up and down. "I've never met a para-investigator before."

I had told him my name and rank when I arrived, but it's surprising how many people make that mistake. I suppose we all wear black, and that's the public image of the paras. "I'm afraid you're not meeting one now," I said. "I'm a plain investigator."

"Oh, right," Kit said.

Kim shook his head. "I told you that, Kit. Investigator Barret-Connor. That's who Geoff said was coming."

Kit smiled sheepishly. "I remember, sorry."

I almost reminded Kim about the "Senior" he'd left off, but I stuck to the interview. "What do you think about the notes? Do either you have any idea who's behind it?"

Kit shrugged. "No idea. I mean, who the heck would want to kill any of us?"

"There's no one who might have a grudge?"

"No," Kit said.

He obviously hadn't thought it over. "What about publicity?" I asked.

He must have been expecting the question, because he answered even more quickly. "No, the corps wouldn't do that."

"What about Jase himself?"

"Jase?" Kim laughed. "God, no. Jase is...he's a strange guy sometimes, you know, but death threats against himself? No way."

Kit nodded. "There's no point, is there? I mean, I guess if the corps had threatened to dump him or something, yeah, but..."

"But he's the one who wanted to go." Kim shrugged. "He doesn't care anymore."

Kit straightened up on his elbows. "Unless. Unless the corps—"

"Mm-mh," Kim said warningly, and Kit shut up.

"Unless the corps?" I prompted.

Kit was staring at the rug, now. "Nothing."

"Unless the corps wanted to scare him into coming back?"

"No. I didn't mean that." Kit looked appealingly up at Kim. "It wouldn't work, would it?"

"With Jase?" Kim smiled. "Never. Not a chance. If he thought that was the reason he'd just be, you know, more likely to do exactly the opposite. He's like that." The smile faded and he looked at me narrowly. "You don't think *we* did it, do you?"

I just raised my eyebrows slightly and waited. One of the Para's tricks.

"We didn't. Like I said, it'll just make Jase more determined to go, if he thinks the corps or *anyone* is threatening him. If we wanted to try to change his mind, we'd talk to him, we wouldn't play stupid games like this."

"So what about fans?"

Kim settled back, obviously yielding the floor.

"Could be." Kit rubbed at the side of his mouth for a couple of seconds before he snatched his hand away, as though he'd remembered being told off for worrying the rash. He looked down at the cushion and rubbed that instead. "There are plenty of nutters out there, and you get used to that really quickly. Some of them don't even think we're real—it's because of all the CGI performers around. I've had people ask for a *copy* of me. Which is pretty freaky. And there's a lot of—" He looked up. "Sex messages. Most of it's harmless stuff. Teens wanting to marry us and-or sleep with us. Or their mums, of course."

Kim chuckled. "Yeah, lots of those. Even screened, there's the odd one that's, you know, weird. Creeps us out a bit. But mostly we read them to each other and laugh."

That led almost naturally to one of the questions I'd wanted to ask. "Is there any kind of personal relationship between Jase and either of you?"

Kit looked puzzled. "You mean, like, are we friends?"

Before I could clarify what I meant, Kim burst out laughing. "No, idiot, he means *friends*."

Kit's expression cleared. "Oh! *Friends*. I like him, of course, but if you mean were we sleeping together, then no...not really. I don't do that. Boys, I mean."

I must have looked surprised, because Kit smiled. "I guess you've seen us on stage, right?"

I thought of the recordings of 343 playing in the corps reception area. "You seemed rather friendly."

"I promise you, I'm straight."

Kim nodded. "Look, it's a demographics thing, you know?" His voice took on a slightly harder, more practical edge, and he suddenly sounded much older. "We were—are—pitched as a primarily teen concept. Girls like to see boys flirting with each other on stage. Bit of hammed-up kissing, you know, all that sort of thing. Then there's the more subtle stuff like sitting close in interviews, holding hands for a couple of seconds at awards ceremonies. Switching around who's touching who. It turns them on, so they buy more music, they watch the interviews, they buy the books to see if they can find out any more."

"It's all in our contracts," Kit added. "We all signed up for it. If you want to get ahead in this business, you have to learn to do what you're told. Okay, it isn't really me, but I got used to it."

I could hear an echo of my father's voice in my head. *No tune, the words don't make sense. They seem to think it's enough to have pretty boys wiggling their hips.* Looked like they were right. "And what about Jase? How did he feel about it?"

Kim stifled a laugh and poked Kit's shoulder with his toe. "Yeah, Kit. How did he feel about it?"

For the first time, Kit looked uncomfortable. "Like Kim said, he can be a bit weird. He crawls in bed with me in the middle of the night, sometimes. I guess I should kick him out, but—" He buried his face in the bolster for a moment. "I don't want to hurt his feelings. And he's usually high. On totally legal stuff," he added quickly. "And, uh..."

Kim hadn't stopped smirking. "And?" I asked.

"I might've let him suck me off a few times. Like, when there were girls around and we were all high. When things were kind of mixed up. As long as there's a girl up top with you, does it matter who's down there? I mean, I don't even know it's him until later, not most times." Kit lifted his head. "And I never do it back to him."

From the sofa, Kim was still watching him, now smiling with an almost fond expression. I got the impression this wasn't a new set of justifications.

Now Kit was flushing slightly. "Okay, maybe it sounds weird to you, Investigator, but it doesn't mean anything. Brand image, yeah? The girls always talk afterwards and the rumors are all over everywhere a few days later. Management loves basically unsourceable stuff like that. It's just PR."

I admired the logic. At least the Para would enjoy reading the IIP for this, whatever he felt about wasting I&I time on corporate string-pulling.

"Kim?" I asked.

He got the question at once. "Me and Jase? Yeah. Well, you know. Nothing that ever meant anything—not the sex. I like the guy, but we were just..."

"So how would you describe your relationship?"

"Occasional, and mostly when there were no fans around." I'm not sure what my expression said at that point, but whatever it was made him smile. "You must think we're all sex-obsessed. But, you know, I'm—" he frowned briefly. "Twenty-one. And we're a top-selling trio. What would *you* do?"

I had to smile. "Take advantage, I expect."

"Right. There's just so many girls—or guys, if that's what you like—that you get used to sex on demand. But they're fans. You've still got to perform, you know? Keep the right image." He rested his feet on Kit's back and smiled. "I mean, Kit *likes* putting on a show. Don't you?"

Kit smiled too, although he looked suddenly tired. "Yeah, always."

"He sticks to the fans. But me and Jase...sometimes you just get sick of it and all you want is the sex, without worrying about how you're representing the brand. Just stress relief. That leaves paying for it—which sends management round the bend because of the PR—or each other."

There was a pause. This didn't seem like a fruitful line of questioning, and I wasn't sure what to try next.

"Have you got the messages?" Kim asked suddenly.

"They're in the case file, yes."

"Can we see them? The corps wouldn't let us."

I thought it over. There was always a chance that they'd spot something in them that the corporation security people hadn't seen. There was no need to check with the Para, because I knew what he'd say: it's not our job to mollycoddle fucking corporate brats. Or something like that, more or less politely depending on who was there to hear him.

"Of course."

I separated the text out from the rest of the file and handed over the screen to Kim. Kit jumped up off the floor and crowded onto the sofa with him. They certainly sat a lot closer together than I would with someone with whom I had a purely professional relationship. Close enough that if I'd tried it with Sara they would've had to stretcher me out of I&I afterwards.

Kit read the messages out loud, frowning slightly. Reading did look to be something of a strain for him.

"'I know Kit wants me with him. He took my number and I saw how he looked at me. Why did you make him stop replying to my messages? Please don't make him stay away from me. C.'"

Kim looked up quizzically. "Is that it? We get stuff like that all the time. People who think they know us and the evil PR guys at the corps are keeping us locked up so we can't get to them. You'd never believe how many girls have tried to tell Geoff that Kit's their childhood sweetheart. Or their long-lost brother."

"There is more," I said to Kit.

"Okay, second one. 'Did you tell Kit about the first message? Of course you didn't. It doesn't matter. I know we belong together and one day you'll have to accept it too. You think he's a baby and you need to protect him, and it's not true. He can do anything he wants to. C.' Third one. 'You can't keep him locked up forever. Why won't you let him call me? I know all about him. I know where he lives, what he eats, what he wears, when he sleeps. He's mine and no one can keep me away from him. C.' Oh, okay." He looked at Kim. "That's a bit creepier."

Kit hesitated, and Kim took over for the last note. "'You can't let them break up. If he won't keep them together, I'll make sure Jase pays. I'll stop him from leaving, for good. Don't you believe me? Here's proof: a, g, one, six—'"

Kit looked up. "That's our security code! For the old place!" His voice was a breathless squeak.

"Signed the same. C." Kim was still staring at the screen. He mouthed something that looked like "fuck."

"That's why they moved you here," I said, wanting to calm them.

"But if they had the code for there, they could get the code for here, too," Kit said.

"Yeah," Kim said. "Otherwise why give away that they knew it? And there's security here, but this sounds, you know, seriously nasty. They must've been pretty sure they could get to us some other way."

"I'm sure the corps is doing everything they can," I said. "After all, you're valuable employees."

"Yeah." Kim scrubbed his hand through his hair. "We *were*. Before Jase got on his artistic high horse. *Fuck*."

"Kim!" Kit protested.

"Yeah, well, we won't have to worry about our language for long, if either the corps doesn't put us back on stage or some maniac offs me and Jase because they want you to be their wide-eyed little love puppy." He threw the screen down on the sofa. "It's always the girls, you know. Deranged *bitch*. When they find her I'll fucking—"

He cut off as Kit clutched his arm.

"*Kim*." Kit's voice dropped to a whisper. "You *know* they listen. *Please*."

A monitored room. Perhaps I should've guessed, but I hadn't even thought of it. That put a whole new slant on everything they'd told me, and I cursed myself for letting the corps set up the interview—a penalty of trying to rush the case along.

"Now that you've seen the messages," I asked, although the question felt pointless now, "do you have any more idea of who might be behind them?"

Kim shook his head. "And believe me, I'd tell you if I did. Creepy shit like—all *right*, Kit," he snapped, and Kit subsided midprotest. "Creepy stuff like this. I want whoever's doing it found."

"It's . . . horrible," Kit said. He shivered, and Kim put his arm around his shoulders and pulled him closer—it looked quite genuine, almost unconscious. "I'm glad they don't let us see that kind of thing. I don't want to know about it."

"I wish I'd known," Kim said. He scanned the room. "She's right about one thing—they treat us like kids."

I decided to wrap it up. If I wanted to talk to them again, I'd arrange somewhere more private.

"What happens to you if Jase doesn't come back to the group?" I asked as a final question.

"The corps'll look after us," Kit said. He sounded utterly confident. "Of course, it would be better if Jase came back, but we'll get recast with another third, or we go on as a duo. We've already got music we can use."

I looked at Kim, who raised his eyebrows slightly and said nothing.

Before I left, I remembered the autographs. The importance of keeping on Sara's good side isn't something I'm ever going to forget.

I'd set my comm for emergencies only while I was interviewing Kit and Kim. Outside the heavily guarded perimeter of the residential complex, I checked for messages and found two. One set up a time and place for an interview with Jase the next day—no corporate escort offered this time—and a second was from the systems analysis section about the suspect messages.

The delayed meeting was awkward, as it meant another day on the IIP. However short an investigation the Para wanted, I could hardly close it down without speaking to the target of the threat. I wondered if Cheung was delaying deliberately to make our involvement more convincing.

In better news, the message analysis was complete—from the tone of the brief report, I suspected the simplicity of the case had disappointed.

Syntactical analysis suggested that the messages were from a single sender, although their brevity put a rather loose confidence on the result. More solidly, the first three had traced relatively easily to a single sender, a fifteen-year-old girl in Roosendaal called Christina Hauptman. The fourth came from a public comm in the same town.

I sent a message to the nearest I&I branch to pick her up, and went back to I&I to file my IIPs and follow my new lead.

As far as their security files went, there was absolutely nothing remarkable about Christina, her family, or her friends. There were no personal or professional ties to any of the players, no unexplained sums of money appearing in any likely bank accounts. Her parents had noncorporate-graded jobs in the catering industry. By the time I'd finished going through the files I had half a mind to call I&I Antwerp and cancel the pickup.

When Christina finally appeared on my screen, against the backdrop of a gray-walled interview room that might have been downstairs rather than a few hundred kilometers away, she appeared just as unremarkable as her file suggested, although predictably terrified.

I spent a long hour trying to coax the information out of her, and wishing that I could borrow Mistry for ten minutes. It was rather a relief that the girl had turned out to be so far away, as she spent twenty-five minutes of the interview crying hysterically, and five throwing up, including once all over the investigator. At fifteen there was no legal requirement to have a relative present, but in the end I told I&I Antwerp to put her in a holding cell while they found her mother or someone else who could calm her down, and then call me back.

Sometimes the I&I reputation is a real handicap. Just then it was particularly annoying, since not only was it delaying my interview, but I was in a building where the interrogators spent half their time complaining about how their Procedures and Protocols had been gutted beyond uselessness. More to the point, I had a date after work with my then-girlfriend—whose name I'm ashamed to say I have forgotten—which was a second attempt after we'd had to cancel the previous week, again due to a case. I called her and negotiated a second postponement.

It took another hour before I could return to my witness.

When I explained to Christina's mother that the whole issue was messages sent to 343, Ms. Hauptman looked pained. I had the strong impression that she wanted to ask me what the hell I&I was doing wasting its time and her tax money on pop singers. I couldn't, unfortunately, tell her that we all felt much the same way.

On the plus side, Ms. Hauptman, thank goodness, seemed to understand that the best route was to cooperate fully, clear up the misunderstanding, and try to keep any mention of the interview out of their security files. Actually, it was her confidence that the situation *would* turn out to be a misunderstanding that tipped me into believing Christina's denials.

"Three," Christina kept repeating. "I sent them three. I just want them to know how much I love him."

She gave me approximate dates for the messages, and an almost word-for-word description of the contents that suggested she'd spent a lot longer crafting them than the results might justify. "A friend," also a 343 fan, had explained to her how to anonymize the messages once Jase had stopped replying to her. She also told me in detail about how she'd been to a truly frightening number of 343 concerts— as her and her family's c&p files confirmed—and how out of all the audience there, Kit had *looked* at *her,* and when she'd managed to get front-row tickets, he'd touched her hand, *twice.* She'd also got his autograph five times, won a meet-and-greet competition where she'd had hugs from all three (although poor Jase and Kim received rather perfunctory mentions), and waited around outside a lot of hotels. Sometimes, the only thing you want is for the witness to *stop* talking.

When, in a last desperate attempt at progress, I showed her the contents of the last message, the blood drained from her face. I thought for a moment I had something. Then she looked back at the screen with wide, tragic eyes.

"They...they're breaking up? No! It's not true!"

Her mother looked, if anything, even more pained. It was probably going to feel like a long journey back to Roosendaal.

Chapter Two

The next morning, the Para caught me on the way into my office. He was holding a screen and he didn't look happy.

"Your IIP's still open, B-C. I thought I told you that I wanted it shut down. Nagra needs some help. Are you getting anywhere?"

The question suggested he hadn't actually read the IIP. Not that I'd dare say that to his face. "One of the threatening messages is a ringer, dropped into an existing sequence. That means it must have been done by someone who knew about the first three messages, and had access to them to trace their origin."

His expression didn't change. "So it's an inside job—say that and close the case."

"I need to talk to a couple more people, that's all, Para. It's a little more complicated than it looked at first: the group's breaking up against the corporation's wishes, and there's a lot of money involved." The Para looked about as disgruntled as I'd expected. "I at least want to know if the subject of the notes feels threatened—if we give them the brushoff and something happens later, we'll end up carrying the can."

The Para pursed his lips and looked back down at the IIP. He paged through it, then nodded. "Okay. If you think there's a case there, keep at it. I'll get a couple more investigators from the pool to fill in for you. If Tillotson complains, I'll remind him who gave me the case in the first place."

I'll say this for the Para—he trusts our judgment and he backs up his team. Around here, that's rarer than honest corporates.

❖ ❖ ❖

The Para doesn't like the word intuition, although I've seen him make enough jumps in logic that *looked* like it from where I was standing. I rarely get anything that I could call intuition, and when I do it's often wrong anyway. So when I get a flash, I remember it, but I try not to put too much weight on it.

On that day, as soon as I saw Jase, I couldn't believe he'd sent the final note.

I'd made better time across New London than I'd expected, and arrived rather early at his flat. When he opened the door he looked different from the stage recording I'd seen, and not even like the picture in his security file. In fact, he looked his age—twenty-four—which he hadn't when he'd last been singing with 343. It was as if he'd gone through a late adolescence. He'd visibly bulked out, some of it fat, some muscle, and he had a rather old-fashioned few days' growth of beard. His straw-blond hair had long, dark blond roots. To me, on an impartial aesthetic level, it made him far more attractive. But then I'm not a teenage girl.

His clothes were smarter and more adult than Kit's, slightly sub-business casual, but neat. He stepped back from the doorway to let me in.

"You must be from I&I." He even sounded older. "I thought you were coming later."

"Yes, I'm sorry. Traffic, but not the usual way around—I can come back, if it's inconvenient."

He looked at me for a moment, like he was considering saying yes, then shrugged. "I'm not busy right now."

The flat wasn't exceptionally large, and it was all open plan: a kitchen, the living area, and a bed on a balcony above. A door at the foot of the spiral stairs presumably led into the bathroom. The place was, in a way, an extremely upmarket version of some of the bedsits I've visited during cases. The kind of bedsit that would belong to a man who until recently had been a third of a top-selling trio. A beautiful piano, made from real wood, stood to one side in the only clear space. Otherwise the place was thoroughly lived in, with clutter on the floor and any available surface, and men's and women's clothes hanging over the balustrade. It was very much a home, and completely the opposite of Kit and Kim's temporary flat.

A woman lay on the red velvet-covered couch, screen in one hand, hairbrush in the other. Tall and leggy, she had waist-length blonde hair and an above-the-knee dress in some kind of clingy natural wool—mohair, I thought, although I'm no expert—that emphasized her figure to expensive perfection. From her pose, her obvious awareness of the impression she made, and her presence in a music star's flat, I guessed she might be a performer or a model.

Whatever she might be, for a moment I felt certain she wasn't happy to see me there. Then the irritation vanished behind a vague, masklike smile.

"Clear out, Ann," Jase said amiably.

She stood without comment. On the way out, he caught her, one hand on her waist, and kissed her on the cheek. It looked part affection and part proprietorial territory marking. Over his shoulder, she looked me up and down, seeming faintly embarrassed. Then she flipped her hair back and headed for the door, snagging a smart jacket from a chair on the way.

"Can I get you a drink?" Jase offered when she'd gone.

"No, thank you."

"Hope you don't mind if I have something."

He poured a glass of cola, then opened the freezer and took out a tub of ice cream. He rolled a careful scoop, then dropped it in the cola. It fizzed loudly, and he licked a spill from the side of the glass. I remembered the taste vividly from my childhood, but I couldn't imagine drinking anything so sickly now.

Jase stuck two straws down the side of the ice cream, sucked hard, then sighed happily. "Rots your teeth and makes you fat, like my mum always told me," he said, then gestured across to the sofa. "Make yourself at home."

The sofa was still warm where Ann had lain. I cleared a space on the table and set down the camera, checking that the feed was good. Jase pulled a chair over, kicking debris out of the way.

"Do you know why I'm here?" I asked.

"One minute, before we get down to business."

I watched as, still with his cola in one hand, he went over to a high set of shelves and rummaged around. He produced a camera of his own, and set it up on the table next to mine. Not any simple camera, but the kind of highly secure, tamper-proof equipment we use.

Jase looked up and smiled. "Hope you don't mind. I like to keep track of what people say. I've learned the hard way that it saves a lot of argument later."

Legally, he had no right to do it, but I didn't want to drag the case out into demands for legal representatives and interviews at I&I. It would annoy the Para no end when he'd wanted a quick closure. "Go ahead," I said.

He sat down, leaning back in the chair with his legs stretched out. "So. Yes, I know why you're here. Geoff the Tosser says we were having trouble with the fans. He wants me back in the fold, 'for protection.'"

"You don't take it seriously?"

He snorted. "Oh, please. It's just corps bullshit, as usual."

"Really?" The ready admission surprised me, and he smiled.

"I don't work for them anymore, Investigator. I'm allowed to have my own thoughts now."

"And what do you think?"

"That Geoff is shitting himself because he finally understands this isn't about another point-oh-one percent, or more exposure, or market positioning, or whatever particular illusion of 'creative control' he was pushing last time I talked to him. He knows I'm not coming back and this is ... well, it's pathetic. Can't blame the man for trying, I suppose, given that the corps will string him up with his own small intestine for losing control of me."

"So you don't take it at all seriously? You can't think of anyone who might have a personal grudge against you, who isn't at the corps?"

206

"Oh, grudges, sure." He paused to suck the straws. The drink was threatening to bubble over into his lap. "If you count the girls and boys I *didn't* screw, and the girls and boys I *did* screw, and *their* boyfriends and girlfriends and parents and . . . well, that's hundreds right there, no?"

An angry partner or parent was a possibility that I hadn't considered. "The threat didn't sound to be related to jealousy or revenge."

"'Course not. Because it's Geoff, or whoever he's got to do it with enough deniability that he'll call in I&I to scare me. Tosser." He grinned around the straws. "Sorry you're having to waste your time with it, Investigator . . . Barret-Connor, right?"

I ignored the sympathy. "We know the first three messages were written by a genuine fan, but the last wasn't. At least she denies it strongly. Would you look at them all and tell me what you think?"

"If you like."

The messages seemed to impress him far less than they had Kit and Kim. Of course, if he was sure the corps were behind it, finding a security code in there meant nothing.

"Usual crap," he said succinctly when he gave me back the hand screen. "Must've been a shock to the poor kid when you lot turned up to ask her questions."

"Did you really exchange messages with Christina?"

"Probably. Or at least, she probably thinks I did. Most of the personalized fan contact is handled by the expert systems, or sometimes by real people pretending to be us. I should think they pegged her as a bit too keen and backed off. The corps walks a fine line between keeping the fans obsessed enough to spend every euro they can whine out of their parents on 343 crap, and avoiding pushing any of them so far they actually hurt themselves, or us. That would be bad PR." His mouth quirked. "Did you show her that last message, then?"

"Yes."

The idea seemed to amuse him. "Ooh, I bet that didn't go down well. I know there are breakup rumors flying, but denial's a powerful force. Did she cry?"

As well as suspect interviews not being any of his business, the question wasn't helping to clear up a case that the Para wanted closed. "So why did 343 break up?"

"Technically, they threw me out, but only after I pushed them into it. I'd had enough. I'm keeping it quiet for now—as a favor to Kit and Kim, and until the contractual closedown period runs out. Twelve weeks where I can still spend my stipend, but on shit they don't like. Wonderful, no?"

"You seem to have done well out of the corps."

He waved around the room. "This, you mean? It isn't mine. Rented cheap from a housing agency looking for some glamor on their list. But, sure, I have some money stashed away, and I won't starve on the streets. The corps's merchandise—

the Kays and me—get a cut, but it's peanuts compared to what we've earned them. Not enough for the shit they put us through. Oh, there's more 'held in trust,' but I doubt I'll see a cent of it, not now. But it's not just the money. I want to do something of my own. I mean, we weren't bad, for what we were, but—" He smiled. "I suppose you never saw us perform?"

"Ah, no."

"Do you know our music at all?"

After Kim and Kit's performance, I didn't want to waste more time. "I saw some recordings at the corps's headquarters."

"What did you think?" When I hesitated, he grinned. "We're better live, honestly. We put on a good show, at least, and I'll admit I loved performing with them. But that's all over now, too."

"Mr. Cheung said that there was a performance scheduled at an awards ceremony."

"I won't be on stage for that. I expect they'll get T-boy to do it." He shook the cola glass slightly, making it fizz. "He's still on contract, so right now he looks more like me than I do. He's been handling the 343 performances and interviews the corps were tied into, and doing a bang-up job, from what I hear."

I had absolutely no idea who he meant, and he smiled at my expression of confusion.

"T-boy—Toby Brown. He'll be in the corporate files somewhere."

The full name did sound familiar. "Another performer?"

"My double. We've all got one, allegedly for security purposes. They do a lot of the outside appearances, when it's hard to provide protection. But they're stand-ins at gigs, too, because they can't cancel just because one of us is ill. Or if we were run over by a rogue transporter, come to that. I always felt sorry for them, though. Bad enough to be a manufactured commodity like me and the Kays. But to be the expendable backup commodity?" He shrugged. "The money isn't great, I don't think, but there's lots of travel and parties, and sex on tap. Actually, they've got their own fans."

The whole setup still sounded oddly improbable, although it was stirring vague memories from occasional brushes with entertainment news. "So this Toby Brown will replace you now?"

Jase frowned thoughtfully. "Maybe. If he's lucky. Like I said, he's been doing a good job for the last few weeks, and normally the no-compete clauses would stop me from performing. But now, if I succeed in going solo the corps won't want to be pushing my image for me. Plus—" He grinned. "I'm not planning to be demographic-friendly for 343. Nothing they hate more than brand confusion."

Which meant that Brown was yet another person with an incentive to want Jase back in the corps. Or permanently out of the picture.

"They must go to a lot of trouble to find doubles," I remarked.

"Not really. The corps took some lucky sods who were close enough to us and paid for the surgery to match them up."

I wondered for a moment if I'd misheard him. "*Surgery?*"

He looked vaguely surprised. "Sure. The corps runs a hell of a plastic surgery facility. I should know, I've spent enough time there. I'm a few years older than the Kays—Kit and Kim—and it's hard staying young and beautiful, especially when you work for vultures."

I hadn't had a chance—or a reason, at that point—to look at their medical files. "You've had surgery, too? Twenty-four seems rather young."

He leaned forwards, pointing towards me with the straws. "Do you know anything about how the business works?"

I shook my head, and he nodded, looking surprisingly grown up. Grim, almost.

"They try to keep it quiet. Basically, they run a shitload of computer-generated artists through an expert system, and then they take the best ones and try them out on real teenagers. And it does work—'Kit' had one of the highest test scores they've ever managed. But they're planning ahead, right? Projecting. By the time they finish polishing the product it'll already be a year or so later, and the market can be fickle. Sometimes, however much the corporations run the scene, there's a big shift in tastes. Like, right now the favorite look's getting more muscular. Some of the bands on the market fringes look like their balls have actually dropped, and they're starting to nibble away at key demographic ear time." He shook his head. "Listen to me. I sound like Geoff the Tosser."

We were getting somewhat away from the topic of threatening messages, again, but I admit I was interested. It's always fascinating to see another system from the inside. "So they chose Kit because he looked like the best projection at the time?"

"No, he didn't. No one could. They chose him because he was close enough. And also because he was young, and he didn't have the right advice, and his parents were greedy and desperate enough that they let the corps turn him into whatever they wanted. He was ten when they signed him as potential, not even twelve when they put together the 343 strategy, and thirteen when they finally finished working on him and launched the group. Fuckers. It makes me want to—"

When he stopped, I waited, wondering if I'd been wrong in my snap assessment that he had nothing to do with the messages. Jase certainly had passion, and more willpower than the other two.

After a moment, he slumped back. "Anyway. Kit was the founder image for the group. He didn't start off with eyes that big and green, or cheekbones that high. He's had body mods, too, over the years—muscle reduction, to thin him down. And the really sad part? Is that he thinks he looks good. What do you think, Investigator?"

The flip answer was that I wasn't qualified to judge the attractiveness of men. However, I gave it some consideration and tried for tact. "He's definitely striking."

"He's a freak. Just imagine how he'll look in thirty years' time, like a sad, middle-aged fucking pixie. Poor little bastard."

I couldn't, in all honestly, disagree.

There was a long silence, then he slurped the straws and shrugged. "Anyway, Kim and I were luckier. We were worked around Kit, and we were always slated to be the more normal, approachable ones. Kim's the Far East market lead-in, so he had the right look already, but he still needed some surgery to get him closer to Kit. I was cast as the older, serious guy with actual musical talent, so mine were mostly 'little tweaks.'" Now, he sounded bitter enough to have done any number of things, from threatening letters upwards. "Of course, there were also the hormone implant 'balancers,' which basically meant they androgenized us chemically."

I thought of the odd, childish softness of Kim's face and wondered why I hadn't thought of that explanation myself. Jase was watching me, swirling the remains of his drink, the ice cream turning the cola to mud.

"It sounds grueling," I said.

"Yeah. It's the day-to-day stuff that grinds you down. The drugs and . . . I'll tell you almost the worst thing—physique. We have—had—to be fit enough to per-form. But no exercise that'd build too much mass, because that wasn't the look when we formed." He raised his eyebrows, which I noticed looked thicker than in the pictures I'd seen. "Doesn't sound too bad, no? But you can't put on weight, so you either take the drugs or you don't eat. I've spent years living on shit I wouldn't feed a dog. I don't think Kit even remembers what real food looks like, and Kim used to have a bad binge-and-purge problem. Can't count the number of times I've heard him throwing up. Then they fixed it with some kind of surgery, so he couldn't do it anymore."

The outpouring of unrequested information after the demonstrated suspicion with the recording interested me. Was it because he wanted to keep me away from other topics, or more that he simply had the chance to talk about these things now? I doubted the corps would approve.

"Not as glamorous as most people think, no? I was always fighting to keep it sane, to resist the pressure to have shit done to me." Jase scraped the back of his fingernails through the scruff on his chin. "I shaved five, six times a day, but those two have got no beards at all. They let the corps's medics kill the hair follicles— they'll never get it back without treatment. In the end, I decided enough was enough."

"So what was the last straw?"

He finished the cola, leaving a sludge of ice cream foam in the bottom of the glass, and set the glass down on the table, careful not to obstruct either camera.

"They wanted me to have a vocal snip—to tighten the cords up, keep my voice lighter. Now, I don't pretend to have the greatest voice in the world, but I worked hard on it, developed it. For a while they processed my voice in performances and recording, but finally someone decided it would be cheaper and easier to just hit the surgical reset button and put me back to how I sounded right at the beginning, like a teenager. Those contracts mean the corps can do a lot, but they couldn't actually put me under a laser without my consent. I said no. They said they'd 'have to reassess the depth of my commitment to the project.'"

"And?" I prompted.

He grinned widely, and made a rude gesture over his crotch. "I told them to kiss my arse and blow me. Did I mention we're not allowed to use inappropriate language? So I got the big E. Formal termination of the contract, effective immediately. They only did it because they thought I'd cave in and beg them to take me back."

"And you didn't?"

"I slapped my signature on it so fast they didn't know what the hell happened. Then when he realized I meant it, Geoff had some kind of heart spasm and ended up in hospital." Now he was chuckling. "Not that I wish any real harm on him but, hell, after what he's put us through, a couple of days looking at white walls might've done him some good, no?"

"So no second thoughts at all?"

"Not a chance. They had six, seven years of my life, and I'm done with them. I'm waiting out the closedown period, and when that's over and they make the official announcement, the next thing I plan to do is get stinking drunk and punch a few journos." He jabbed at the air with both fists, looking reasonable professional. "I've been taking lessons specially."

"And what about Kim and Kit? What happens to them?"

"Oh, if they keep their heads down and the corps agree on a new third for them, 343's got a couple of years left in it. Maybe even more—it's consistently one of the corps's top-ranking products, and Kit's the one strongly brand identified, not me. Eventually, though, they won't be able to keep the wrinkles off them, or too many fans will age out, and then they'll can the group. Someone else might pick them up after that, but the corps is a youth brand." His voice was analytical, but I couldn't tell if the hard edge was callousness or self-defense. "Trios don't last forever, anyway. No one knows why, despite all the research the corporations put into it, but longevity is for solos, or a few lucky quads and quins. Whether I leave or not, before too long it'll become more economical for the corps to get a fresh set of faces than to keep pushing the old ones."

"What if the corps decides not to look for a new third member now?"

"Then they're finished, musically. If you mean what happens to them after that?" He shrugged. "I honestly don't know. Kim will be fine, I'm sure. He's a survivor, like me."

"And Kit?"

"You've met him, right? He has no idea how the outside world works. If he can find someone else to cling to he might pull through, but if he can't..." Jase shook his head. "Put it this way: I wouldn't be surprised if I saw an obituary pop up on a newsfeed some day."

I couldn't help saying, "That sounds rather callous."

"Yeah, it does, doesn't it? But I'm supposed to be telling you the truth, no? There came a point where it was them or me. I'm sorry if Kit suffers as a result, but what's been done to him over the years to make him the way he is, I didn't do it. I can't let the corps use him as a hostage to stop me."

An attitude of self-preservation that would've done any corporate proud. I wondered if Jase had been like this before he'd joined 343, and if his slightly greater life experience before the group had made the difference between him and the others.

"Have either of them told you how they feel about the group dissolving?"

"Well, I haven't seen them since right after it happened, not without a platoon of lawyers and corps minders. The corps doesn't want me contaminating their product." He grimaced. "But I imagine they're pretty pissed off with me. Or Kim is. Probably not Kit. Kit's a surprisingly nice kid still, when you think how desperately fucked up his life is."

A softer edge had crept into his voice, now. "You're going to miss them?" I asked.

"The Kays?" He looked down at his hands, running the pad of his thumb over his nails. He might have abandoned his dietician, but he was clearly keeping up with his manicurist. "I...yeah, in a way. Just them, not the rest of it." He shrugged quickly, and looked up. "I don't know if you've seen us interviewed? It's all scripted to fuck. We say we love each other, and it's written in once every two minutes so it gets caught in the clips. But...they've been my life. So I suppose it's true."

"Is that a platonic affection?" As Jase had said earlier, jealousy—or more accurately fear of loss—might make a plausible motive for the threat.

"Not entirely." The question didn't even make him blink. "Kim and I screwed around, off and on." He smiled, just showing his teeth. "Have you seen him dance? He's very flexible."

"And Kit?"

"Fuck, no." The surprise sounded genuine. "Never."

"Kit told me otherwise. He said that you propositioned him."

"Really?" He shrugged again. "Well, Kit likes to think he's irresistible. I suppose after all that work it would be hard to accept you weren't."

"He claimed you climbed into his bed occasionally, when you were intoxicated."

"Mm. Yeah, okay, I'll put my hands up for that." He scratched the side of his neck. "Weird as it's going to sound, I was never planning to do anything more than hold him and sleep. Kim's not always up for that kind of thing."

212

I couldn't keep the expression of disbelief off my face, but it didn't seem to offend.

"I get lonely when I'm really strung out. Although, you know, I don't think I *could* have sex with Kit unless I was so wasted I probably wouldn't be able to get it up anyway. He is a sweet kid but, like I said before, physically he's a freak." His expression changed, and he was smiling *at* me, his voice dropping slightly. "Besides, I much prefer tall blonds."

Just then, he almost reminded me of the Para, the same switching on of charm jarring with my previous impression. It must've worked wonders with fans.

"He also said that you—" I could feel a slight blush starting under the intensity of his gaze. "That you'd had oral sex on more than one occasion, when there were female fans present who let the story out."

The seductive aura vanished. "No, Investigator, not guilty. Kit reads too much of his own PR. Although—" Jase tilted his head. "Ah. It might have been T-boy. Now I bet *he'd* suck Kit off and let Kit blame it on me. Toby can be a prize wanker when he tries, although I shouldn't say that, since I owe him."

"Owe him?"

"I—confidentially?" he said after a moment.

"Of course."

Jase weighed the decision for a few seconds, then said, "He's the one who hooked me up with Andrews—that's my new manager. Obviously if the corps ever hears about it he's in deep shit, so the only people who know are me, him, and Andrews—and you, now. T-boy started off wanting to be a musician, like me. Only I hit relatively lucky, and he bombed out. So in the end, he got a job as a fake stand-in for a group that's barely fucking real on a good day. He knew Andrews from way back when." He looked at me narrowly. "Didn't Geoff tell you about Andrews?"

"No."

"Hm. Wonder why not." He leaned back in the chair. "Well, the other reason I refused the vocal surgery was because I'd already had a couple of informal meetings with Andrews—well, I say 'meetings.' More like literally whispering in corners in club VIP sections, to keep it away from the corps. Andrews has lots of contacts, lots of friends, and a contract lined up for me with a new corporation."

"And the corps know about it?"

"They do now. But like I said, I pushed them into kicking me out before they found out—enormous piece of luck, especially that they used the no-fault severance. Of course, they didn't think it was going to stick, because I'd come crawling back. Hah. But, seriously, you cannot imagine the penalty clauses if I'd been the one to try to terminate. Noncompetition for fucking ever. Bunch of utter bastards."

"And how well will the new contract pay?" I asked.

"Not too badly. I'm not under any illusions—part of why I'm getting the chance is so they can steal a name from the corps and stick two fingers up at them. How long it lasts depends on me delivering good demographic and sales. In a year I might be out on my newly muscled arse with a failed solo career that'll fuck me forever." He sounded completely sanguine, and I think it was only then that I fully realized how badly he must have wanted to escape.

However, just as he'd scotched my theory that Toby Brown could be behind the threats (unlikely if he were the one who'd given Jase the lead to start a solo career in the first place), he'd handed me another option. Corporate rivalry—that was one of the Para's least favorite motives, and I've never liked it either. There's often a certain solid logic to crimes committed purely for cash, but rivalries can turn into obsessions and the power politics are often beyond horrifying.

"So you're sure your new employer—" I paused, but he didn't offer a name, "—will give you a serious chance?"

He shrugged. "If they have me, they might as well try. That would piss the corps off even more, if I succeed. But even if it bombs out, I'll be okay. I'm not staggeringly rich, but it's all relative. When I first signed the contract with the corps, the only reason I wasn't an indig was that a friend let me sleep on his sofa. I've saved enough to keep me in cola floats for the rest of my life. Who knows, my lawyer might even wring a little more out of those mythical trusts. And, uh—" He picked up the screen Ann had discarded. "I'm trying my hand at writing."

"Fiction?"

"Of a kind. My autobiography." He rubbed the back of his neck. "Pretty fucking arrogant at my age, right?"

"I'm sure it'll sell well."

"I hope so. Luckily, my lawyer also has a degree in literature, so she's helping me with my commas as well as my libel."

"She sounds useful."

"And hot, no?" He grinned at my expression of confusion. "You met her—Ann Marshall."

"Oh!" Not a model or an actress, then. And she hadn't been mentioned in his security file. "How long have you been together?"

"Officially? She resigned from the corps a fortnight after I escaped, and it started not a day before then. In reality, about a year." Jase smiled, warm, reminiscent, and more genuine than any smile I'd seen since I arrived. "We had to keep us a total secret, because 'the image' doesn't allow full-time girlfriends. The funny thing is, deep down I always half suspected she was corps to the core, and they had her keeping a watch on me. I mean, you've met her. She's older than me, she's brilliant, and she had an actual education, and everything she has is on her own merits, not some corps-designed 'product.' But, hey—" The smile, again. "It turned out she liked me for my sparkling personality. Anyway, now we'll be rich and free together. Assuming this sells, anyway."

"Why wouldn't it?" I couldn't imagine the legions of 343 fans dissipating so fast after the breakup that they wouldn't want to hear the inside gossip.

"It might not get the chance." Jase scrolled down the screen, text flashing by too quickly for me to read it—all I could make out were lines in various colors. "The plain black is the stuff no one could object to. That pretty much means 'We arrived in Paris on the fifteenth of May' and 'I like broccoli.' Then there's green, orange, and red depending on whether it's interesting and easily provable, harder to prove but true, or just plain lawyer-bait libel."

There was, indeed, an awful lot of colored text, although most was green. The red made only occasional flashes of a line or two at most. I wondered if that meant it was nearly finished. "Do you have a publisher?"

"Oh, yes. The bidding got pretty competitive. We even turned down a couple of offers on principle, which was fun. There's always room for thieves and plagiarists at the top of my shit list." He grinned. "Andrews is handling the deals for me, of course, but I've seen the contracts. I should do very nicely out of it. Working for the corps at least taught me to read the small print and check the attachments so I know what I'm signing away."

"Could I have a copy of the book?"

His eyes narrowed. "Why?"

"Curiosity, primarily." If the threat against Jase had any substance, the autobiography might show up old enemies—or even be the source of the motive.

"Well... not right now, you can't. If you want to insist, I'll have to talk to Andrews, and Ann. I can tell you now she'll demand bulletproof confidentiality agreements. Some of this stuff is dynamite, and we're hoping to get pre-release serial deals for the best parts."

More delays to the investigation. "I'll let you know."

"Are you talking to Andrews?" he asked, then held his hand up. "Sorry, you didn't know about him, did you. Do you want me to call him and set something up?"

"Today, if possible."

"Sure." He reached for his comm earpiece, then paused. "You're taking this seriously? The threats?"

"The corps was very insistent."

"Nice answer. I do a lot of interviews, Investigator. I should know an evasion when I hear one, no?" He smiled and picked up the earpiece. "I'll call Andrews anyway. He won't mind."

The screen in reception listed the talent management agency and gave its location on the fifteenth floor. Andrew Andrews and Associates. What on earth possesses parents to give their children names like that? As someone saddled with the initials ABC, I sympathized.

The corporate district, and the outside of the building, were a long step down from the corps. However, the offices themselves had the same smart, ultramodern décor that was obviously de rigueur in the business.

Andrews was a large man—tall, heavily built, with huge hands. Actually, his hands were interesting. On close inspection, the fingers were rather blunt, almost stubby. Looking wasn't easy, though. He kept them in motion, gesturing all the time, giving an illusion of elegance that must have taken a lot of study and practice. I wondered if he'd been a performer before he became a manager.

His first words were, "So you've come about the messages? I heard they'd blamed some poor fan for it all."

I sat and set down the camera, waiting until he waved permission. "That line of inquiry has been concluded, for now. Do you think the threat is corporate?"

Andrews raised his eyebrow at the camera. "Surely you can't expect me to suggest that a respectable corporation like the corps would play so dirty?"

"Mr. Andrews, all interview material we record is absolutely secure."

He smiled faintly. "Of course. And I&I is a paragon of incorruptibility."

I'd never heard anyone deliver sarcasm so drily. "Do you think the messages are from the corps?"

After a brief pause, he sat back in his chair and nodded briskly. "Of course. They're trying to frighten Jase into staying. They want him to think I can't provide the same kind of protection they do. Well, it won't work. Jase doesn't frighten easily."

"How did you make contact with Jase?"

"I had the privilege of hearing some of his unproduced music, via a mutual acquaintance. That's what we do here—find opportunities for new talent, push new names to the big corporations."

"Or not so new?"

"I won't deny Jase is the biggest thing we've ever had here." He smiled, surprisingly self-deprecating for a professional salesman. "I have to admit, it's rather exciting to have such a major name. If he's successful, the agency could become a major name, too. All the more annoying that the corps is playing these childish games."

"The corps was insistent they wanted a thorough investigation."

He shrugged.

"And you? Would you like us to press the investigation?"

"To be honest, Investigator, I wouldn't. Jase is a smart young man, and he has a lot of determination, but this kind of pressure, on top of everything else, is hard for him. He didn't show it, I'm sure, when you talked to him. But my job is to protect my client. If there's a threat here, it's not from some anonymous note-writing fan." He waved dismissively. "Allowing the corps to point to I&I as proof there's real danger is just fanning the flames for them."

It was lunchtime when I returned to I&I, so I found myself a quiet corner in a level four coffee room and reviewed the case notes while I ate my sandwiches.

I could see no reason at all for anyone on Jase's side of the breakup to be staging the threats. As far as I could tell, all Jase wanted was a quick and easy exit from the corps.

Far more likely suspects were the corps, or even the remaining two members of 343. Their shock on seeing their security code in the note had seemed genuine enough, but however they came across, they were professional performers who had plenty of experience in presenting a good front to interviewers. Hopefully an I&I interview was a little more intimidating than a soft-soap, scripted music business interview, but maybe not.

Their stories had tallied well with Jase's, with the single exception of the level of intimacy between Kit and Jase. I couldn't understand why Kit would make something like that up. Or, if he hadn't, why Jase had lied to me.

Maybe that was a lack of empathy because I've never wanted to touch a man, still less accept regular blowjobs from my close friends. Maybe if I did and for some reason didn't want people to know, I'd deny it to an I&I investigator. Perhaps because my attractive and highly useful lawyer girlfriend would object. However, Jase hadn't seemed annoyed or disturbed by the suggestion, just amused. Given that, as he'd said, the trio's publicity made a deliberate effort to blur the lines of the relationships between the three of them, it certainly wouldn't harm his career or his prospective book sales.

The story about sexual mistaken identities with his double seemed improbable, but the only way to settle the question was to ask the corps to produce Toby Brown and talk to him about it. More trouble and a longer investigation, for something which seemed like a minor point.

Anyway, on balance, I decided I believed Jase. Looking back, I think it was simply the fact that Jase seemed so much more together and intelligent than Kit that pushed me in that direction. There was the book, to start with, although it was possible Marshall was ghostwriting for him. I did wish that Mistry had been there, because she's better at judging subtle shades of truthfulness than I am. The Para had her busy elsewhere, though. If it ever seemed that important, I decided, I could show her the recordings.

Apart from that, everything pointed to a desperate attempt by someone at the corps to drive Jase back into the fold. On that score, killing him would be profoundly counterproductive, except possibly as a warning to other artists. Even given all that I knew about corporations, I found that idea hard to credit.

So I closed the case. My assessment: there was no serious threat to Jase, and the case didn't merit I&I resources. I didn't actually say the corps was behind it. I phrased it as "a possibility of corporate sabotage," which left it open to be from an outsider. I sent a message to Geoff Cheung and offered to liaise with Justice and hand the case over to them if the corps wanted to pursue it further, but I didn't hear back from them. Possibly it was because I included a personal note to the effect that if anything did happen to Jase, I&I policy would dictate a close scrutiny of *all* corporate parties.

The case closed with my name on it, even though the Para signed it off as head of the team. Looking back, I know there's more I could have done. If I had the case to run again, there's more I would do. But life isn't a sim, where you can just start the program again if something goes wrong, and sometimes the sad truth is that innocent people suffer for the mistakes of others.

Chapter Three

Ifrowned when Sara put the mug down on my desk, and then harder again as the biscuits made a neat little pile beside it. Chocolate biscuits.

"What do you want?"

I'm not usually that tactless, but it's water off a plastic-wrapped duck's back to Sara.

"I heard you had an invitation." She smiled sweetly, utterly unabashed. "To the New London Music Awards on Wednesday."

The news had travelled faster than I'd expected. "I'm not sure if I'll go. The rules about gifts from suspects and witnesses—"

Sara rolled her eyes. "As if anyone ever pays attention to *those*."

"Senior paras don't. They can get away with it."

She shrugged. "Okay, it's a good point. But you closed the case a month ago. And Jase wasn't a suspect, right? And, well, I did hear that you'd split up with that nice...what was her name, again, sorry?"

I studied her for a moment. "I suppose you *didn't* hear it was just a single invitation?"

"You're kidding me. No plus one?"

"'Fraid not."

At least she left me the biscuits.

❖ ❖ ❖

The note with the invitation had said "343, last chance to see...—J," and nothing else. I assumed this meant Jase was still going through with his plans to leave the corps.

As it turned out, a small delay at work combined with a much larger traffic snarl-up caused by a burst water main (that's when you can tell the difference in traffic priority between an I&I car and a normal taxi) meant that I was late to the ceremony. Hurrying in, I didn't even have time to be impressed by the plushness of the entertainment complex. When I finally reached it, the vast central hall did make me pause. The walls were solid screens, floor to very high ceiling. I couldn't even make out the roof—it was hidden by the brightness of the lights, although I could see crisscrossing walkways. There were dozens of tables. I hadn't appreciated how major an event it was. The name ought to have tipped me off—the less assuming the name, the more important the corporate event, generally. It looked more trans-European than local.

The meal was almost over, although the staff quickly brought me a plate of extremely good food. Andrews sat me down to his left, and introduced me to the other entertainment industry people at the table. Ann Marshall was there, to his right, with an empty seat between them, but other than her I couldn't tell you a single name.

"Where's Jase?" I asked.

"He went backstage—he said he wanted to talk to Kim and Kit." Andrews took a square of cardamom chocolate and bit it in half. "I told him the corps's minders wouldn't let him see them."

Jase hadn't returned by the time the lights dimmed in the room and the stage area lit up. The screens lining the walls came up in a dull, glowing red-gold, sunset images fading in and out, morphing between the New London skyline and interior views of a bedroom. You might even know the song, which is one of the few 343 tracks that still pops up from time to time, called "Watching You Sleep". The tune is pleasant enough, although if you listen to the lyrics, they're honestly rather disturbing. Maybe they just sound that way if you've worked on enough kidnappings and similar cases.

Anyway, as soon as 343 stepped out, I had a feeling something was out of place, but it took me a few seconds to realize what. The real Jase was up there, between Kit and Kim, his arms linked with theirs, all three smiling for the crowd as the applause rose and the music started. Clean-shaven, with his hair styled to match the others, dressed in a loose costume crisscrossed with reflective stripes, Jase looked completely different from the man I'd met.

The three of them made their way to the front, still arm in arm. An unofficial farewell performance, although no doubt everyone in the crowd had heard the rumors and were speculating. I looked around, gauging the crowd's reaction, and I noticed Andrews doing the same thing.

I turned back to the stage just as 343 moved apart into their separate spotlights. A moment later, someone shook my shoulder, hard.

When I turned, Andrews was pointing up towards a metal catwalk—high up, halfway back down the length of the vast room, with a perfect view of the stage. He shook my shoulder again, leaning in so I could hear him over the music.

"There's someone with a gun," he said, the words so incongruous that for a moment they made no sense. Then he pushed back his chair and started for the stage. I couldn't see a damn thing where he'd pointed, but I went after him anyway. Marshall had stood up, too, I think, but she didn't follow us.

Needless to say, as we reached the edge of the stage, security came dashing to intercept us. From behind were the beginnings of confusion—a rising noise from the crowd abruptly drowned out as the music started. Up on the stage, the three had separated for the beginning of their set. With the lights in their faces, they probably hadn't even seen us. I got caught up by a couple of security guards, who tried to stop me. I waved my I&I ID and pointed back up at the walkway, shouting as best I could over the music to look for a shooter. I'm not sure which it was that got their attention, but they let go of me, and I kept going, heading for Kit and Kim as Andrews seemed to be aiming for his own client.

Andrews was ahead of me, so I actually saw him hit. The first shot fired took him right in the back and it was nothing short of a miracle that it didn't kill him outright. He'd put himself between Jase and the gun, and the impact sent him forwards into Jase. I was close enough that I heard Jase grunt with surprise as he half caught Andrews and they both went down.

More figures were racing in from the back of the stage to protect the valuable merchandise, and I heard shots from ground level, which must've been armed security. Kim had flung himself at a couple of bodyguards and I waved at Kit to get into cover, too. He was simply standing there, in a spotlight, his mouth and eyes wide open, looking less human than ever. The music cut off suddenly, but the noise from the stampeding, screaming audience almost drowned out the next gunshots. I hoped like hell that the hall exits were large enough to cope, or the panic could do far more damage than the bullets.

I spared a glance around. This time I saw a muzzle flash from up on the walkway, a suggestion of a concealed figure behind it. I didn't get any details before I looked back to Kit. Finally he'd started to move, and I called out again when I realized he was heading *towards* Jase.

Then, as I thought at the time, someone bumped into me—a shove against the side of my right leg hard and unexpected enough to send me sprawling. Funnily enough, it didn't occur to me immediately that I might've been shot. It didn't hurt at first, not even as I hit the ground, but the second I tried to stand again, *then* I knew. The pain was absolutely blinding—focused in my thigh, but washing out through my whole body, making it hard to breathe. I couldn't have got up if there'd been a line of shots marching across the stage right toward me, but fortunately for me there wasn't.

It felt very, very strange. I knew I was hurt, that I'd almost certainly been shot, but I seemed unable to do anything logical or useful with that idea. I lay for what felt like ages but must have been less than a minute, staring at the stage under my nose and wondering when the pain would stop, and when someone was coming to help me. When I finally realized it wouldn't and they didn't seem to be, I managed to roll over and look around.

Andrews lay on the stage, with enough people around him to stop me from seeing his face. Another group surrounded a second body not far from him, and from a sleeve I could see, it was obviously one of the trio—I assumed Jase. From that direction I could hear an absolutely horrible noise, someone choking on blood or vomit, and a frantic voice repeating, "Clear his airway, clear his airway!"

The rest of the trio had disappeared already, although a few trailing guards at the back of the stage suggested where they'd gone. Another guard sat on her own, clutching her upper arm and looking shocked. I suppose we were both too far down the value scale to rate immediate attention, or, to be fair, it was plain that there were two people far worse off than us.

Gingerly, I checked my leg. I've never liked blood—some people would say I'm in the wrong job, but it's less common than you'd think—and there was plenty of it around. Nothing gushing, though, so I decided panicking wasn't needed just yet. There was a surprisingly small, neat hole in the side of my trousers slightly towards the back where the bullet had gone in, and another one, not quite so neat, where it had come out the front. In between them, of course, was the damage to me that I couldn't see, but which I could most definitely feel. The only good news was that when I eyeballed the trajectory, it didn't seem to pass through any bone.

I waited until I heard a voice call down from the walkway to say there was no trace of the shooter, then I fainted. If you ever get shot, I thoroughly recommend it.

There's a blank in my memory for a while after that. I remember a few snatches, mostly of people moving about above me, and of my leg hurting like hell. I know I was conscious for longer than I remember, because I learned afterwards that I said and did things that I don't remember at all. I think my mind decided I'd be better off not knowing.

Somehow, my professional training held up. After I passed out for the first time, a couple of the venue security guards noticed me hit the floor and came over to check me out. They woke me up, and I told them to stop everyone in the crowd from leaving, including all the corporate and VIP guests but also the guards and event staff and anyone else in the building, and to call I&I and tell them what had happened. I don't remember doing this. Nor do I remember waving my I&I ID at them, telling them this was an investigation in progress, and being pretty explicit about what happened to people who obstructed an I&I officer.

I must've been reasonably impressive, because they did it. Venue security had locked down the complex's perimeter exit gates at the first shots, and the guards I'd detailed contacted the security station in time and stopped them from opening the place up. They herded everyone back inside the building, into the hall, and locked the doors.

Apparently it was chaos. The next thing I remember clearly is someone shaking me awake and trying to get through to me that there were hundreds of pissed-off and important people who wanted to know why they couldn't get back into their corporate cars. I made an effort, then, and pulled myself together. I was still on the stage, with the guard who'd been shot in the arm, and I wondered where the other wounded people I'd seen had gone. There were a couple of medics with us, and the one beside me was putting things away in a case. He'd put pads on my leg and wrapped it up, and the pain had decreased considerably, which suggested drugs, but there was still too much blood around for comfort. My trousers lay beside me, the right leg sliced up from ankle to waistband, and I could see one of the bullet holes in it.

There were tears on my face, and I wiped them away while I looked around. Across the stage were two other smeared pools of blood much larger than mine.

At that point, I nearly lost my nerve and told them to let everyone go. I felt sick from the residual pain and the thick smell of blood, my head was spinning, and I couldn't get my thoughts organized. Mostly, though, it was because I just couldn't face the idea of talking to angry corporates when I didn't have any trousers. Stupid, isn't it?

I didn't give up, though. I pointed to the other blood pools, and I knew it was bad news from the way the medic's face changed to professional sympathy.

"They've already been taken to hospital."

"What's their condition?" My throat felt hoarse, like I'd been shouting.

"I honestly don't know, Ainsley."

I must have told him my first name at some point. It's not my favorite thing about me—something I have in common with the Para. "Senior Investigator Barret-Connor, I&I," I said, and his eyes widened a fraction. "And this is an investigation in progress."

"The boy—" he said, and waited until I nodded, wondering which one of 343 it was. "He was hit in the head, but from what I know, he has a good chance. They stabilized him well before they took him away. The older man was in bad shape: he was shot twice in the back and his lung is severely damaged, possibly also his spine. I think they had to put a neural induction pack over his heart."

"Is he going to die?" I asked.

"Investigator, I really don't know. I'll get in touch with the hospital and find out—he might still be on his way there."

So with two potential murders on my watch, I had to start work, with or without trousers.

I asked the medic—who was muttering about hospital for me, too—if I was fit to stay, and eventually he conceded that I was if I didn't try to run around. I assured him there was no danger of that. I called I&I, who'd already been alerted, and told them to officially reopen the IIP, and that I needed a full forensics team and enough investigators and scanners to DNA ID and interview a large crowd. Then I told a guard to go backstage and find me something to wear, and to start setting tables up, and a queueing system with ropes so that the I&I people could process everyone as fast as possible.

There was something nagging at me, and I couldn't think what it was. I asked the medic and security guard to get me to a chair, and then I tried to work out what I'd forgotten, but it just wouldn't come. When you've been shot, your body seems to decide it has better things to do with its resources than analytical reasoning. I felt hot and cold, and the pain in my leg kept sharpening, like a reminder that I ought to be lying down and whimpering quietly. I persuaded the medic to give me something extra to calm it down, which turned out not to be a good thing.

I'd just had the shot when I was distracted by the arrival of the trousers. They were maroon, and they had long stripes down the side that shimmered in enough colors to constitute a danger to epileptics. But they were wide and they went on over the pads on my leg and, frankly, anything was better than nothing. After that, I told the guards to bring anyone to me who was making too much of a nuisance. I went through my I&I heavy routine—I'm better at it than you might think—with an assortment of corporates. All the ones I saw I let go to the head of the queue for IDs. It kept them quiet and started building the queues slowly.

After a while, the I&I pool staff started to arrive, and I relaxed for a couple of minutes because I wasn't in charge anymore. And then people were looking at me expectantly and I remembered that, yes, it *was* my investigation.

It took another fifteen minutes before I realized I couldn't cope. Whatever the medic had given me for the pain had begun doing something very odd to my short-term memory. Turned out that it was something I shouldn't have been given. There was an omission from my file at Central Medical Records, which isn't uncommon, or so I understand from the interrogators.

As long as I was talking to corporates I was okay, as I was basically relaying the same information over and over. Giving fire-and-forget orders and organizing the interviews was another thing entirely. I kept repeating things with slight variations and confusing the hell out of people. If I'd been more with it I would've stopped and found an investigator to delegate to, but of course I didn't realize what the problem was, not until I talked to people afterwards. The medic kept bothering me—I must've looked like hell—and I kept waving him off because I had so much to do.

I did feel like absolute 24-carat crap, though, and the world had developed a gentle rocking that made me want to throw up.

It was one of the best sights of my life when I saw the Para crossing the room with Alex-Ann Jameson beside him. The Para was wearing civilian clothes and his expression went from pissed off to amused in the time it took him to walk across the hall and see me—and my trousers.

When he reached me he looked slowly around the room, at the long lines and the interviews and equipment, and nodded. "Good job, B-C," he said. "Well done." An automatic response while he started getting a handle on the situation, but I remember being incredibly pleased.

Then he looked down. "B-C, what the hell are you wearing?"

"I was—" Suddenly, I lost my grip on the whole business of sentence structure. "My leg. I was shot in the leg. There was—tried to kill..." I felt unbelievably stupid, and embarrassed, again mostly because I didn't understand why the world had suddenly become so difficult to handle.

The medic was trying to get his attention. "Excuse me—?"

"Senior Para-investigator Toreth," he said, and showed his ID. My vision was so unfocused that I couldn't make out anything on it, and that, more than anything, made me realize something was wrong with me.

Before the Para could say anything more, the medic took him aside. The man didn't get out more than a couple of sentences before the Para was asking questions, very crisp, and nodding sharply. He glanced at me once or twice, then lifted his hand to stop the medic, and came back.

"You're going to hospital," he said to me in a tone that under normal circumstances I wouldn't have dreamed of questioning.

Flying sky-high on unexpected drug side effects is not normal circumstances for me. "No. I'm—I've got to stay. I'm—lead in—inst—invit—" The lead investigator, when I couldn't even manage to say it.

He raised his eyebrows. "Don't worry, B-C, I won't mess up your case."

I was still trying to produce some kind of apology when the stretcher arrived.

I wouldn't want to say that the Para cares about me in any personal way. He appreciates the professional job I do, that I'm an effective member of his team. I wouldn't want to say, actually, that he cares about anyone. He's good at pretending, better than many of them, but fundamentally it's a para thing. Without it, they couldn't do the job they do.

We all do it to some degree, but for them the disconnect is bigger and a lot more all-encompassing. I love my family, some of my friends, many of my girlfriends—I love them, and I've been known to say it to them. But there are billions of people in the world I don't know, and if any random one of them died and someone told me, I wouldn't be devastated. The difference with the paras, and even more so with the interrogators, is that they feel like that about everyone. Most of them aren't capable of loving or caring. Some of them flat-out hate people in general. Maybe it sounds like a harsh judgement, but it's true.

Not that the Para is completely cold. There's Sara, for one thing. Even there, I wouldn't say "cares." He's incredibly possessive about her, you could almost say jealous sometimes, but I've seen him do things that I'm sure must have hurt her deeply, and I know he saw it and that it didn't bother him. There's Doctor Warrick too, and . . . well, I've met him occasionally, but I'm definitely not qualified to pass any opinions on what goes on between them. Let's just say that the appearance of a regular partner in the Para's life was something that would have picked up a substantial pot of winnings if anyone had ever even thought to bet on it happening.

There are other people who . . . stand out from the crowd for him, I suppose might be the best way to put it. A handful of the other senior paras are people he'll do a favor for without keeping a careful count—perhaps just because there are so many debts going so far back that it would be impossible. The rest of us, the core of his regular team, we make an impression sometimes, and it would annoy the hell out of him if any of us got ourselves killed or left I&I (and those would be about equivalent, as far as he's concerned). Like I say, he's possessive, and he doesn't appreciate it when our efficiency is impaired, or we get caught up in office politics, which can get quite vicious at I&I.

Beyond that, I've seen him furious about cases, about the times when we can't carry them through to the end because of politics or corporate pressures. It's the unsolved cases in our record, though, and the damage to his pride that hurts, not anything to do with justice or the victims, whoever they might be. I'll say it again—he doesn't care about people.

I still do, though, sometimes even about the people we have to deal with during cases. It's not always a good thing.

Chapter Four

❖

I hate hospitals, but then that's a given, isn't it? Have you ever met anyone who likes them? At least, unlike many people, I don't mind the smell too much. It's similar to the interrogation levels at I&I. I've spent enough time down there that it's familiar, if not exactly comforting. Still, I'd far rather have spent the night at home, on a more comfortable bed and without being constantly woken by people who wanted to check if I was sleeping.

Luckily, by the time the memory-scrambling effects of the painkiller—and the nausea from the other drugs they gave me to counteract the first one—had worn off, my leg had been treated. I don't remember whether I tried to leave and get back to my investigation. I have a suspicion that I did, but I never asked. There didn't seem to be any point looking for extra embarrassment.

Infuriatingly, the next day the hospital wouldn't discharge me until they had a definitive blood test saying the side effects had cleared from my system and I was back to normal. My mother arrived—bringing clothes—and then my father. They were both upset, of course, and it was odd to have their suddenly focused parental concern, again, after leaving it behind when I reached adulthood. We managed without any major scenes, though. My mother wanted me to come back to Strasbourg with her to recuperate, then ordered me when I declined. Even if technically I could have asked for medical leave, there was the case, so we compromised on her coming to stay with me for a few days.

When the Para arrived just before lunchtime, he looked rather ragged around the edges, and I wondered how much he'd slept, if at all.

"How's the case?" I asked with due trepidation.

"Well, if this is corporate PR, then they've done a hell of a job. It's all over everywhere, and someone's already leaked the fact that we closed down the initial investigation." He dropped into the chair by the bed. "And if the corps are behind it, then they're pulling a hell of a bluff, too."

"They don't want corporate security to handle it?"

"They're demanding we put everyone we've got on it. Tillotson isn't happy, because it's still not a political case, but there are rumors that they're threatening legal action if they aren't satisfied with the results."

I felt sick again, definitely not because of the drugs. "Could they do that?"

The Para shrugged. He didn't look overly concerned, which reassured me far more than his answer. "I have no idea. I've never heard of a corporation successfully suing I&I. We'd just better make sure we get the investigation right this time."

I can't tell you how much I appreciated that "we," but relief did come with a twinge of disappointment. "If you want to give it to Nagra, or take it yourself, then I understand."

He looked at me assessingly. "Are you still high?"

"I'm sorry, Para?"

"If I wanted to give it to Nagra, then she'd have it, whether you understood or not. What I want to know is if you're fit to keep running the case. The medic won't give me an opinion either way."

I didn't hesitate. "Yes, I am."

"Fine. I can spare Jameson to help you, so let her do the running around." He stood up. "Tillotson told me to take charge personally, by the way."

I nodded. Office politics, which was just what we needed in the middle of what was already enough of a mess.

"He doesn't run my team, though." The Para's smile didn't touch his eyes. "If someone at the corps is trying to play us over this, I want them. And if they don't find that *satisfying*, they can sue us from inside a re-education center."

"Yes, Para."

After he left, I lay for a while and fretted about office politics. I don't know whether I&I is worse than most places, but the stakes can be very high. Too often we're stuck between corporations, or corporations and departments, and no one has any love lost for us. On the other hand, if you spend all your time second-guessing and trying to keep out of trouble, then there's no way to get your job done. I let myself fret for five minutes, and then I tried to put it out of my mind.

With some painkillers that didn't send me out of my skull, and a brace on my leg with neural inducers to limit muscle contractions to safe limits, I found I could struggle about with the help of a pair of crutches. I felt rather silly, and a day or two's rest would have worked better for me, but the Para had asked me to do something for him and the team.

I went to I&I first. It was midafternoon by the time I got there, and news of the previous night's events had obviously spread, because my appearance caused little surprise but a lot of murmuring as I crossed the General Criminal central office. Sara was up and out of her seat before I made it halfway to her desk.

"That autograph should be worth a bit more, now," I said as she came up to me.

"Forget the autograph. Are you okay? Toreth said it wasn't serious, but . . ." As she spoke, she looked me over head to foot, like she was counting limbs.

"I'm fine. All patched up, now, and they say it shouldn't even scar if I follow the treatment plan properly."

She looked so worried, it was actually rather touching. I swear, there were tears in her eyes. And then she said, "You could've been killed."

The funny thing was, I genuinely hadn't thought about that, not until she said it. I couldn't produce a reply, but I suppose I must've looked as shocked as I felt, because she put her hand on my arm.

"I'm sorry. Stupid thing to say. Shouldn't you be resting?"

"No. I just came in to read the IIPs from last night and this morning." And get my bearings before I jumped back into the investigation. "And, um, I'll need an interview camera."

"You sit down in your office, and I'll sort it out. Where do you want to go?"

"I should talk to Kit and Kim. And Jase. If I can, anyway. And I need to talk to Jameson, if she's around."

She nodded, efficient Sara again. "I'll find them all, and arrange a car."

Alex-Ann Jameson was the long-delayed replacement for Lucia Wrenn. The rest of the old team tried to remember not to mention Wrenn's name in front of the Para, and I think for a while he was down on Jameson because her presence reminded him that Wrenn had, as he saw it, betrayed him personally by her decision not to come back after the revolt. I couldn't blame Lucia for it. She'd been at I&I when the attack happened, and she was in one the last groups of people who got out before the building was secured by the resisters. I've never had a chance to speak to her about what happened to her or what she saw, but I've heard enough from other people to wonder what decision I might've made about coming back, if I hadn't been luckier.

Anyway, it had taken the Para a while to bring the investigative team up to strength, which could partly be blamed on the staffing shortages, but was probably also due to his residual irritation. I'm sure Jameson must've noticed he treated her differently from the rest of us. I thought for a while that if she didn't leave, the Para might still replace her with someone else to break the link with Wrenn's memory, but Jameson stuck it out, and in the end he seemed to get used to her.

I liked Jameson as soon as I met her. She came to I&I from Justice, a couple of years before the revolt, something not unknown but fairly unusual. She has enormous dedication and enthusiasm for her job; I've rarely known her to grumble about staying late or working at a weekend. She never talks about her personal life and it surprised me, actually, when I found out from Sara that she had not one but two registered partners, and a child. Presumably her partners must be tolerant of her long hours or, I suppose, equally busy.

Physically, she's short, muscular, and incredibly energetic. She taps her feet and fiddles with anything left lying on a desk, and she hates sitting still. I couldn't tell you her hair color without checking her security file, because it never stays the same for long, and she has a liking for flashes and patches. She always keeps it short, though, which helps her to walk the edge of I&I rules about investigator presentation.

Jameson offered to go to the hospital for me, and part of me wanted to say yes. Not just because of the pain in my leg, but because I felt reluctant to face 343 and the corps. I told Jameson to stay at I&I, collating results as they came in, and to start working on the corporate sab angle.

I was slightly surprised to find that the corps owned a part share in an extremely upmarket private hospital, although perhaps I shouldn't have been, after my conversation with Jase about cosmetic surgery. The corps itself, combined with New London's other entertainment corporations, probably generated a lot of medical business.

At the hospital it was easy to spot Kit's room. There were four bodyguards flanking his door, watching the corridor with reasonably professional alertness. They certainly spotted me—the crutches and the uniform made it easy for them. I started towards the room, but halfway there I saw Jase.

He was sitting alone in an alcove, on one of a semicircle of low seats, head back against the wall, hands hanging loose between his thighs. He looked exhausted, and I realized he was still wearing the costume from the performance, complete with bloodstains. The reflective applique seemed horribly out of place.

As I hesitated, he spotted me and stood up at once.

"I'm sorry, Investigator. You have no idea. It's my fault."

"What is?"

"The whole thing. Fucking—fucking corporate sabs. If I hadn't tried to get out, they'd have left us alone." He looked down at my leg. "Are you okay? I'm so sorry you got caught up in it."

"You think the corps was trying to kill you?"

"Of course! Who else would be shooting at me?"

"At you?" I said.

"You were there. Andrews—" Jase held out his arms, like he was catching someone. "He was right in front of me. If he hadn't run up on stage, I'd probably be dead."

"Jase, who knew you were planning to perform?"

"No one. I didn't tell a soul, not even Ann. Not that I don't trust her, but she doesn't like me talking to the corps, and I had to ask Geoff to let me backstage. But I didn't even tell him I wanted to do the show until last night. Honestly, I didn't think it would work out. I expected Geoff to say no to letting me on stage, but he didn't, and Kim and Kit were up for it. It's funny—I just about squeezed into T-boy's costume, and..."

His voice trailed off, and I waited.

"It wasn't me?" Jase said. He sounded more confused than relieved.

"It doesn't seem likely. You were sitting still at the table in plain view all evening."

"But Kim and Kit only came out to perform." He nodded. "They were the targets, then?"

On the one hand, it seemed like the logical conclusion. But what was the motive? "That doesn't make much sense, either. Not to me."

"Well. Maybe the corps figured if the trio was done, then they'd take the insurance payout. Or maybe it was a warning to the rest of their acts to stay in line." He paused, then shrugged, looking slightly sheepish. "Jesus. I sound like a nutcase fan, don't I?"

Given that I'd considered the same possibilities, I could hardly agree completely. "It seems a touch extreme."

"Yeah. From an organization that drugs kids and turns them into human sculptures. Sure it does. I could tell you stories about some of the things—"

He turned away as the door to Kit's room opened. An older couple came out—Kit's parents, whom I recognized from their security files. They looked upset, but there was something hard-edged about them, too. There were discussing something in low, serious voices which seemed oddly businesslike and out of place. Jase had characterized them as greedy, and judging by their appearance, either they did pretty well for themselves or they'd taken their share of their son's success.

They stopped when they saw us, and Jase went over to them.

"Bobby, Jayne, I'm so sorry. I never—"

They walked away without a word, blanking him completely. Jase watched them go, scrubbing distractedly at his hair. It looked thick with product, left over from the stage show.

"Have you seen Kit?" I asked.

"They won't let me. Kim's in there with him." He hesitated. "I've only been here for an hour. I was at the other place, with Andrews. He doesn't have a hundred corps people looking out for him, or—" He waved a circle. "A facility specializing in making bodies beautiful."

"How is Andrews?"

"I'm not his registered contact, so they'd only tell me so much. But he's a mess. I did see him. He was unconscious most of the time—he opened his eyes once but I don't think he recognized me. And then he went for surgery again, and they said he'd be out for a fair while afterwards, so there didn't seem to be any point staying. Are you going to see Kit?"

I nodded.

"Good. Tell him I'm sorry, please. Tell him I love him, and I'm going to keep trying to see him until the bastards let me in."

The declaration was delivered with total seriousness, and no trace of embarrassment.

The guards obviously had orders to let I&I personnel through without question.

Kit was in the bed, the left side of his head and face concealed in protective plastic. Kim sat beside him. His attitude didn't look comforting, though—Kim was leaning forwards, and Kit looked to be trying to pull away. When I opened the door, they both froze, then relaxed again.

"It's the investigator from I&I," Kim said. "The one who said there was no threat."

The urge to apologize was almost overwhelming. "Case assessments are based on the available evidence."

Kim pointed to Kit's face. "So how does *that* rate as evidence?"

"We've reopened the case, of course." I turned to Kit. "How are you?"

"He's going to be *fine*," Kim snapped. Before I could ask him not to interrupt my questions, Kit turned awkwardly towards me, moving his whole body because his neck was braced.

"Look at this." His voice was muffled, like he couldn't move his jaw. "Look!"

Fumbling, he pushed a screen into my hand. I glanced through the medical procedures listed on it. I'm not a doctor, but I do have some training and experience. What was on the screen went far beyond repairing the damage the ricocheting bullet had done to Kit's expensive face. It looked as though the corps was taking the chance to do some more cosmetic work on its product. As far as I could tell, some of it was aimed towards undoing the earlier work, at least in part. I remembered Jase saying that the body-shape fashions were changing.

From one point of view, it should've been reassuring for Kim and Kit. On first inspection, again given my limited knowledge, it looked like expensive treatment. I couldn't imagine the corps wanting to extend its investment on this scale if they planned to dissolve the group.

At the bottom of the screen the request for patient authorization was still highlighted, waiting.

"Mum and Dad say I should go through with it," Kit said when I laid the screen down.

"And they're right. Come on. This is just 'cause you're hurt and tired and people keep bothering you." Kim glared at me, then stroked Kit's hand. "Just let them do what they have to do. Look, I'm being booked in, too, while you're out of commission. Muscle sculpting for me, and you know how much that hurts."

"I don't want to do it anymore," Kit whispered. Tears tracked down his bare cheek. "I just want them to fix my face, that's all. Not the rest."

"If you don't do it, we'll both be out of a job," Kim said flatly. "Right now we're a good story. A *valuable* story. We'll have another release set if you get all pretty again, but not if you don't. There are a thousand girls outside this minute waiting to hear you're okay."

He wasn't joking. The I&I car had struggled to make it through the crowd spilling from the pedestrian areas into the road. I'd wondered why the hospital security hadn't cleared them away, but then I realized—publicity.

"Kim..." Kit said weakly.

"They're recasting Jase. I've talked to Geoff." Kim leaned down over the bed and dropped his voice to a whisper. "You do it, Kit. You sign the fucking consents. If you don't, the corps will cut you loose. Where are you going to go if you don't have the corps? Do you think *Jase* is going to ride in on a white horse and save you? He doesn't give a shit about either of us. I thought you would've figured that out by now." Kim gestured around the room. "Who pays for all this if the corps doesn't? Do you want to blow your savings on reconstruction?"

Kit looked up at me. His one visible eye was bloodshot and watery. "What do *you* think?"

That floored me. I've never been good with sudden questions. "Um. I think— I'm not qualified to give you an opinion. I'm investigating the case, nothing else."

There was a long silence, then he nodded, and reached out for the screen.

It's funny what stands out, what you remember about a case and about the people involved. And like I said, I've been told I have a protective streak, usually by people who don't approve of it. I'll never forget the expression on Kit's face, like he'd just that moment realized how alone he really was. For a second I badly wanted to take the screen away from Kit and tell him he didn't have to go through with it, that he could find a life for himself outside all this corporate insanity.

I didn't do it, of course—I couldn't. I had a job to do, and so far I hadn't done it very well.

"I suppose that looked pretty harsh," Kim said.

"It's none of my business," I said.

"It's the best choice for him." Kim shrugged. "Okay, yes—and me. And the corps. No one wins if he turns into some scarred recluse."

We were in the hospital cafeteria, drinking coffee from chic off-white china in a soothingly lit space that looked like the kind of expensive restaurant where I'd only take a serious girlfriend.

Kit had said he wanted to be alone for a while, and with the forms signed Kim seemed happy to leave him. When he'd gone outside to talk to the guards, I'd belatedly passed on the message from Jase, and that had seemed to calm Kit down more than anything else. When I left the room he was already sleeping. Outside, I'd found Kim arguing with the guards. He wanted them to leave us alone while we went for a coffee. When they refused, he managed to persuade them to sit a few tables away. I wondered what he wanted to say to me that he didn't want the corps to know about.

To start with, he seemed to want to justify his behavior.

"Kit needs to be told what to do, that's all," Kim said. "He's fragile, you know? He didn't used to be. But it's been getting worse for a while now. One day he's going to have a real breakdown. Being alone would destroy him."

"Have you told the corps?"

"I don't need to. They've got psychologists on our case all the time. And right now, I don't want to give them any more reasons to kill the group. Figuratively speaking," he added as my eyebrows went up.

"Would they really drop Kit?" I asked.

"Of course, if they thought he couldn't follow through. It's a business, Investigator, and we're a product. No, a commodity. You know the difference, right?"

"Yes. So what now?"

"T-boy's getting his promotion at last. Geoff says they're announcing it in the next week or so. I'll have a while doing appearances with T-boy, then a few weeks of surgery and recovery that I'm really not looking forward to. The projection looks okay, as long as they don't make any mistakes. They don't, often. And anyway, I've got about as much of a choice as Kit does." He stared down into the black coffee in front of him, and then blew on it. "You're good to talk to, you know? Not the corps, not media, not the business, not a fan. Ordinary. I don't meet many people like that these days." He looked up. "I used to have friends, when I was a kid. I wonder what happened to them?"

I resisted the urge to say "they grew up." Kim's childish appearance was very much surface. "Have you ever thought about leaving the corps?"

The melancholy in his eyes cleared. He leaned closer, voice lowering. "Yes. That's why I wanted—you've been talking to Jase. Do you think, if I asked him, he'd be willing to consider a duo?"

I was about to tell him the truth—that I very much doubted it—but as I drew breath he kept talking.

234

"I've been thinking it over, and it could be really good. We work well together. And we look good together, too, although I imagine that's not how he's planning to pitch things. But if he's got a contract...I mean, I don't know who it's with, but maybe he could talk to them, you know? What do you think?"

So much for his concern about leaving Kit alone, was what I really thought. But I also knew the Para would give me the bollocking to end all bollockings if he caught me playing mediator for this bunch of warped pseudoadolescents.

"It's not my job," I said. "You'd have to approach him. He was here, in the hospital, trying to see Kit. He said he'd stay until he had."

"Yeah? No one told us, of course. If I can get him into Kit's room, he'll *have* to talk to me." He grinned, and put his hand on my forearm, squeezing. "Thanks."

I went through all the questions I had lined up, and got the answers I'd expected—Kim claimed he had no more idea now than he had before who might be behind any attempt on his, Kit's, or even Jase's life. For the present, I decided to believe him.

Other people's families fascinate me. When I was a child, I always thought my home life was so dull. Now, of course, I'm grateful that it was stable, and that my sister and I were so well loved that we never even noticed the fact. We just took it for granted, which is how it should be.

There were other things we never noticed, too—tensions that must have been there. Our parents divorced a few months after Sophie finished university. I suppose they thought that at that point they'd done all they could for us and they might as well do what they wanted. There were no big scenes, no recrimination or arguments at all. They're still friends.

My father started dating almost immediately, and was quite quickly remarried to a woman my age. She looked remarkably like the women I date, the ones that the rest of the team claim not to be able to tell apart. I liked her, but I wasn't surprised when they split up. She lasted two years, and since then he's already managed to squeeze in another few girlfriends just like her. It must run in the family.

My mother says she's had enough of relationships. She has her career as a division head at the Department of Transport, which, yes, is pretty prestigious. She's also gone back to breeding miniature dogs, something she did before I was born, and doing even more crosswords, always a passion of hers. She generates them by hand, an insane waste of time when they can be done so easily automatically, and sends them to me. I make my own crosswords to send her in return. Every time I think about cheating, and every time I don't do it. That's what I've inherited from her.

However, divorces and everything, we're still a family. We all get together every New Year and on birthdays—even dad's current girlfriend is always invited—and have a genuinely friendly and enjoyable time. So, even after splintering, my family still inexplicably manages to be dull. Or, as my mother would say, civilized.

When I decided I wanted to join I&I, my parents were nothing but supportive. It wasn't what either of them would have chosen for me in their ideal worlds, but neither of them would have dreamed of pressuring me into following their wishes over my own. My mother was disappointed that I went for Int-Sec over the DoT, but I think she understood, and respected, that I needed to fall a bit further from the tree.

Having ambitions for your kids, or even living vicariously through them, is one thing. The idea that someone could take a child of their own and, in effect, sell him to a corporation...well, in that case, perhaps fascinating isn't the word that comes first to mind, but it is interesting to try to imagine the thought processes behind the actions.

When the corporation handed Kit's parents the first list of surgical procedures, did they hesitate before they signed? Did they tell themselves that it was all for the best for him? Did they try to explain it to him? Or did his wishes simply not enter into the equation?

Of course, none of that was inside the scope of my investigation. But I couldn't help wondering.

I arrived back at I&I and found Geoffrey Cheung waiting for me. I'd expected to have to go back to the corps, probably to an unfriendly reception, so his voluntary appearance at I&I rather threw me. I asked Sara to arrange an interview room for us, while I took some more painkillers and backed them up with strong coffee.

The weeks since I'd last seen Cheung hadn't been kind to him. He looked more haggard than ever, and he'd definitely lost weight. He fidgeted constantly, but the plain interview table gave him little scope for fiddling. I'd brought a coffee for him, too, and he looked pathetically grateful for it. At least until he took a sip—I&I coffee isn't up to corporate standards.

I settled myself into the chair, trying to find a position that wasn't too distractingly uncomfortable. "I'm sorry for what happened to Kit. When we closed the case, there was nothing to indicate this might happen."

To my surprise, he seemed to accept the apology immediately. "I understand."

"So what can we do for you, Mr. Cheung?"

"I thought you'd want to talk to me, and the corps wants to make it clear that we're cooperating a hundred percent with your investigation. Obviously, we want to do anything we can to help."

I'm sure he knew as well as I did that corporate cooperation is never obvious. "Did the corps have any security present at the event?" I asked, hoping for at least some additional footage, or a search of the venue that could pin down when the gun was placed.

"No. The NLMA organizers dealt entirely with venue security. No corporations had personnel present."

"None at all?"

"Events like that aren't considered a risk. You said it yourself, Investigator. Almost all product-targeted threats are PR-driven. Yes, of course we have some sabbing, but it's information based, or aimed to generate negative PR. Can I speak off the record?"

I nodded. Certainly, in a wider sense, he *could* speak off the record, although not with an I&I investigator in an I&I interview room.

"There's...you might call it an unofficial understanding inside the business that product isn't targeted physically. Vendettas don't help anyone's bottom line."

"Well, perhaps someone decided to step outside the agreement. Do you still deny any involvement with the threatening message regarding Jase?"

"Absolutely. If it was generated within the corps, then it was done without any reference to me." He sounded sincere, but I did notice that now he was denying prior knowledge, not the possibility of the corps being behind the messages. "Frankly, I would've told them that with Jase it was counterproductive. They should've known that in any case, from the 343 files."

"You read the report I sent?" I asked, and he nodded. "Whoever sent the threat had to have had access to information held by the corps, beyond knowing the security code. The location of the sender of the first three messages, for example."

Cheung shook his head wearily. "Investigator, if we'd sent the threat, I'd tell you. I've had people looking into it since last night, and if we find how the information leaked we'll be taking steps to deal with the source. But you're looking in the wrong place, and while you do those boys could still be in danger."

Faced with flat denial, what more could I do? I wondered what my chances were of getting a commercial confidentiality warrant strong enough to let us poke around in the depths of the corps's communication records.

"Did you know in advance that Jase was planning to perform?" I asked.

"No." With no trace of hesitation, he added, "I was the one who agreed to it, though."

"Oh?"

"Yes. Jase called me a few days before the event and begged me to let him backstage to talk to Kim and Kit." He had started to drum his fingers on the table, beside his still half-full coffee cup. "I was reluctant—I thought it might unsettle the other boys. In the end I allowed it, with suitable supervision. Then when I saw him on the night, he said he wanted 343's last performance to be the real 343."

"And you agreed."

"After some thought. I did wonder—hope—that with the breakup announcement scheduled for the next day he might finally be having second thoughts about his future. Statistically, his chance of a solo career with success even touching that of 343 is negligible. The services we provide to our artists are some of the best in the business."

Suddenly, they were artists, not product. "So you didn't worry he might do something to embarrass the corps?"

"Actually, no. I asked him straight up and he promised he wouldn't. Believe me, I know how he feels about us, but I trusted him not to mess things up for Kit and Kim—or to give himself a bad reputation."

Jase had said that live performance was his favorite aspect of 343. But at the hospital, he'd shown no change in his attitude towards the corps. "You'd really take him back?"

"Investigator, 343 is an enormously profitable brand. We have lifecycle strategies in place for all our product, and that includes their closedown. Ideally, we shift fanbase to another product within our stable, at least until they move out of our demographic. 343 had good long-term projections, but even another year or two would let us complete their cycle in a controlled way, with better fan retention."

That dovetailed well with Jase's estimate of 343's prospects. "And what about your personal stake?"

Cheung was silent for a long few seconds, then he said, "Last week, Jase coming back was pretty much my only chance to save my career at the corps. That's why I gave in to him—it couldn't hurt, and any straw was worth clutching at. The truth is, they'd only let me stay to handle the closedown because no one else wanted to touch the mess."

"They'd definitely decided against continuing with Toby Brown?"

He nodded. "Some weeks ago. I argued in favor, of course. Fan acceptance testing was broadly positive, and I'm sure it could've been improved with the right marketing. But my opinion wasn't worth much then, and the feeling was that the risk to the corps's image was too large."

Brand confusion, as Jase had called it. "And what if Jase hadn't planned a solo career?"

"Oh, well." He brightened slightly. "That would've been a different matter. I could've put together a strong case for Toby to—" He stopped dead.

I had terrible training scores in level two verbal interrogation, and even my level one results were nothing special, but at that moment, I thought I'd done all right. I let the silence stretch out, giving Cheung plenty of time to think about what he'd said.

"I didn't try to kill him," Cheung said at length. "I didn't try to have him killed. We knew nothing about it. *Nothing*. It's an insane suggestion."

I didn't dispute that directly. "I heard today that the corps's now planning to replace Jase with Toby Brown and keep 343 in business."

"No. I mean, yes, in light of the huge positive PR boost we spent last night re-evaluating the projections and—" He lifted his hands from the table, palms towards me. "I didn't plan *any* kind of shooting, okay? Fatal or otherwise."

That was a possibility that hadn't occurred to me, yet—a supposedly bloodless PR stunt gone messily wrong. Or even a less bloodless stunt that had gone right. Would the corps risk potentially killing Kit because having him maimed would be profitable? I felt I was probably allowing Jase's venom and paranoia to color my judgment. On the other hand, I've known corporations do even less savory things without hesitation, and if the choice was between 343 ending unprofitably, and a chance of a high payoff with the risk of killing Kit...

Cheung sat back, his hands now still. I saw his gaze move around the room. We weren't down in the interrogation levels, but a gray, windowless interview room isn't the most hospitable place to be. That's how they're designed.

"Mr. Cheung?"

"This wasn't done by the corps," he said firmly.

"To your knowledge."

"I—" He swallowed. "I don't believe we'd do such a thing. We don't work like that. It's completely outside our corporate culture."

Not the most compelling argument I'd ever heard, and I felt sure the Justice systems would give it about as much weight as I did, should I need a waiver at any point. "Let's hope you're right, Mr. Cheung. Because we'll be looking closely at the possibility."

For reasons I've never understood, I&I's architects chose to put the forensic labs along with pharmacy up on the sixth floor—or at least they did in part. Sometimes the items they have to deal with are too large to fit in even the large access lifts, such as vehicles or shipping containers. For those, the forensics have another area on the ground floor at the back of I&I. You might wonder why they didn't come up with a more sensible arrangement during the rebuilding after the revolt. To be honest, I've wondered the same thing. I suppose logistics weren't in the forefront of people's minds.

Forensics had survived the revolt better than a lot of I&I. Even resisters on the rampage can spot that people in lab whites probably aren't interrogators. However, they'd had a lot of equipment wrecked, and at the time of the 343 case they were still rebuilding. The first lab I looked into was occupied by a maintenance crew refitting the place.

The IIP listed the assigned senior forensic specialist as Jovita Marin. She'd only been in the division for a few months, but I'd worked with her once already and I felt confident my scene was in good hands. She'd come to New London from I&I Madrid, which had been one of the messiest stories of the unrest. The building caught fire early in the attack, and when the automatic systems didn't contain it the resisters closed up the building and let it burn. There were a lot of stories afterwards—firefighter vehicles blocked from approaching, I&I staff driven back into the flames or shot, that the resisters had even refused to open the emergency cell evacuation routes. I have no idea what might be true, because the investigation afterwards was, obviously, not public.

Sara once told me that Marin had been out at a crime scene that day, much as I was at Justice when our building was attacked, but that was all I knew. I'd never raised the topic with Marin. What can you say to someone, really? Sympathy seems completely inadequate.

I found her in a lab that looked to have just finished its refurbishment. One or two pieces of equipment were still shrouded in plastic. Marin seemed surprised to see me.

"The initial report will be finished tomorrow," she said with the faintest hint of reproach in her voice. "We're working as fast as we can. You were there, Investigator—it was a huge scene."

"I thought I'd pop up and see if you needed anything from me." I propped myself on my good leg, and lifted a crutch to demonstrate. "I'm supposed to be keeping myself mobile."

"Oh, right. Well, then. No, I think we have everything." She pointed at a row of sealed plastic tubes. "That's your personal bullet, there, fourth from the right. We dug it out of the stage. Of course, they came from a disposable, so the bullets do nada other than confirm it was the only rifle in the building, which it was—automatic and computer controlled."

"I thought I saw someone up there."

She shrugged. "I'd say that's unlikely. Maybe you saw the recoil block and aiming mechanism? The whole thing was concealed in a plain case attached to the walkway that presumably dropped open on target detection. It looked more or less like the venue's major lighting junction boxes—not an exact match, though, so the sabs were confident, sloppy, or cheap, take your pick. The gun is fairly low end."

It's a perennial problem with sabs. Any of them who have any sense—which is any sabs who do more than one job—buy cheap black market weapons and destroy them after a single use. Or, as in this case, leave them at the scene so that the sabs are a long way away before anything kicks off. Even auto-aiming guns are mechanically simple, and most are created to order. All 3D print equipment is supposed to have a molecular code to tie product to printer, but sabs know that, too, and they're usually removed or faked. Like a lot of what we do, it's an arms race between them and us, in this case literally as well as metaphorically.

240

"Do you think you'll get anything else from the gun?"

"Not yet. Standard catalytic coating, so I don't expect anything from the outside. I sent the control module down to Systems, and they're working on recovering the rifle instructions. It depends on how well they can reconstruct the storage."

I've seen gun control systems reduce themselves literally to liquid to prevent evidence from being reconstructed. "Did the self-destruct method have a lot of matches in the system?" Maybe we could narrow the search like that.

Marin shook her head. "This time we can't blame the sabs. I wouldn't hire the venue security guards to do a search, but at least one of them was a good shot. Good, or lucky—or unlucky, depending on how you look at it. They returned fire, and there was a direct hit on the data store."

"Deliberately?" I asked in surprise. It seemed like a staggeringly risky way for someone to try to destroy evidence, but just because something is stupid doesn't mean that it won't be tried or, occasionally and infuriatingly, succeed.

"That's your area, Investigator. Anyway, the store was wrecked, and it's probably encrypted anyway. But the thing wasn't cutting edge, so if they can reconstruct the store they'll probably drag something out of hiding." She raised her eyebrows. "*Probably*. Don't come back later and tell me I promised anything."

"I won't, don't worry."

"Hm." The sound had a disbelieving note to it. "I do still have people at the venue doing DNA sampling, but I wouldn't hold out much hope. Every name so far's someone who had a legitimate reason to be there last night or in the past. We concentrated on the walkways and access routes and now we're expanding. But those complexes have so many temporary employees and other people with access—" She shrugged.

"You're doing your best," I said. "If the evidence isn't there, it isn't there. Looking harder won't make it appear by magic."

She smiled. "Now I remember why I liked working with you. Everyone's usually so impatient up here. I think it's the cold climate."

"We need to keep moving to keep warm." I hesitated for a moment, then I said, "I heard they finally made up their minds about the I&I Madrid site."

She nodded. "They're rebuilding. I'm...surprised. Clearing the underground levels will be..." She clicked her tongue. "I imagine it'll take a while."

"Will you go back, when it's complete?"

Marin looked down at the rows of bullets on her bench, then shook her head. "New London isn't so bad. I think I'll get used to the cold, in the end."

Chapter Five

❖

I'd planned to stay late, but physically, I just couldn't do it. Instead I went home and let my mother make a fuss over me. Sophie called from Lucerne; we had a nice chat, and I talked to my niece, who was then just about old enough to recognize me on the comm and babble away. Around 9 p.m. I tried to look at the IIP again, but the words just didn't make any sense. I gave up and went to bed.

The next morning, I took a taxi to I&I, leaving my mother engrossed in a call with the woman who was looking after the dogs while she was away.

I'd only been there for an hour or so when Jase and Ann Marshall arrived. I happened to be out in the main office, limping my way back from the toilets, so I saw him arrive. All signs of the trauma were gone, and they looked like a polished celebrity couple. Even at I&I, where I would've thought most people were too old for the 343 demographic, he caused a stir. He walked through it as though he couldn't hear the whispers. Maybe after so long they genuinely didn't register. In my office he asked how I was and helped me sit down, and then he and Marshall sat opposite. Jase put a camera down on my desk without even looking at me for permission.

I cleared my throat. "Those are banned inside the building. Inside the whole Int-Sec complex, actually. Not just banned—illegal."

He paused and looked up. "No one said anything when we arrived."

The Para would've blown a fuse about presumptuous corporate tossers. I just told him that if anyone challenged them on the way out, I'd given permission.

"Thanks." He handed over a folded screen. "You said you wanted to see the book—in case it could help. Here it is."

"I'd like you to sign a confidentiality agreement," Marshall said.

Jase nodded. "But if you won't, you can have the thing anyway. It's locked onto this screen, but at the end of the day we can't stop you from taking it. All I can say is, please don't."

I watched the text scroll, colored lines flashing by, and it suddenly reminded me of something. "Is this how you always mark your text? With different colors?"

"Yes. I like colors—I find them easy to handle. Actually, that's how music looks in my head. It always has, since I was a little kid. Sound-color synesthesia, it's called." He shrugged. "Gives me something at least mildly interesting to talk about in interviews, although the corps didn't really like *that,* either."

Marshall cleared her throat. "The economic impact is completely outside mandatory treatment levels, but someone who was looking hard for content provision violations could call it normalizing a neurological defect."

Jase frowned slightly—I imagine he'd hoped to leave that kind of consideration behind at the corps. "Anyway, I always write music with colors, yeah. On paper, usually—not because I'm trying to pretend I'm an old-fashioned artist, it just works better for me. I like to have a load of pens, match the colors, write over things and cross them out."

"Would it surprise you to know that I've seen some music written like that before?"

For a moment Jase looked at me blankly, then he grimaced, squeezing his eyes shut. "Ah, *hell.* No, it wouldn't surprise me. I told the idiot to transcribe them right away."

Marshall glanced at the camera on the table, then leaned over and switched it off. "You didn't do anything illegal, Jase."

"I know, but—" He sighed. "Investigator, when I said I hadn't seen the Kays since the breakup...that wasn't quite true. Sorry. Kim came over to me at a party one night—slipped his minders—to ask me to think again. I—well, obviously I couldn't. But I felt bad for the Kays, leaving them in the lurch, so I wrote Kim some songs and had a friend pass them along. They were all ideas from before I got the chance to jump ship. 343 material, not what I want to do now."

I wondered if Kim had caught up with him again, at the hospital, to make his proposal. "Does the corps know?" I asked.

"God, no. There's no way the corps would let me have anything official to do with 343. But Kim's a better writer than people would tell you—he can take the credit. There's enough for a release set, and if they want more fillers I can write some. And I'll get my percentage, which will come in handy."

"You have a contract?"

"Nah." He waved a lazy circle towards the camera. "But if Kim doesn't come through, I've got recordings of the conversations where he agreed. And of a few other things he wouldn't want put about. Like I said, recording saves arguments later."

"What if the corps takes the material from them and gives it to a new group?"

For a moment he went still, then he shrugged. "That won't happen. I'd get it back, one way or another." He sounded very certain.

"But if Kim is supposed to have written it, won't the corps own it?"

"No," Marshall said. "We have every single note Jase has written since he signed the termination on file at two independent legal firms and an artists' rights association."

Jase smiled slightly, with his mouth only. "Like I said, Investigator, I hate plagiarism. People get destroyed by it—corporations take their work when they can't do a damn thing about it." His smile turned bitter. "Life's laid out along a learning curve, right?"

"I'm sorry?"

"The first time I really let myself see what the corps was like. It started... someone sent me a demo recording. It slipped past the screening. I thought they were pretty good, so I passed it on to Geoff. A few weeks later we got two of the songs back, credited to in-house writers. You know 'Watching You Sleep', right? That was one of them. One of our biggest hits. Of course, they'd screwed it up, too, changed the lyrics. The original had this great underlying self-awareness of just how unhealthy it is to want someone in your control every second of their lives—which is a lot like working for the corps, no? We tried to put some of that back in the visuals, with the microcameras, but—" He shrugged. "That wasn't really the point. The point was, the corps stole it."

Marshall, I noticed out of the corner of my eye, was looking slightly pained. Maybe she didn't want Jase letting all the juicy secrets out in advance.

"As soon as we got the track, I took it to Geoff, then I went higher up, but no one would do anything. And the worst thing was I couldn't even remember the poor bastards' names to contact them and tell them. Shitty, no? They trusted me with their fucking souls and I let them down. Eventually, when I'd made a few more friends in the right places in the corps, I had someone find the names for me and I sent them every cent I earned from the stuff. But—" Jase scrubbed his face and sighed. "Everything they ever gave us could have been the same. Stolen. The corps doesn't understand how much something you create *matters*. They just see little people they can rip off without consequences."

"Is this in the book?"

"Yes. I can back all that up, so they can sue me if they want to make headlines when I win." He shook his head, mouth twisting in disgust. "And I've got proof of much more, but we can't use it all. It came from an inside source, someone they'd be able to find. Violating corporate confidentiality like that would break someone if they were caught."

Remembering his comment about libel and commas, I took a stab in the dark. "Would this person be—" I glanced at Marshall.

"That would've been a breach of my contract," Marshall said firmly.

Jase raised one eyebrow slightly, the message clear.

"How seriously do you think the corps would view these revelations?" I asked.

"You mean, seriously enough to kill me?" He frowned, biting his lip. "Honestly? I think I'd be flattering myself if I said yes. This kind of shit comes up all the time. Music distribution needs a content license from the Public Media Division, so the corporations have the business stitched up so tight it doesn't matter what a few disaffected whiners say. No one will read that chapter, anyway—not enough sex and pharma. A few people might pick up on it and make a fuss, but the corps could bury the story with PR for far less than it'd cost to hire a pro sab team to hit me."

"So you've changed your mind about blaming the corps for this?"

"I—" He hesitated, then threw up his hands. "Fuck, I can't think who else it could possibly be. And I know it seems like I wasn't the target, but they've got no reason to want Kit or Kim dead. If I'd died on that stage, then the coverage would've been incredible and they could've recast me without worrying about what I might do to 343's image. Maybe they were always planning to shoot me during the set, even sitting at the table. More dramatic impact, no?"

"Maybe," I said. In my experience, corporate sabs are more concerned with efficiency than drama, but they also do what they're told by their clients. I wondered about floating the possibility of a pure PR stunt, but all I could see it doing was reinforcing Jase's existing prejudices. "Is there anyone else who might have a reason to hurt anyone in 343?"

"The corps have to be behind it," Jase said firmly. "Are they trying to get you kicked off the case?"

"No. They want a full investigation."

"Oh." Jase slumped back in the chair. "Then... I don't mind telling you, Investigator, this is scaring the shit out of me. I'd convinced myself that the messages were just the corps trying to play me, but guns aren't a game. If it isn't them, then how the hell do I keep myself safe? Especially with Andrews in hospital."

"I'm sure the agency will come through with security soon," Marshall said soothingly. "If not we can look into a private arrangement."

"Soon." He grimaced. "Hopefully soon enough. No, no, Ann. It's okay. I know they're doing their best." Jase turned back to me. "Once I'm finally with the new corporation, of course, they'll have all the security I need. I was supposed to be signing on Monday, but it's been delayed, under the circumstances."

I hadn't considered all the ramifications of the shooting. "Will this make a difference to your new contract?"

"Well... maybe," Jase said. "Andrews is the senior partner at the agency, but I assume one of the other agents will take over my management if—well, if he dies. But I suppose AAA could fold without him, and then any unsigned contracts they negotiated would be worthless."

He looked surprisingly relaxed about it. I suppose he'd already thought it all through for himself long before I suggested it. "And what if they decide to drop you?"

"They won't. And if they do, I'll find someone else. Right now I'm big news, which should help."

"There'll be other options," Marshall said. "Even if they're less than perfect."

Jase picked up his camera, toying with it. "In a way, it doesn't make any difference. It was never a sure thing, so this just lengthens the odds against me, no? I've already left the corps. The only thing they can do now is kill me, and they'll have to, because I'm not going back."

Once more, I believed him, and Geoffrey Cheung had apparently felt the same. But had someone else at the corps thought differently? Andrews, after all, was the one who'd actually been shot. Had *he* been the intended target all along? It was hard to see how that could've been arranged.

"Thanks, by the way," Jase said suddenly.

"I'm sorry?"

"For passing that message along at the hospital. That was kind of you—I know it isn't exactly your job."

"So you spoke to Kit or Kim?"

He nodded. "Kim's a wizard at escaping his security, and he got me a few minutes with Kit, too. It was good to see him. I mean, bad in how messed up he is, but...good."

"Did they discuss their futures with you?"

"You mean, did Kim try to sell me his half-baked duo idea? Yes." Jase shook his head, smiling wryly. "It's ridiculous. I didn't think I'd ever say it, but he'd be better off sticking with the corps and the recast."

"Why?"

Marshall cleared her throat. "Trio to solo is difficult enough. Trio to duo, especially losing the brand-identified artist, is invariably a commercial disaster."

"I see." Kim presumably knew that, too. It didn't say much for his faith in a recast 343 if he was desperate enough to try to talk Jase into career suicide. "Well, thanks for bringing me the book. You'll call me if you think of anything that might help?"

Marshall nodded, and Jase mirrored it, more fervently. "Fuck, yes."

Some people would tell you that it's criminal to make any complaints about the way the Administration works, or about Europe's government in general. Of course, that's ridiculous, and it's generally only said by people whose real motive is a desire to be free to incite unrest by spreading harmful anti-Administration rhetoric, the majority of which is based on lies and distortions. The truth is that all Administration departments have channels through which any European citizen can directly raise issues of concern. If they prefer to remain anonymous, then the elected representatives at the Parliament of the Regions have whole offices dedicated to investigating problems. That way, valid concerns can be identified and addressed.

Content provider licenses are one of the key pillars by which Administration comms networks are kept clean of the sorts of unverified rubbish that could harm good government. No one benefits if the citizens of Europe are exposed to resister propaganda.

The whole licensing system was reformed and tightened up about twenty-five years before the 343 case, after footage purportedly taken inside a high-level re-education center was spread across Europe. As a result, the Unification Day holiday a few days later was marred by widespread demonstrations, some of which became violent. The Service was called in to protect property and innocent bystanders, and tragically, some of the protesters were killed or injured, an example of the awful consequences that can stem from unrestricted information dissemination.

These days, corporations who provide any kind of news distribution service are held to strict standards of public responsibility, and can be fined enormous sums for causing social harm, even if unintentional. A small corporation that would be incapable of paying the fine for even a minor content violation has, in a way, very little to lose. So in general it's only larger corporations with a strong financial footing who are granted licenses, especially the riskiest types—for example, to provide any kind of public forum where ordinary people can create content without editorial checks.

Beyond that, all corporations who provide comms services are deemed to be responsible for the content transmitted over those services. There are some exception for corporate networks that are cleared to carry corporate grade encryption, but they are still monitored by the Data Division, and practically speaking, a corporation whose network was caught carrying illegal traffic would find themselves in a very difficult situation when they next applied to the Communications Systems Assessment Division for a license renewal.

The content provider system had survived the recent unrest, even though I heard there was an amnesty for unlawful communications made during the trouble itself. Ending movement notification was one thing, but no Administration Council, however liberal-minded, would be willing to open up Europe to the kind of destabilizing forces unlicensed content and comms could unleash.

Of course, even though the reasons for it are sound, I can't deny some people do suffer from unfortunate, unintended side effects. This is what Jase meant when he said that corporations have the music distribution business under tight control, and why without a contract with a licensed provider his career would be over. But content is content, and while it would be lovely if something as harmless as pop music could be exempt, it would only open the whole system to abuse.

The initial scene forensics report arrived not long after Jase and Marshall left. I read it through closely, and with a detachment that surprised me. Although it had happened only two days before, the memory of the stage, soaked with blood (and some of it mine), was fading into being just another crime scene.

As Marin had predicted, both the gun and the area around it had so far proved forensically useless. Professionals like that don't thoughtfully leave obvious evidence for us. Systems was still working on recovering the gun control data, but that might be equally unhelpful, beyond giving us a definitive target ID. The rifle could have been there for any length of time, although practicality suggested it had been placed during the laying out of the hall for the awards. That meant more hours of internal surveillance footage to scan in the hope of seeing something suspicious.

I'd just finished reading it all when the Para arrived for a case conference. He hadn't asked for it, but I'd had Sara set it up anyway. I wanted to let him know that I was on top of everything, despite being injured. And, just possibly, after the mess I'd made by closing the original investigation, on some level I wasn't feeling so confident in my lead investigator skills.

He didn't ask me why I'd wanted the conference, just listened while I ran through the events of the day. He has a cool, thoughtful way of watching you talk which makes you want to keep going, to find the right thing to say, and which is very disconcerting. I imagine that it's even more so down on the interrogation levels.

When I finished, all I got was a nod, and an "I see," before he finally looked away and started reading through the IIP. I sat and tried not to fidget. My leg had begun to itch in an absolutely infuriating way, right under the brace which was keeping it straight. Fortunately, I didn't have to wait too long before he nodded and closed his hand screen.

"Good work," he said. "Do you have a definite target yet?"

"No. The location of the gun fixes the target area as the stage, but it could be any of 343—Jase, Kit, or Kim—or even Toby Brown. We'll have to wait for Systems to finish the forensics."

"Right. By the way, have you talked to Corporate Fraud?"

I shook my head. "I was going to ask Jameson to do the financial backgrounds, Para."

"Pass it over to CF—I'll authorize the budget. They can dig much deeper than we can, much more quickly." He stood up. "I'm seeing Tillotson this afternoon. I'll tell him you have everything under control."

"Thank you, Para," I said, somewhat taken aback by the abrupt end of the conference.

He grinned. "Don't worry, B-C, I'll be keeping an eye on the IIP. Just try not to get yourself shot again."

Sara was at lunch, which reminded me that I ought to eat something myself. My mother had boxed up some lunch for me, so I took it along to the coffee room, just to keep moving. The morning in my office had stiffened my leg up horribly.

Now, I'll freely admit that I never much liked Chris Doyle, and I was glad when he left the General Criminal section. We had a professional working relationship, and we functioned perfectly well as part of the same team, but I didn't enjoy sharing a case with him in the same way I have with other junior paras.

A lot of people would tell you that Doyle reminded them of the Para, but from my point of view, I'd say they were fooled by the superficial similarity of build and coloring, and a certain sense of latent violence in Doyle which the Para certainly has, too.

Doyle wears a surface layer of charm and friendliness, but he always made it fairly clear that he thought we investigators existed to do things for him, never the other way around. He saw us as the second-class citizens at I&I, which is ironic, because he was a talented investigator himself, if sometimes impatient. It just so happened that, in addition, he possessed the skill set for interrogations.

I know that Mistry felt the same. I'm not sure if the Para didn't see it, being a para-investigator himself, or if he didn't care because Doyle certainly did his job well.

Sara liked him. It's the only time I can remember the two of us disagreeing about someone on the team. But he always treated her with scrupulous friendliness, because he knew exactly how much the Para valued her. Naturally, after Doyle left the team, he did very well for himself over at Political Crimes. When he came back to General Criminal after the unrest as a brand-new Senior, I had hoped it wouldn't be a reason to see too much of one another.

Luckily, because I was "only" an investigator, he didn't seek me out. So I was surprised when he sat down next to me in the coffee room.

"That woman who turned up to see you," he said without preamble. "Blonde, nice arse?"

I put down the lunch box of tartiflette, which had just reheated itself nicely. "You mean Ann Marshall?"

He snapped his fingers. "That's her. Is she a suspect?"

"No, she's a lawyer."

"Oh, she can't be both?" His voice had that slight edge of superiority that annoyed me so much. So slight it was impossible to call him out on it, but it was there.

"Is there any reason she should be a suspect?" I asked evenly.

"You tell me. I recognized her from an old case over at PC. About four years ago, I think. Resisters were moving money around with invoices for fake services. We had to look at about ten corporations before we rounded everyone up, and she was definitely at one of them. Special security contracts."

Special security—often, but not always, a euphemism for corporate sabs. "There's nothing in her security file about an investigation."

"Her corporation was completely cleared. Not the same one that she works for now, though—I took a look at your case. Nice tidy IIP, by the way, Investigator."

"Thank you, Para."

"Anyway, it was just a thought. She worked on security contracts, and you have people with bullet holes in them. There might be a connection there."

"Absolutely." I picked my lunch up again. "Thanks for letting me know."

"Any time. At least it could give you an excuse to pull her in for an interview, right?" He winked at me as he stood up. "And if you need someone to interrogate her..."

I told Sara what the Para had said about getting help from Corporate Fraud.

"I'll call Phil Verstraeten," Sara said without hesitation. "If there's anything there, he'll find it."

While I didn't know the man personally, the team had worked with him and his boss, Senior Finance Specialist Elizabeth Carey, several times before, including on the investigation which ultimately led to the closure of the Selman kidnapping. It's one of the big regrets of my career that I wasn't involved with that case. I have some of the reflected glory from being on the Para's team, but I didn't actually take part.

Andrews was still unconscious and listed as critical at the hospital, which left me one more important interview to conduct. I asked Jameson to make sure that Corporate Fraud had access to everything they needed, and limped off.

Like the real members of 343, Toby Brown lived in a secure corporate-graded building. I suppose that overenthusiastic fans might not be discriminating when they spot their objects of adoration, and certainly Brown and the other faux 343 artists looked so much like the originals that I had no trouble at all crediting Jase's stories of exotic cosmetic surgery.

Kit II and Kim II (as I couldn't help thinking of them even at the time—I admit that right now, I'd have to check the files to find their real names) were unsettling in the way that any extremely good replica of a real person can be. They looked like almost, but not quite, perfect portrait sculptures, only in this case modeled from living, breathing flesh. The uncanny valley in human form.

Brown was even more disturbing, like coming across someone you knew when they looked very different. Perhaps if I'd met him first and Jase second, Jase would've seemed like the strange one, but perhaps not. I think I found something fundamentally unsettling about the intensely fine-tuned perfection of face and body which Jase had managed to scrub away in only a short time off the corporate

250

leash. According to Brown's file he was older than Jase, but he certainly didn't look it.

Their three-bedroom flat was far from subsistence housing, but it was about equally far from the expansive luxury of Kim and Kit's temporary accommodation. It was a little cramped for three, but in a good area of central New London rather than out in the cheaper suburbs. I imagine that the stand-ins had to be conveniently on hand in case of corporate emergencies.

There was a stack of bags in the hall, I noticed when I arrived, with a guitar case on top. Was the corps worried about the safety of the doubles, or was it connected to Toby Brown's sudden promotion?

At least they knew where the coffee was and how to make it. Kit II filled mugs with an efficiency I couldn't imagine his counterpart ever achieving, and led me through to the small living room.

Although I would've said up until then that 343 was paper-thin corporate product, meeting their doubles made me re-evaluate them slightly. Although they looked so similar, they did lack a certain presence, and I understood quickly why these were the backups and the boys I'd met before the front line. They were obviously bewildered by events and extremely wary of talking in front of an outsider.

My introduction and initial questions were met with monosyllabic answers from the three of them.

"Are you leaving here?" I asked, trying to find a topic that would get them to open up. "The bags in the hall."

Kit II and Kim II exchanged glances.

"They're all mine," Brown said. "I'm moving in with Kim tomorrow, or maybe the day after. I need to be there by the time they make the recast announcement, anyway."

"What about you?" I asked Kit II. "Will you be performing while Kit's in hospital?"

He looked down. "No."

"We don't have anything scheduled right now," Brown said. "Just some appearances." He sighed. "Would you like to come and see the view?"

"T..." Kit II said.

Brown raised his eyebrow. "Bit cold for you two, I should think. You'd better stay here."

I'd expected a balcony, although I didn't remember seeing any on the outside of the building. Instead, Brown took me up onto the roof—fortunately, there was a lift. I couldn't imagine much of a view of anything other than more flat, gray spaces with air recycling units and pigeons. I went over towards the edge, anyway, but I'd only gone a few meters from the door when I realized Brown hadn't followed me.

"Take a look if you want," he said. "I'll wait here."

I went back to him. "You don't like heights?"

"Fucking hate them. Have you ever seen a 343 show? No, I suppose not. They love flying rigs. Sometimes I think they do it just to fuck with me when I need to stand in for Jase. But it's safe to talk. I don't think even the corps can be bothered to monitor up here."

Just then, a pigeon landed on the top of the small structure that covered the access lift. It peered down at us, and Brown laughed.

"Hello, birdie. Have you got a camera hidden under your wing?"

The pigeon gave a soft, warbling coo, then started to preen its breast feathers. "It looks innocent enough," I said.

Brown laughed again. "I wouldn't put it past them, though. I don't know for sure if the flat is monitored, but—" He shrugged. "We get more freedom than the real 343, but not a lot. Image first, you know. Always, image first."

"So what did you want to tell me?"

He put his hands in his pockets—he hadn't picked up a jacket on the way out, and with his almost total lack of body fat, he must've been freezing. "I don't know. But I wanted to do it where I don't have to worry about the corps. Whoever it was at the NLMA, they were shooting at me, right?"

I looked at him with surprise. "Why do you think that?"

"We were all watching on the screens backstage. I saw Andrews get hit—he was right in front of Jase. If they were aiming at Kit or Kim, they were the world's worst shot. Unless someone else knew Jase was planning to perform?"

He sounded almost hopeful, and his face fell when I said, "Jase says not."

"Shit. Well, then, that's what I thought."

"Do you know of anyone who'd want you dead?"

When you think about it, it's an odd question ask someone, and I've asked it of a lot of people over the years. Either about themselves, or about someone else who was no longer around to answer the question in person. Some people are genuinely baffled, some have one clear answer, and some have so many names they don't even know where to start. Quite often, though, especially where there are corporate considerations, even the people who are dead sure (if you'll excuse the pun) have no intention of sharing with I&I.

Toby Brown frowned thoughtfully, rubbing his chin in the V between his thumb and forefinger. I waited patiently, but in my head I could hear the Para scoffing at the performance.

"No idea at all," he said finally, to my utter lack of surprise.

"Not the corps?" I said.

This time, the frown looked genuine and alarmed. "Do *you* think it was?" he said.

"Other people seem keen to point the finger at them."

"And by 'other people,' you mean Jase." He relaxed. "Man, I like Jase, but

252

he's ... bitter. So incredibly bitter. He probably blames the corps if there's no toilet paper left on the roll. I'm not saying the corps are saints, but everything he's got comes from them. Their backing, their demographics, their marketing."

"So he should be grateful?"

"Why not? At least a bit. I am."

So grateful that he'd slaughtered the corps's prize cash cow by giving Jase a way out. "How well do you know Andrew Andrews?"

This time his face didn't give anything away, and I wondered if this question was the reason why he'd wanted to talk to me up here. "The agent? Not well. Professionally, that's all. He represented me, years ago, before the corps signed me up."

"I believe you've been in touch with him more recently than that."

He glanced up at the pigeon, even though I hadn't noticed it move, then shrugged. "I see him at events sometimes. We say hello."

"Jase told me that you'd introduced him to Andrews."

"*Fuck*," Brown said, loud enough to scare the bird above us into flight. "Sometimes he's such an arse."

"He asked me to keep it confidential."

"Yeah, but you still put it in your—your report or whatever, didn't you?"

"The Investigation In Progress, yes. But those files are internal to I&I only."

He gave me a skeptical look. "I've seen what the corps can do. And Jase knows that, too. That's what I meant about him. No fucking gratitude. Now that he's out, he doesn't care about us. If the corps ever heard about it, *I'd* be out five minutes later, flat on my arse, recasting or not."

"So why did you risk putting him in contact with Andrews?"

"It's simple enough. I want his job. Every so often one of the backups gets lucky—their front guy manages to overdose, or offs himself, or cocks things up so badly that management kicks him out. Jase wasn't ever going to do that. He's too clever. But I knew how much he wanted to get out, so—" Brown shrugged. "There's nothing wrong with helping a friend. Listen, how is Andrews? No one ever tells us anything, and they put the flat on a blackout so we can't even get any newsfeeds."

"He's in intensive care." According to Jameson's call to the hospital that morning, he'd been taken back into the operating theater for further emergency surgery that morning, which didn't sound good. "They can't give a definite outcome, but his condition's critical."

"So he might still die?"

I nodded.

"Huh. Wow."

I couldn't read his expression. "Wow?"

"Just. You can be there one day, gone the next, just like that. It's mad, really, isn't it? All for some shitty music made for teenage girls to learn how to wank over." He sniffed. "I hope they appreciate it."

"Mr. Brown, as you say, you do seem to be a likely target. There's nothing to say that whoever tried to kill you won't try again. So you're absolutely sure you don't know who it might've been?"

"Don't you think I'd tell you if I knew?" he said.

There was no need to give him an honest answer, so I simply said, "If anything occurs to you, get in touch with us right away."

"Sure," he said. "Right away. If the corps will give me a comm, anyway. Was that everything?"

My leg was aching, probably from the cold wind, and I wanted to get back inside a nice warm I&I car, or preferably back to my office where I'd stupidly left the painkillers on my desk. There was just one more thing that I thought I'd take the opportunity to clear up, though. "When I spoke to Kit and Jase before the incident—"

"Oh, right. When you closed the case because there wasn't any threat."

Clearly, some news leaked through. "Yes. When I spoke to them before, there was some confusion about their relationship. Kit indicated to me that he'd had sex with Jase; Jase denied it. Jase thought you might have something to do with that?"

He laughed. "Oh, man. Yeah, that's me. Kit is so weird. He says he's straight and—" Brown shrugged expansively. "I'm not a mind reader. He fucks plenty of girls, I do know that. But he has this ridiculous obsession with Jase. He thinks one day Jase is going to fall in love with him, or some stupid crap like that—adopt him, maybe—and they'll live happily ever after making music in a penthouse overlooking the Thames Park. Which is insane, because Jase would cut his own prick off before he'd stick it in that little—" He stopped himself abruptly, and I wondered what he was about to say.

"But you wouldn't?"

"I don't have to want to marry him, or even look at his face, to mess around when he's blitzed. And I promise you, whatever stories he's making up for you, he knows it's me. Fuck, I've sucked him off when Jase wasn't even in the country, never mind the same hotel. He can lie there moaning 'Oh, Jase' all he likes, but he knows it's my mouth. Sometimes I make him say 'Good night, Toby' afterwards, and he does. Then he toddles off, probably to cry his poor popstar self to sleep in a huge fucking suite, while I go back to my shitty little room next to the bodyguards and the makeup team." Brown jabbed his finger towards me to emphasize his final words. "He. Knows."

I stared at him, rather wishing I hasn't asked the question. It didn't seem relevant to the case, and it was just so...distasteful. I know, with the life I lead and the things we have to see, perhaps I was overreacting. But the contempt in his voice sickened me.

"Well," I said finally. "Thank you for clearing that up."

"No worries," he said complacently. "Really, you can't trust anything Kit says. Nutty as a fruitcake, all the way through."

I walked with him to his flat door, but I didn't go inside. As soon as I stepped out of the building, I called Sara and asked her to add Toby Brown to Corporate Fraud's financial trawl. I hoped at least I could find some illegal debts or unpaid taxes.

My pessimism in regards to Andrew Andrews's health was proved correct late in the afternoon, when an automatic notification from Central Medical Records arrived to announce his death. The morning's surgery had failed to stem further hemorrhaging, and another emergency intervention had been required. He'd died in theater, before they'd even begun to operate. Even modern medicine still has its limitations.

I flagged his file to have the autopsy completed at I&I, and I set up some basic checks on the medical staff present around the time of his death, but it was the slimmest of outside chances. Even the most cursory inspection of his medical file suggested that a sabbing attempt would've presented terrible value in terms of risk versus reward.

In one way, it had no immediate effect on the case. We'd had no expectation of being able to interview Andrews in the near future. It did, however, put a definitive end to that line of inquiry.

With that cheering news, I decided to call it a day.

Chapter Six

❖

I spent the next morning back at the hospital, not for the case but for a check on my leg. The medics told me I'd been doing far too much, and that if I didn't rest I could be left with residual muscle damage, maybe bad enough to need replacement grafts. Remembering Kim's lack of enthusiasm for muscle work, I promised to be more careful.

Although it was Saturday I'd still planned to spend some time at I&I. Unfortunately—or, I suppose, fortunately—I'd accepted my mother's offer of company at the hospital, so she'd heard the medic's opinion. She directed the taxi home, and I didn't argue. Secretly, I was glad for the rest. I called Jameson to explain, and then spent the day on the sofa with my leg elevated, watching the IIP like a hawk as the reports and interviews slowly made their way in.

There's often a stage in an investigation when the initial interviews have been completed and you need to sit back and wait for information to appear. In certain cases, where there's a clear suspect to pursue or a kidnap victim to locate, it can be excruciating to have to wait while other people do their jobs. Even when there's a dead body that won't get any more dead for a day's delay, there's the knowledge that the perpetrator could be covering their tracks.

There's nothing to be gained by sitting wistfully outside the experts' labs or offices, though, like a dog waiting for a treat. People have their own priorities to set, and another case in another section may be legitimately more urgent.

I explained this to my mother, probably more times than was necessary over the course of the weekend. She listened with progressively less patience, and in the end she declared a pressing need to check up on her dogs on Sunday morning, leaving me to stew on my own. I tried to read the autobiography Jase had given me, but the depressing banality of stardom drove me back to sab activity reports. I gave the book to the I&I evidence analysis system instead.

My mother came back in the late afternoon, bringing a vast stock of groceries with her. In the evening I taught her how to play blackjack, which kept us both nicely distracted until it was time for bed.

"Your IIP is destroying my childhood," Sara said mournfully when I arrived for work on Monday.

"What?"

"It's so depressing. I had a favorite group once, you know—Backsync. I'm sure *you* don't remember them."

Actually the name was vaguely familiar, but I shook my head anyway. It doesn't do to disappoint your colleagues.

"Told you. Mind you, I haven't thought about them in forever, either. But for a couple of years I even I had a dedicated screen on my bedroom wall. My mum and dad bought me a show ticket for my twelfth birthday." She sighed reminiscently. "I went with some of my friends from school. My best friend, Georgie, she had the most *insane* crush on, um, Scott? I think it was Scott. He was the one who stood at the back and didn't say much in interviews, but Georgie was like that. She always had to be different."

"You liked the lead singer?" I guessed.

Sara smiled. "I'm not telling. Anyway, the point is, I had no idea about all this stuff that was probably going on behind the scenes. No wonder they split up."

"Well." What could I say, really? It seemed odd to apologize for my case, but in the end I did say, "I'm sorry."

"Oh, don't worry. I'm being stupid, I know. Just seems like nothing's the same anymore these days." She cleared her throat. "Anyway, how's your leg? You went back to the hospital, right?"

"Yes. It's much better." Rather late, it suddenly struck me why Sara had seemed so upset to see me on crutches. I knew she was still sensitive about the revolt, and it must have been a shock to her to see someone—one of the team—injured again. "The medics said it should be back to normal in no time."

"Smashing news." She smiled sweetly at me. "You go sit down, and I'll bring you a coffee."

Later in the morning, Phil Verstraeten sent a message to say he'd finished the first look into the case financials. I expected a report, but he offered to come up to General Criminal to talk me through his findings. I suspect he's had a lot of experience with people assuring him they'll understand the details, and then turning up at inconvenient times to clarify points with him. It's a hazard of being a specialist, I suppose.

I called the Para, and asked if he wanted a financials case conference. He told me he was busy, which made me feel rather better about myself.

So it was just Alex-Ann Jameson and myself in my office, watching as Verstraeten linked his data onto our screens. I'd asked Sara for more coffees, and got them—I wondered if the sympathy points would expire before or after I could stop wearing the brace.

"Thanks for being so quick," I said to Verstraeten.

"I can't take all the credit, I'm afraid. The corps was surprisingly helpful, considering that we didn't have any warrants."

"They do keep telling us how much they want a thorough investigation," Jameson said.

"Well, maybe they do. Of course," he added apologetically, "I didn't find anything that looked like sabbing payments. But it's a huge corporation, with a complex assortment of contracts. I'm sure if there were sabs being paid anywhere I could stumble across them, they wouldn't have been so cooperative."

I nodded. "How about Andrew Andrews and Associates?"

"Very helpful, too." Verstraeten snorted his odd laugh. "Although in that case, if Andrews hadn't been out of the picture it might've been different. AAA definitely isn't a triple-A corporation. They're living... well, not completely outside their means, but on the edge of them. Late rent payments on their offices, that kind of thing. They've been hit by the general decrease in opportunities and increase in caution and in-housing after the, ah, recent troubles. If they failed sometime in the next year, I wouldn't be surprised."

I thought of their offices, which hadn't suggested imminent failure. On the other hand, image was everything.

"How significant is Jase to them, then?" I asked.

"Very. If he's a success, then AAA will have a good income stream. Even the standard bonuses from the contracts they already have lined up for Jase are substantial: his content distribution deal—that's with a corporation called Old Style Label, by the way, which is in fact rather new—his book, some potential product imaging deals. AAA will take a healthy cut of all of those."

"So Andrews had a big incentive to keep Jase on board and safe," I said.

"Yes." Verstraeten brought up a new screen, a list of business names. "Now, AAA seems clean enough, but Andrews himself has a checkered business history. AAA is the core, although the 'Associates' have a steady turnover—most of them leave for good corporations, though, which says something about AAA's reputation. Andrews has also had interests in a large number of other, smaller, short-lived entities. At least ten, but I suspect I could link him to more if I looked longer. One or two had corporate status, because there was a corporate partner who brought it in, but most of them didn't. And Andrews was always in the background in terms of their day-to-day operations."

"All bankrupt?" I asked.

"No. That's quite interesting, actually. They operate for a short while, often rather profitably, and then the money is taken out by Andrews and the other partners, and the business is wound up."

"Laundering?" Jameson suggested. "Cover companies for sabbing contracts?"

Verstraeten stared at his screen for a moment, then shook his head. "Could be either, or something else completely. It doesn't quite ping any patterns in the system. They're described in various ways, mostly themed around content brokering or entertainment industry consultancy. They had dealings with a slew of different corporations in the music sector, and I'd need a lot of warrants to check if all the invoicing was legitimate. I'm not sure we have grounds to get them, either."

And how likely were long-dead companies to be relevant to the awards ceremony shooting? "Does he have anything like that operating now?"

"That could've paid for your sabbing, you mean? I don't *think* so." Verstraeten's expression suggested that not being able to answer definitively gave him acute indigestion. "I had the same thought, and I looked hard for it, but the last one was closed down—rather abruptly, compared to previous companies—about five months ago. Nothing since."

"Oh." I shared a disappointed look with Jameson. "Do you have anything else suspicious on Andrews or AAA?"

"Maybe. I found a series of cash withdrawals from the AAA accounts, by Andrews, tagged as misc expenses," Verstraeten said, his eyes fixed on the screen. "Now, if you analyze the agency's historical expense claims, these fall outside the usual patterns. The amounts themselves are even more interesting. Small corporations are especially tightly restricted when dealing in cash these days, so the thresholds for flagging by the Central Bank are low. These withdrawals are designed to game the flagging system—which is a bit of a science in itself."

"How long ago?" I asked.

"Ten weeks ago, a month ago, and three weeks ago. So, three weeks before the initial threat, and then three and four weeks after it. Or looking at it another way, the last withdrawal was thirteen days before the shooting."

"Not a perfect pattern for a corporate sab," Jameson said.

I nodded. "I like the cash payment, though."

"True," she agreed. "A classic sign of someone paying fairly low-rent sabs if there's no payment mechanism included in the deal—so classic, hardly anyone tries it anymore."

"Just so," Verstraeten said. "The system agreed it was an unusual pattern. It ranked sabbing as about equal with blackmail. Less likely but possible is illegal debt, or a new expensive hobby—pharma, sexual partner, that kind of thing." He shrugged diffidently. "Sometimes it's impossible to get a good fit without making some assumptions."

"Blackmail?" I frowned at the screen. "Um. By Jase? No, that doesn't make any sense. Andrews would have jumped at the chance to get Jase."

"And if Jase wanted money, there's no reason for Andrews not to simply pay him through the agency," Verstraeten added. "He's made regular expenses payments as it is, ever since he signed a nonbinding understanding with Jase. And, of course, the cash transactions may have no connection at all to the shooting."

I nodded. "Jameson, go talk to the associates, please. See if they know anything about the withdrawals, or at least if any of them look nervous when you start asking questions."

"Right. I'll see if they realize how shaky the finances are, too," she said.

"And now that we have some potential payment dates, we can run through known sabs, look for anyone going quiet or with a comms connection to Andrews. Thanks, Verstraeten," I said a little belatedly.

Verstraeten cleared his throat. "I do have a couple of other names you might be interested in."

I apologized for preempting him, and he ducked his head.

"Not at all, Investigator. This one's a bit tenuous, anyway, I'm afraid. A new account pops up in Ann Marshall's name not long after the first withdrawals. Now, the money going in doesn't match up with Andrews's withdrawals, but someone is paying in cash—no traceable transfers. It's possible this is only one account, and she has more under another identity we haven't found yet. I'll keep looking. The other name is Toby Brown. Sara said you want me to run him, too? Now, you'll like this."

He pulled up a new file while we waited. I always enjoy watching someone else enjoying their work, and you've never seen job satisfaction until you've seen Phil Verstraeten with some financial records on his screen.

"According to his c&p, he's been spending a lot less than usual lately."

"He's cutting down on expenses?" I suggested. "He was expecting to be unemployed."

"Ah. Now, on the surface you might think that. But the key is the pattern. For example, taxis don't take cash payment, so they have to show up in the c&p. See, here, here, here, this set down here—all journeys to entertainment complexes, shopping complexes, that sort of thing. Running a co-local c&p pulls up a selection of his friends, no one suspicious. But he's there for an hour, a few hours, and then there's another trip home, and in between, virtually nothing."

He sat back and smiled.

"Corporate expenses?"

Verstraeten shook his head. "I called the corps—they were surprisingly helpful once again. Apparently all the artists on contract have stipend accounts, and the corps let us see the records for 343 and the backups without demanding a warrant. Brown spends up to his limit every week without fail, but the last few weeks he's been building up a surplus and moving it to his main account. Which is perfectly legal, of course, as the corps already pays the tax due."

"So?" I prompted.

"So?" He looked at me blankly for a moment, then his face cleared. "Oh! I'm sorry, Investigator. He's almost certainly come into money—cash—that he doesn't want to put into his account for whatever reason. He's spending it wherever he can, so his regular salary and stipend build up. It's an old-fashioned kind of laundering, you could say."

"Can we prove it?" I asked.

"Oh, I should think so. He doesn't seem to have been very smart about it, on the whole. He's been spending in some top-grade complexes, so I'm sure there's security recordings of cash payments."

I looked at Jameson, and she nodded and made a note on her screen. "I'll get right on it."

"With enough transaction data, I can significantly narrow the error bars on the estimates of how much Brown received," Verstraeten said. "If you think that's worthwhile..."

"Thanks," I said. "If it isn't too much of an imposition on your caseload?"

"Oh, not at all. Investigator Carey said she's happy to help." Verstraeten stood up. "Thanks for calling me in. It was a fun little exercise. It isn't often I get cooperative corporations, apart from anything else. Give me the sales data, and I'll send you the figures."

Jameson arranged a visit to Andrew Andrews and Associates. She found them in the middle of a day-long meeting about the future of the corporation, but happy enough to take a break to talk to her.

No one could explain the cash withdrawals, but equally no one seemed surprised to find out about them. Andrews, it appeared, had run his corporation on a need-to-know basis, and been held somewhat in awe by his junior partners. Jameson described them as "like baby ducks that had lost their mother." She also picked the duckling most likely to move to the front of the flock as someone called Brit Nikolsen, and I added her to the list of people to be investigated more thoroughly. Cui bono, as they say.

She made an unlikely candidate, though. She would've not only needed to know, or guess, that Jase was planning to perform, but she would've also needed to predict that Andrews would spot the gun and run up on stage to protect his investment. There are, as any corporate could tell you, far more predictable ways to remove an annoying obstacle from one's career path.

Chapter Seven

❖

On Tuesday afternoon, Systems finally retrieved the gun's instructions. The systems specialist I talked to over the comm was keen to tell me about the technical difficulties caused by the venue security officer's bullet.

"I can't give you everything," he said at the end. "But I did manage to partially reconstruct the targeting data, which Marin said was the main priority, correct? Everything we do have points to a corps employee called Toby Brown."

"Just him? You're sure?"

"I'd say 95%. There were parts of the store we couldn't reconstruct, so anything in there is lost for good."

"Any identifying information for the sabs, or the source of the target data?"

"I'm afraid not. One thing that stood out is that the pattern recognition for Brown is low quality. I'd say it was taken from recordings. Most sabs will set up surveillance, get a good solid read on the target with professional biometric imaging tools, and then use those for the auto-aimer. These are good enough, but not perfect. Not what I'd want, if I was trying to kill a moving target in a poor-quality environment."

"I suppose that's why it shot at Jase instead of Toby."

He nodded. "They share enough fundamental details, like height and bone structure. But it even used the positions in the routine as target data. It's sloppy work."

I thanked him, and then Jameson abandoned her long list of Toby Brown's spending locations to read over the full report with me. Jameson and I were still discussing what to do next when the Para opened the door without knocking.

"B-C, did you see the gun analysis?"

"Yes, Para. We're just looking at it."

"So was I. There's an inconsistency in the witness statements from your table," the Para added as he pulled a chair over to my desk and sat down.

Clearly, he wasn't taking as hands-off an approach to the case as I'd thought he might be. I wondered if he was getting an alert with every new piece of evidence that dropped into the IIP.

"I checked them all myself, Para. The transcripts are accurate." I'll admit I was feeling touchy.

"I didn't say they were wrong." From this distance, I can see that he was being extraordinarily patient with me during the case. "I said they were inconsistent."

"Where's the problem, Para?" He wasn't the only one who could be patient.

"Here." He paged back to my own statement. "You say Andrews saw the gun before it started shooting."

"Yes. He said, 'there's a gun' or 'someone has a gun,' something like that." I was glad I'd had someone take my statement at the time—the next day, everything was rather hazy.

" 'There's someone with a gun.' " The Para looked up. "No one else at the table heard him."

I thought back as well as I could. "No. The music had started by then. I don't think anyone else could've."

"Mm." He nodded. I don't think, looking back, that he actually doubted my statements. I think it was just an automatic check he might've applied to any eyewitness. "Then look at the timing on the recording covering your table and compare it to the gun deployment data."

I pulled up the information. For a moment I thought it might be a simple clock error. But when I skipped forwards, the sounds of the shots on the security recording synchronized perfectly with the gun telemetry.

While I'd been working on my own screen, the Para had set up the 3D model of the hall for the seconds before the shooting, complete with line-of-sight markers for the figures representing Andrews and myself, but I didn't need to watch the reconstruction run to see what inconsistency he meant.

"You're right," I said. "Andrews shouted and started towards the stage, but when I looked up I couldn't see anything on the walkway. I only spotted the gun later, after the shooting started. I assumed I just missed it the first time, but..."

"Exactly. When Andrews reacted, the target system hadn't acquired yet. The box was still closed—there was nothing *for* him to see."

"So." I paused, thinking it through. "So the only explanation is that Andrews knew about the hit in advance. And he sat there, waiting, until—" Until something no one was expecting had happened. "He saw it was the real Jase on the stage!"

"The wrong target." The Para nodded.

He looked pleased, and I understood why. It's the kind of realization that brings a real buzz of adrenaline, better than anything Daedra can cook up. One fact jumps out of a mass of reports and analysis, and suddenly the jumble of case details starts to fall into place.

"Right." I sat up straighter, even though it made my leg throb. "So why would

Andrews want to kill Brown? Was Andrews even behind it himself, or did he just know that it had been arranged?"

"Good questions," the Para said, meaning *you find the answers,* and stood up.

Jameson had sat unusually still throughout, with her knees neatly crossed and her mouth closed. When the Para had gone, I raised my eyebrows pointedly at her, and she smiled. "You didn't look like you needed any help."

"Thanks," I said dryly.

My leg had stiffened up badly, so I struggled onto my feet, and did circuits of my desk until the muscles were working more easily. Then I sat on the edge of my desk which, being higher, was easier to get up off again.

"So, our current working theory is that Andrews shot himself in the back while trying to stop his own sabbing attempt," I said.

Jameson nodded. "Basically, a really complicated and expensive way to commit suicide. And rather sad."

"But can we prove it was his plan, or just that he had prior knowledge? How are we doing with the money?"

"Well, assuming that the payment into Ann Marshall's new account was all she received from Andrews, we have to divvy the rest up between Toby Brown and these hypothetical sabs. I'm still working on getting details from the shops, bars, and what-have-you that Brown visited, and it'll take time. He didn't stint himself, that's for sure."

"But it's still possible some of it went to sabs, either directly or through an intermediary?"

"Actually, I was just thinking about that." Jameson uncrossed her legs, planting her feet firmly on the floor. "It could all have been done by Andrews himself, you know. Buying a gun like that isn't so hard, and it would explain the poor quality targeting data."

"How would he get it into the venue?"

"It's an entertainment complex, not a high-security zone. We don't have a hundred-percent coverage for his movements that afternoon, either."

I nodded. "Maybe his short-lived companies were connected to sabbing contracts after all."

"Right," she said with confidence. "I bet it was him. That explains why the payments fell outside normal sabbing patterns."

"Even if that's true, it still doesn't tell us why," I said. "Justice won't close it in our favor without more evidence, or a motive strong enough to boost the confidence."

That's the sort of consideration that's supposed to be important for the team at I&I—solid case closures. I'm known as a good team player. Part of my mind, though, was thinking about Kit in his hospital bed, an innocent victim who deserved some kind of justice.

While I wasted my time on professional idealism, Jameson was doing some more practical thinking. She squinted thoughtfully across the office, running her finger back and forth across her top lip. I don't think she was even aware she did it when she was thinking hard.

"Well...suppose Cheung was actually right about something?" Jameson said at length. "Suppose Jase was having second thoughts about leaving 343?"

"Andrews was making sure he didn't have anything to go back to, you mean?" I contemplated the idea. It didn't seem likely, but Andrews had expressed worries about the pressure on Jase. "But then why only fire at Toby Brown? Kit would be the natural target."

"Unless there's more data in the gun they couldn't recover. Kit could've been in there, too."

The idea that the bullet had somehow selectively removed all trace of Kit from the data store seemed rather far-fetched, but I could sympathize with the desire to squeeze the evidence into a more logical shape. I sighed. "It's a shame we can't ask Andrews about it."

"Not him, no, but other people might still be involved," she said.

"Like who? Not any sabs, according to you."

"Well, maybe not. But how about Ann Marshall, for one? She wouldn't want Jase to go back to the corps any more than Andrews. She left her job and took the product with her. Places like the corps don't forgive that kind of thing—it's practically sabbing, in a way."

I nodded slowly. "Chris Doyle told me she used to work in special security contracts."

"Well." Jameson folded her arms. "There you go, then. Maybe they were working together."

I remembered Marshall at the dinner, standing up just after Andrews and myself. Was she simply reacting to us, or like Andrews, had she realized that Jase was in danger?

"We should talk to her again," I said. "Formally, this time."

Jameson nodded. "Or more than just talk."

I popped—well, struggled—outside to see Sara.

"What kind of damage waiver do you think I could get for Ann Marshall?"

I know it sounds like an odd question to ask an admin, but after dealing with so many submissions, Sara has a great eye for what Justice will and won't grant. I'm sure the Para or most of the other para-investigators and interrogators could do it just as well, but Sara is always my go-to.

I'd prepared a summary of the evidence to send to Justice with the application.

I leaned on the desk while Sara read it and then checked Marshall's security file.

"She lost her corporate status when she left the corps, which is good. But..." Sara looked up. "Is that really everything you've got on her?"

"Yes. My main suspect died on Friday."

"Ah. Honestly, then, I'd say apply for an upper second-level waiver, and find the best interrogator you can."

Not what I'd wanted to hear, but there's no point getting good advice and not taking it. "Do you have time to write it up?"

She smiled. "Of course. I don't think we'll get it back until tomorrow, but I'll let you know the minute it comes in." She patted my hand. "Why don't you go home early, B-C? You still look wrecked."

Chapter Eight

❖

Sara was right, as usual—on both counts—and the waiver came back as approved the next morning. I decided to take Doyle at his word and asked him to run the interrogation. He promised to drop by my office as soon as he could to discuss it. After three hours, and several unanswered messages automatically redirected from his comm, I decided I was wasting my time and went out into the main office to talk to Sara yet again.

"I've been trying to get hold of Senior Para Doyle," I said diplomatically. "Maybe his admin lost my messages."

"Oh, I shouldn't think so," she said cheerily. "Have you met Diann? It's her first I&I posting, but she's got all the systems down pat already. Of course, it's easier to pick the rest up now that the interrogation habituation courses are so much shorter, but she's very organized."

"Doyle's ignoring me," I said.

Sara grinned. "Probably. Don't worry, I'll see what I can do."

Doyle arrived fifteen minutes later. Faced with the concrete prospect of another interrogation to add to his presumably busy day, he'd apparently lost some of his enthusiasm for Ann Marshall's attractive rear.

"Do you have any actual evidence for me to work with?" he asked, once he'd finished reading the section covering Marshall in the IIP. "Is there anything more about the money? Sab payments taken from it?"

"We can't link the payment directly to sabs, but Andrews spent a lot of money in a short space of time, and in that same short space, Marshall acquired a brand-new account with a healthy balance. And then a sabbing attempt occurred."

"Hm," he said.

"The c&p shows that they had private meetings."

"She's this music bloke's lawyer; Andrews was his agent. If the c&p says she took a taxi to Andrews's flat a few times, that isn't what I'd call evidential."

His dismissive attitude would've been marginally less annoying if he hadn't been the one who'd suggested Ann Marshall as a suspect in the first place. "She called several security providers, using the term loosely."

"According to your IIP," he said, with a slight stress on the "your," "she mentioned looking into arranging private security for Jase if the Andrews Agency didn't come up to scratch."

"But she made calls before the shooting, too. And some of them . . . well, technically they're legit security providers, but only because no one's caught them yet."

"So she'll say she was concerned after the threats, and she wanted serious protection, not good-looking blokes in suits."

I frowned at him, and I'll admit my tone was snippier than I'd normally use to a senior para. "It's usually the lawyers' jobs to try to talk down the waiver, you know."

Doyle sighed. "Fine. What level is it, again?"

I doubt he'd actually forgotten in the minute since he'd looked at the file. "I had to put in for an upper second."

"Fuck me. Why don't you just tell me to bring her coffee and cake and ask her nicely?"

"You can start with the motive," I suggested. "That's solid, at least."

He snapped the hand screen closed. "I know how to do my job, Investigator. Let me know when she's here."

Dressed in a paper interrogation outfit, with her hands cuffed in front of her, and escorted by two guards with firm grips on her arms, Ann Marshall looked like a different woman from the one I'd met at Jase's flat, or who'd walked confidently through the General Criminal office.

I was watching the interrogation on the screen in my office. Generally I stay away from interrogations, but when I'm lead investigator I like to keep a closer eye on things. Especially when someone like Chris Doyle is handling one of my prisoners.

"Did you search her?" Doyle said to the guards.

The guard grinned. "Very thoroughly, Para. We didn't find anything."

"Oh, well. Maybe next time, eh?"

Bumping the waiver, that's what they'd started to call it. It's always happened to some degree, but the term itself originated around that time, in the wake of the rewriting of the Procedures and Protocols, when bumping was especially popular. Section N interrogations had been banned, but a prisoner could be given a full body search as many times as their interrogator ordered. There was no more neural induction, but the right kind of restraint for the right amount of time could be just as painful, especially with too many salts and not enough water to help the cramps along. Prolonged sleep deprivation was a lost high-waiver technique, but repeatedly moving a prisoner from cell to cell during the night because of the cleaning schedule was just their bad luck.

Technically, bumping is probably in violation of the P&P. But you can't blame the interrogators, who were only trying to do their jobs in the face of a sudden dearth of the tools to which they were accustomed. You could point a finger at Justice, I suppose, but the reps didn't want a drastic fall in their case closure and conviction rates any more than we did, so formal protests were infrequent and disciplinary action even rarer.

Anyway, Marshall looked shaken, which you'll understand if you've ever seen I&I guards conducting a prisoner search.

"Put her there," Doyle said genially, and gestured not at the chair with restraints in the middle of the room, but the chair opposite him at the small table. I saw the flash of relief on Marshall's face.

When the guards had her seated, one left and one stayed, standing by the door.

"Are you all right?" Doyle asked Marshall. There was no sign of the faint contempt underlying his apparent friendliness that I'd noticed earlier. Clearly he made more of an effort in an interrogation than he did with his supposed colleagues in the coffee room.

"I'm fine," she said, and I saw her hands clench. "Fine."

"They can be a bit rough, I'm afraid, but you wouldn't believe what gets smuggled in here sometimes. It's for your benefit as much as ours. Sometimes prisoners do silly things to themselves."

In other words, what we do here is so bad, people commit suicide to avoid it. Marshall looked like she'd taken the point.

"Now." Doyle smiled warmly across the table. "Do you want a cup of coffee? Tea?"

"Tea?" she said, more surprise than request.

"Right. Milk? Sugar? Neither?" Doyle turned to the guard. "Black tea, and get me a coffee with milk. Or whatever the nearest thing to milk is they've got down here."

"Right, Para."

"Someone explained your rights to you when you were booked in," Doyle said as the guard left. "Was it clear enough?"

There wouldn't have been many rights for her to memorize, which was an unfortunate side effect of quitting her corporate job for love. With no right of access to a lawyer, some time in the next twenty-four hours a Justice rep would be assigned to her, but I'm sure Marshall knew better than to place much hope on that option.

269

Marshall tried a smile. "I'm a corporate contracts lawyer, Para-investigator, but I still just about remember the basics of criminal law."

"Mm," Doyle said. "Well, this is your damage waiver. I'm sure you know what that is." He laid a hand screen on the table. "Upper level two, which means that alongside verbal questioning techniques we're allowed to administer the listed range of drugs, via the routes prescribed and within specified risk tolerances, to ease this conversation along. If necessary, at least. Do you understand?"

"Yes." I noticed her head make a tiny movement as she stopped herself from looking at the array of injectors and drugs to one side of the room.

"Good. But hopefully we won't need any of that. If you just answer truthfully, we can get through without any more unpleasantness."

The guard reappeared with two thin paper cups.

"Thanks," Doyle said. He took his coffee and waited until Marshall had her cup held awkwardly in her cuffed hands. He lifted his own cup halfway, and even in her current circumstances, politeness forced her to take a drink before he did. Socialization is a funny thing, with some funny uses.

"Right," Doyle said. "We can—wait just a moment."

He stood up and went to the far side of the room. He tapped his comm, then subvocalized something—my name, I assume, because a moment later I heard his voice in my ear.

"B-C? Have you got us on screen?"

"Yes, I have. Why?"

"No reason—I noticed someone was watching the feed from upstairs, so I guessed it would be you. I'm just killing some time now that she's waivered. Did you watch the search, too?"

"No."

He smiled, visible to the camera but not to Marshall. "You should've—I did. Nice arse, like I said."

Back at the table, Marshall was sipping her tea nervously, splitting her attention between the guard on the door and Doyle.

"You know," Doyle said, "I bet if she was visiting a corporation she didn't trust, she'd know better than to drink anything. Strange how they don't think it applies here."

"I suppose it's because they're expecting you to use an injector."

"Yeah. Keeping them off-guard is much better, though. They don't resist the effects, and when the waiver's bloody useless you have to do what you can."

I almost told him he was starting to sound like one of the full-time interrogators. Instead I offered as sincere an "I appreciate it, Para," as I could manage.

"Well, I did offer. And at least she has susceptible genetics, with a good strong dose, anyway. Mind you, relying on guards to measure dosage is what put Hinch's prisoner in the ICU last week. Don't worry, though, he woke up in the end." He glanced over his shoulder. "That's probably long enough to get started. Thanks for letting me know," he said out loud, and Marshall's head jerked towards him.

I saw her take a deep, settling breath as he returned and sat down. Doyle had a mouthful of coffee, and she shadowed the motion, probably without even realizing it. Whatever was in there would be making her more compliant in every area.

"Ah, right, yes. Ann Marshall. I don't know if you remember me? Para-investigator Chris Doyle."

She gave a small shake of her head.

"That's okay. Sometimes people only see the uniform. I remember you, though." He picked up his hand screen to consult it, then put it down. "You were working at Sécurité Absolute."

"Oh," she said, and finished the last of her tea, delaying. "Yes. The investigation, of course."

"Bit of a change of career, moving from sabbing to music."

She shook her head firmly. "I worked in security provision. Nothing to do with corporate sabotage."

"Really?" Doyle's tone was still friendly. "We looked at a lot of your invoices and contracts in the course of the previous investigation. I refreshed my memory before I came down. You should see how many of those people you worked with seem to have got mixed up in sabbing since you hired them."

"I don't know anything about that." She scrunched up the paper cup, squeezing it between her fingers. "We only worked with people with absolutely clean records."

"Mm. Interesting you needed to bring in anyone at all, when you had such a big staff."

"Our own security personnel were trained to handle a certain level of risk."

"In other words, window dressing."

"Definitely not. They were good." She smiled, relaxing visibly as she talked. "Well, some of them. A lot of clients do know they aren't important enough to need serious protection, and there's an element of image management. But sometimes clients felt they need a more...robust level of personal security. I dealt with the providers."

"Counter-sabbing, provided by sabs?"

"No. Security. I matched up clients with people who'd make them feel comfortable, negotiated contracts, that kind of thing. Nothing more."

"I see. Well, let's leave that for the moment. When we looked at your financial affairs, we found a new account. Cash deposit. Here, let me show you."

He turned the screen towards her, displaying the account details.

"It's just an account," she said. "I have several."

"Really? Any more than these?"

"Um." She blinked a few times, and looked closer at the screen. "No. That's everything, I think."

"So why that account? Why now?"

"It's just for the—" She visibly caught herself midsentence. "I don't remember, exactly. I like to keep my money working, so probably it had attractive benefits for new account holders."

"Ah, right, I see. Sounds very sensible. I'm crap with money. The stuff just spends itself, somehow. Maybe when we're done here, you could give me some advice."

His tone was casual, but I could see him watching her, gauging her responses with professional precision. If she'd been in the interrogation chair then the monitors would be providing readings for him, but working like this was more art than procedure and protocol. Teasing the best he could out of a waiver he thought was inadequate, for someone else's case—as I said, Doyle wasn't my favorite colleague, but he did his job extremely well.

Doyle sat back in his chair, apparently reading his hand screen with great attention. I switched the camera view so I was looking over his shoulder. He clearly hadn't been joking about watching the body search, because he'd saved a few pictures, which is unfortunately common practice down there. After a minute or so, he flicked them off his hand screen and started looking at plans and photos of flats. Either it was to do with his own casework, or he was accommodation-hunting on I&I time. I wouldn't like to speculate.

What he was also doing was giving the drugs more time to work. After a few more minutes, Marshall wiped her fingers over her cheeks, which had developed a faint flush, and then her forehead. I switched the camera view back as Doyle looked up.

"It gets a bit hot down here sometimes," he said. "Something to do with the air cycling system. We keep talking to the maintenance people, but they don't care as long as their rooms are cool."

She nodded. "It's okay. I'm all right."

"Good. Now." Doyle frowned, puzzled rather than threatening. "You see, we have you, who dealt with sabs in the past. We have a mysterious new account full of money. And we have a sab hit at the awards ceremony. Maybe you can make sense of that for us? Did some of your old friends help you out with a more recent problem?"

"I know nothing about what happened at the NLMA. It doesn't hurt the corps that Andrews is dead, but we didn't do it."

"Oh, come on." Doyle smiled, still disconcertingly friendly. "You know Andrews wasn't the target. They were trying to kill Toby Brown."

She looked more confused than frightened, now. "But I wouldn't damage corps merchandise. That's ridiculous. And Kit and Kim were up there, too. Do you have any idea how much they're worth? The corps would be furious if I put them in danger."

I couldn't stop myself tapping my comm. "She shouldn't be talking about the corps like that," I said to Doyle. His face didn't flicker, but I imagine he didn't welcome the interruption from an investigator.

"Why do you care about the value of corps assets?" he asked. "Your security file says that you resigned."

"Yes, technically. But—" She scrunched up her face, and rubbed at her right eye. Doyle glanced up at the camera, and raised his eyebrow slightly. "I still work for the corps. That's why I have that money. It's my salary—and a bonus, for being off-book. So, you see, it's nothing to do with sabbing. Nothing at all."

"Well." Doyle regarded her with measured skepticism. "That's definitely an imaginative story."

"It's absolutely true!"

"So why the hell did you decide to fake a resignation?"

"Jase. I was supposed to help keep him in line. The corps knew he was interested in me, and Geoff asked me to—to get closer to him. He still blindsided us with the contract issues, so I went with him, to find some way to persuade him to return. He isn't easy to work on—he's smart, and suspicious. But it's my job to protect the corps's product, whether it's Jase or Toby Brown." She sighed softly. "You know, Jase is sweet. I'm very...*fond* of him. But he'll be better off with the corps. Statistics—the statistics for corps acts who try to go solo are terrible. Terrible."

"So you've been doing everything you could to get him back with the corps?"

"Yes. I even sent the message—the threat, from Roosendaal. I told Jase I was going to Groningen for a couple of days, to meet a new prospective distributor, but it was easy enough to use the comm on the way. I suppose you could check that, right? You must have some way of doing it, even without movement notification?"

Even with drug-dulled inhibitions, suspects don't often make suggestions like that unless they're telling the truth. I started the c&p anyway, while I listened.

"Geoffrey Cheung told us the corps knew nothing about the message," Doyle said.

"Cheung." She snorted. "He's an idiot. Do you know what Jase calls him? Geoff the Tosser. So true. And Cheung isn't just screwing up his own career, either. This mess is all his fault, antagonizing Jase over the snip. Why would they tell Cheung anything, when he was on his way out? Of course, after all the drama he might even keep his job."

"Do you think *he* could be behind the shooting?"

She actually burst out laughing. "*Geoff?* He doesn't have the balls."

The c&p results didn't take long to find. She'd been moderately clever, booking a train route that went through Roosendaal, allowing her to break her journey there without raising any flags, but it annoyed me that we hadn't spotted the possibility. Of course, we'd had no reason to suspect Marshall before.

273

"The Roosendaal trip checks out," I said over the comm.

Doyle bent his head over his hand screen. "Do you believe her about the rest of it?" he subvocalized.

"I think so."

"Yeah, me too." He looked up and smiled. "Thank you, Ms. Marshall. See, I thought we'd be able to get this cleared up. I'm afraid you'll have to wait in holding for a short time, while we verify what you've told us."

She smiled back, with obvious relief. I wondered if she'd ever realize what Doyle had done to her. "I understand. I'm glad I could help."

While, unbeknownst to her, Ann Marshall waited for the effects of her interrogation to wear off so we could release her, I pondered what we'd learned.

The corps played hard, and were willing to resort to extremely underhand tactics to control their product. I didn't feel I'd learned much there.

Ann Marshall had admitted to sending the threat against Jase, but I doubted the corps would thank us for bringing that to light. Besides, since Marshall was unofficially employed by them at the time, there might be some legal wriggle room to argue that she was empowered to send the message in the course of fulfilling her instructions. Marshall might not have any right of access to a corporate lawyer, but that mattered less when she was one herself. Cases rejected by the Justice analysis system are the worst kind to have on your record. If the corps had known about her plan to send the message, then they'd been wasting our time by insisting we investigate, but anyone involved would simply deny it and place the responsibility back on Marshall. I couldn't get waivers for the whole of their staff.

And anyway, none of it seemed connected to the shooting in any way that I could see.

That left me with only one possible way to get to Andrew Andrews—through his intended victim. If I could pin down a solid personal motive for wanting Toby Brown dead, that might be enough to ascribe the sabbing entirely to Andrews and give the case positive closure.

I couldn't find an interrogator with time free to run Brown through a level one. Doyle unsurprisingly declined—I don't think Toby's arse appealed to him at all— and Interrogation wasn't feeling receptive to a request from an investigator with a low-priority nonpolitical case like mine.

"The Para and Nagra are out of the building," I said. "We could wait until they get back."

"I expect they'll be too busy, don't you?" Jameson said.

The edge to her voice made me look at her in surprise. "What?"

She shook her head. "Nothing, never mind. Well, I suppose it doesn't matter whether we find an interrogator or not, anyway," she added philosophically. "We don't have any solid reason to apply for a waiver."

"A witness waiver, maybe," I said.

"My old Para used to say witness waivers were for people who were too lazy to do a proper interview. He loved a good level two."

I'd never met her last boss; as far as I knew, he'd been killed in the revolt, which was somewhat ironic if he'd preferred verbal interrogations over what resisters would call "brutality."

"Unfortunately, I barely scraped an interrogation pass," I said. I don't do too badly with people who want to cooperate, but anyone can see the difference between one of my interviews and, say, the Para's.

"I did all right," she said. "At investigator standard, anyway. Why don't we both talk to him? I'm sure if we put our heads together first we can come up with a plan."

I know perfectly well what Jameson was hinting at about the Para and Nagra. At the hospital, I'd felt pleased that the Para still trusted me to close the case, even though I'd messed up. The other way of looking at it—Jameson's way—was that he wanted to keep the case at arm's length because it was a stinker. That's why he was watching the IIP and dropping in every now and then to nudge the investigation along, but making it quite clear that I was running the case.

If the worst came to the worst, Jameson and I would be the ones held responsible for failure. I'd screwed up by declaring Jase was in no danger; she was the newest, most expendable member of the team. I should think most people at I&I would agree with Jameson's assessment of the situation, even Mistry and the others. They all have enormous respect for the Para and the work he does, and for the way he runs his team, but none of them would expect him to take a bullet for us, metaphorically or otherwise.

It's true that when I&I was controlled by Socioanalyst Carnac and the Service after the revolt, the Para risked his life to save I&I, or at least to stop it from being destroyed, which isn't quite the same thing. I'm not sure how many people ever really understood how close we all came to disaster. But even knowing that, I had to agree with Jameson to a certain extent. The circumstances were very different, and Jameson and I were dealing with nothing more than some sticky internal politics. Our careers were certainly at risk of being sacrificed to smooth over relations between division and corporation, and it was up to us to save them.

Just because we didn't have a real interrogator didn't mean we had to give up the rest of the trappings. The general public are often hazy about the exact job distinctions at I&I, and the unrest had left I&I with a surplus of interrogation rooms relative to interrogators.

I had Toby Brown picked up—from his old flat, which presumably meant the corps still hadn't finalized his promotion—and brought down to level D. Prisoners often find the corridors alone to be intimidating, and I dressed the interrogation room up with a few packets of wrapped injectors.

Brown had obviously paid at least some attention at the mandatory arrest training course I assume the corps must put its staff through, because the first thing he said when he sat down at the table was, "Shouldn't I have a—a waiver, or something?"

"You aren't under arrest," I said. "Mr. Cheung said the corps wanted to cooperate fully with the investigation."

"Oh, yeah, of course." He relaxed back in the chair, his hands on his thighs. "Well, here I am, fully cooperating. What can I do to help?"

"How was your relationship with Andrew Andrews?" Jameson asked.

"Relationship? You mean was I sleeping with him?" Brown looked mildly horrified. "God, no."

She smiled briefly. "I actually meant, did you get along well?"

"Why shouldn't we? I mean, yeah, of course we did. I put him and Jase in touch, remember?"

"Yes, I do remember." Jameson expanded her hand screen. "Now, there are some discrepancies in your recent financial activities that we'd like you to explain. Some purchases, for example."

Jameson had cherry-picked the most expensive of his cash-splurge shopping trips, so she had some nice security footage to show him of him handing over handfuls of euros in exchange for clothes and jewelry.

"We know the money came from Andrew Andrews," she said with great confidence, and only a slight disregard for the truth.

Fortunately for us, he didn't deny it. Stating a supposition as a fact is a tested technique with a good success rate, so long as you avoid overly suggestible interviewees. "It was an introduction fee, that's all. For doing the go-between work with Jase. Totally legit."

"And he chose to pay you in cash installments for this service," Jameson said skeptically.

"Well, yeah. I didn't want to risk the corps finding out, did I? People reckon they monitor all our accounts." He might not have been clever enough to hide his windfall from Corporate Fraud, but he'd obviously prepared this story in advance.

"Look, he was happy to pay. He stands—stood—to make way more from Jase than he gave me."

"So happy, in fact, that he took out a sab contract on you," I said.

He stared at me. "What?"

"There's no doubt about it. You were the target, and Andrews arranged the sabbing."

"Wow. No shit?" The wide-eyed surprise was impressive, but I don't think the idea was much of a surprise to him. It did explain his reluctance to discuss his suspicions on the roof. "Well, what can you say? Corporations, right? They don't like paying people what they owe."

"So he paid you two installments, and then changed his mind?" Jameson asked, now frankly disbelieving. "Seems to me it would've been cheaper to call in the sabs right away."

"Yeah, I suppose so. Still, he must've changed his mind, mustn't he? I guess you'll never find out, now that he's dead. *I* don't know anything about it."

He looked between us with earnest truthfulness, and I wished I had the training to use a neural scanner. Of course, accurate scanning needs a selection of assistant drugs that I don't have the qualifications to use, either.

Luckily, there were other approaches, even if they might be slightly less ethical. I sat back a little, yielding the floor to Jameson.

"Mr. Brown, I'm afraid I don't believe you. The first payment was made some time after Jase and Andrews signed their understanding. Jase didn't mention anything about a payment to you, and there's no official record of it in the AAA accounts. I'm afraid we're going to have to look into this whole matter in more detail. *Much* more detail." Jameson looked at him significantly.

He frowned. "Like how much more detail?"

"Well, probably a search of your flat, a close examination of all your comms for the past few months to try to verify your story." This part of the interview had been Jameson's idea, and she laid it on with relish. "We can talk to everyone at AAA, and your fellow doubles—"

"Oh, come off it!"

"I'm sorry?" Jameson said.

"So the corps finds out what I did, and I get the sack just when they're going to announce the recast? Thanks a fucking bunch."

Jameson looked at me. "What do you think?"

"That might be an unfortunate consequence, I suppose." I shrugged. "It isn't relevant to our investigation, though."

"All right!" He held his hand up. "You win. This is how it happened, God's honest truth. All I wanted at first was Jase out of the way. No money, just a chance at a break, right? I fucking deserved it. And the performances went great, but after a couple of weeks it started to feel like the corps were just winding things up.

Eventually I straight-out asked Geoff, and I can always see through his bullshit. 343 was over. It pissed me off—it wasn't fair, you know?"

It seemed to me like he'd made his own bed. "How does this relate to Andrews?" I asked.

"I wanted some compensation, that's all. Something for putting myself through so much shit for all these years. Do you think *we* have anything held in trust, like Kit and Kim'll get? Fuck, no. So when Geoff said 343 was finished, I went to Andrews and...I asked him for some money."

"Just asked him?" Jameson said.

"Why shouldn't that have been enough? Maybe we didn't have a signed finder's fee agreement, but so what? He could've made a fucking fortune from Jase."

I was about to say something, when Jameson nudged my foot with hers under the table. We both regarded Brown steadily across the table, keeping our faces impassive. He started to shift in his chair, and for the first time he glanced across the room at the interrogation chair.

"Okay, look." Brown leaned forwards, lowering his voice. It didn't matter; the room mikes were more than sensitive enough. "Andrews wasn't exactly Mr. Clean Hands, either. He ran a scam finding music from nobodies—offering them an option deal, telling them he needed demos to show around the corporations, and when it was much too late they'd find out they'd signed over all the rights. He sold the music, and dropped the writers. He had a good ear, too."

"And Jase didn't know about it?" Jameson asked.

"Obviously not. Jase wouldn't piss on a content thief if they were on fire, never mind do business with one."

I remembered Jase's extremely clear views on thieves and plagiarists. "And how did you know about Mr. Andrews's sideline?" I asked.

"Because he did it to *me*. I was signed with AAA, and then this small agency approached me, saying they'd heard some of my material, they could get me a big break. You know the shit they spin." He looked rather embarrassed. "And, yeah, I know. I was stupid to fall for it. But years after it happened I ran into this girl who'd worked at a few of the scam agencies. I recognized her from the one that'd ripped me off, and so I...made friends with her. She was angling for an in with the corps, and I thought, you know, make her some promises, see how she liked getting played. But eventually she mentioned Andrews's name, and I realized how he must've been running it. Setting up little agencies, closing them down as soon as one got a bad reputation. He was a clever fucker, at least."

It all seemed to match Verstraeten's findings. I said, "And you didn't do anything about it at the time?"

"No. When I met this girl I already had the 343 gig with the corps. I didn't want a reputation as a troublemaker. And, okay, it was a shitty thing for Andrews to pull, but it's a tough business, I got over it. I knew Jase would do his nut if he found out, though. He's funny about that stuff."

"Did you have any proof?" I asked.

"Not a lot. But I knew I wouldn't need much. Jase is totally paranoid about people stealing music. He'd believe it."

"So you used the information to blackmail Andrews?" Jameson said. "On multiple occasions?"

"Like I said, I asked him for a bit of money, that's all, just a couple of times. Only what I was due. An introduction fee, some back payment for those songs he stole. I brought up the other shit to—to help him do the right thing."

"The right thing," she said. "I see. And when you introduced Jase to Andrews, did you already have that recourse in mind?"

He frowned. "That what?"

"Did you plan to use Andrews's past to get money from him?"

Brown shifted in his seat. "I suppose I might've thought about it. I mean, yeah, of course, why wouldn't I? I'd be stupid not to. Look, like Jase always says with his fucking camera obsession, it's good to know things about people. I was just sick of getting screwed over."

Taking money from Andrews like he'd taken sex from poor Kit, because he had power over them, because he felt—genuinely believed, I think—that the world owed it to him. At least now Kit wouldn't have to tolerate him anymore.

"Blackmail is a still a crime, Mr. Brown," I said. "Premeditated, in this case."

"But—" He stared at me uncomprehendingly. "Andrews tried to have me fucking killed! And he's dead, anyway."

And both, ultimately, because of the blackmail. I only regretted that there was no way to hold Brown responsible for the sab attempt.

"Not legally relevant," I said. "We have plenty of evidence, and your entirely voluntary confession of extortion against a registered corporate entity, Andrew Andrews and Associates. By introducing Andrews to Jase, you deliberately—"

"Listen, I can just pay the money back," he said urgently. "I still have most of it. It's packed up in my bags, I can show you."

"You deliberately manipulated your victim into a position where you could put pressure on him. The Justice systems will have to process the file, of course, but I don't think there's any way you'll avoid re-education."

"What the *fuck*?" He stood up, then sat back down abruptly as the guard by the door took a step forwards. "I want a lawyer!"

"You'll get a Justice rep, for now. But don't worry, I'll let the corps know you're under arrest." And no doubt they'd have his corporate status revoked by the end of the day. I turned to the guard. "Take him to processing."

"Very nice!" Jameson said when Brown was gone. She stood up, almost bouncing on the balls of her feet. "Couldn't have gone better, really."

"Thank you for your help," I said.

Jameson shook her head. "I think you would've been okay on your own."

"I told you, my interrogation training grades were—"

"Training was a long time ago, B-C. Don't get hung up on the numbers. You're better than you think you are."

I regarded her with surprise. "Honestly?"

"Honestly." She certainly sounded sincere enough. "If you don't believe me, maybe you should sit the tests again and find out."

She helped me up—even the chairs without straps on level D are somewhat uncomfortable—and we went back upstairs to celebrate our success with coffee and biscuits.

Chapter Nine

The next day, as we were finishing off the financial reports, Sara brought me an entirely unexpected message—a call from Jase, asking me to meet him at his flat. Insofar as I'd thought about him at all, I'd assumed he'd be busy with his new contract and the changes at AAA.

The building door opened as soon as I activated the comm outside, and Jase was standing at the open door to the flat by the time I limped there. His scruffy beard was growing back in after he'd shaved it for the concert, but that wasn't the only thing that made him look desperate—his clothes were untidy, and his eyes bloodshot.

"Thank fuck," he said. "Come in."

It took me a while to settle myself on the low couch. By the time I'd found a comfortable angle for my injured leg, Jase was seated opposite me, his hands clenched together. His trademark camera was nowhere in sight.

"What's so urgent?" I asked.

"It's the corps. The pre-release book samples leaked. It must be one of the content providers we were talking to—a corps insider with a contact there, maybe. And now they know that Ann was the one who gave me information for the book. They say they have *proof.* God knows how, but they showed it to her."

"Does it matter, now?"

"To me? No. To Ann, it's her whole career. She didn't just break her contract, she violated the corporate accords. She'll never hold a corporate-grade job again. She'll probably lose her certification to practice. So of course now they're pressuring me to go back." Jase sounded utterly despairing. "They'll drop the breach of confidentiality against her if I do. Geoff laid it out for me. I could've punched his smug, stupid face. Oh, there's some sweeteners. Another percent or two, more say in the music." He laughed harshly. "Which is all bullshit, of course. I'll have to do whatever the fuck they tell me to do. Sorry. Whatever the *heck* they tell me to do. And we'll plug on until I'm too fucking old and Kit's a basket case, and then we'll be binned like any other rubbish. Nonrecyclable."

"I'm sorry," I said.

"Not anywhere near as fucking sorry as me, I can promise you. I can't believe... after all this. After Andrews. I talked to the associates yesterday, and everything was okay. Brit Nikolsen is taking over running the agency—I like her, she's got a good head. We were going to go ahead and sign the new contract as planned. And then this." He lifted his fist, as though he were going to smack the table, and then let his hand drop. "*Fuck.*"

"What about taking your chance to escape?" I said, thinking of his attitude towards Kit and Kim. "You said you wouldn't let the corps threaten you."

"Well, no. But this is my fault. Ann quit for me. I talked her into putting some of that shit into the book, when she thought it was too dangerous. No one wrote a script to tell me to say I loved *her.*" He sounded as determined as when he'd talked about escaping the corps. "I owe it to her at least not to fuck up her entire life, no?"

And yes, I did feel a twinge of... if not guilt, then responsibility. Maybe the corps had planned this all along, but if not, then it had probably been precipitated by Toby Brown's arrest. A last, desperate play made by the corps to keep the 343 profits rolling in, and I wondered whether it was with or without Ann Marshall's consent.

"Why did you want to see me?" I asked.

"I don't know. Well... I thought, just maybe, there's something you could tell me. Something I could use. Was the corps not involved in the shooting at all?" He looked at me pleadingly. "I was wondering if maybe once Andrews died, the corps pulled some strings and had everything blamed on him."

"I'm afraid not. All the evidence we have points to Andrews contracting the sabs." I didn't think that at this point it would help him to know why.

"Oh. Oh, right. So... I guess that's it, then. Last throw of the dice came up double one. Back on the merry-go-round." Jase tried to fake a smile, but his voice cracked. He slumped back, staring up at the ceiling, and the lights caught the glint of tears in his eyes. "Oh, God," he said softly. "I don't think I can bear it."

The beautiful flat was silent. I tried not to feel as sorry for him as I did. He had more money than I would ever see, genuine fame and fortune. He had Ann Marshall... at least for as long as the corps assigned her to him.

"There's something you ought to see," I said reluctantly.

He cocked his head, so he could see me with one eye. "Oh?"

Accessing an interrogation recording from outside the I&I or Justice buildings needs an extra layer of authentication, so I can't say I didn't have time to think about what I was doing. Jase had no business seeing that file, and I had no business showing it to him.

He took the screen and watched it through in silence. I'd already cut the file around Ann's confession, so there was no need to let him listen to Doyle's conver-

sation with me, or see his attempts at amateur porn. It was a standard Justice submission, in fact, which eliminates unnecessary clutter. Jase flicked the scene back,
and Ann's voice repeated:

I work for the corps.

I was supposed to help keep him in line.

Jase is sweet. I'm very... fond of him. But he'll be better off with the corps.

Jase is sweet. I'm very... fond of him.

I'm very... fond of him.

I thought for a moment he was about the throw the screen down in disgust,
but then he handed it back to me. "Classic." He shook his head. "Classic fucking
corps. I'm such an idiot."

"No. No, you—"

He looked up. "Was she drugged?"

"It was absolutely inside the waiver. I could show you the—"

"No." He cut me off again firmly. "I just meant—she was definitely telling
the truth?"

"Yes. Her interrogator was confident, and so was I."

"Right. So, yeah, I am an idiot. Bastard corps. Bastard..." He wiped the heels
of his hands carefully under his eyes. "I need a drink. Do you want something?"

"No, thank you."

While he went off into the kitchen area, I cut the connection to I&I and folded
my screen. As I said, I'd known when I took out the screen what a risk I was taking.
Listening to him opening the fridge and pouring the drink did, however, give me
some time to think about how I could possibly explain it to the Para, if it ever
came down to that. In a formal resignation message, probably.

Jase came back with a glass of cola—topped off, I suspected, with something
stronger—and used it to wash down a couple of small tablets. When he sat down
again, his eyes were dry.

"Well. It's better to know, right? Better to know the truth. It'll give me some
exciting new material for the book, anyway."

"You can't mention the interrogation," I said hastily. The possibility, stupidly,
hadn't even occurred to me.

"No?" He looked at me measuringly, then nodded. "Mum's the word, I
promise."

"It had better be," I said, trying to put a little para-investigator aura into my
words.

Jase didn't seem noticeably fazed. "Anyway, I can still tell part of the truth.
Name my source. It certainly looks like she broke the accords, no? I don't see the
corps telling people differently. Um." He took a deep swallow of the cola, and
blinked at the fizz. "Right. I have to call some people, now—Brit Nikolsen, first,
to tell her I need a new lawyer."

"I should get back to I&I," I said.

We stood up, and he shook my hand, squeezing warmly. I think if he hadn't still been holding the drink, he might've hugged me.

"Thank you again," he said. "I can't tell you how much I appreciate this. I'll make sure you get tickets for my first solo show. VIP."

"Please don't," I said. "You don't owe me anything. Really."

He looked taken aback for a moment, then he smiled. "Okay, sure, I understand." Setting the cola to one side, he rummaged around on the table until he found a printed publicity image. He signed it, and offered it to me. "How about that? You never know, it might be worth something one day."

Chapter Ten

❖

I didn't submit the files to Justice right away. We were still hunting, with ever-diminishing chances, for any trace of the sabs who'd placed the gun at the awards ceremony, or the money that Andrews had almost certainly used to pay them. Phil Verstraeten's thorough analysis of Toby Brown's spending (plus the cash we'd found packed away in his bags, still stacked in the hallway of the doubles' flat), compared against the money Andrews had taken out of AAA, had left us with a discrepancy large enough to buy a *very* cheap sabbing contract, or possibly an overpriced disposable rifle. Jameson still liked her theory that Andrews had bought and placed the gun himself, but I suspected we might never find out which of us had won the bet.

I'd deprioritized the IIP, though, which is why the alert didn't show up on my screen. Instead, Sara knocked on my door and opened it while I'd only made it halfway through "Come in."

"Did you see the news about 343?" she asked.

"No. They officially announced the breakup, then?"

"Not exactly."

She came over to my screen and brought up a link, and the two of us watched the news clip play.

It looked as though it had been recorded by one of the fans outside the corps's private hospital. High above a window opened, and a figure appeared, half his face concealed by something white. From all around, the delighted cheers and calls rose. Whoever was holding the camera was shaking it around so much that even the compensation tracking optics struggled to keep a clear, focused image. It still looked wrong to me, though, and I realized why a few seconds later when another window opened and an identical figure appeared. The crowd quieted, puzzled, and then I saw that the person at the first window wasn't Kit, but Kim with something wrapped around his head. He pulled the towel off and whirled it around, and someone near the camera called, "Oh, *boys*."

Kit leaned out, left hand on the ledge, waving to the crowd below. Then he shifted, bringing one knee and then the other up onto the sill. Kim vanished abruptly from his window.

I breathed, "No."

"Mm-hm," Sara said.

Kit stood up. A hand appeared for a moment at his hip, but it was too late. He jumped, throwing himself forwards, arms spread.

They'd slowed the next section of the clip, of course, zoomed in tight on the blurring tumble of limbs and hospital gown. At least they'd cut the sound. I suppose it had been deemed too graphic for inclusion. I could imagine it, though—the screams changing from excitement to horror, hopefully loud enough to mask the solid, wet impact. As the crowd scatted backwards, the recording fixed shakily on the body lying still on the pavement before hospital security began clearing the witnesses away.

Sara blanked the newsfeed. After a few seconds, she said, "I suppose that's definitely it, then. No more 343."

"He was the brand identifier," I said, like a particularly uninspiring epitaph, and Sara frowned at me. "Sorry. Case jargon."

For a moment, I wondered how Kit's death would affect the value of Sara's autograph, but this time I didn't say anything.

I interviewed Kim back at the expensive flat, now more silently empty than ever. Partly it was to dot every last *i* and cross every last *t* in the IIP, after the hash I'd made of the initial investigation. There wasn't any doubt about the events, though—the corps had the whole hospital room under surveillance. Justice had already ruled it to be an accidental death, which I'm sure pleased the corps from a publicity point of view. (A valuable result for them, you might say—or possibly even good value.)

Mostly, the interview was the sort of morbid curiosity that kept the clip of Kit's jump circulating endlessly in a sea of speculation and analysis. Oddly, very little of that speculation seemed to focus on the mental and physical trauma inflicted on him over the years by his employer, and I wondered if that would change when Jase's book was released. The corps, presumably, would already have damage control planned.

As I sat down in the living room, I spotted the pink bolster lying discarded over by the keyboard.

"I just wanted your account of events for the file," I said to Kim. "This is a purely voluntary interview."

"Ask away." Kim plumped down into the thick cushions, sitting with his legs crossed. "I already went over it with the Justice officers."

"Why were you there?"

Kim shrugged. "To see Kit, that's all. I'd been there most of the day—I thought he could use the company. My schedule's been pretty empty since you arrested T-boy."

"Who suggested the stunt with the towel?"

"Kit. He said he wanted to have some fun with the fans, tease them a bit." Kim leaned towards me. "He didn't plan to jump, I'm sure. Whatever people are saying. Kit would never think of doing something like that. It was just a—he meant to stand on the ledge, I think, so they could see him better."

I knew he was only saying what he'd been told to say—and under the watchful eye of the corps—but the erasure of even the last willful act of Kit's life unexpectedly annoyed me. "You guessed what he was going to do, Kim. You ran over and tried to stop him."

"I thought he was leaning too far out, that's all. I was worried, in case he had an accident."

"Kim—"

"No." His jaw set, perfect lips firm. "That's the truth. And that's all I'm going to say about it."

And this was a voluntary interview, with someone who had just lost a friend. "Of course. Can I ask, did Kit know 343 was finished?"

I thought for a moment he wouldn't answer, but then he said, "Yes. Geoff wasn't going to tell him, at least not until he was feeling better. But then the corps cancelled the extra surgery they'd scheduled for us, and one of the medics let it slip. So he worked it out on his own. Although I think he already knew—Jase gone, Toby headed for re-education. The corps had no choice. I thought Kit would freak out completely, but he seemed okay about it."

"Really?"

I held his gaze until finally he looked down at his fingers, twisting the corner of a cushion. "I don't know. I couldn't tell with him anymore. I just assumed the psychologists would have it all in hand for the closedown."

Maybe the corps had cut back on that expense, too, along with the cosmetic surgery. "So what happens to you?"

Kim let go of the cushion corner and patted it smooth. "The corps is terminating my contract," he said with equanimity. "Once we're done with the postfuneral PR, anyway. I'm not much of an asset for the brand anymore."

"You don't sound too upset."

"No. I'm getting the held-in-trust payout, in full. Which is practically unheard of in the history of the corps, so I'm not complaining. There's even some kind of bonus. Trauma compensation, or whatever they want to call it."

Hush money, in other words.

"And Kit's mum and dad will get his share, I think," Kim added. "I suppose that's something for them."

"Confidentially clauses?" I guessed.

"Lots. But who wants to hear about us, anyway? We'll be old news soon." He looked around the room. "It'll be nice to have my own place at last, you know? My own life. I'm not even sure what I'll do next—I'll just have to see how it goes."

He seemed out of place already in the soulless perfection of the corps's flat, even though I couldn't say what had changed about his appearance. I remembered Jase's opinion that Kim was a survivor, and I suspected he was right.

If. If, and might.

If I hadn't closed the case that first time, if I'd found out about Toby Brown's blackmail earlier, the sab attempt might never have happened.

If I hadn't broken the rules and accepted that invitation to the New London Music Awards, Andrews's role may never have come to light, and Toby Brown might've saved 343.

If I hadn't shown the interrogation to Jase, and he'd rejoined 343 to save Ann Marshall, Kit might not have died.

There were myriad other factors, of course, at every stage. I don't know if you could say I was responsible for anything that happened, but I was certainly involved. And not just as an investigator, dispassionately assessing events after the fact.

Funnily enough, although I'm not proud of everything I did, the case didn't look too bad on my record or Jameson's. There was the unfortunate closing of the initial investigation, of course, and we didn't find the sabs, if there were any, but sadly that's often the case. In the end, we placed the commissioning of the NLMA attack squarely on Andrews, with the unexpected bonus of Brown's blackmail conviction. So it looked positive, and no, image isn't everything, but it does count.

Contrary to Kim's opinions about their newsworthiness, for a while the events of the case came up every so often: when Jase released new music, when he tried his luck as an actor, when he married another popular solo artist some time later, and when they divorced. In time he was successful enough that generally his management could keep the old 343 story well in the background. Kim surfaced less often, and the last time I remember seeing his name was in connection to his then-girlfriend's fatal overdose on illegal pharmaceuticals, from which he was cleared of any involvement.

Of course, my colleagues would always make sure I knew about it whenever one of "my" 343 was rating high in the news. Eventually, though, even the elephantine memory of the I&I coffee room let them slip into the past, to my relief.

I never finished reading Jase's book, not the original he gave me, or the one that was published, with all the green, orange, and red toned down to black, and a new section promising "the shocking truth" about 343's breakup. I didn't see the point, when I already knew it. Letting go of mistakes, leaving the past behind—that's something we all have to learn to do. I do still have the image he signed for me, though. I didn't frame it, but I did put it in a protective sleeve, and every so often I'll come across it in a drawer. "You showed me the truth that set me free—Jase." I didn't find out until much later that it was a line from a 343 song, but apart from that, I suppose it doesn't make a bad testimonial for an I&I investigator.